LUMBERJ
BONUS TRACKS

LJ

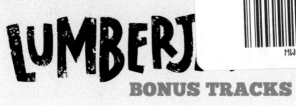

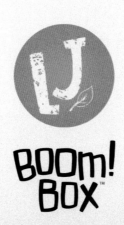

BOOM! BOX™

BOOM! BOX™

LUMBERJANES BONUS TRACKS, March 2018. Published by BOOM! Box, a division of Boom Entertainment, Inc. Lumberjanes is ™ & © 2018 Shannon Watters, Grace Ellis, Noelle Stevenson & Brooklyn Allen. Originally published in single magazine form as LUMBERJANES: BEYOND BAY LEAF SPECIAL No. 1, LUMBERJANES: MAKIN' THE GHOST OF IT SPECIAL No. 1, LUMBERJANES: FAIRE AND SQUARE 2017 SPECIAL No. 1. ™ & © 2015-2017 Shannon Watters, Grace Ellis, Noelle Stevenson & Brooklyn Allen. All rights reserved. BOOM! Box™ and the BOOM! Box logo are trademarks of Boom Entertainment, Inc., registered in various countries and categories. All characters, events, and institutions depicted herein are fictional. Any similarity between any of the names, characters, persons, events, and/or institutions in this publication to actual names, characters, and persons, whether living or dead, events, and/or institutions is unintended and purely coincidental. BOOM! Box does not read or accept unsolicited submissions of ideas, stories, or artwork. #RICH - 771147.

BOOM! Studios, 5670 Wilshire Boulevard, Suite 450, Los Angeles, CA 90036-5679. Printed in USA. First Printing.

ISBN-13: 978-1-68415-216-2 eISBN: 978-1-64144-030-1

THIS LUMBERJANES FIELD MANUAL BELONGS TO:

NAME:_____

TROOP:_____

DATE INVESTED:_____

FIELD MANUAL TABLE OF CONTENTS

LUMBERJANES
FIELD MANUAL

For the Intermediate Program

Prepared for the
**Miss Qiunzella Thiskwin
Penniquiqul Thistle Crumpet's**
CAMP FOR  HARDCORE
LADY-TYPES

"Friendship to the Max!"

A MESSAGE FROM THE LUMBERJANES HIGH COUNCIL

miss
Quinzella
Thiskwin
Penniquiqul Thistle Crumpet's
Camp for
HARDCORE LADY TYPES
FRIENDSHIP to the MAX!

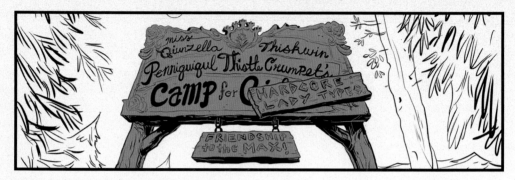

There are many things in life we may expect—birth and friendship and the inevitable arrival of spring, among others. These things become such an established part of the rhythm and rhyme of our lives that we are no longer surprised to see the crocus bloom, or to wake up each morning to the rising sun, once again bold and warm and waiting for us on the horizon.

These natural wonders become the regularities of life. They give us comfort and hope, but it can also be important to learn to embrace the things in life that we do not expect—the things that leave us taken aback, surprised and shaken.

Whether it is a change in your family life, or your friendship circles, or something new developing at school, it can feel initially like an upset, most especially when you have grown accustomed to the particulars of life as you have known them. These rhythms can feel as unshakable to us as the shifting of the seasons. And when something changes, you may feel as if your world is spinning.

Start first by breathing—you hold within you a tide as powerful as the Pacific Ocean, that ebbs and flows and carries you safe home again. Hold to that if things are moving too quickly for you. Then, look through your life carefully: what has changed? What is new? What is the same as always? Who is there with you to hold your hand?

After all, even the first moments of your life—the gasp of air, the shock of cold and bright and loud outside your mother's womb—was a surprise to you at the time, and it has led to so much good.

THE LUMBERJANES PLEDGE

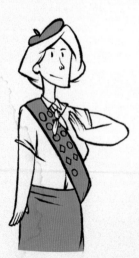

I solemnly swear to do my best
Every day, and in all that I do,
To be brave and strong,
To be truthful and compassionate,
To be interesting and interested,
To pay attention and question
The world around me,
To think of others first,
To always help and protect my friends,
[redacted]
And to make the world a better place
For Lumberjane scouts
And for everyone else.

THEN THERE'S A LINE ABOUT GOD, OR WHATEVER

LUMBERJANES™
BONUS TRACKS

Created by Shannon Watters, Grace Ellis, Noelle Stevenson & Brooklyn Allen

Beyond Bay Leaf

Written by
Faith Erin Hicks

Illustrated and Lettered by
Rosemary Valero-O'Connell

Colored by
Maarta Laiho

Makin' The Ghost Of It

Written by
Jen Wang

Illustrated by
Christine Norrie

Colored by
Maarta Laiho

Lettered by
Aubrey Aiese

Faire and Square

Written by
Holly Black

Illustrated and Lettered by
Marina Julia

Las Estrellas Del Campo: Edición Lumberjanes

Written by
Gabby Rivera

Illustrated by
Gaby Epstein

Lettered by
Jim Campbell

Sphinxes, and Riddles, and Wishes, Oh My!

Written by
Kelly Thompson

Illustrated by
Savanna Ganucheau

Colored by
Joie Brown

Lettered by
Mad Rupert

Cover by
Chynna Clugston Flores

Pin Designs
Kelsey Dieterich and Scott Newman

Designer
Kara Leopard

Assistant Editor
Sophie Philips-Roberts

Editors
Dafna Pleban & Whitney Leopard

*Special thanks to **Kelsey Pate** for giving the Lumberjanes their name.*

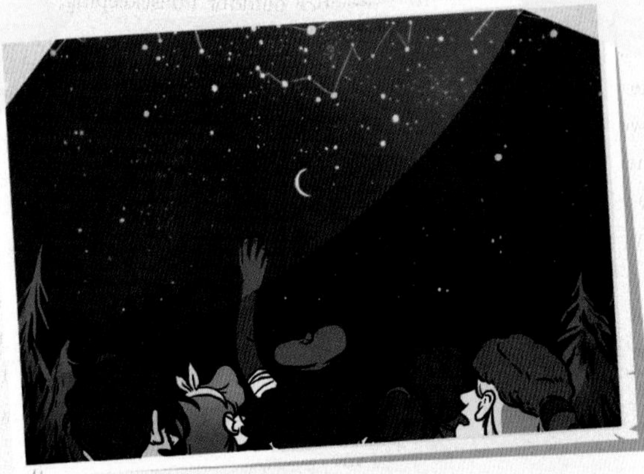

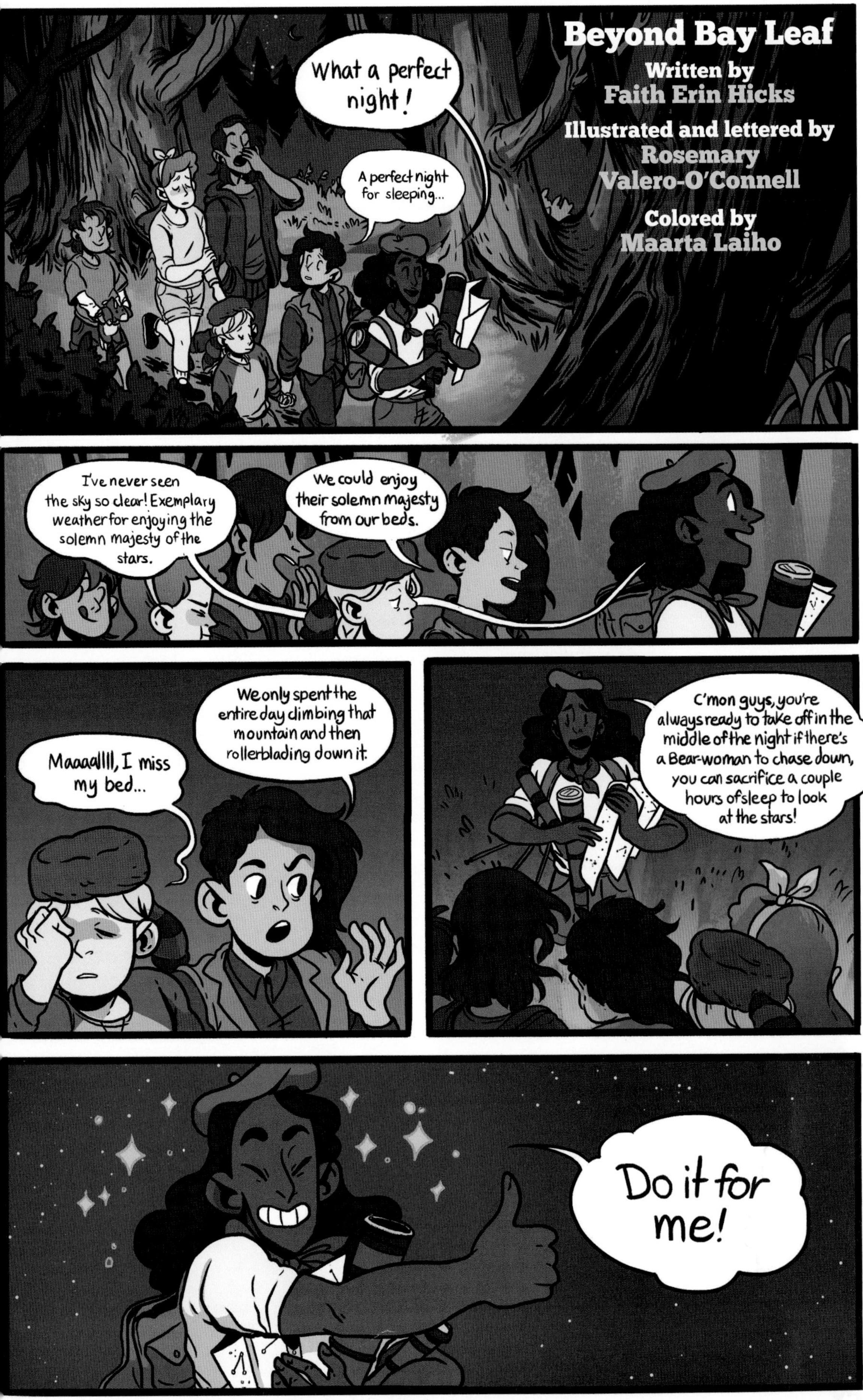
Beyond Bay Leaf
Written by
Faith Erin Hicks
Illustrated and lettered by
Rosemary
Valero-O'Connell
Colored by
Maarta Laiho
What a perfect night!
A perfect night for sleeping...
I've never seen the sky so clear! Exemplary weather for enjoying the solemn majesty of the stars.
We could enjoy their solemn majesty from our beds.
Maaaallll, I miss my bed...
We only spent the entire day climbing that mountain and then rollerblading down it.
C'mon guys, you're always ready to take off in the middle of the night if there's a Bear-woman to chase down, you can sacrifice a couple hours of sleep to look at the stars!
Do it for me!

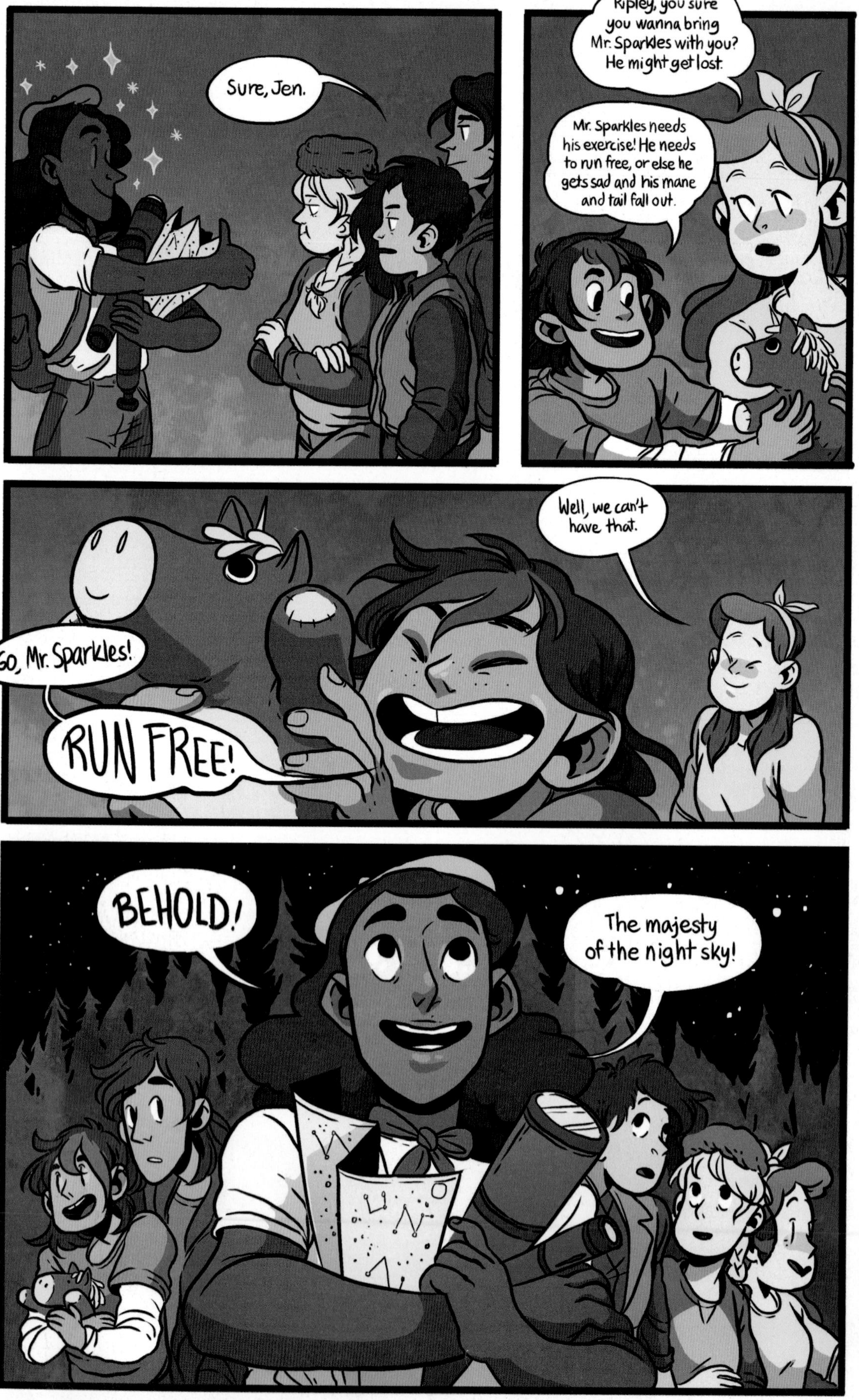
Sure, Jen.
Ripley, you sure you wanna bring Mr. Sparkles with you? He might get lost.
Mr. Sparkles needs his exercise! He needs to run free, or else he gets sad and his mane and tail fall out.
Well, we can't have that.
Go, Mr. Sparkles!
RUN FREE!
BEHOLD!
The majesty of the night sky!

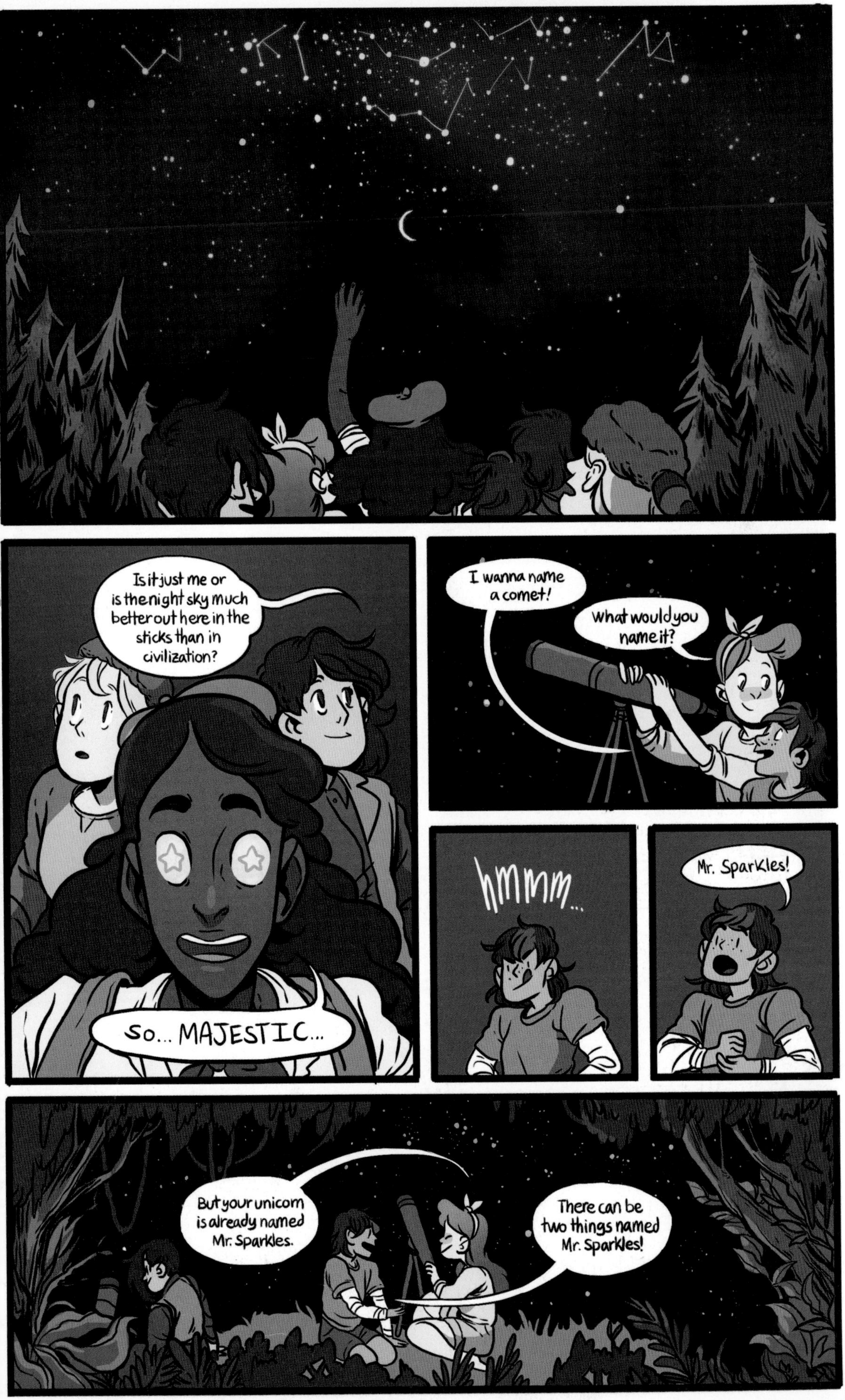
Is it just me or is the night sky much better out here in the sticks than in civilization?
So... MAJESTIC...
I wanna name a comet!
What would you name it?
hmmm...
Mr. Sparkles!
But your unicorn is already named Mr. Sparkles.
There can be two things named Mr. Sparkles!

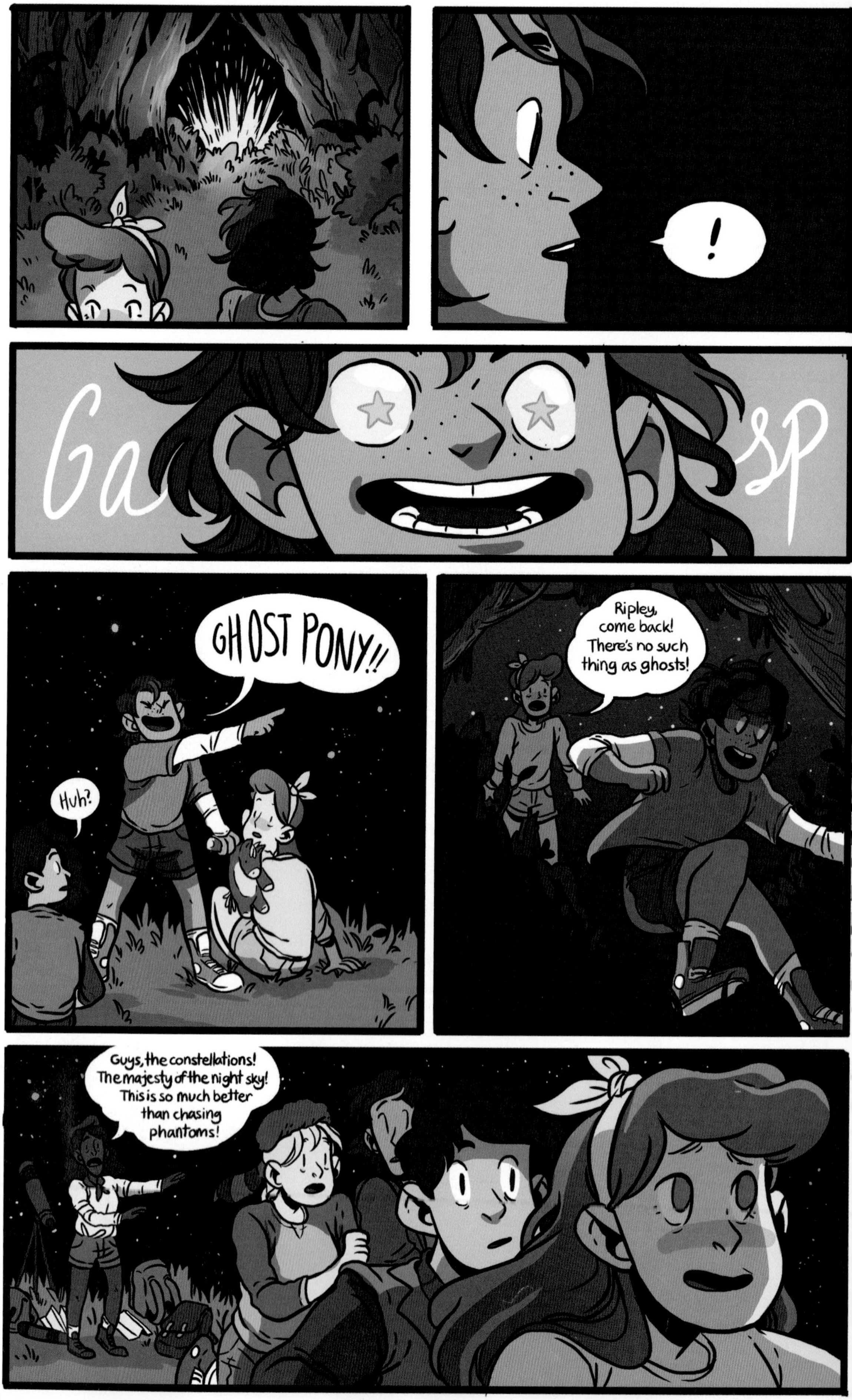
!
Ga
sp
GHOST PONY!!
Huh?
Ripley, come back! There's no such thing as ghosts!
Guys, the constellations! The majesty of the night sky! This is so much better than chasing phantoms!

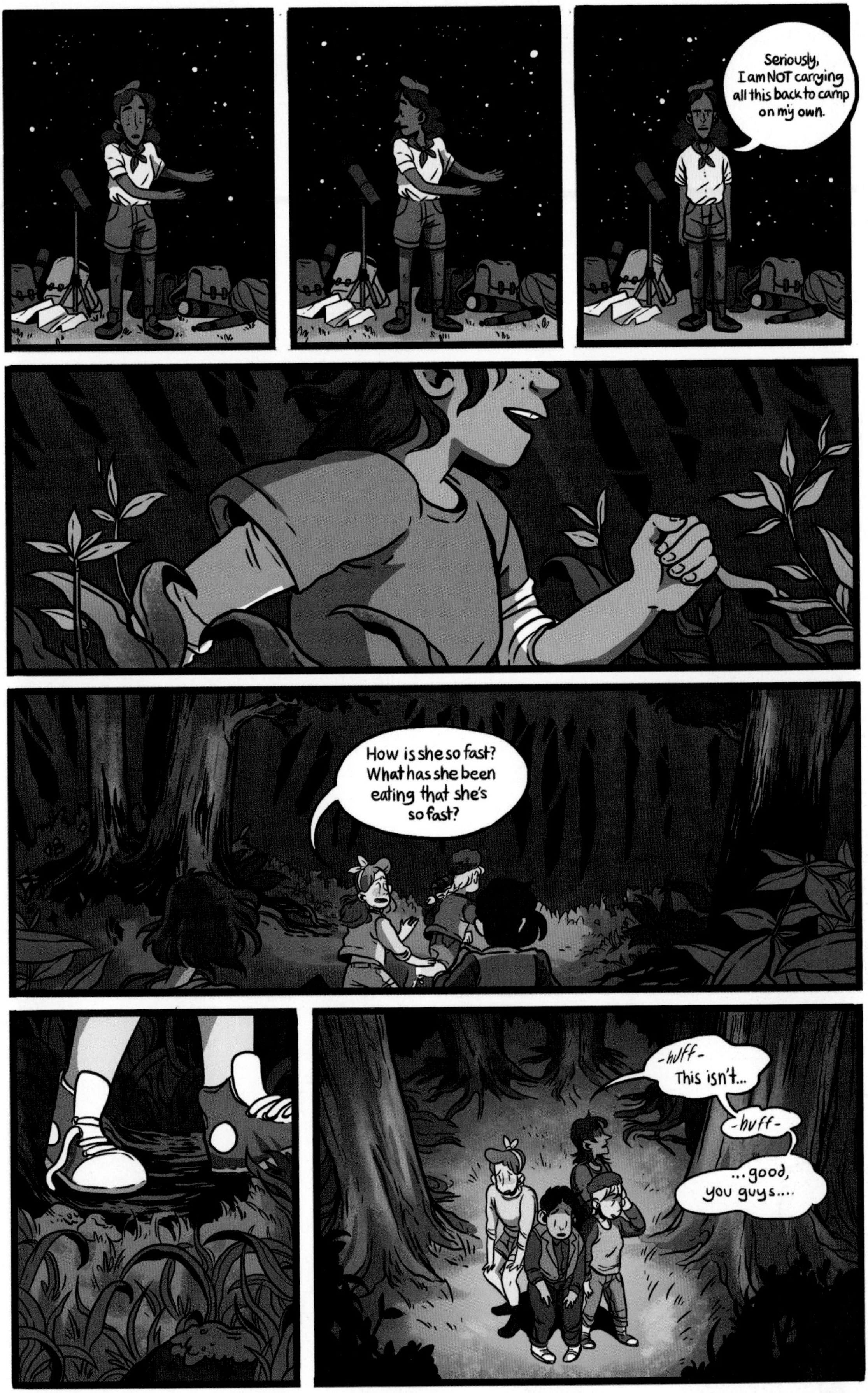
Seriously, I am NOT carrying all this back to camp on my own.
How is she so fast? What has she been eating that she's so fast?
-huff- This isn't...
-huff-
...good, you guys....

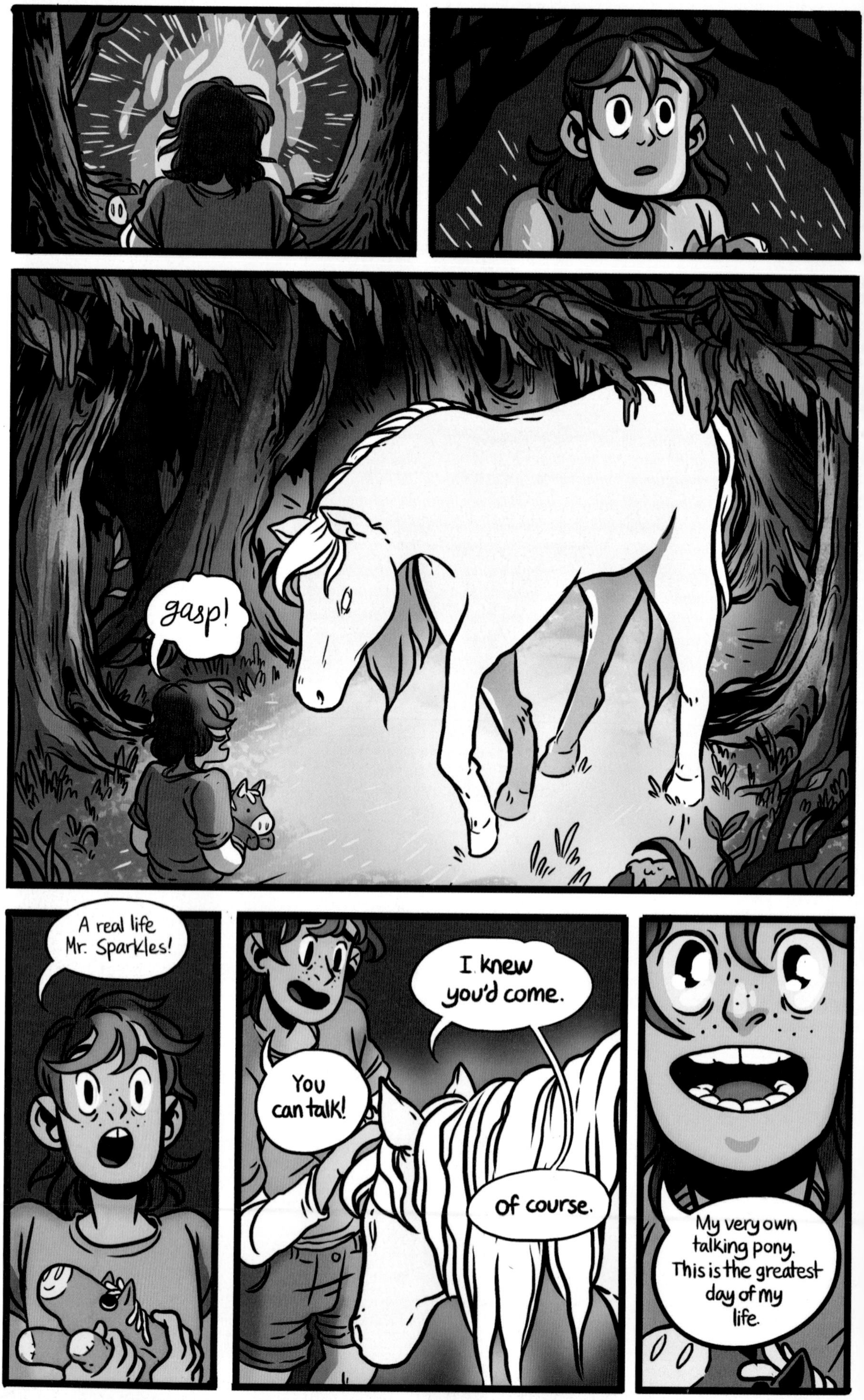
gasp!
A real life Mr. Sparkles!
You can talk!
I knew you'd come.
Of course.
My very own talking pony. This is the greatest day of my life.

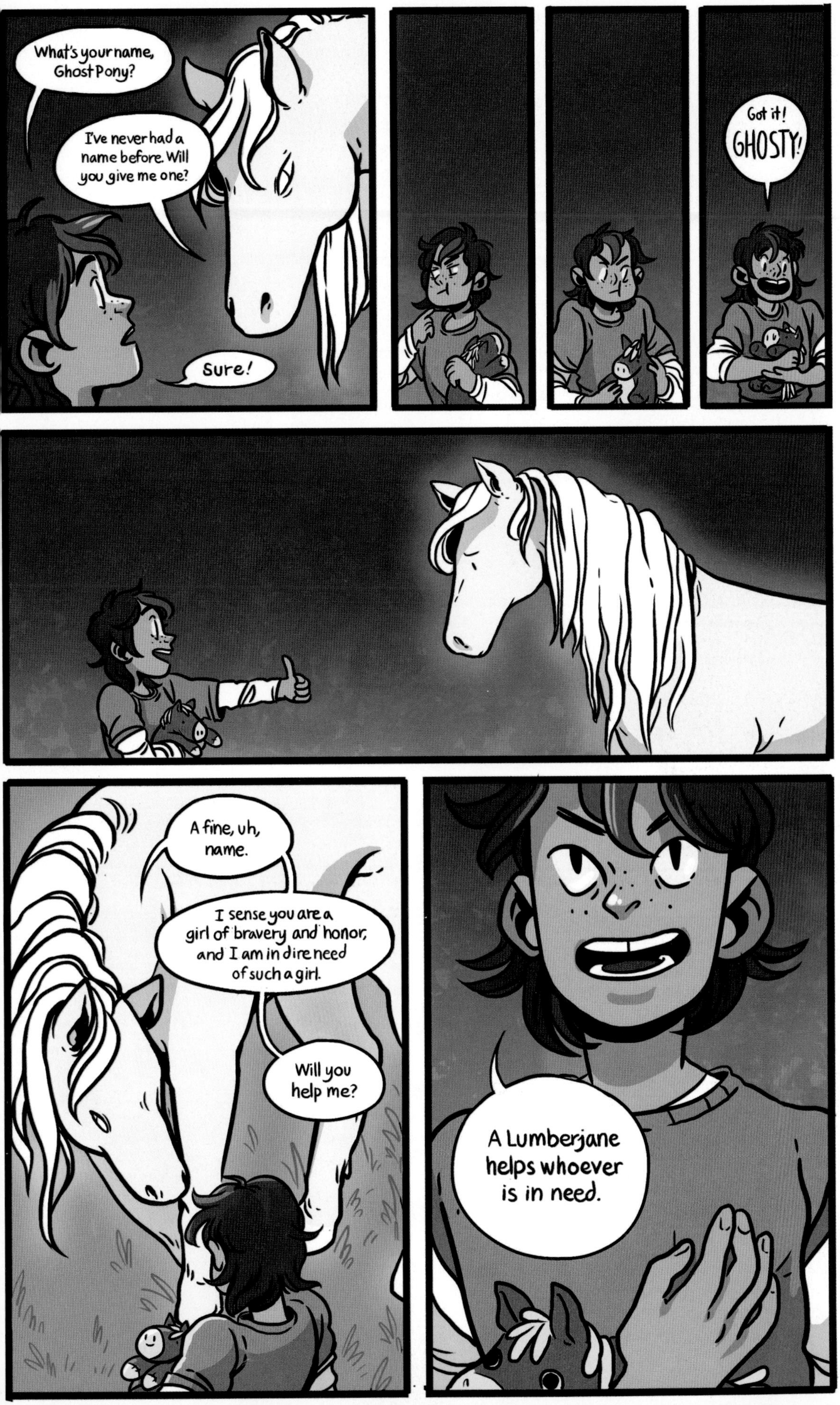
What's your name, Ghost Pony?
I've never had a name before. Will you give me one?
Sure!
Got it! GHOSTY!
A fine, uh, name.
I sense you are a girl of bravery and honor, and I am in dire need of such a girl.
Will you help me?
A Lumberjane helps whoever is in need.

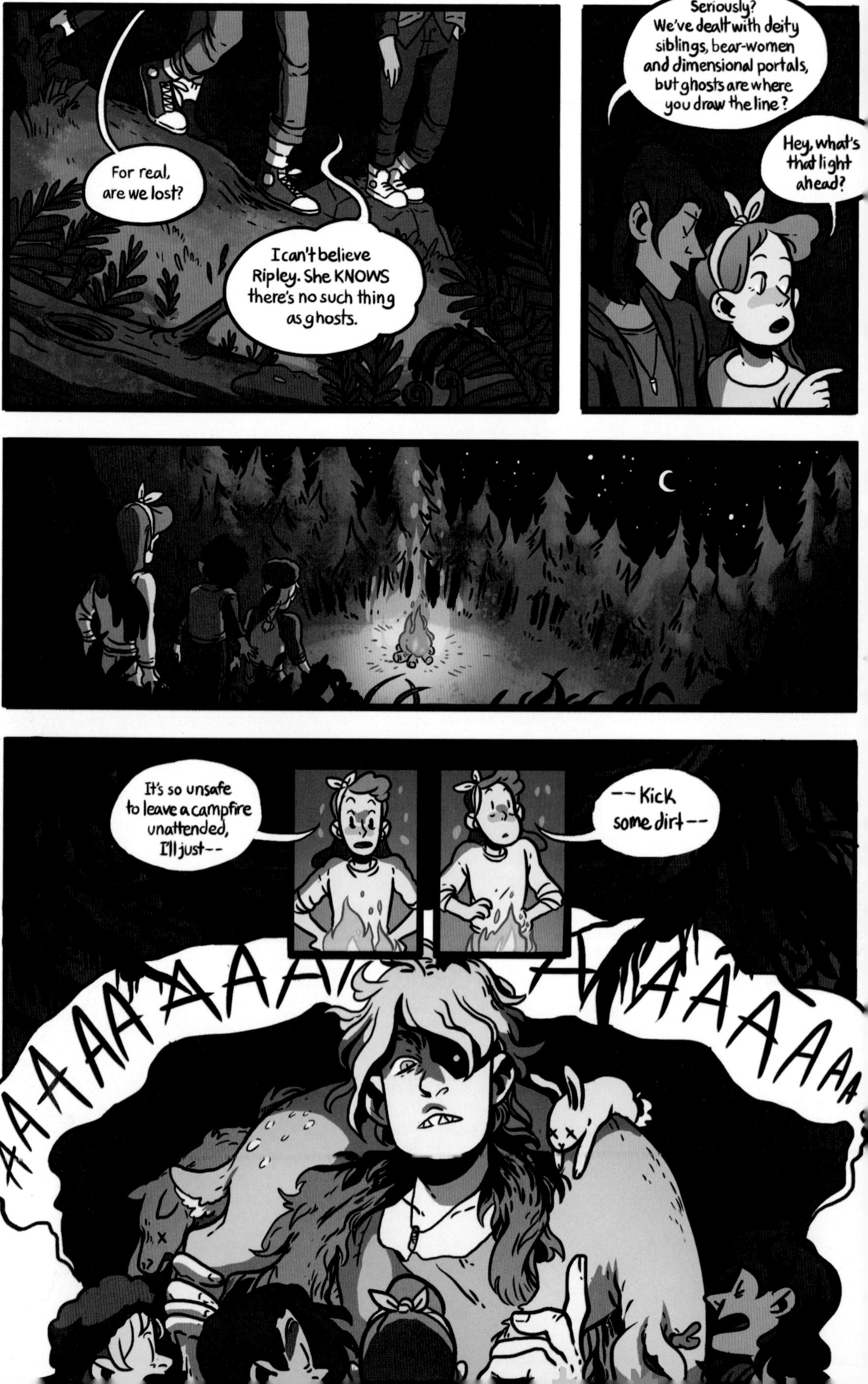
For real, are we lost?
I can't believe Ripley. She KNOWS there's no such thing as ghosts.
Seriously? We've dealt with deity siblings, bear-women and dimensional portals, but ghosts are where you draw the line?
Hey, what's that light ahead?
It's so unsafe to leave a campfire unattended, I'll just--
--Kick some dirt--
AAAAAAAAAAAAAAAAAAAAAA

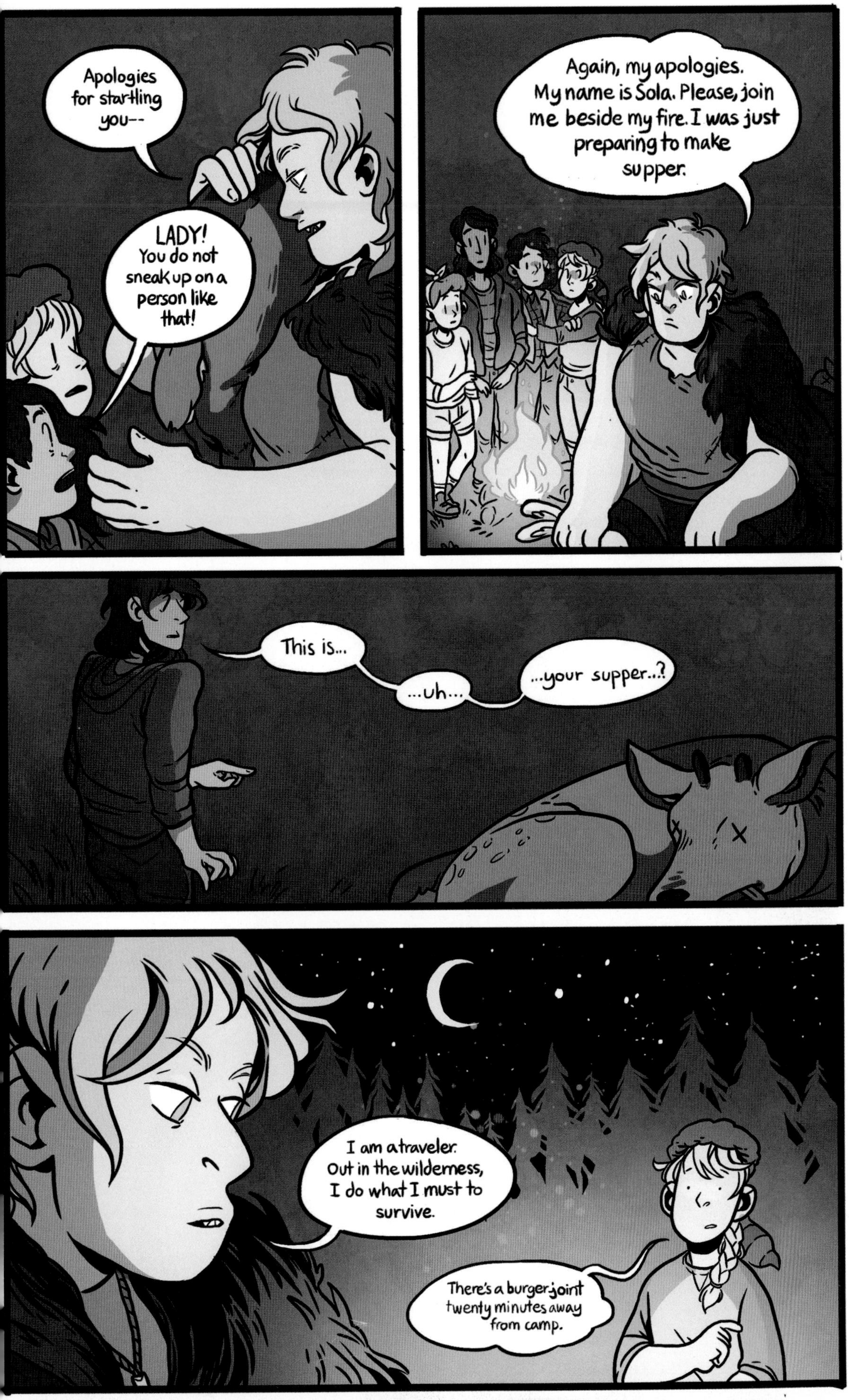
Apologies for startling you--
LADY! You do not sneak up on a person like that!
Again, my apologies. My name is Sola. Please, join me beside my fire. I was just preparing to make supper.
This is...
...uh...
...your supper...?
I am a traveler. Out in the wilderness, I do what I must to survive.
There's a burger joint twenty minutes away from camp.

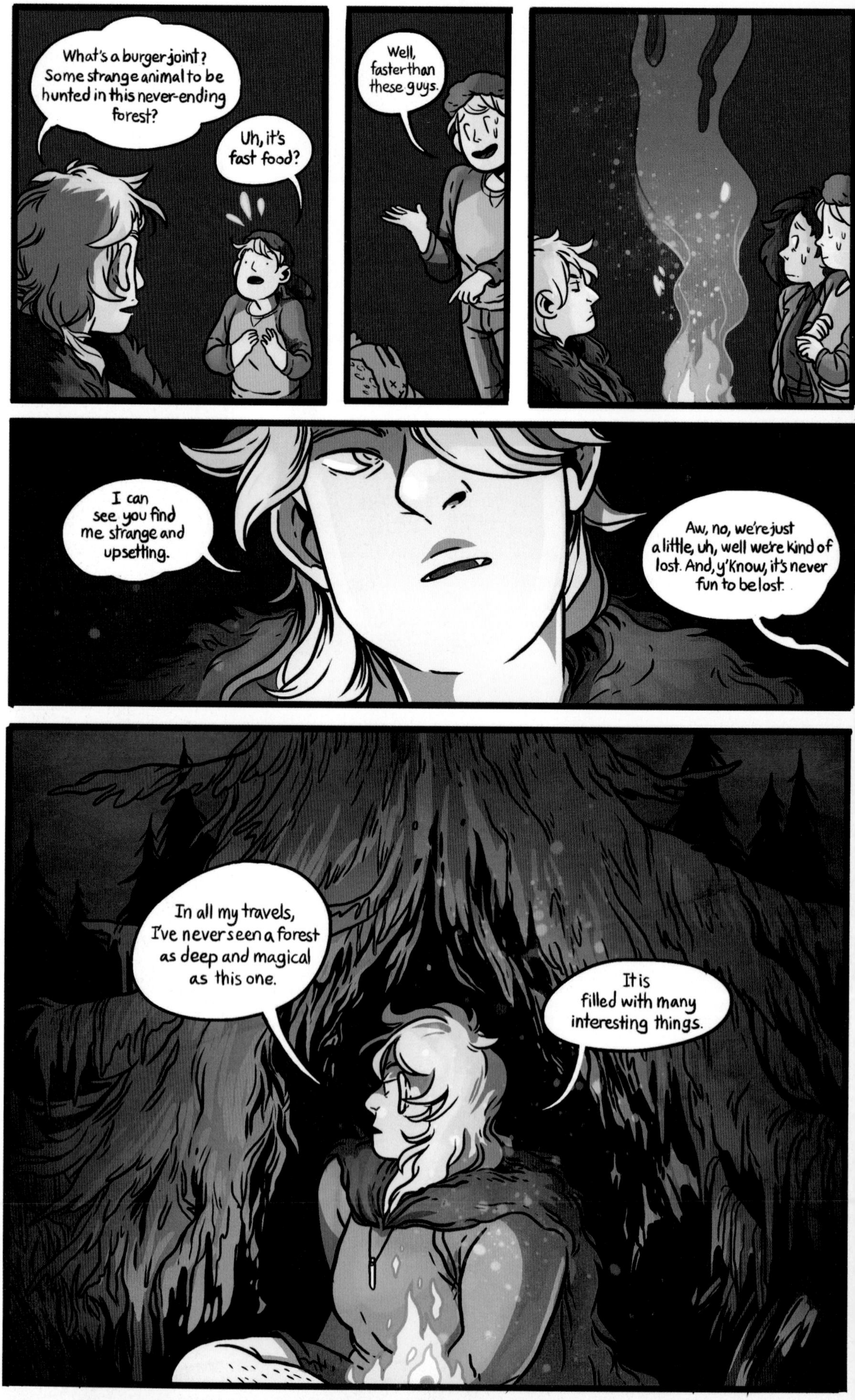
What's a burger joint? Some strange animal to be hunted in this never-ending forest?
Uh, it's fast food?
Well, faster than these guys.
I can see you find me strange and upsetting.
Aw, no, we're just a little, uh, well we're kind of lost. And, y'Know, it's never fun to be lost.
In all my travels, I've never seen a forest as deep and magical as this one.
It is filled with many interesting things.

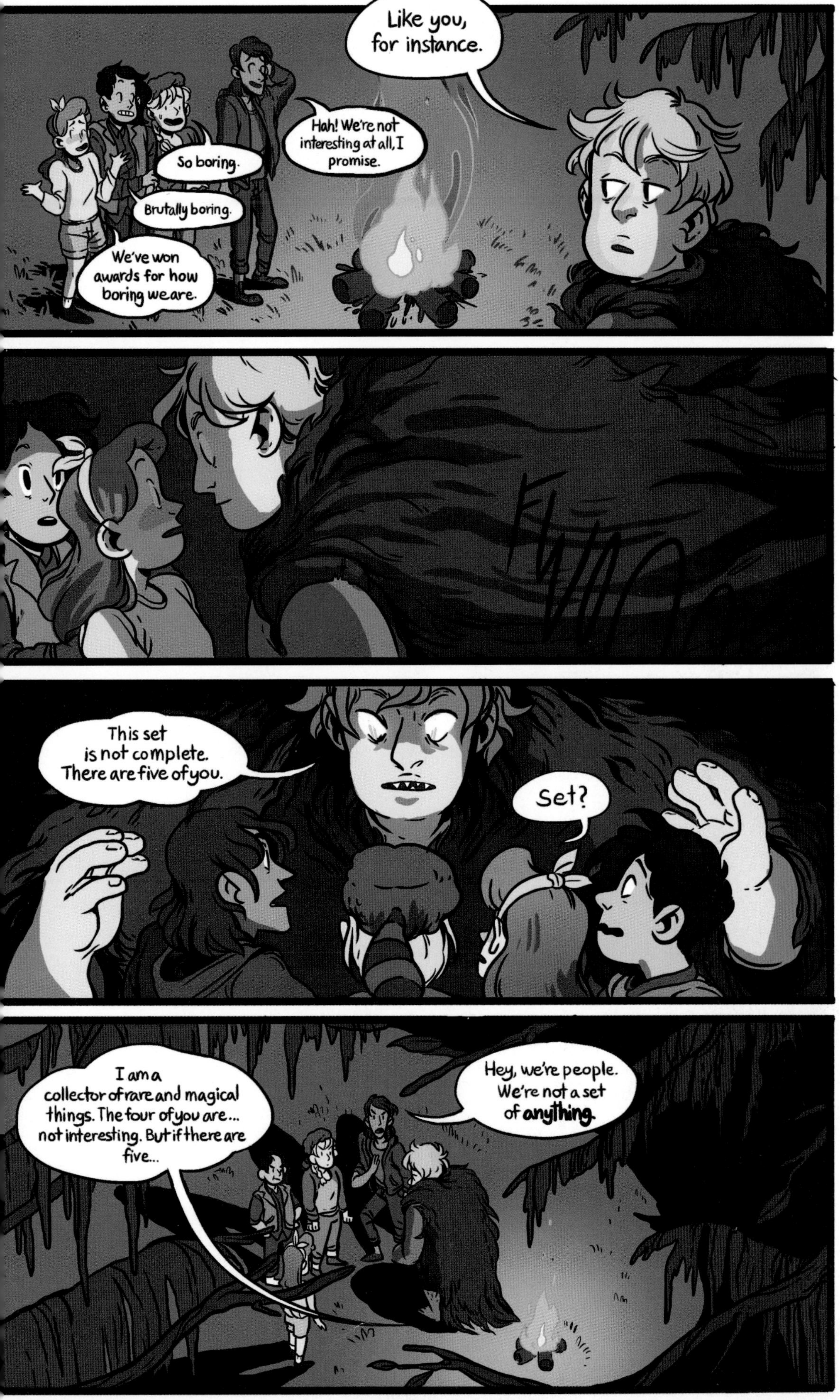
Like you, for instance.
Hah! We're not interesting at all, I promise.
So boring.
Brutally boring.
We've won awards for how boring we are.
This set is not complete. There are five of you.
Set?
I am a collector of rare and magical things. The four of you are... not interesting. But if there are five...
Hey, we're people. We're not a set of **anything.**

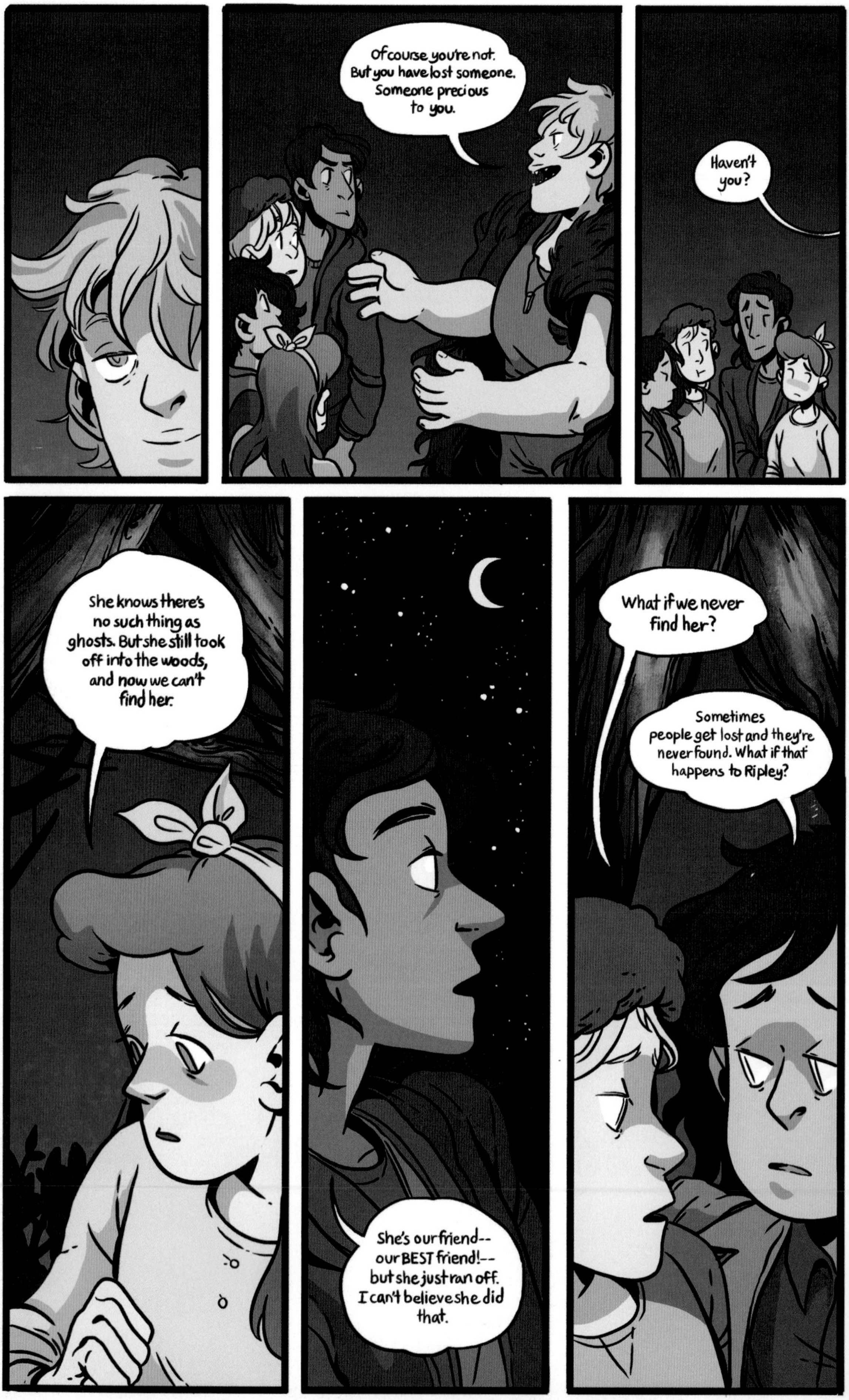

Of course you're not. But you have lost someone. Someone precious to you.
Haven't you?
She knows there's no such thing as ghosts. But she still took off into the woods, and now we can't find her.
She's our friend--our BEST friend!--but she just ran off. I can't believe she did that.
What if we never find her?
Sometimes people get lost and they're never found. What if that happens to Ripley?

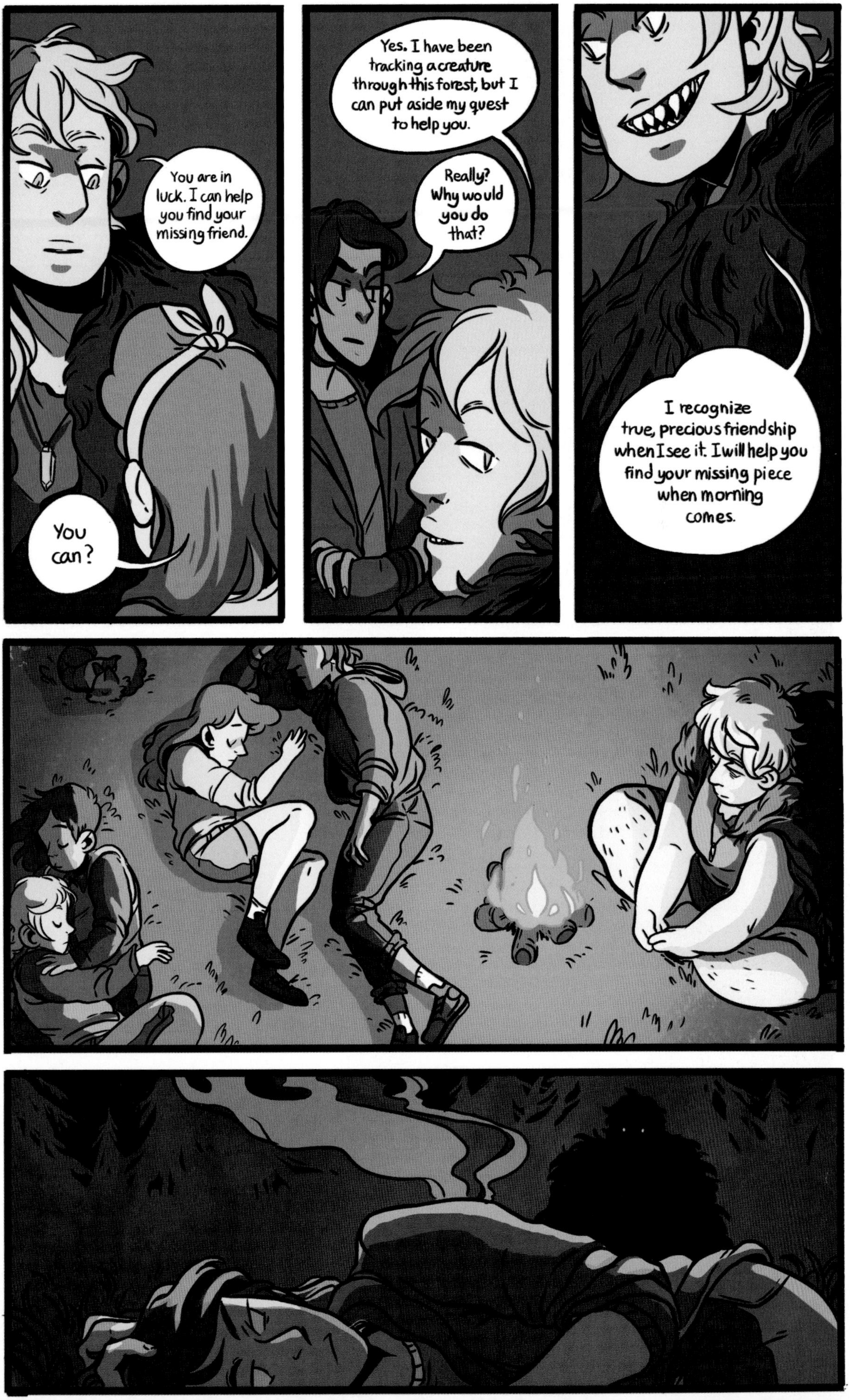
You are in luck. I can help you find your missing friend.
You can?
Yes. I have been tracking a creature through this forest, but I can put aside my quest to help you.
Really? Why would you do that?
I recognize true, precious friendship when I see it. I will help you find your missing piece when morning comes.

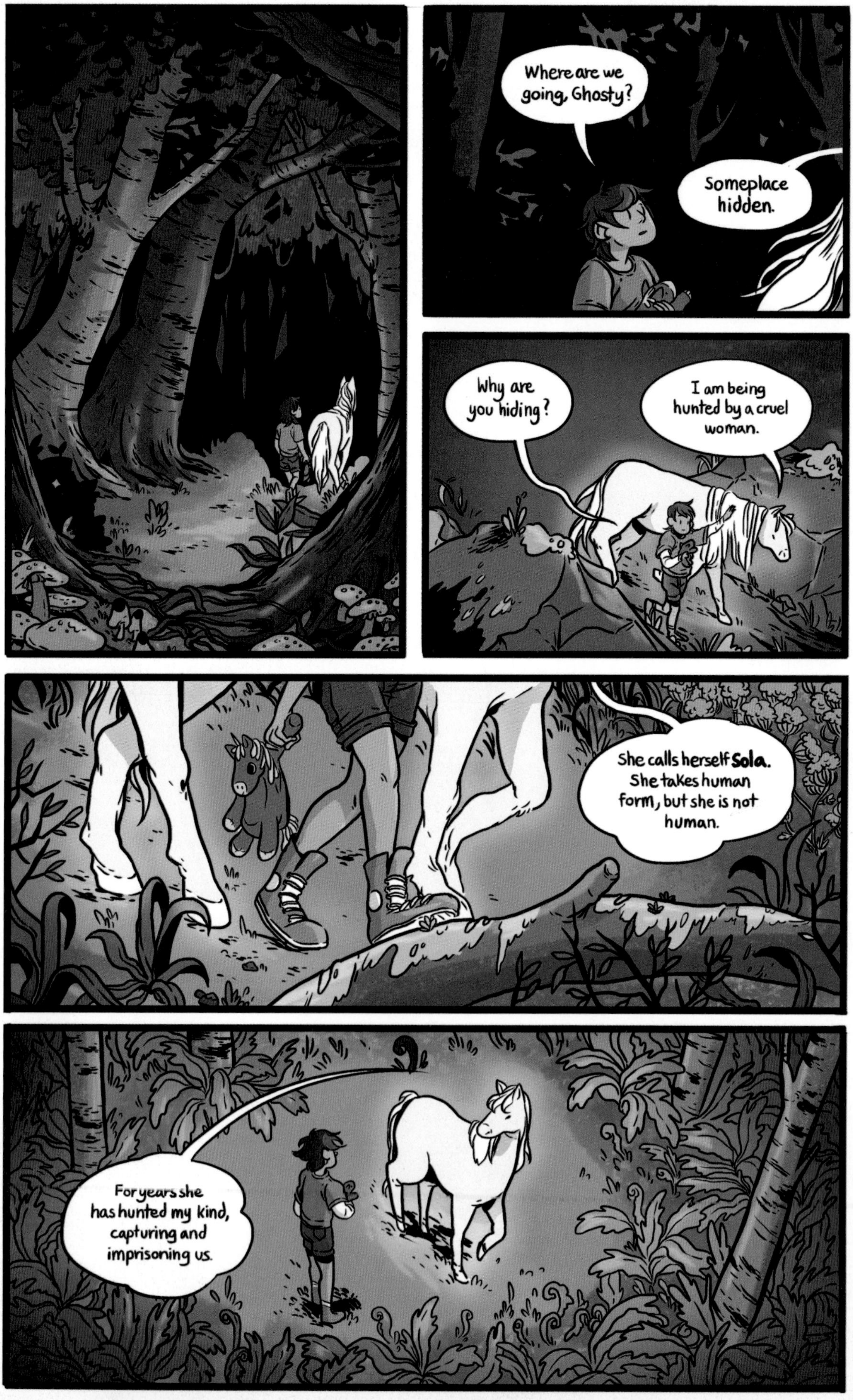
Where are we going, Ghosty?
Someplace hidden.
Why are you hiding?
I am being hunted by a cruel woman.
She calls herself **Sola.** She takes human form, but she is not human.
For years she has hunted my kind, capturing and imprisoning us.

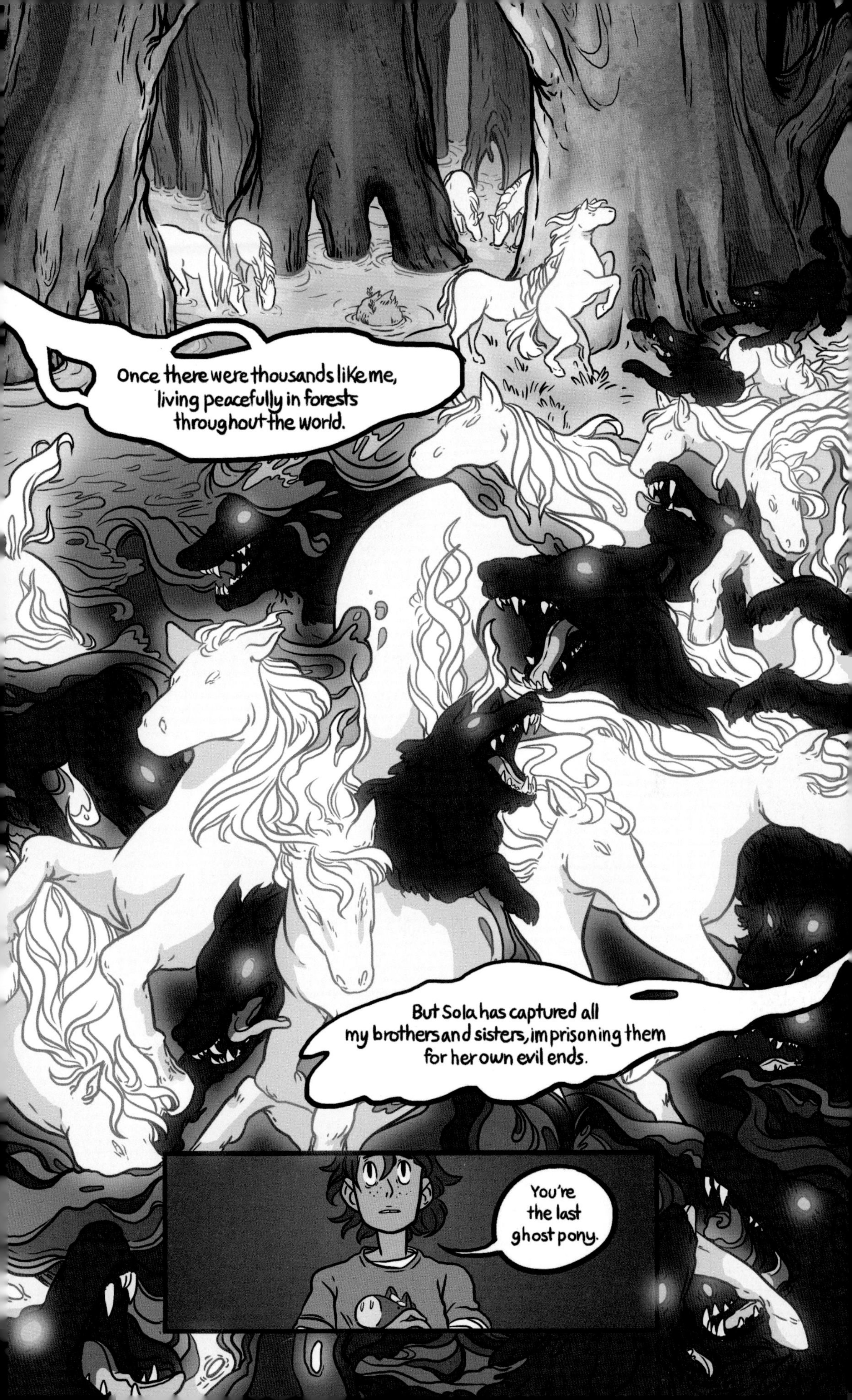
Once there were thousands like me, living peacefully in forests throughout the world.
But Sola has captured all my brothers and sisters, imprisoning them for her own evil ends.
You're the last ghost pony.

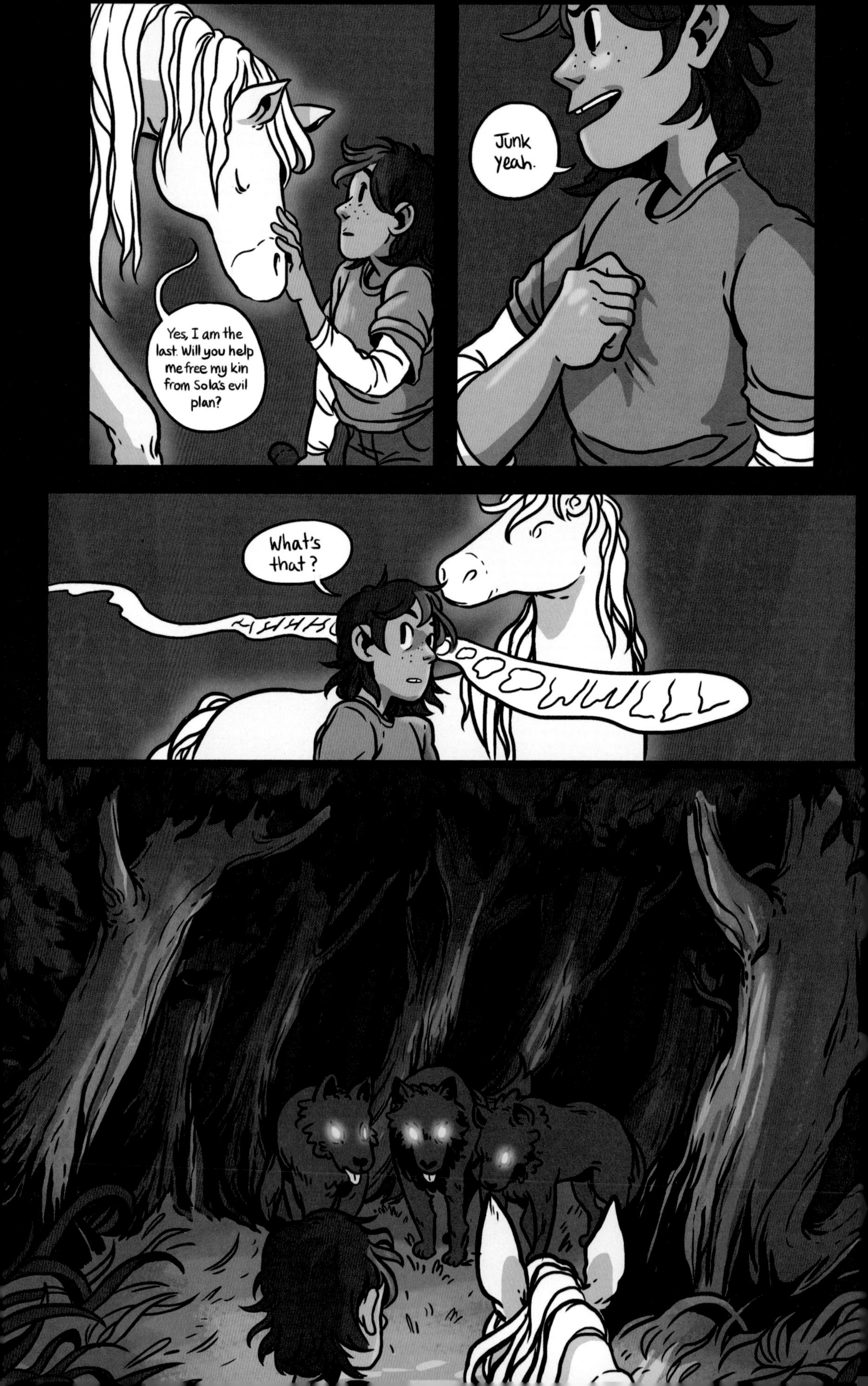
Yes, I am the last. Will you help me free my kin from Sola's evil plan?
Junk yeah.
What's that?

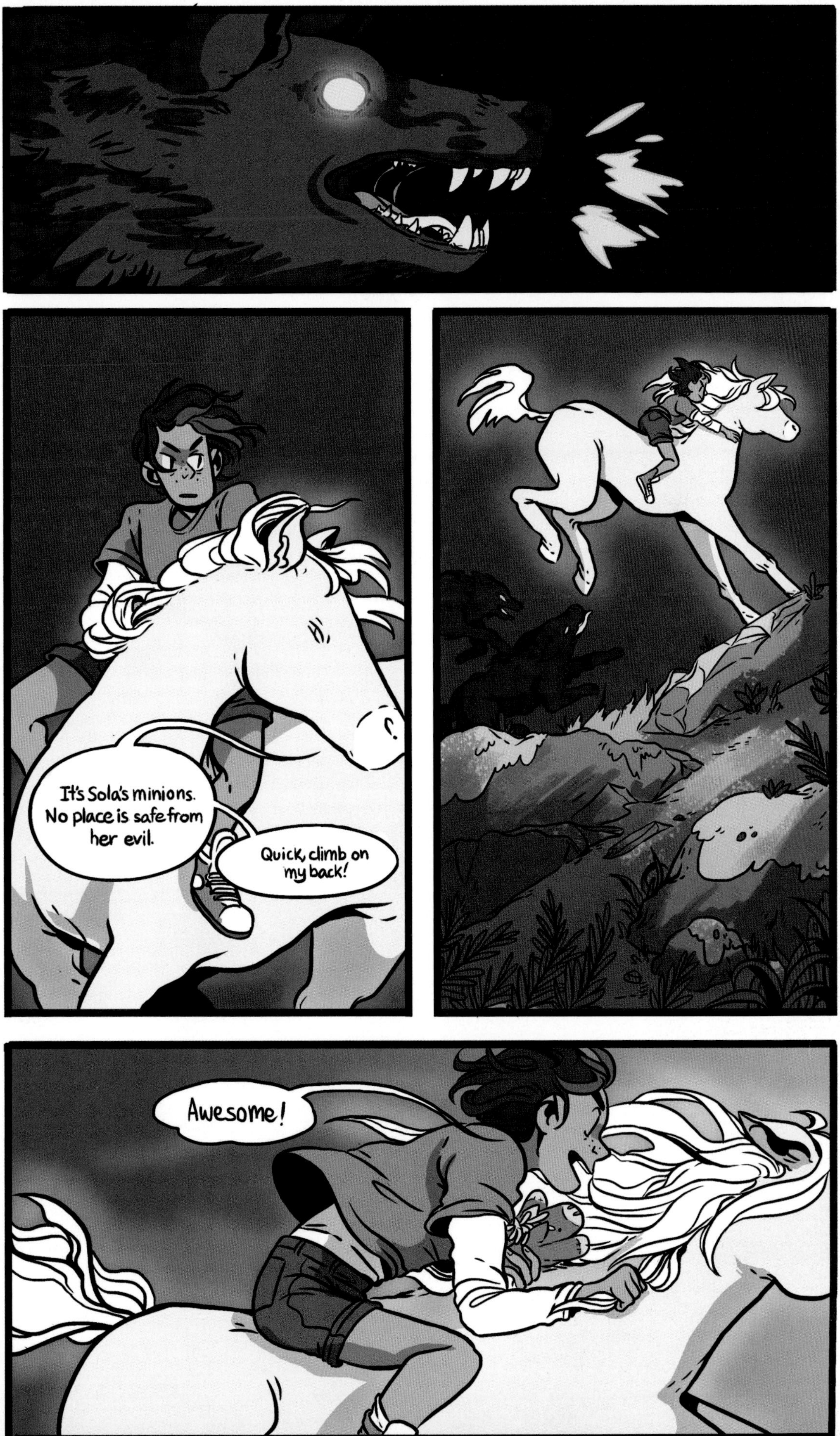
It's Sola's minions. No place is safe from her evil.
Quick, climb on my back!
Awesome!

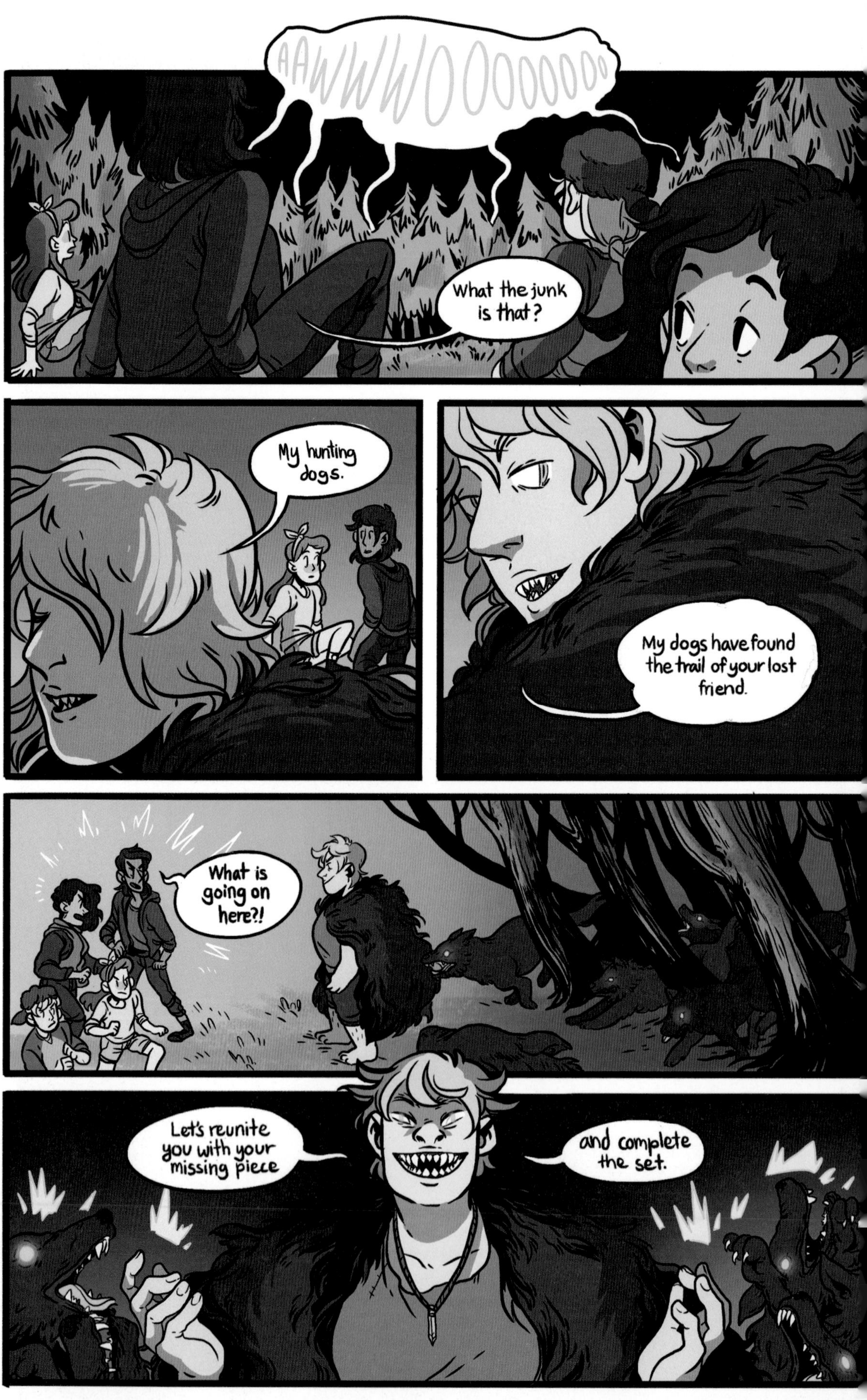
AAWWWOOOOOOOo
What the junk is that?
My hunting dogs.
My dogs have found the trail of your lost friend.
What is going on here?!
Let's reunite you with your missing piece
and complete the set.

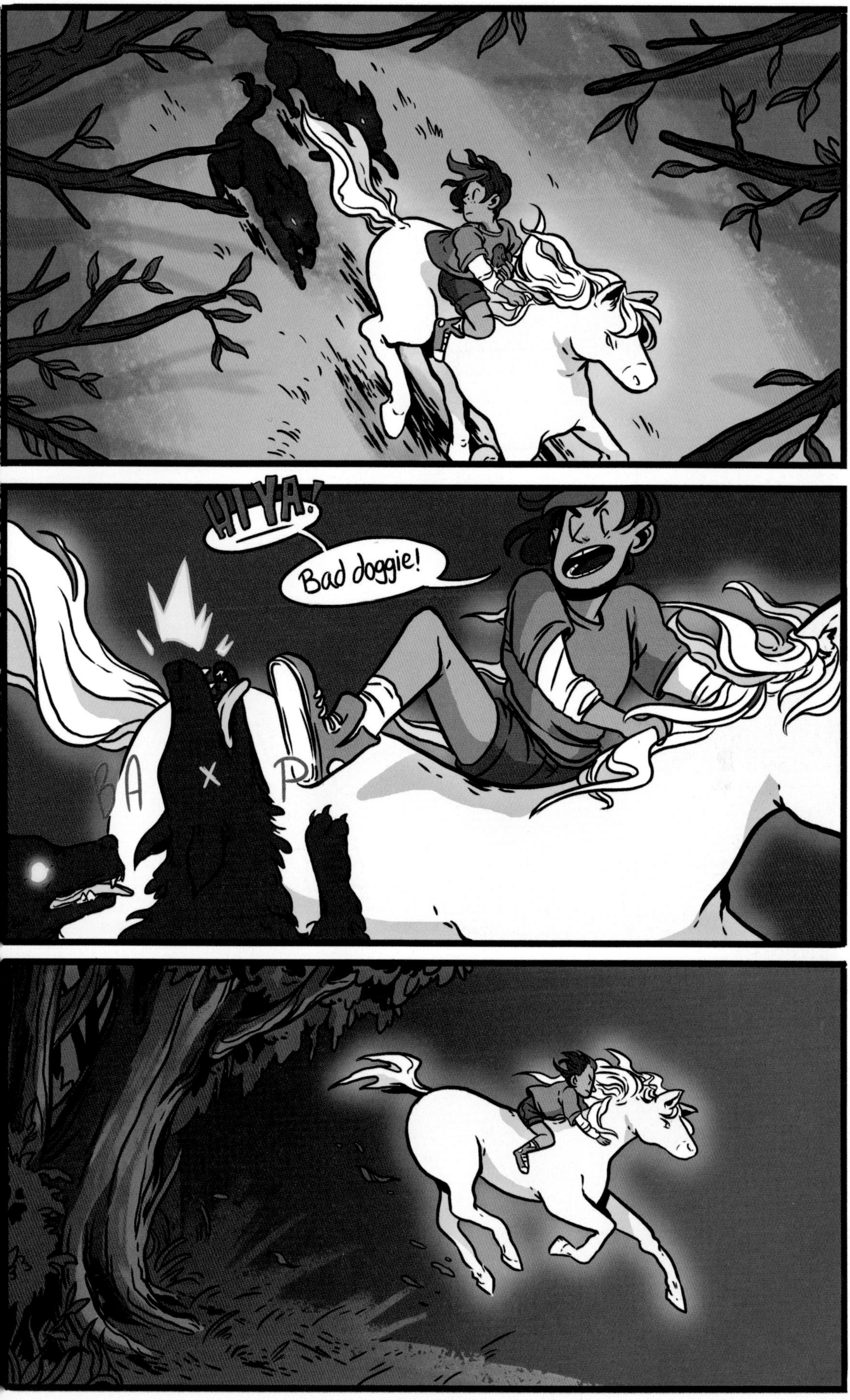
HIYA!
Bad doggie!
BAP

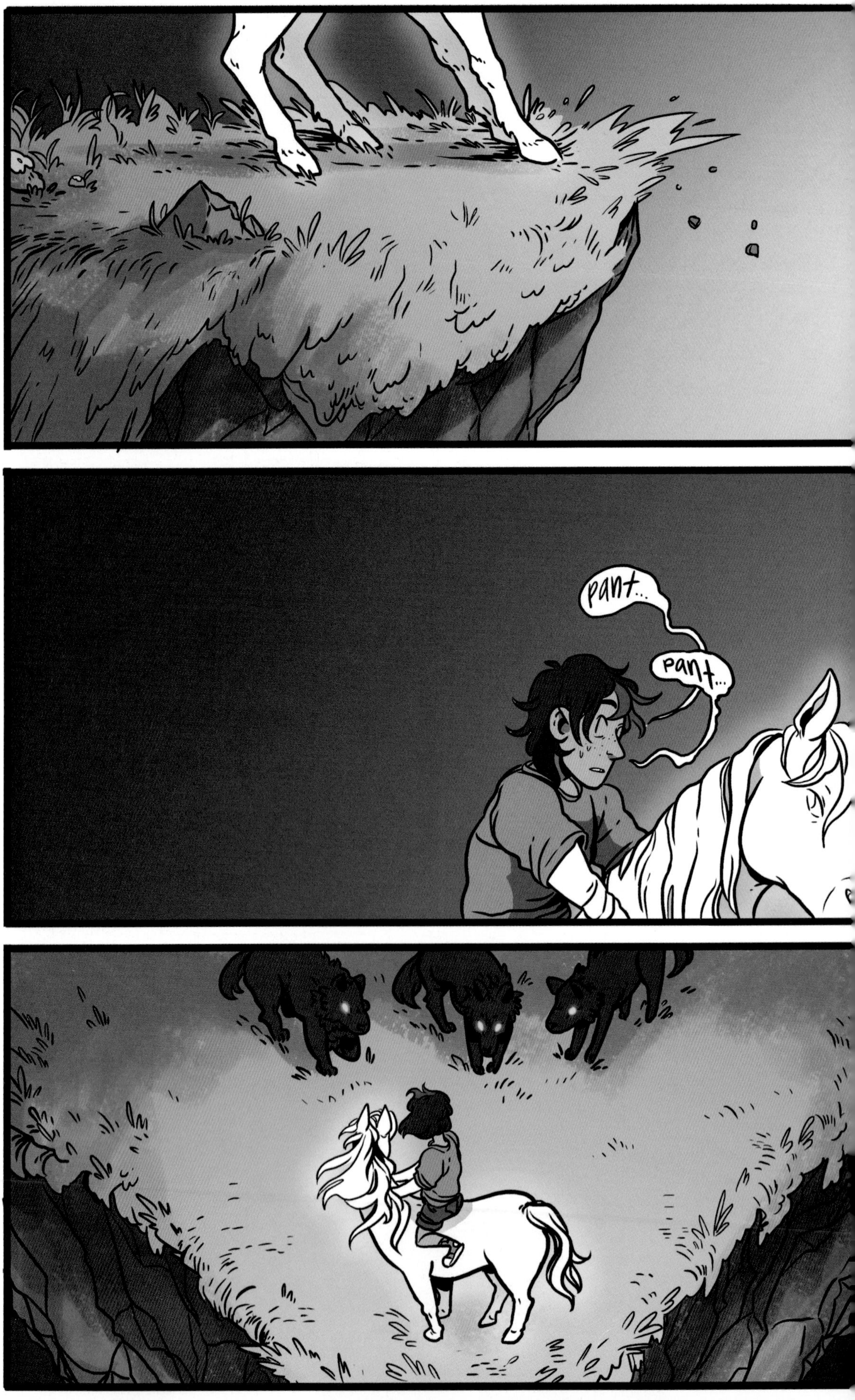
pant...
pant...

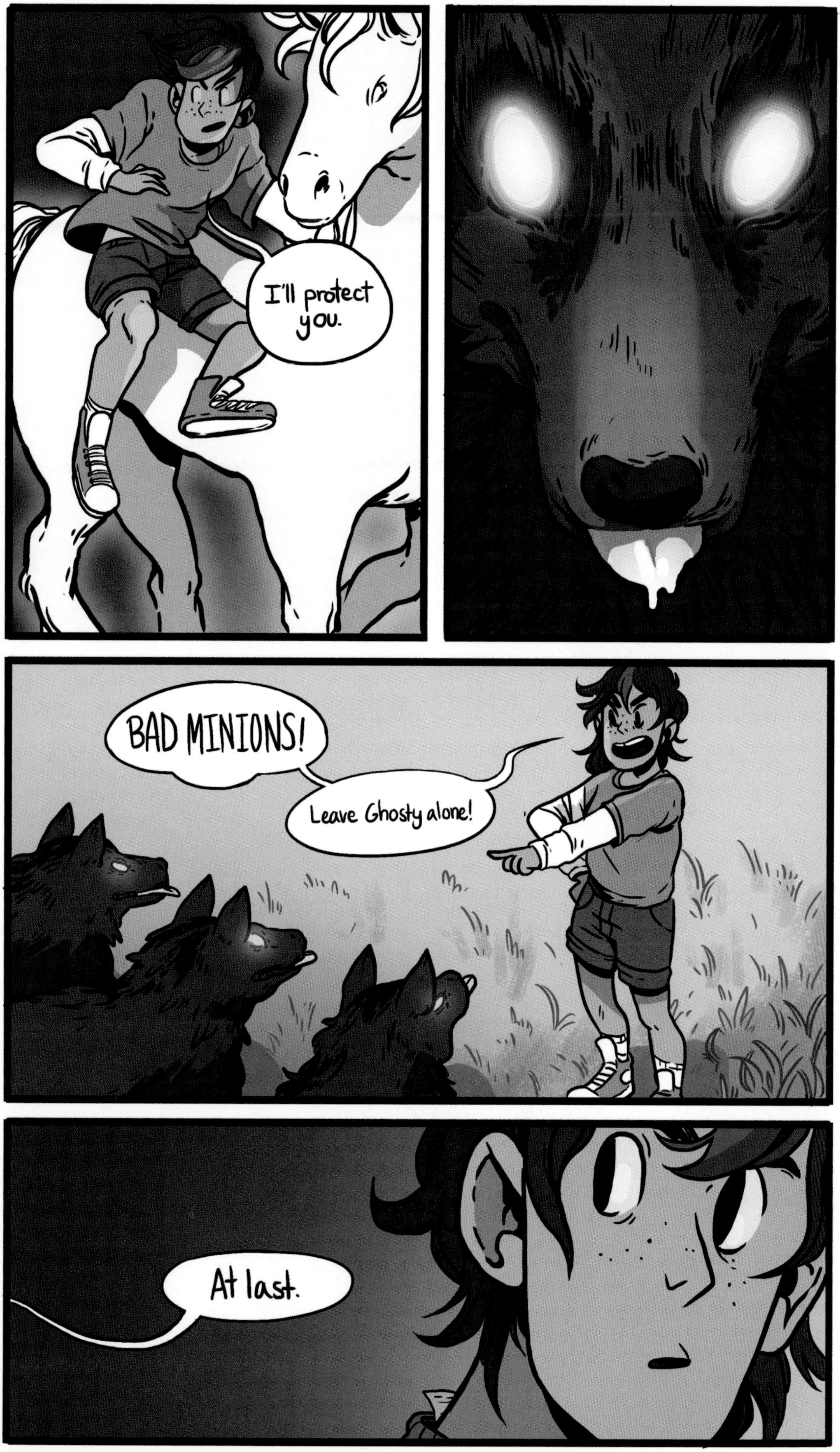
I'll protect you.
BAD MINIONS!
Leave Ghosty alone!
At last.

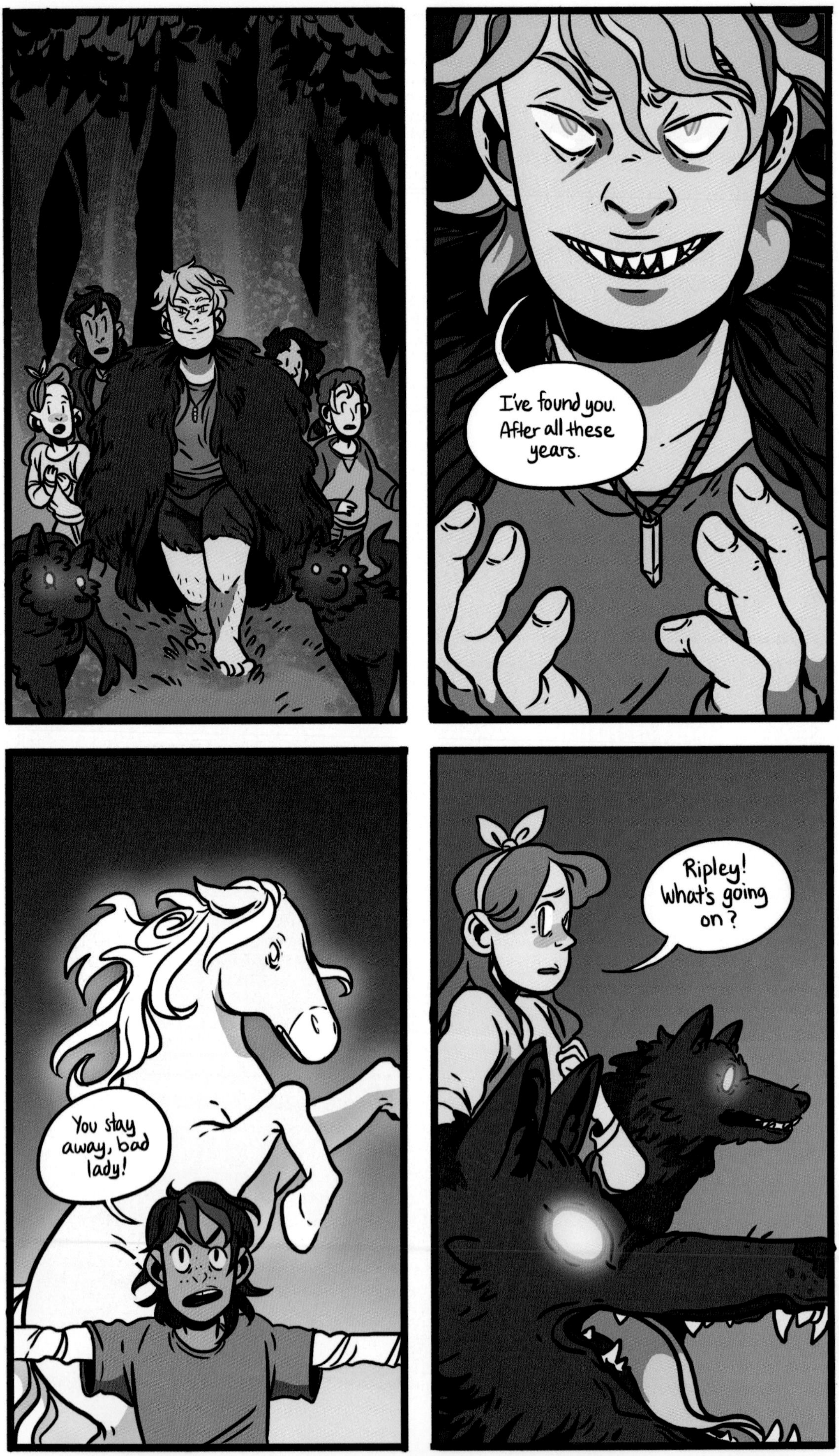
I've found you. After all these years.
You stay away, bad lady!
Ripley! What's going on?

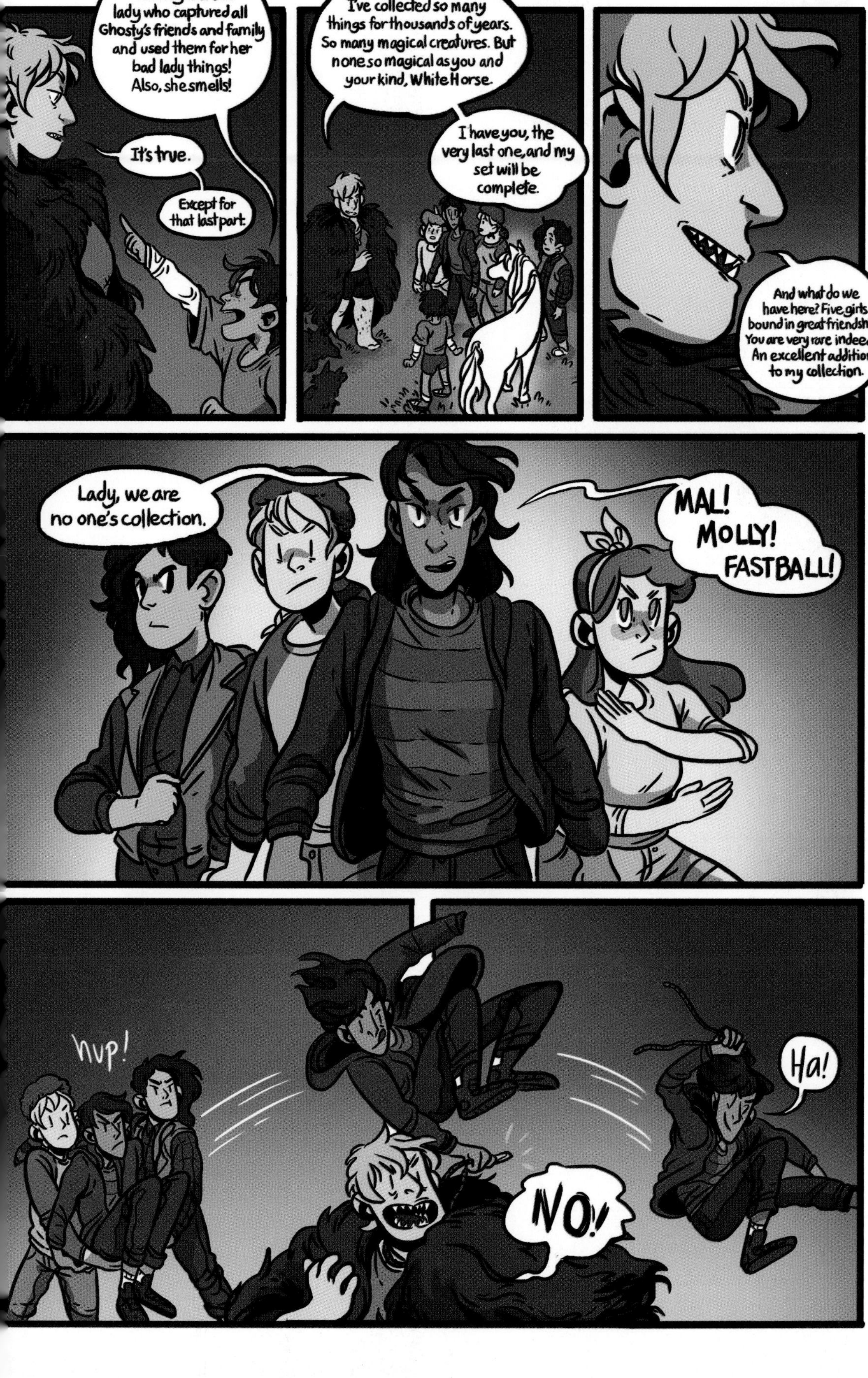
That lady is a bad lady who captured all Ghosty's friends and family and used them for her bad lady things! Also, she smells!
It's true.
Except for that last part.
I've collected so many things for thousands of years. So many magical creatures. But none so magical as you and your kind, White Horse.
I have you, the very last one, and my set will be complete.
And what do we have here? Five girls bound in great friendship? You are very rare indeed. An excellent addition to my collection.
Lady, we are no one's collection.
MAL! MOLLY! FASTBALL!
hup!
Ha!
NO!

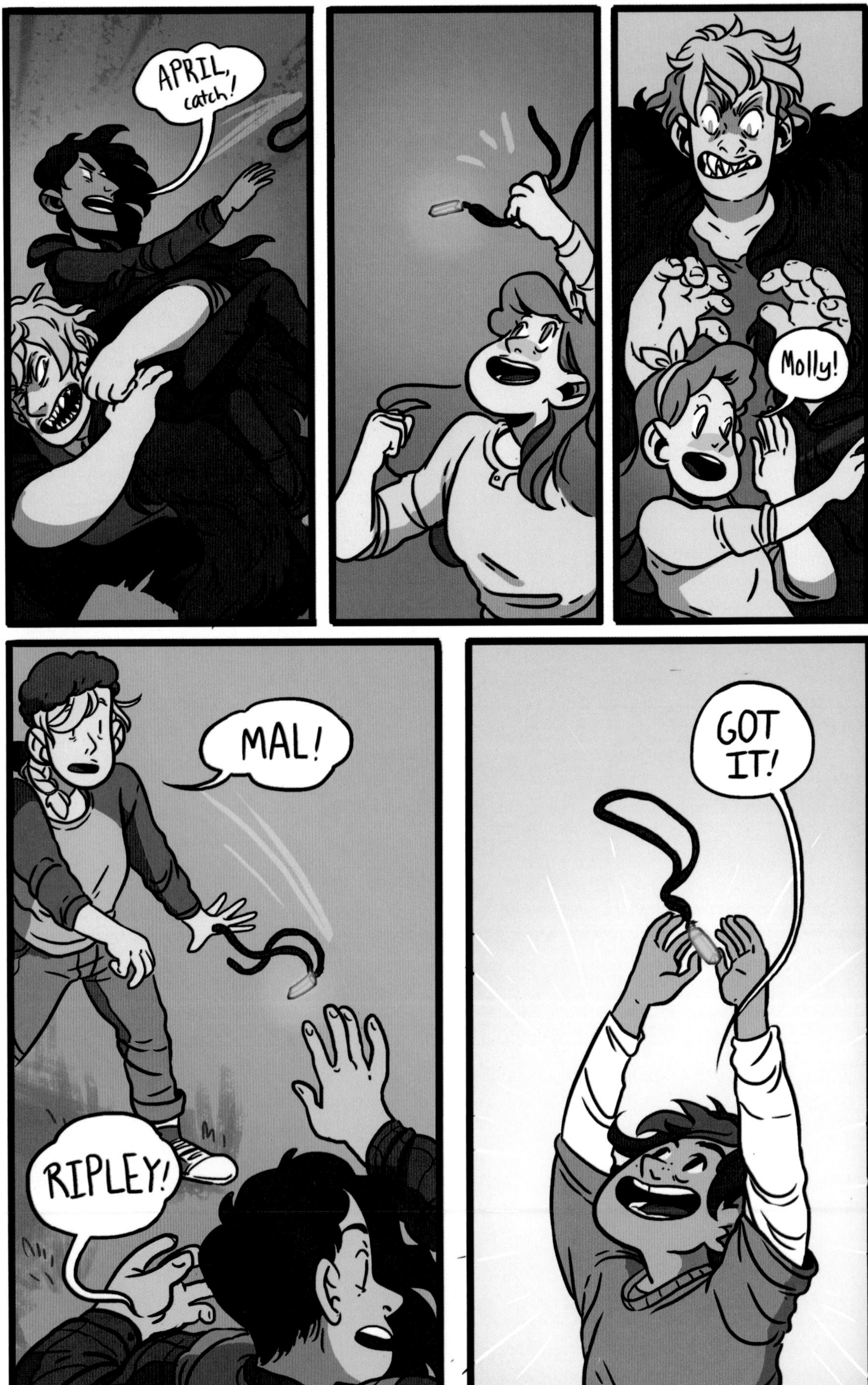
APRIL, catch!
Molly!
MAL!
RIPLEY!
GOT IT!

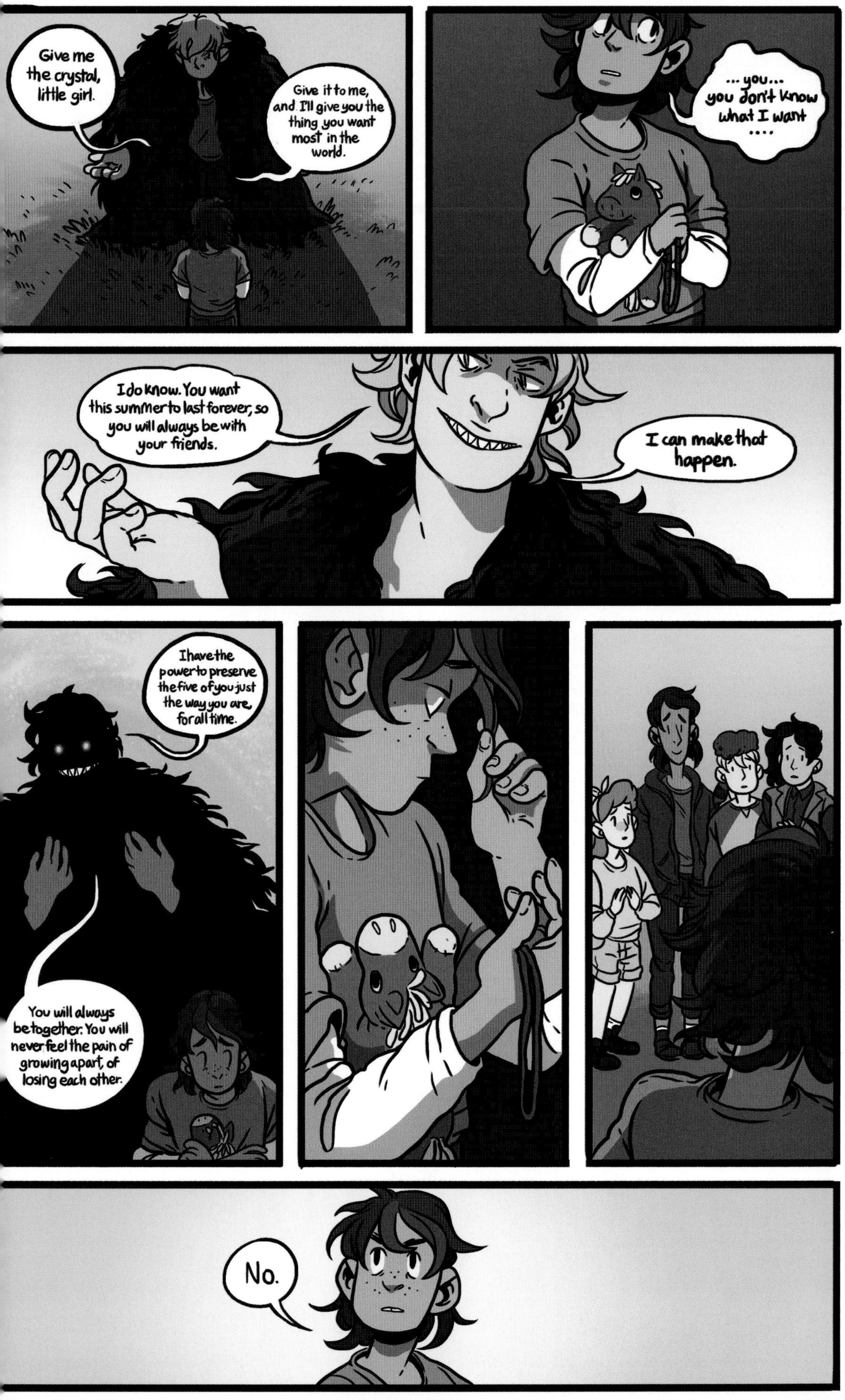
Give me the crystal, little girl.
Give it to me, and I'll give you the thing you want most in the world.
... you... you don't know what I want ....
I do know. You want this summer to last forever, so you will always be with your friends.
I can make that happen.
I have the power to preserve the five of you just the way you are, for all time.
You will always be together. You will never feel the pain of growing apart, of losing each other.
No.

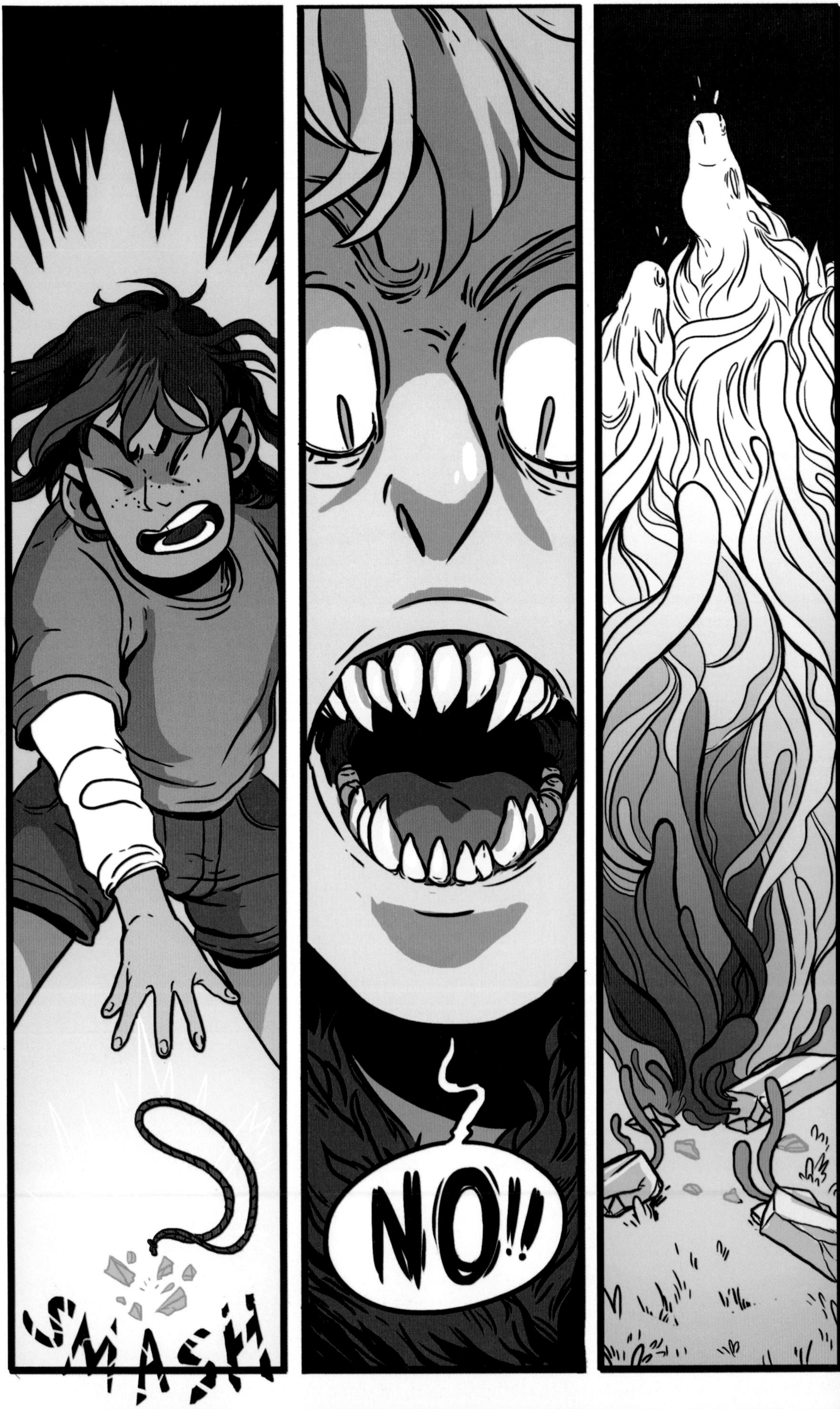
SMASH
NO!!

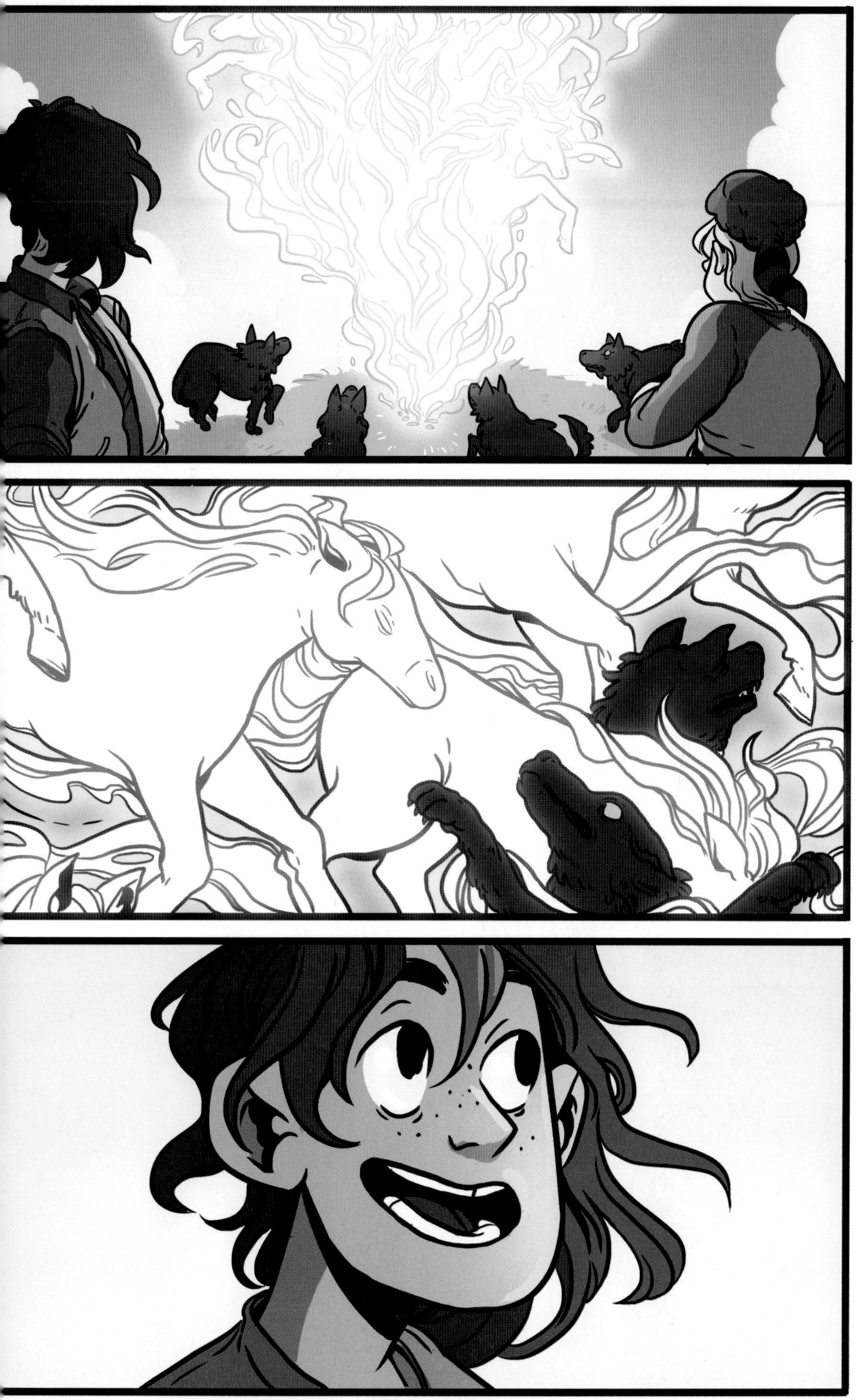

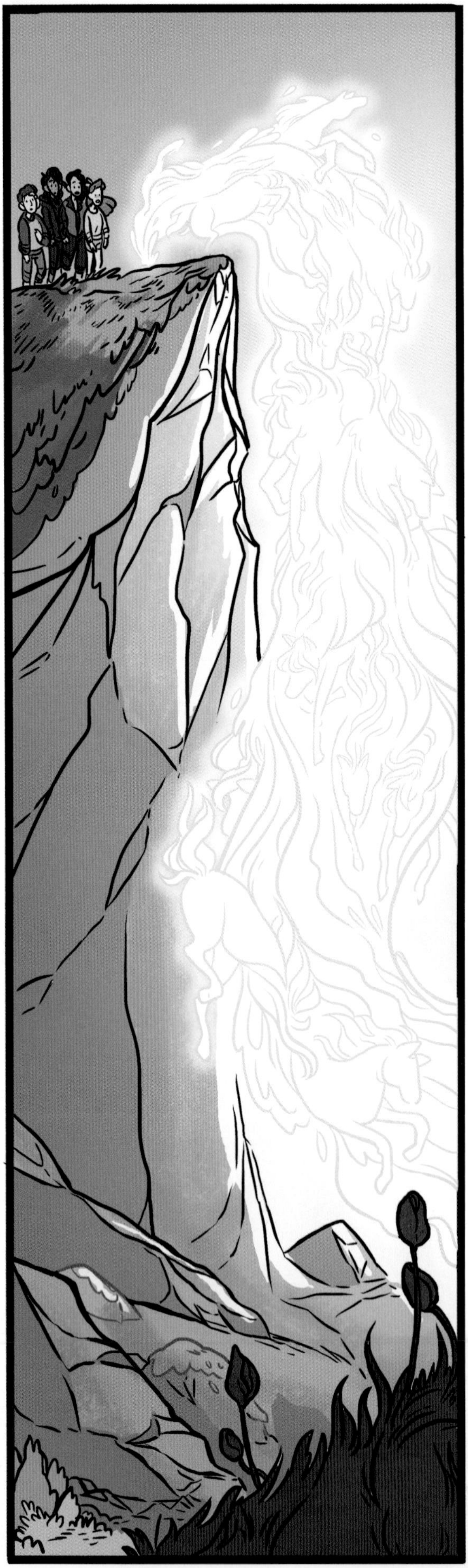
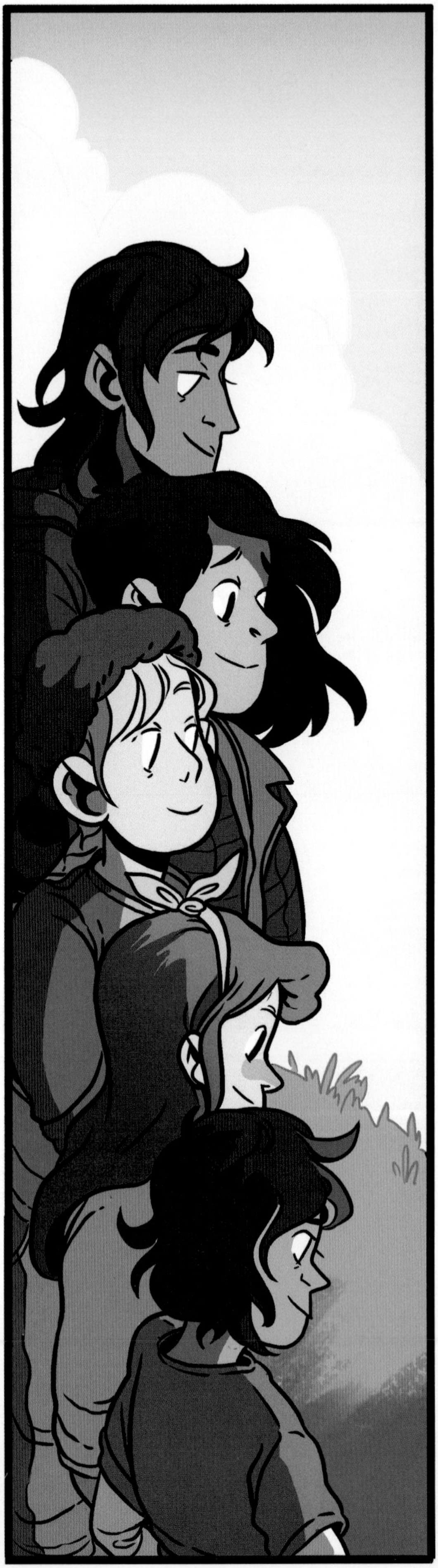

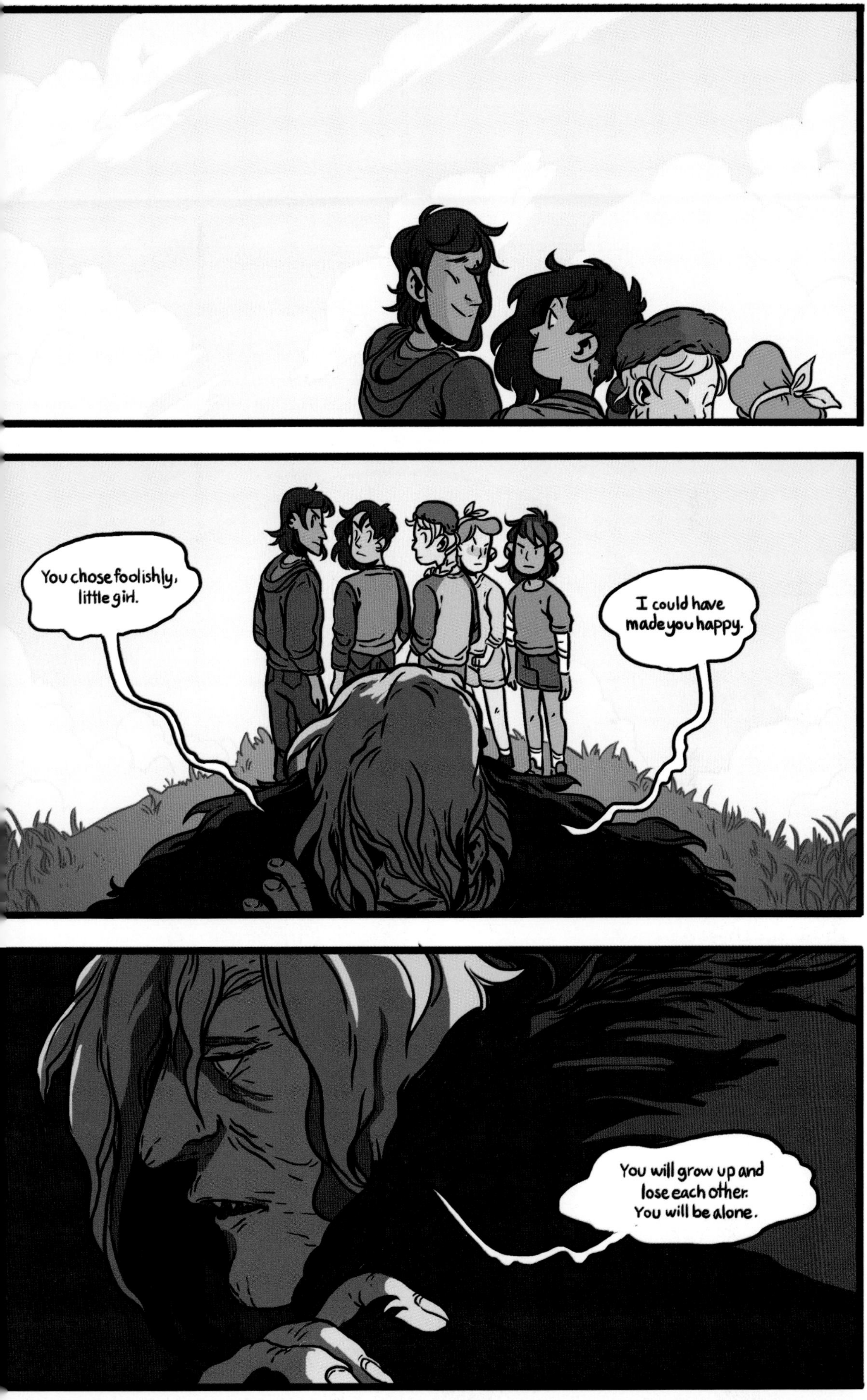
You chose foolishly, little girl.
I could have made you happy.
You will grow up and lose each other. You will be alone.

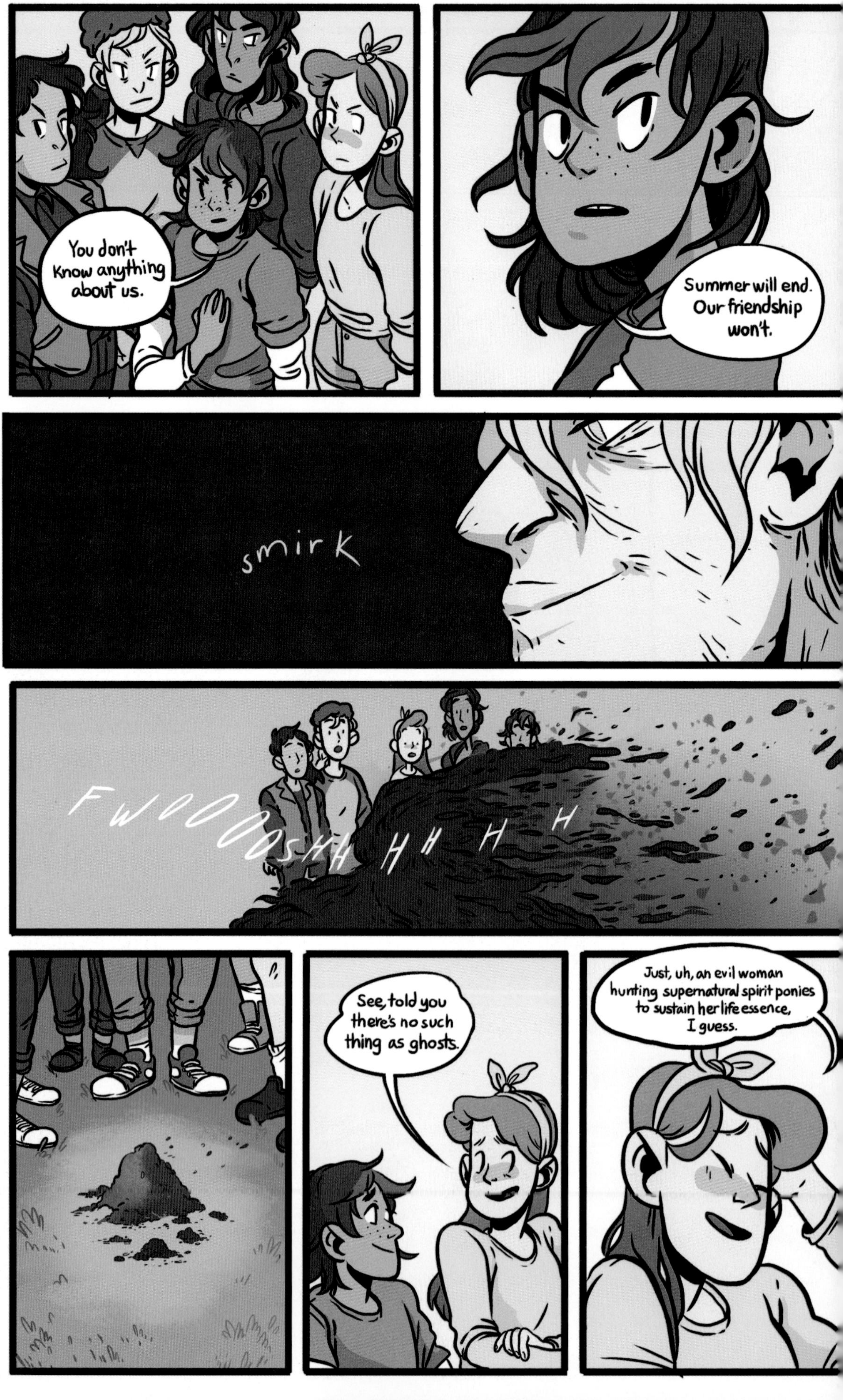
You don't know anything about us.
Summer will end. Our friendship won't.
smirk
FWOOOOSHHHHHH
See, told you there's no such thing as ghosts.
Just, uh, an evil woman hunting supernatural spirit ponies to sustain her life essence, I guess.

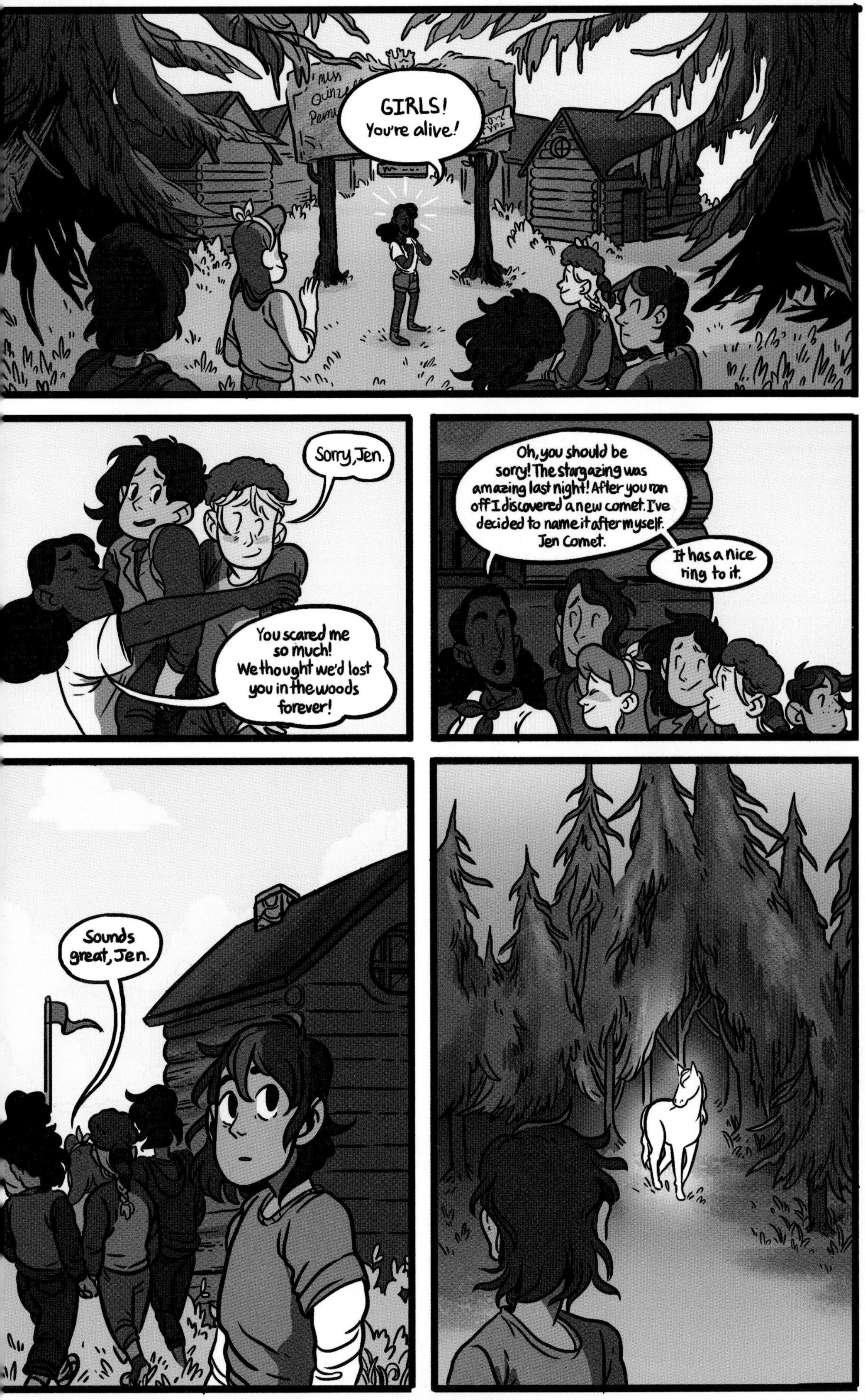
GIRLS! You're alive!
Sorry, Jen.
You scared me so much! We thought we'd lost you in the woods forever!
Oh, you should be sorry! The stargazing was amazing last night! After you ran off I discovered a new comet. I've decided to name it after myself. Jen Comet.
It has a nice ring to it.
Sounds great, Jen.

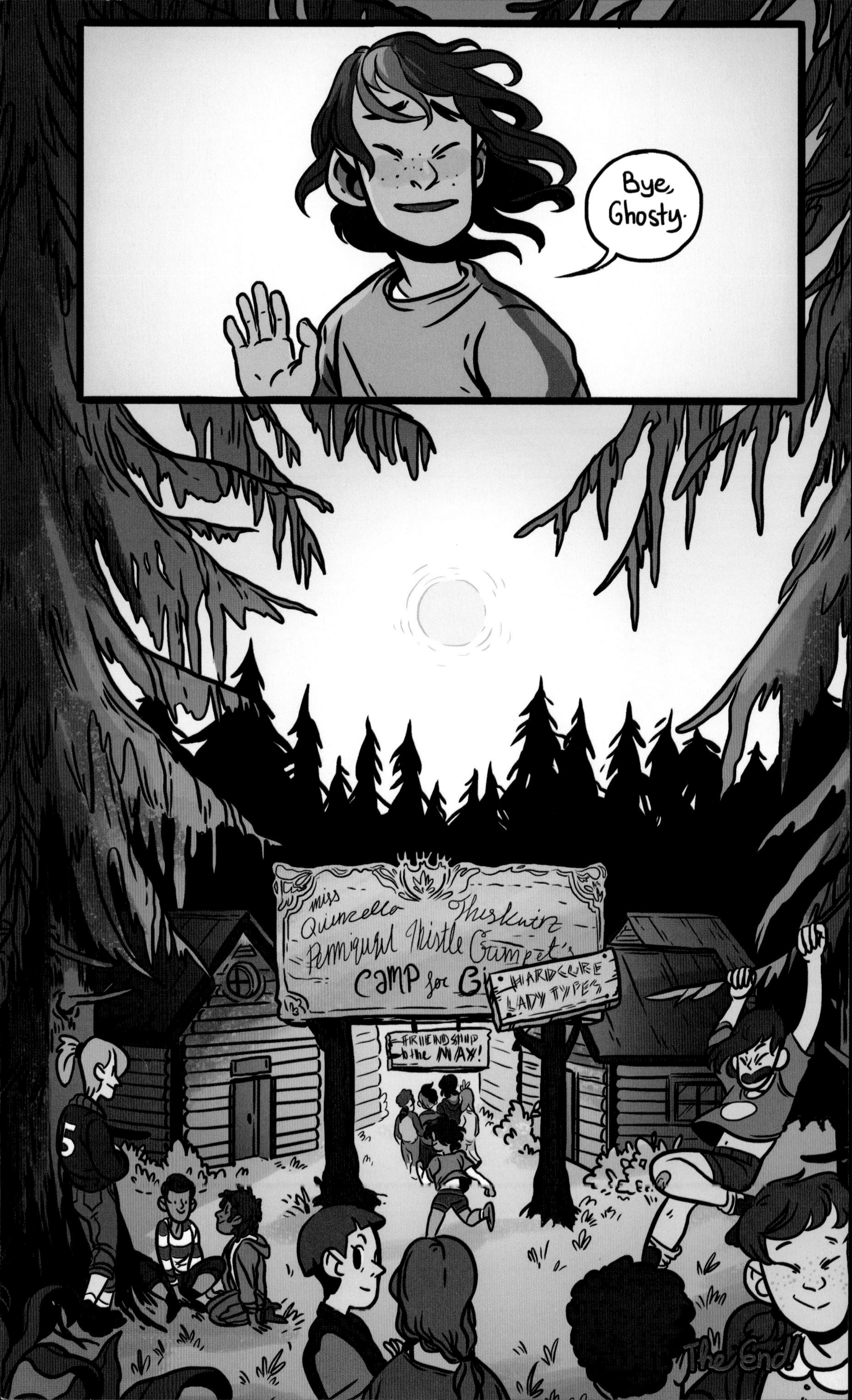
Bye, Ghosty.
miss Quinzella Thiskwin Penniquiqul Thistle Crumpet's CAMP for Gi
HARDCORE LADY TYPES
FRIENDSHIP to the MAX!
The End!

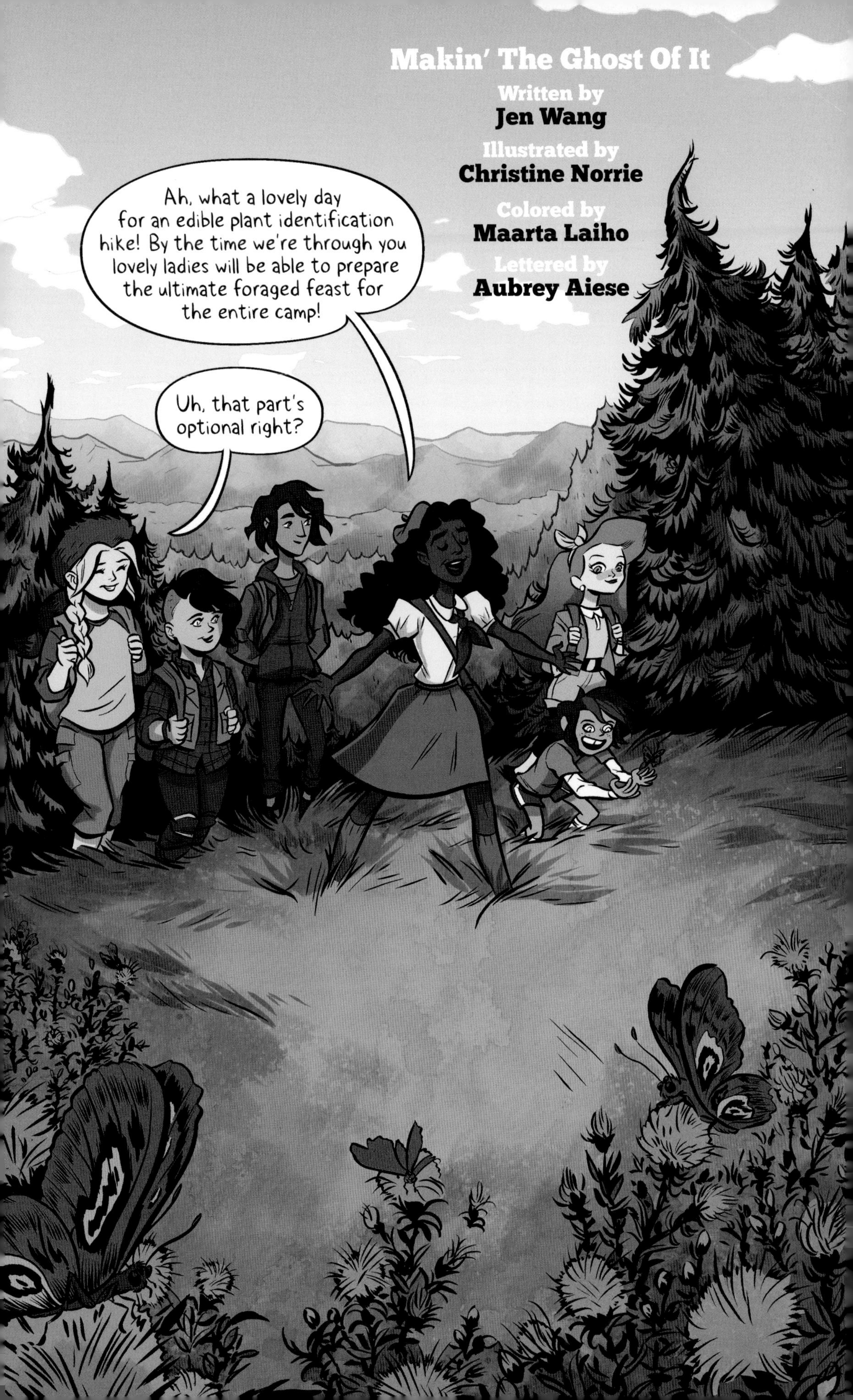
Makin' The Ghost Of It
Written by
Jen Wang
Illustrated by
Christine Norrie
Colored by
Maarta Laiho
Lettered by
Aubrey Aiese
Ah, what a lovely day for an edible plant identification hike! By the time we're through you lovely ladies will be able to prepare the ultimate foraged feast for the entire camp!
Uh, that part's optional right?

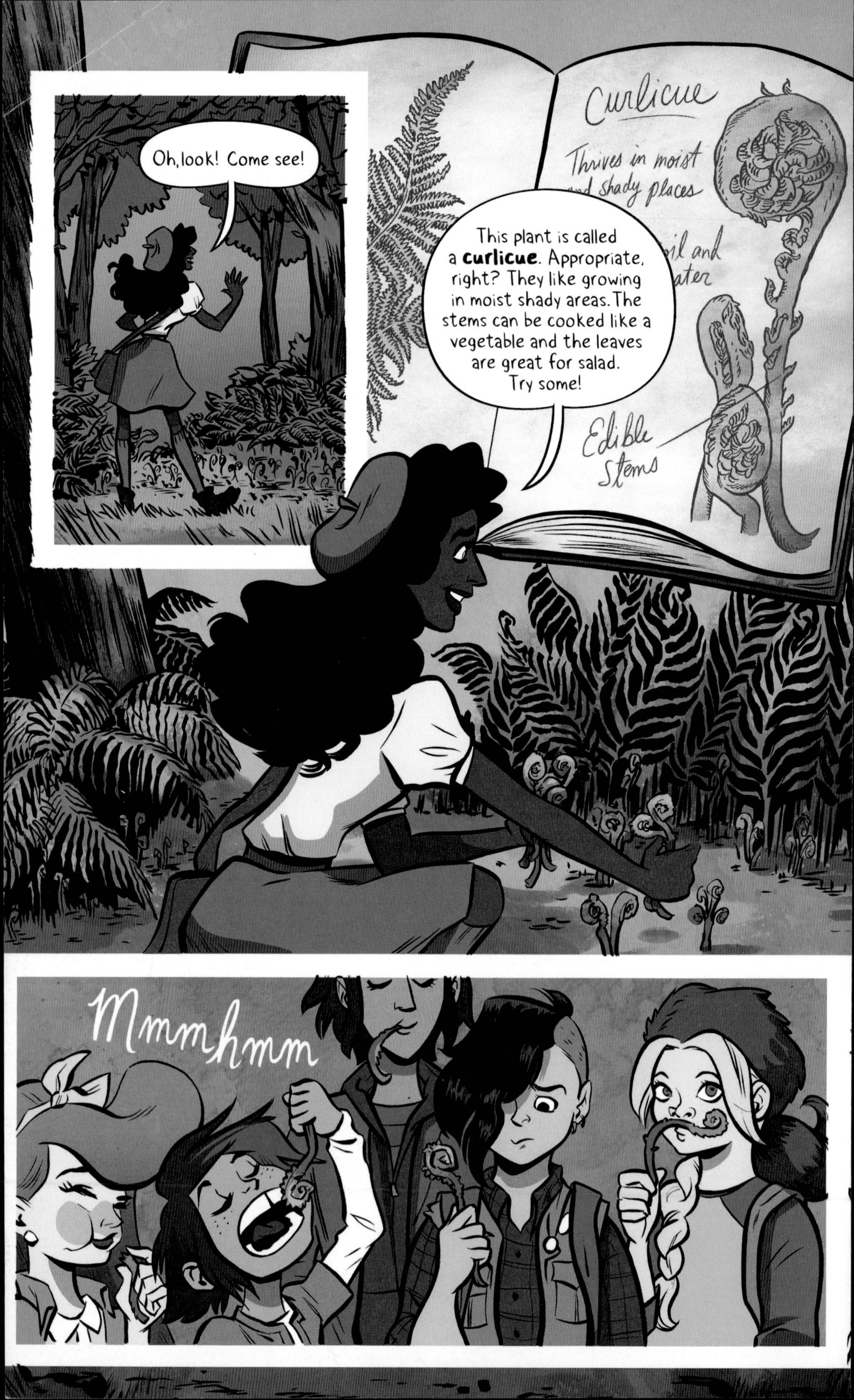
Oh, look! Come see!
Curlicue
Thrives in moist
shady places
Edible Stems
This plant is called a **curlicue**. Appropriate, right? They like growing in moist shady areas. The stems can be cooked like a vegetable and the leaves are great for salad. Try some!
Mmmhmm

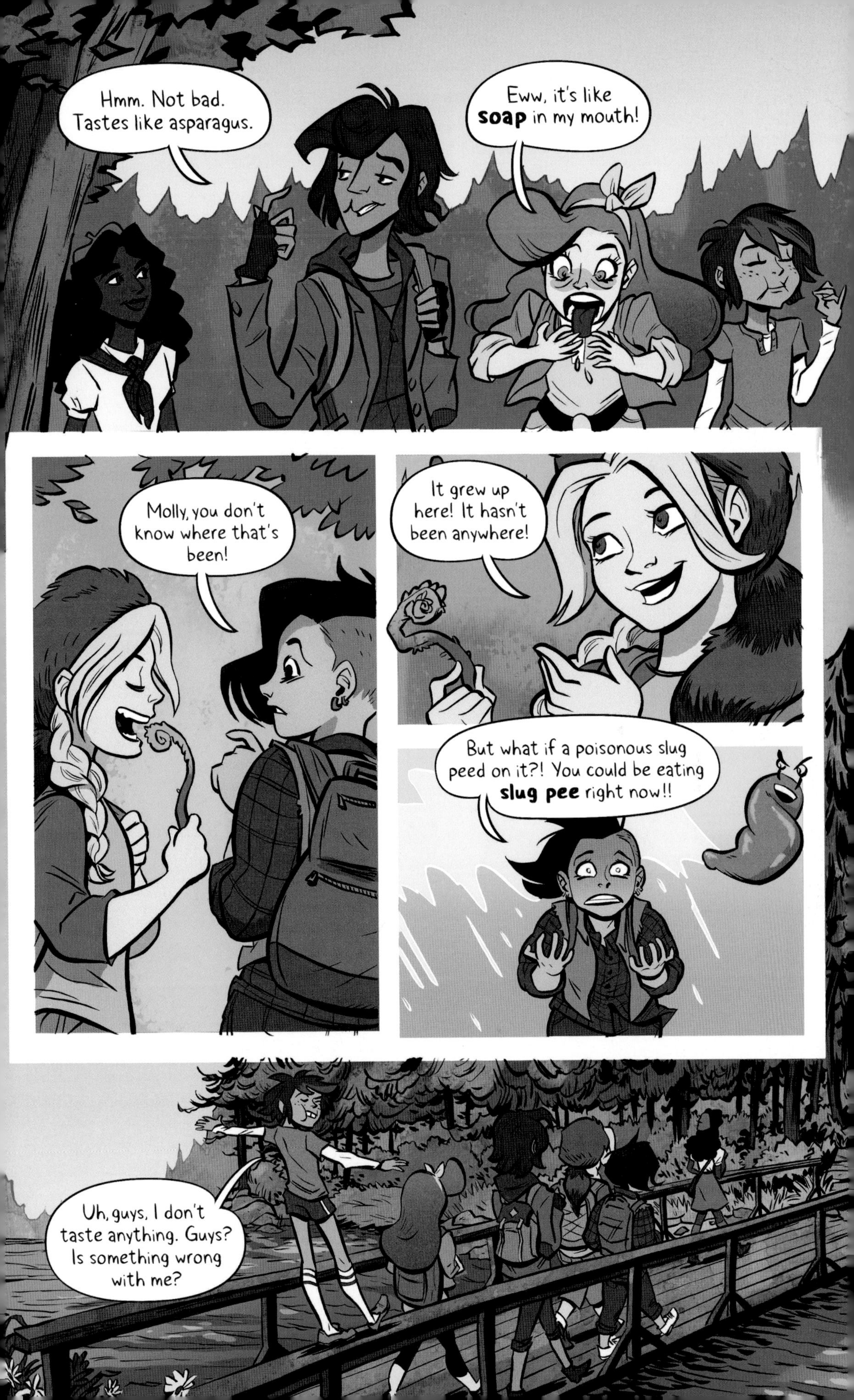

Hmm. Not bad. Tastes like asparagus.
Eww, it's like **soap** in my mouth!
Molly, you don't know where that's been!
It grew up here! It hasn't been anywhere!
But what if a poisonous slug peed on it?! You could be eating **slug pee** right now!!
Uh, guys, I don't taste anything. Guys? Is something wrong with me?

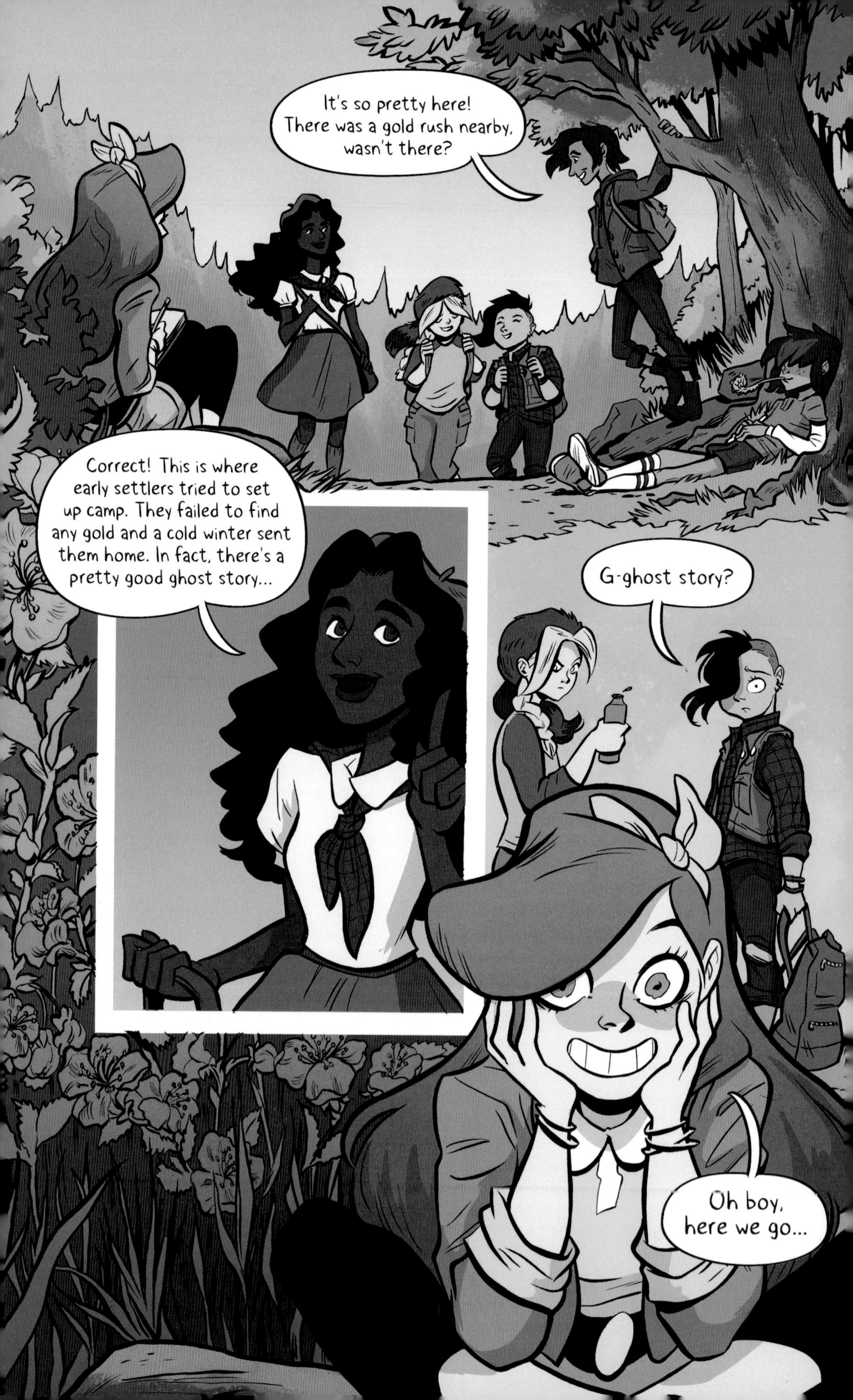
It's so pretty here! There was a gold rush nearby, wasn't there?
Correct! This is where early settlers tried to set up camp. They failed to find any gold and a cold winter sent them home. In fact, there's a pretty good ghost story...
G-ghost story?
Oh boy, here we go...

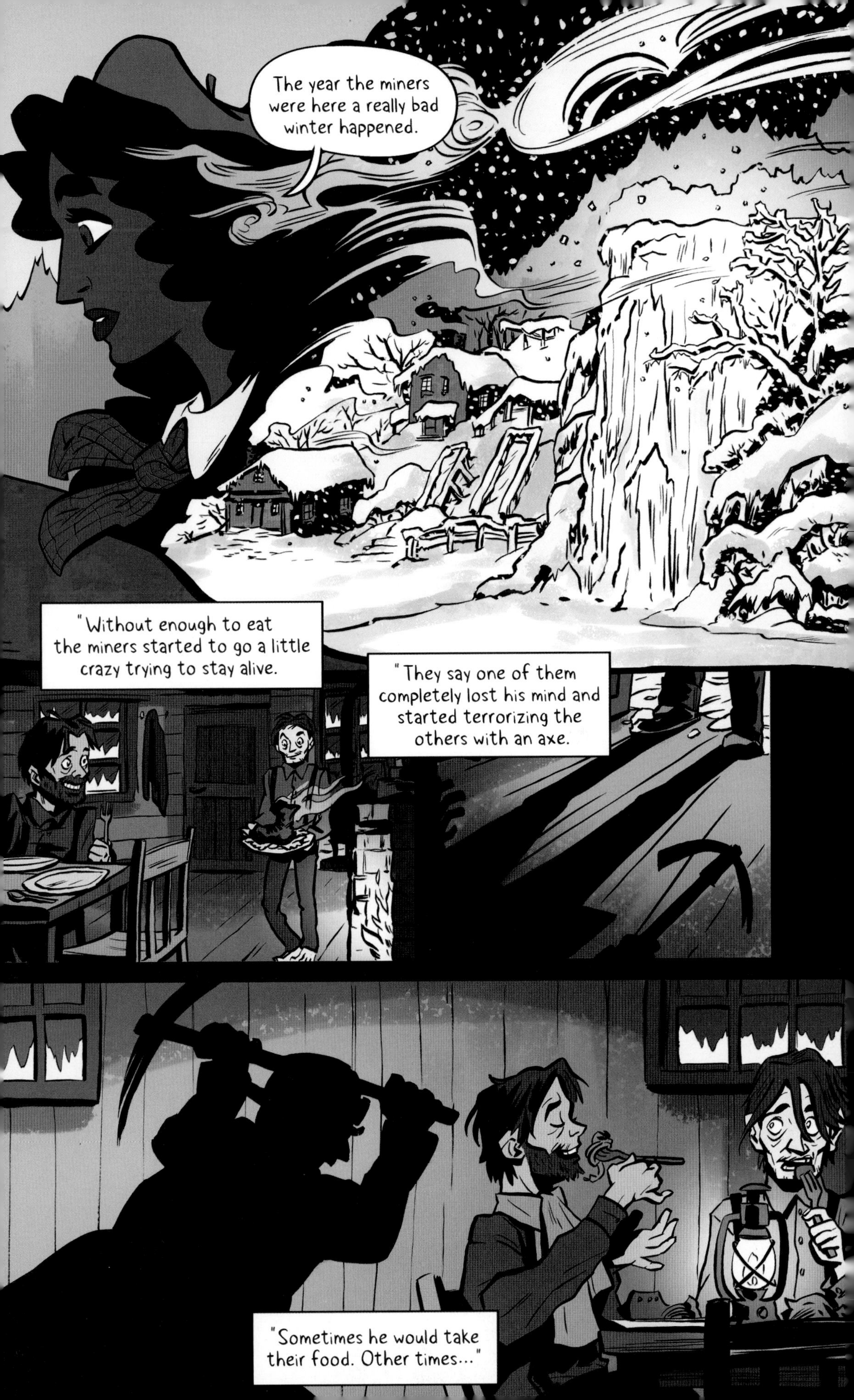
The year the miners were here a really bad winter happened.
"Without enough to eat the miners started to go a little crazy trying to stay alive.
"They say one of them completely lost his mind and started terrorizing the others with an axe.
"Sometimes he would take their food. Other times..."

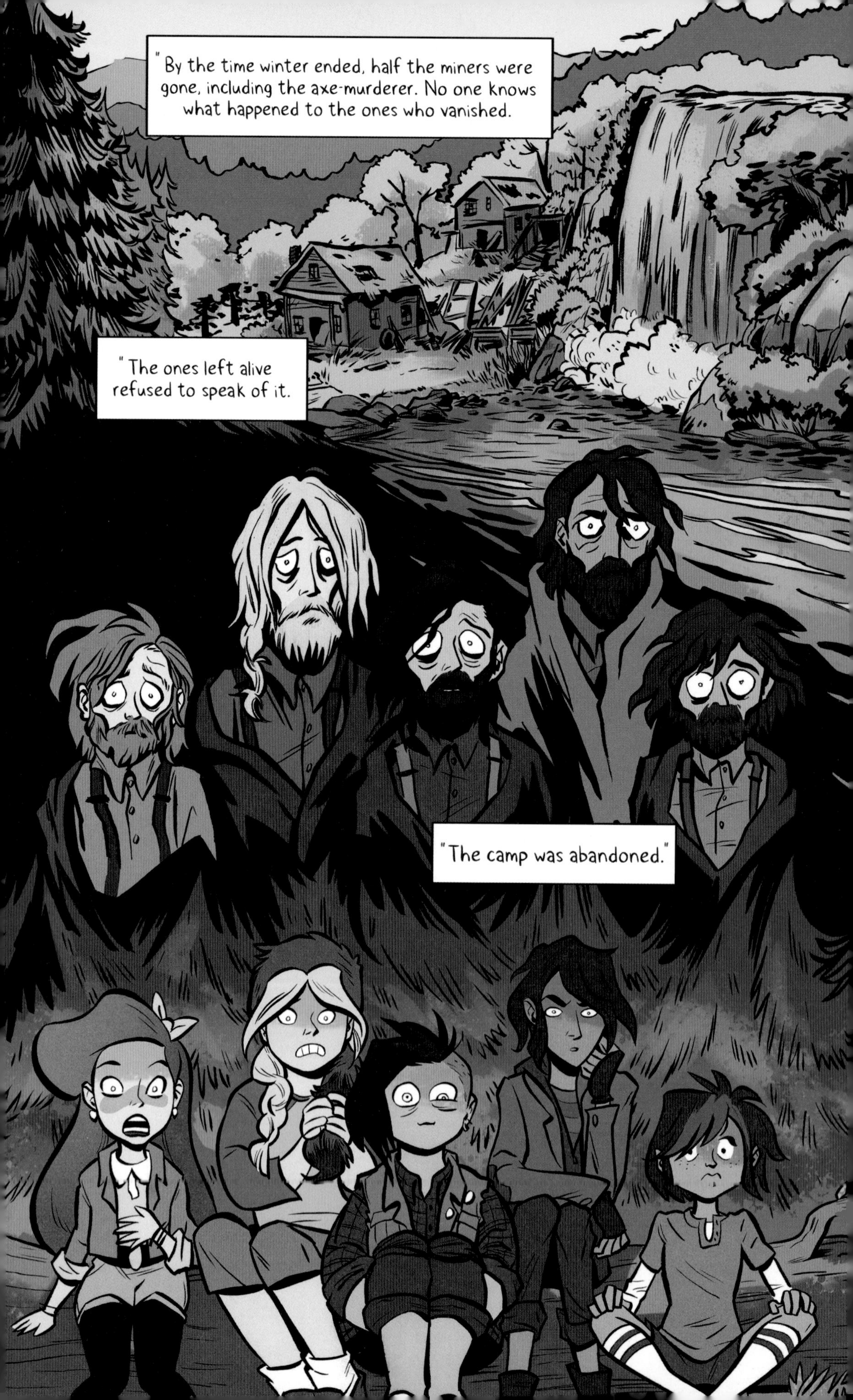
"By the time winter ended, half the miners were gone, including the axe-murderer. No one knows what happened to the ones who vanished.
"The ones left alive refused to speak of it.
"The camp was abandoned."

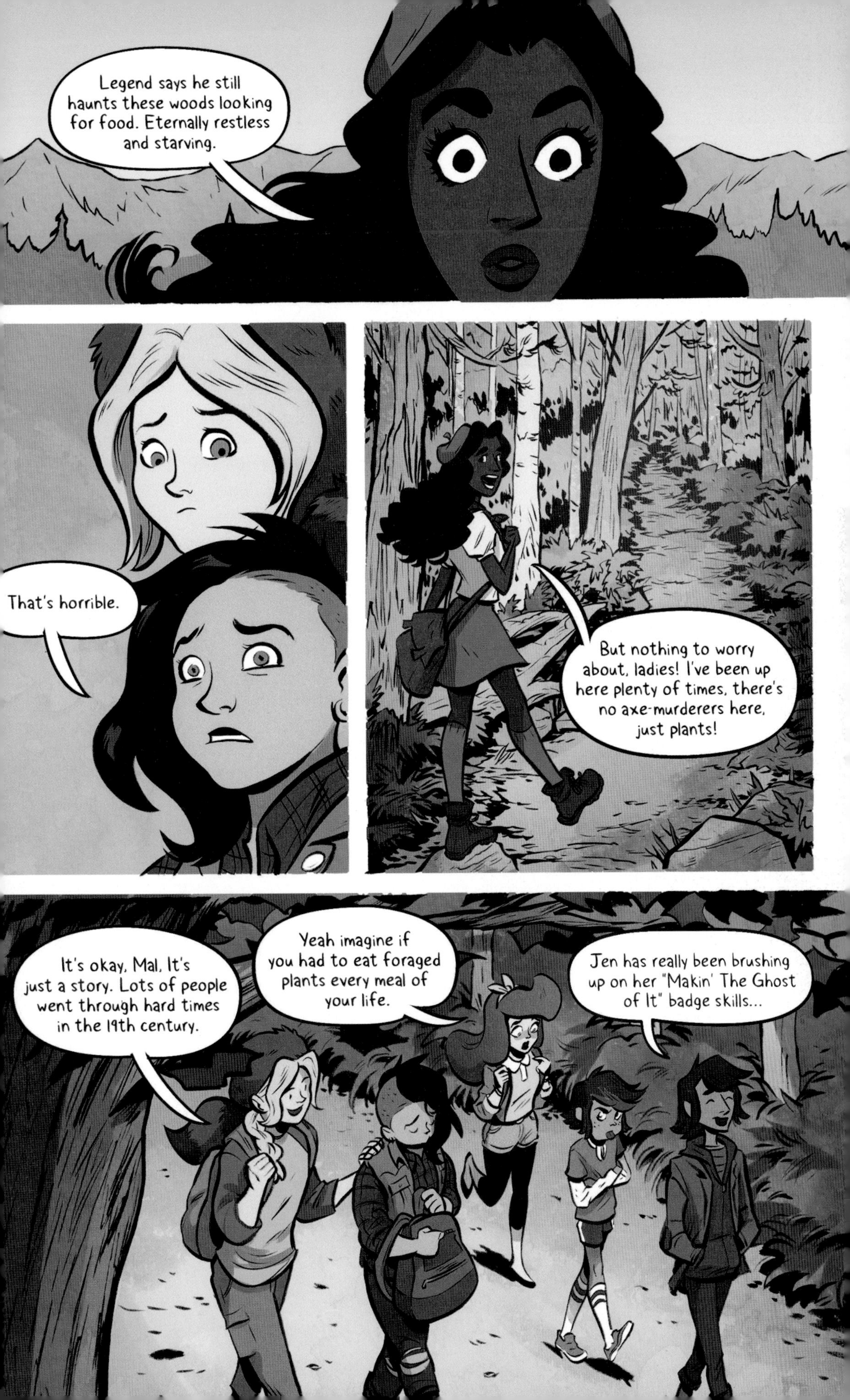

Legend says he still haunts these woods looking for food. Eternally restless and starving.
That's horrible.
But nothing to worry about, ladies! I've been up here plenty of times, there's no axe-murderers here, just plants!
It's okay, Mal, It's just a story. Lots of people went through hard times in the 19th century.
Yeah imagine if you had to eat foraged plants every meal of your life.
Jen has really been brushing up on her "Makin' The Ghost of It" badge skills...

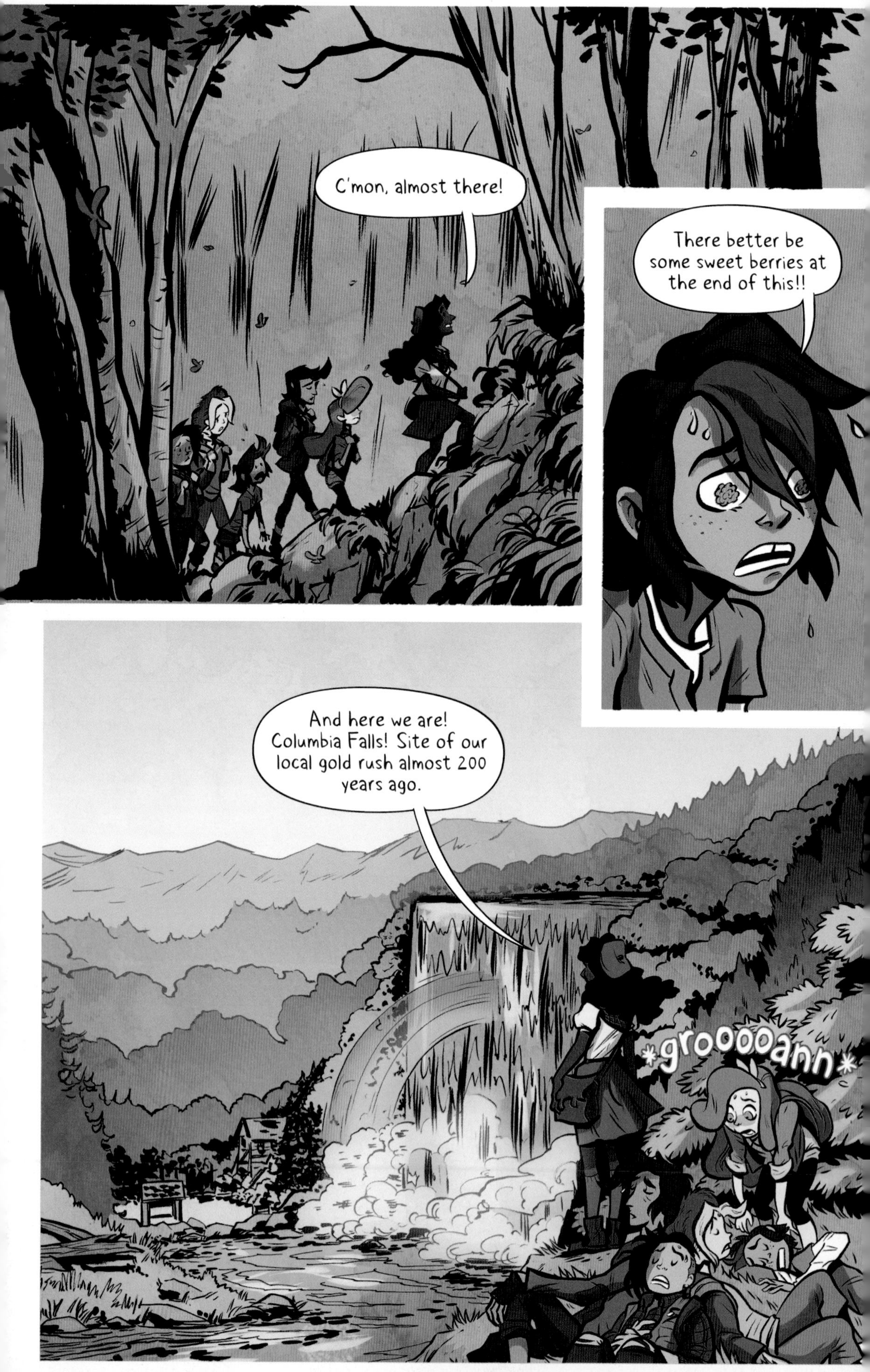
C'mon, almost there!
There better be some sweet berries at the end of this!!
And here we are! Columbia Falls! Site of our local gold rush almost 200 years ago.
grooooann

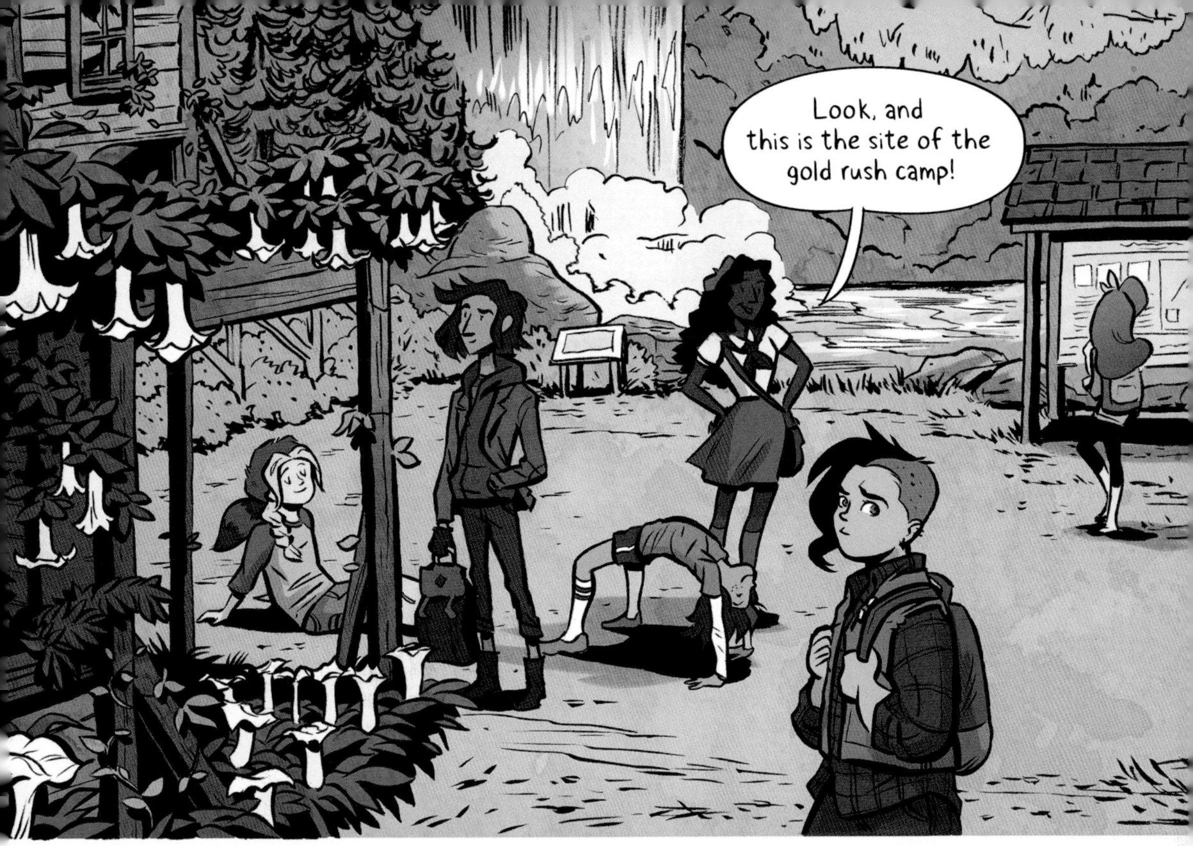
Look, and this is the site of the gold rush camp!

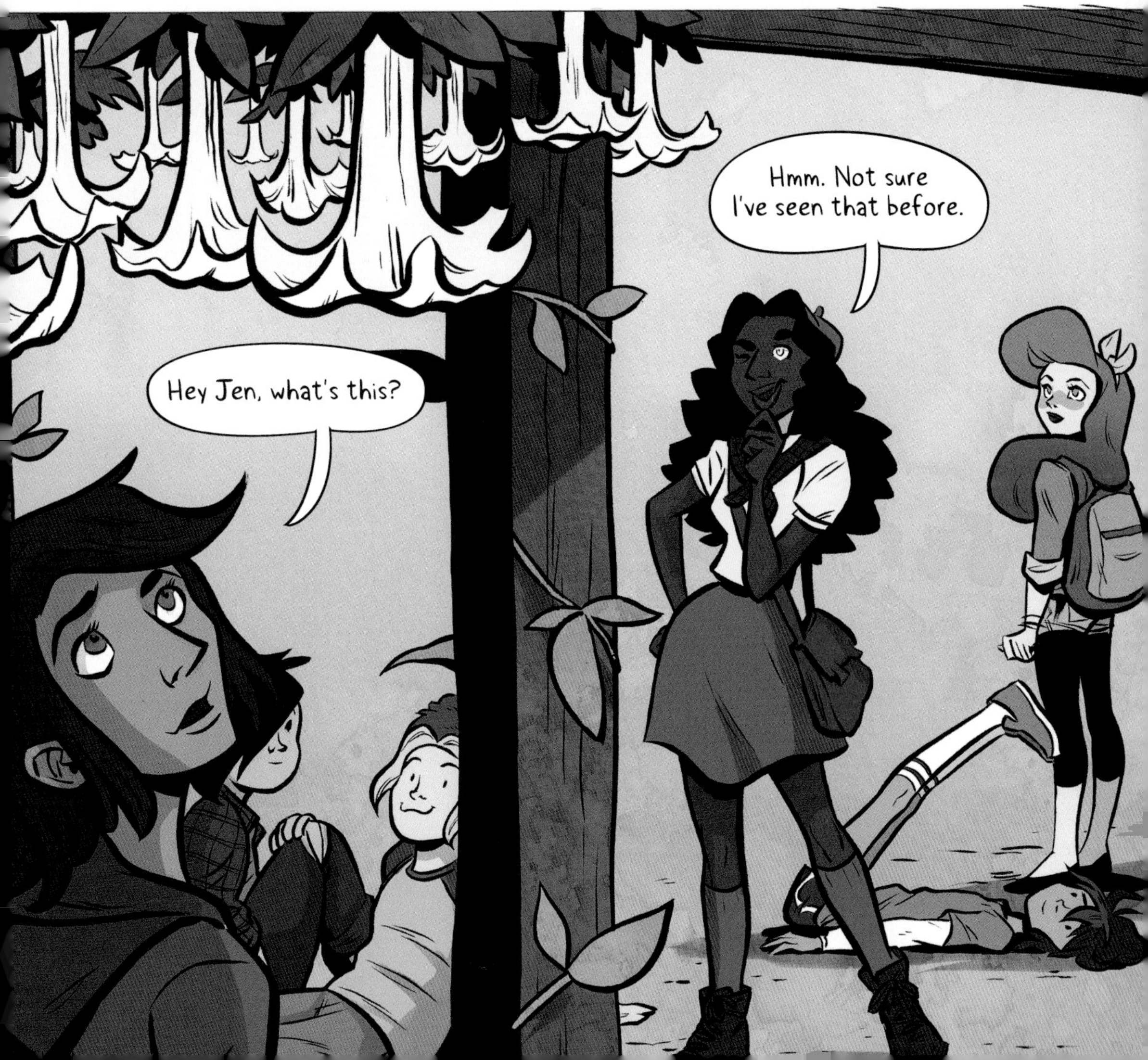
Hey Jen, what's this?
Hmm. Not sure I've seen that before.

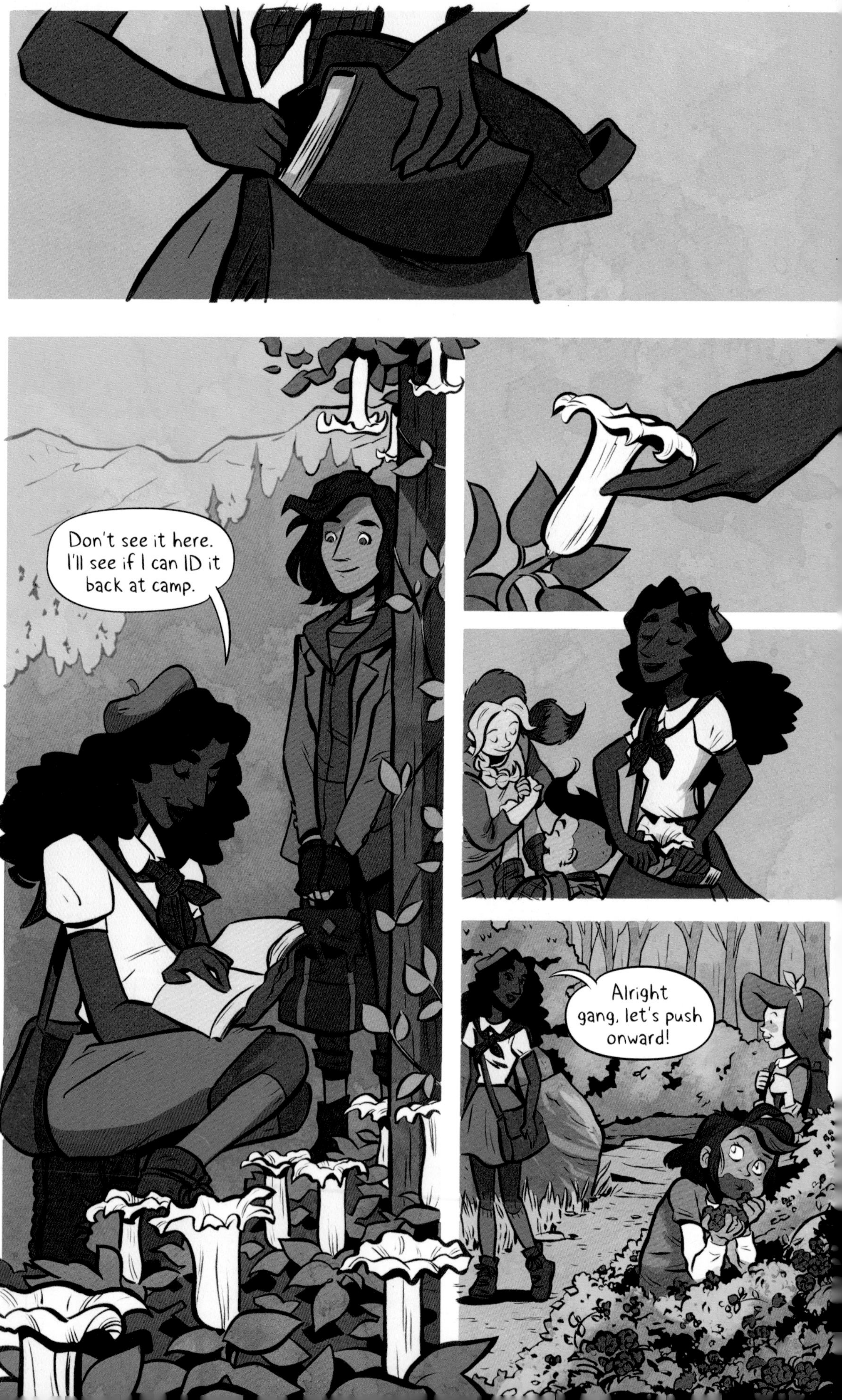
Don't see it here. I'll see if I can ID it back at camp.
Alright gang, let's push onward!

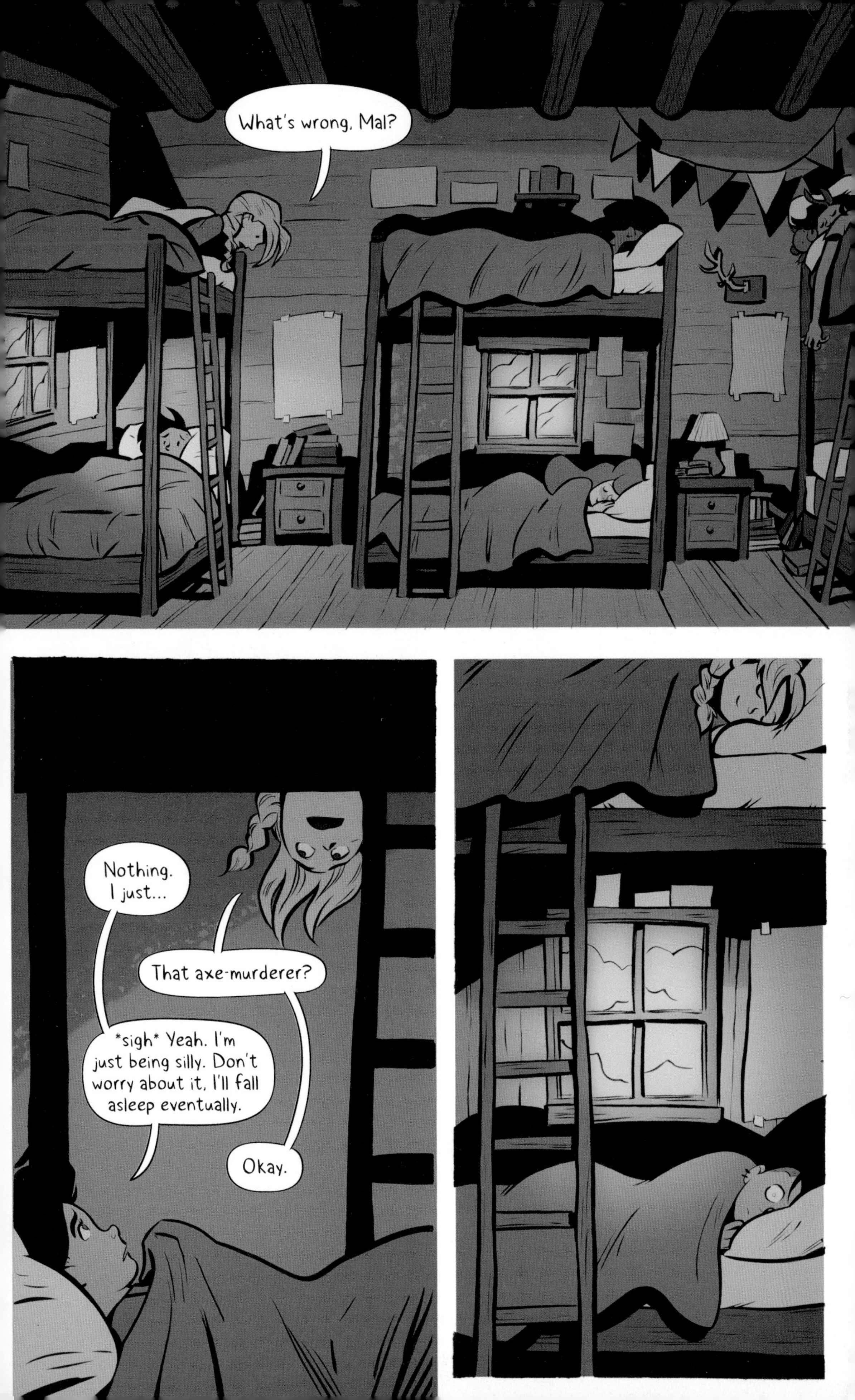
What's wrong, Mal?
Nothing. I just...
That axe-murderer?
sigh Yeah. I'm just being silly. Don't worry about it, I'll fall asleep eventually.
Okay.

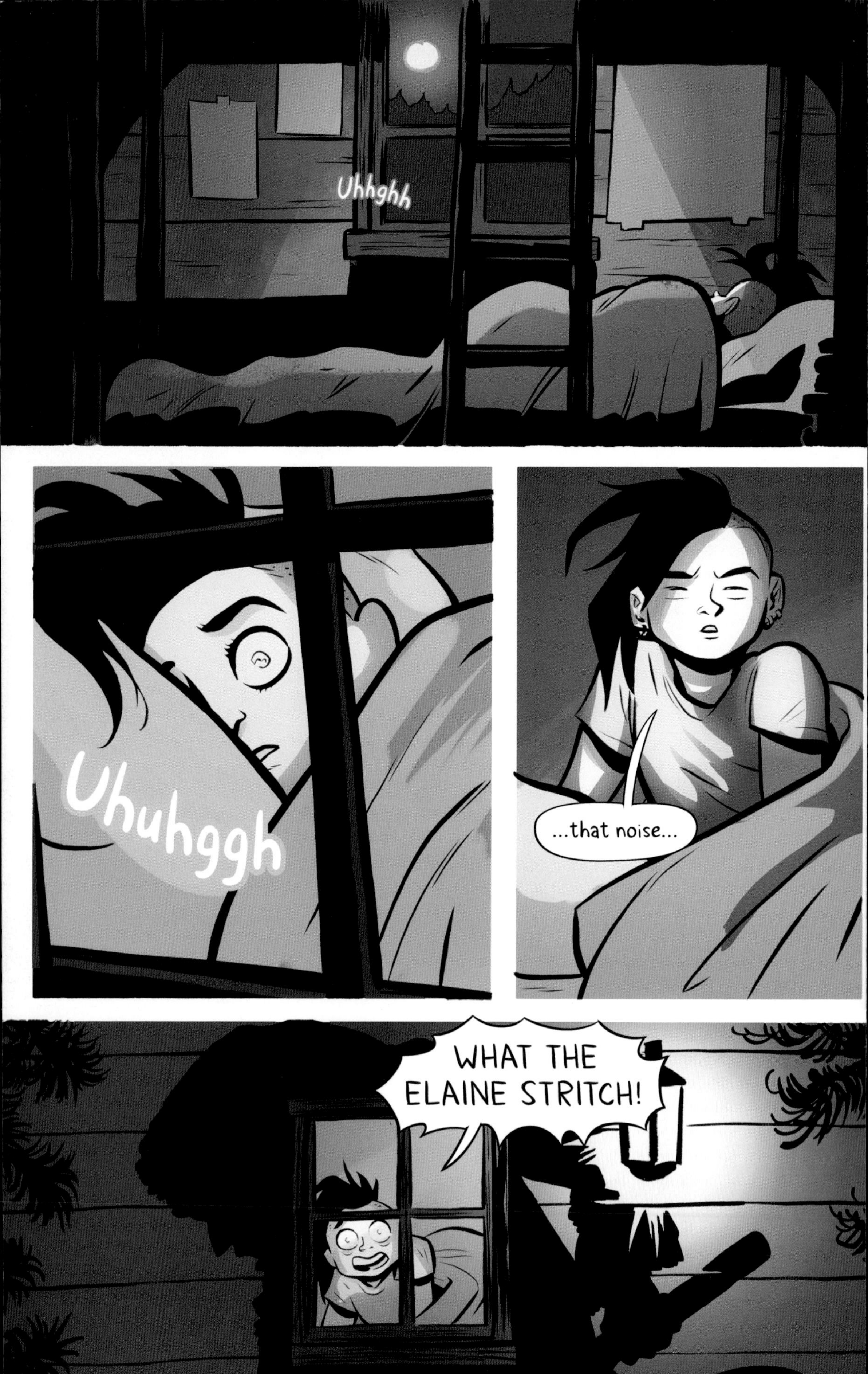
Uhhghh
Uhuhggh
...that noise...
WHAT THE ELAINE STRITCH!

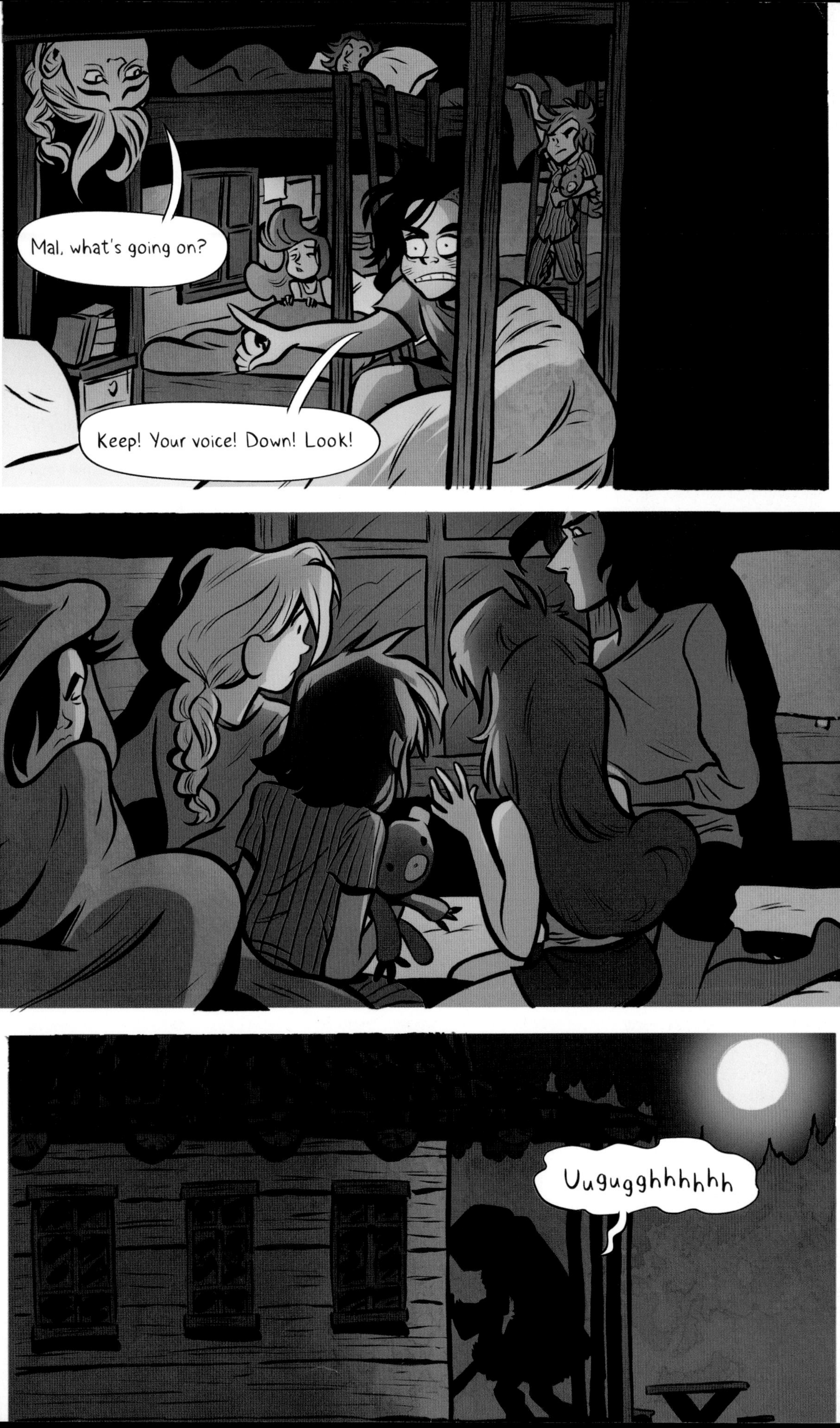
Mal, what's going on?
Keep! Your voice! Down! Look!
Uugugghhhhhh

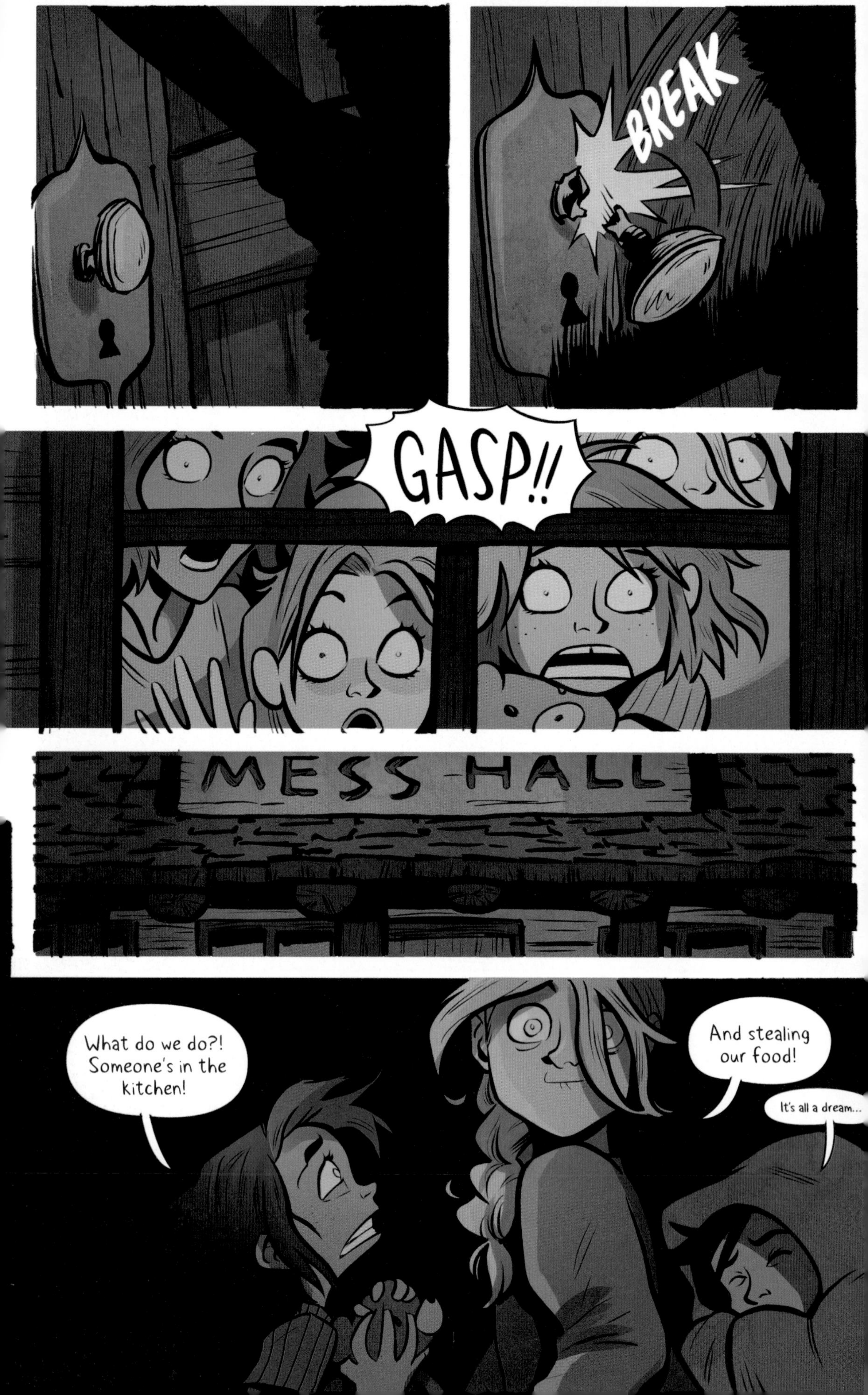
BREAK
GASP!!
MESS HALL
What do we do?! Someone's in the kitchen!
And stealing our food!
It's all a dream...

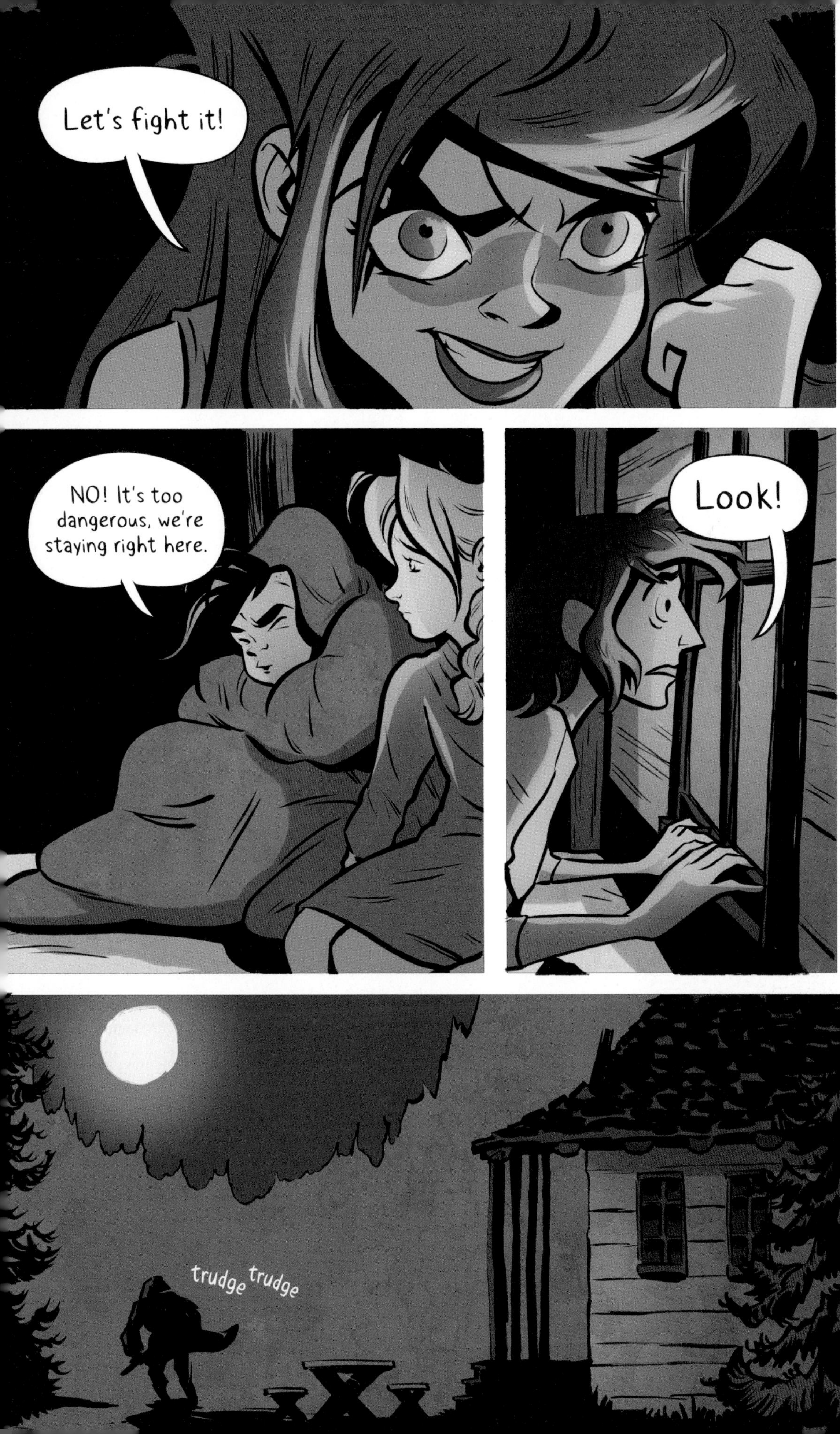
Let's fight it!
NO! It's too dangerous, we're staying right here.
Look!
trudge trudge

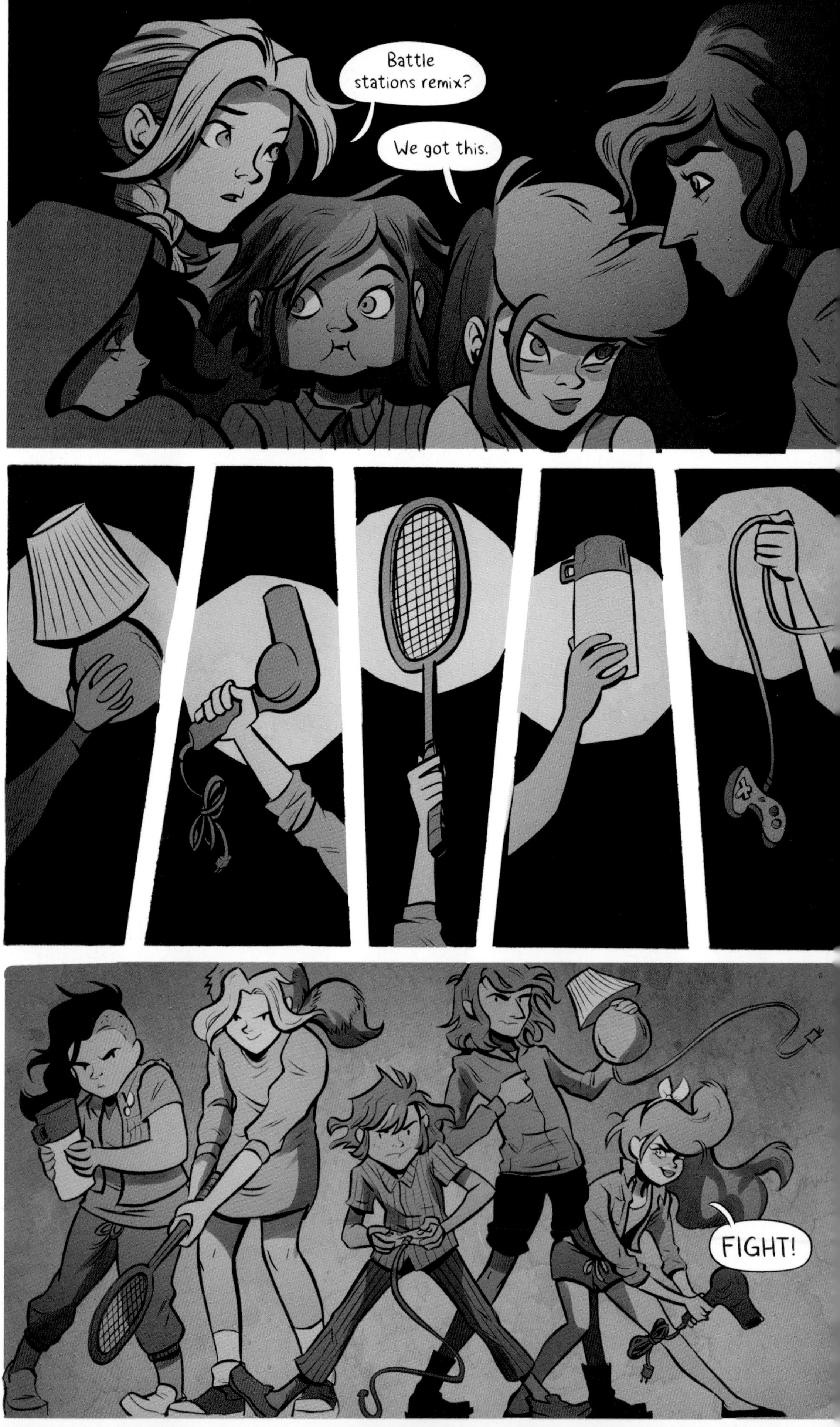
Battle stations remix?
We got this.
FIGHT!

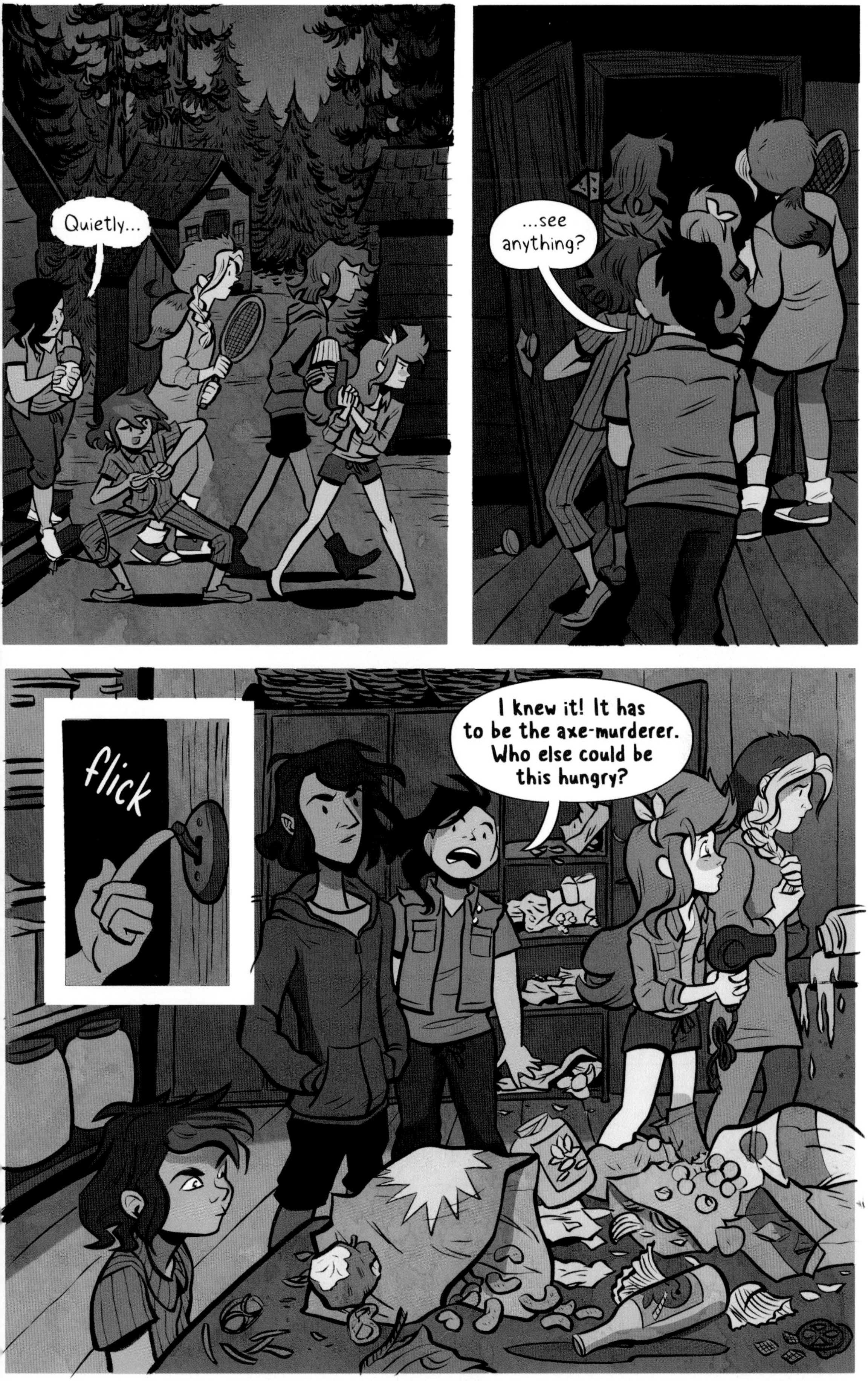
Quietly...
...see anything?
flick
I knew it! It has to be the axe-murderer. Who else could be this hungry?

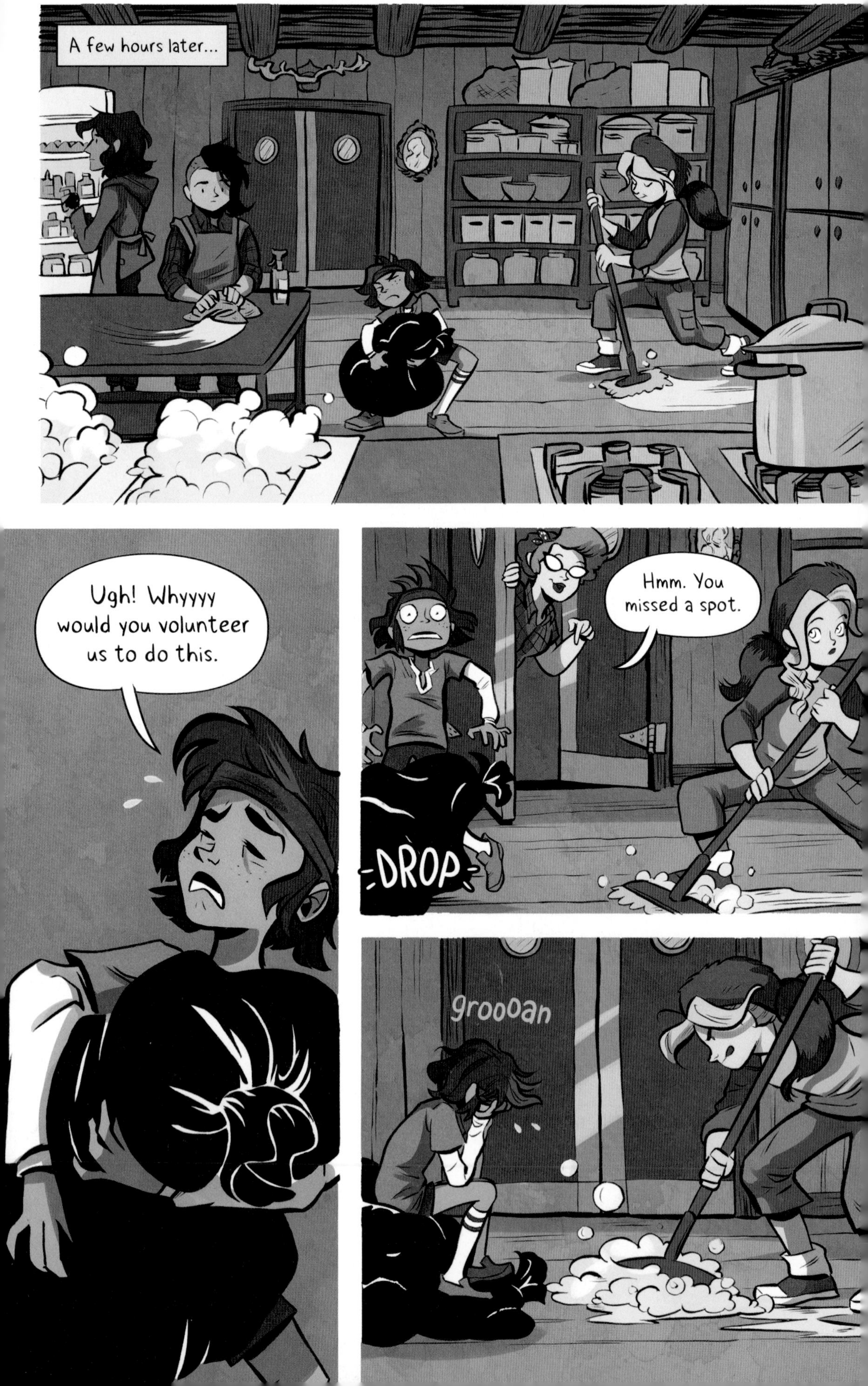
A few hours later...
Ugh! Whyyyy would you volunteer us to do this.
Hmm. You missed a spot.
DROP
groooan

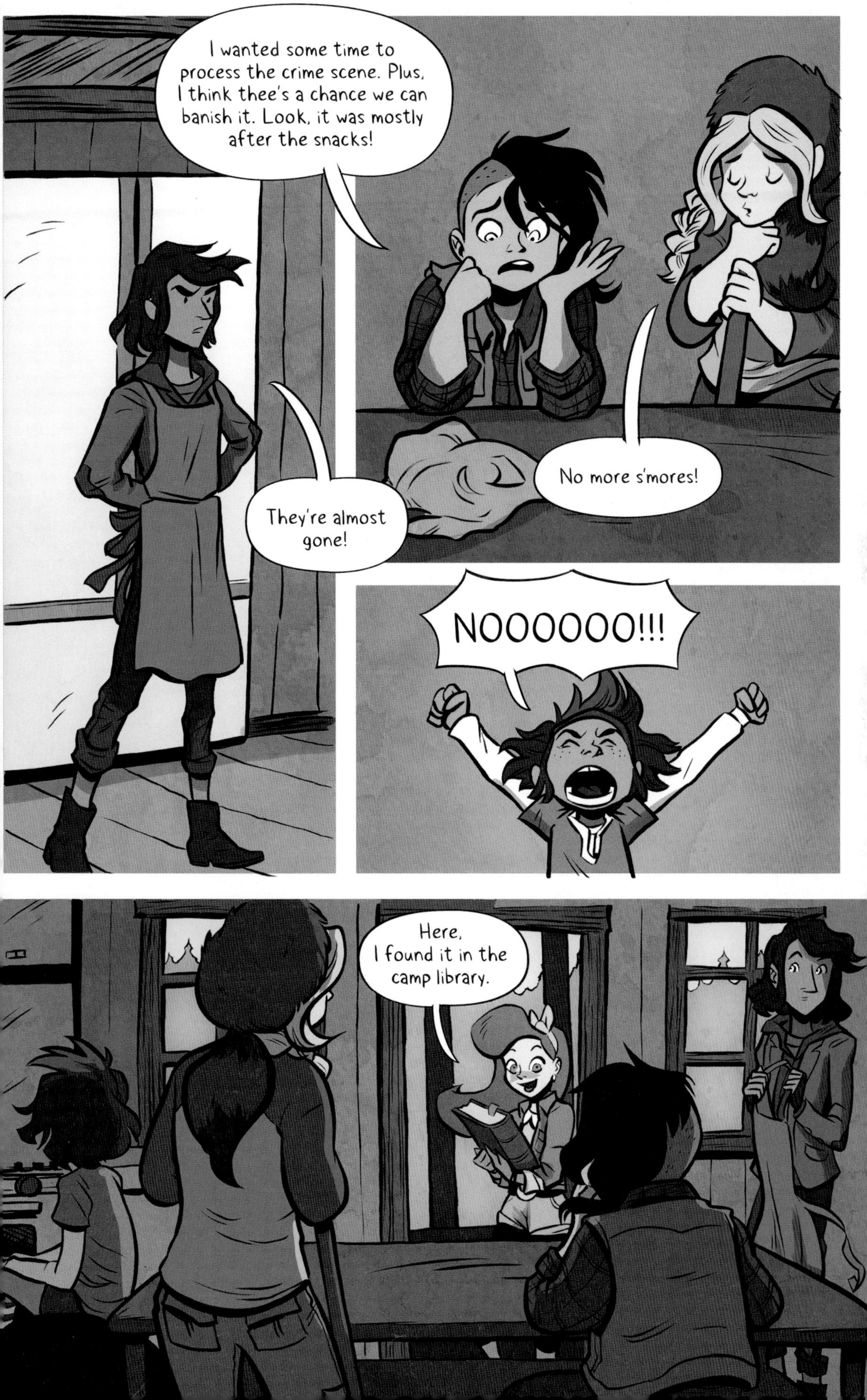
I wanted some time to process the crime scene. Plus, I think thee's a chance we can banish it. Look, it was mostly after the snacks!
They're almost gone!
No more s'mores!
NOOOOOO!!!
Here, I found it in the camp library.

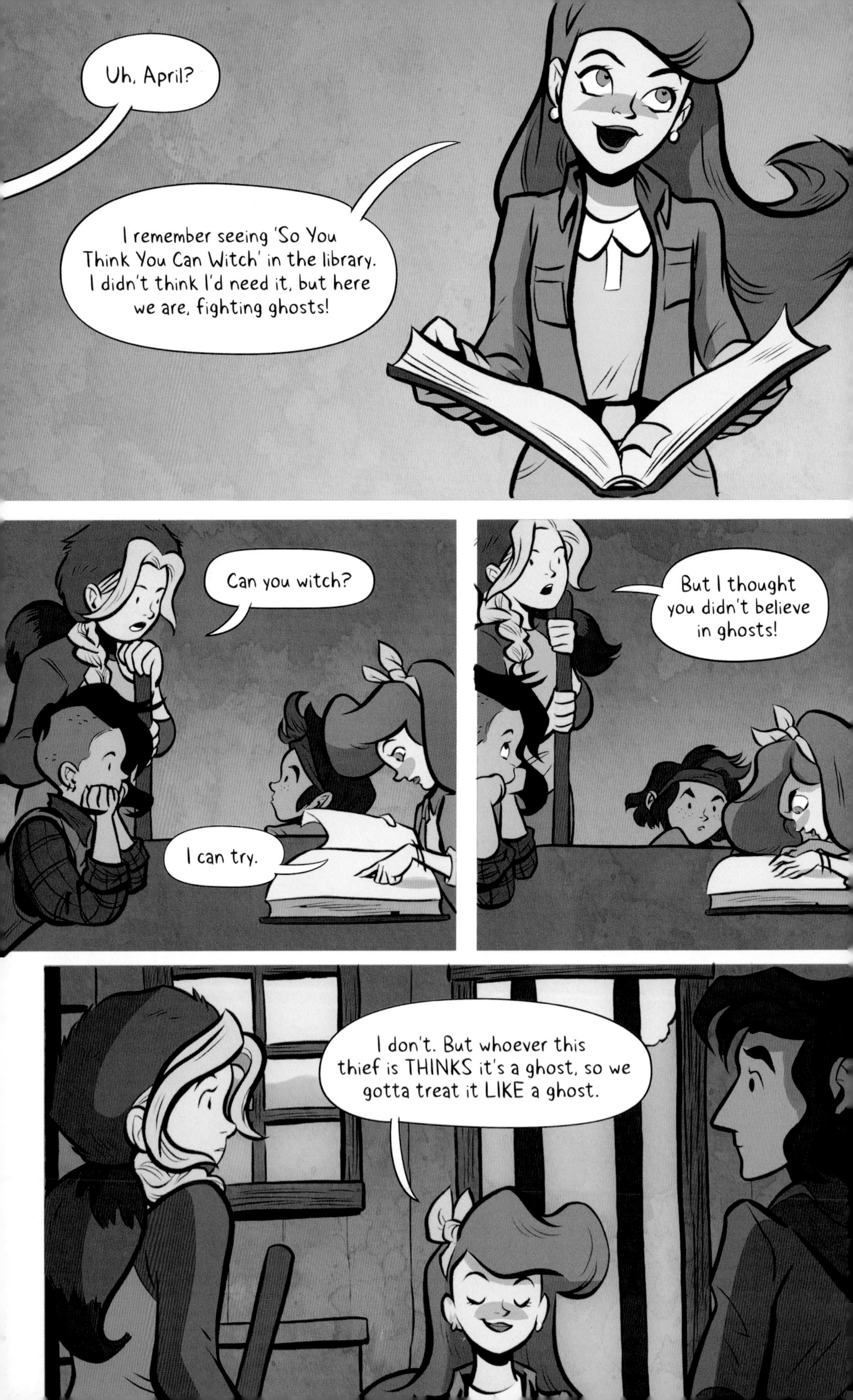
Uh, April?
I remember seeing 'So You Think You Can Witch' in the library. I didn't think I'd need it, but here we are, fighting ghosts!
Can you witch?
I can try.
But I thought you didn't believe in ghosts!
I don't. But whoever this thief is THINKS it's a ghost, so we gotta treat it LIKE a ghost.

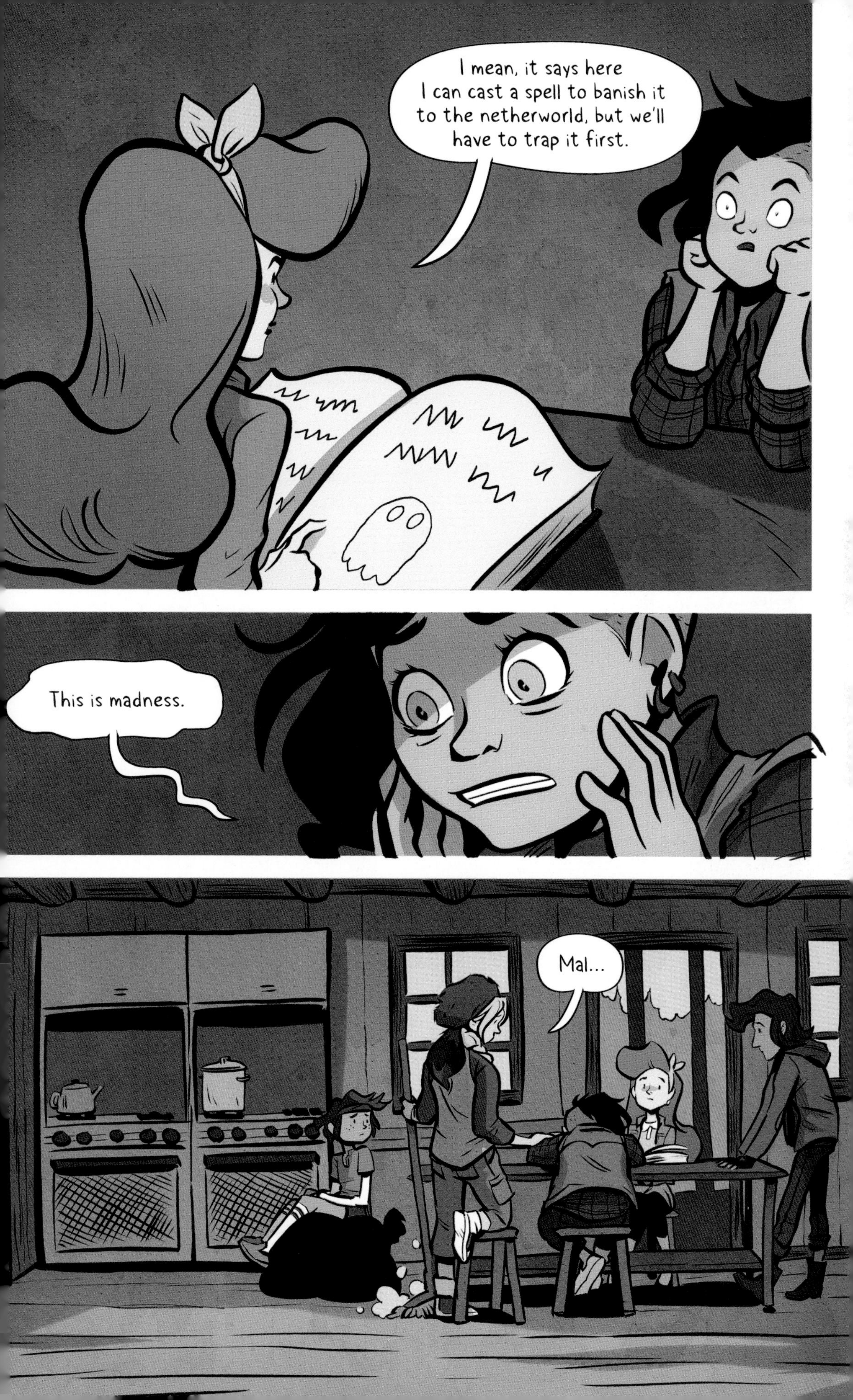
I mean, it says here I can cast a spell to banish it to the netherworld, but we'll have to trap it first.
This is madness.
Mal...

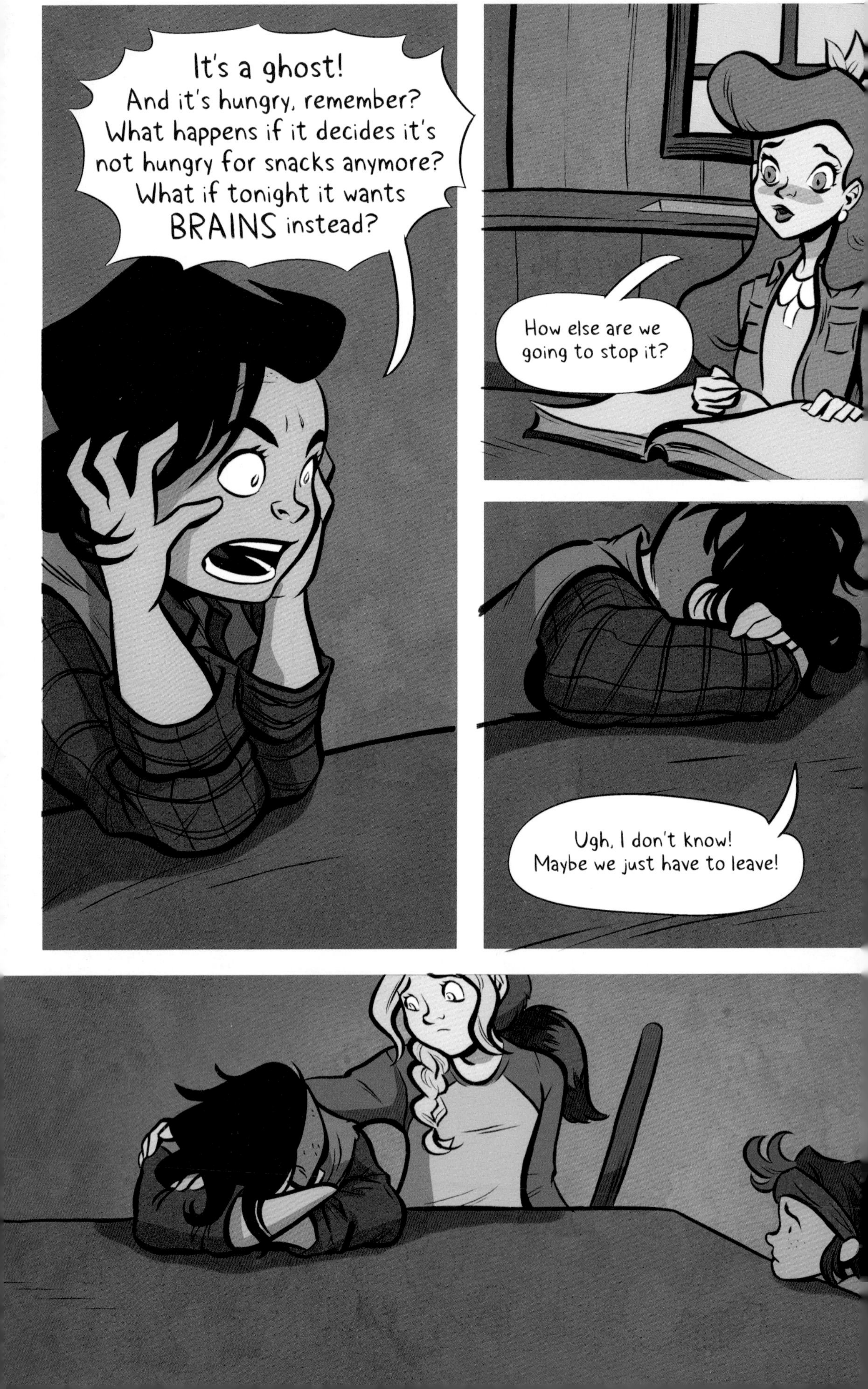
It's a ghost!
And it's hungry, remember?
What happens if it decides it's
not hungry for snacks anymore?
What if tonight it wants
BRAINS instead?
How else are we
going to stop it?
Ugh, I don't know!
Maybe we just have to leave!

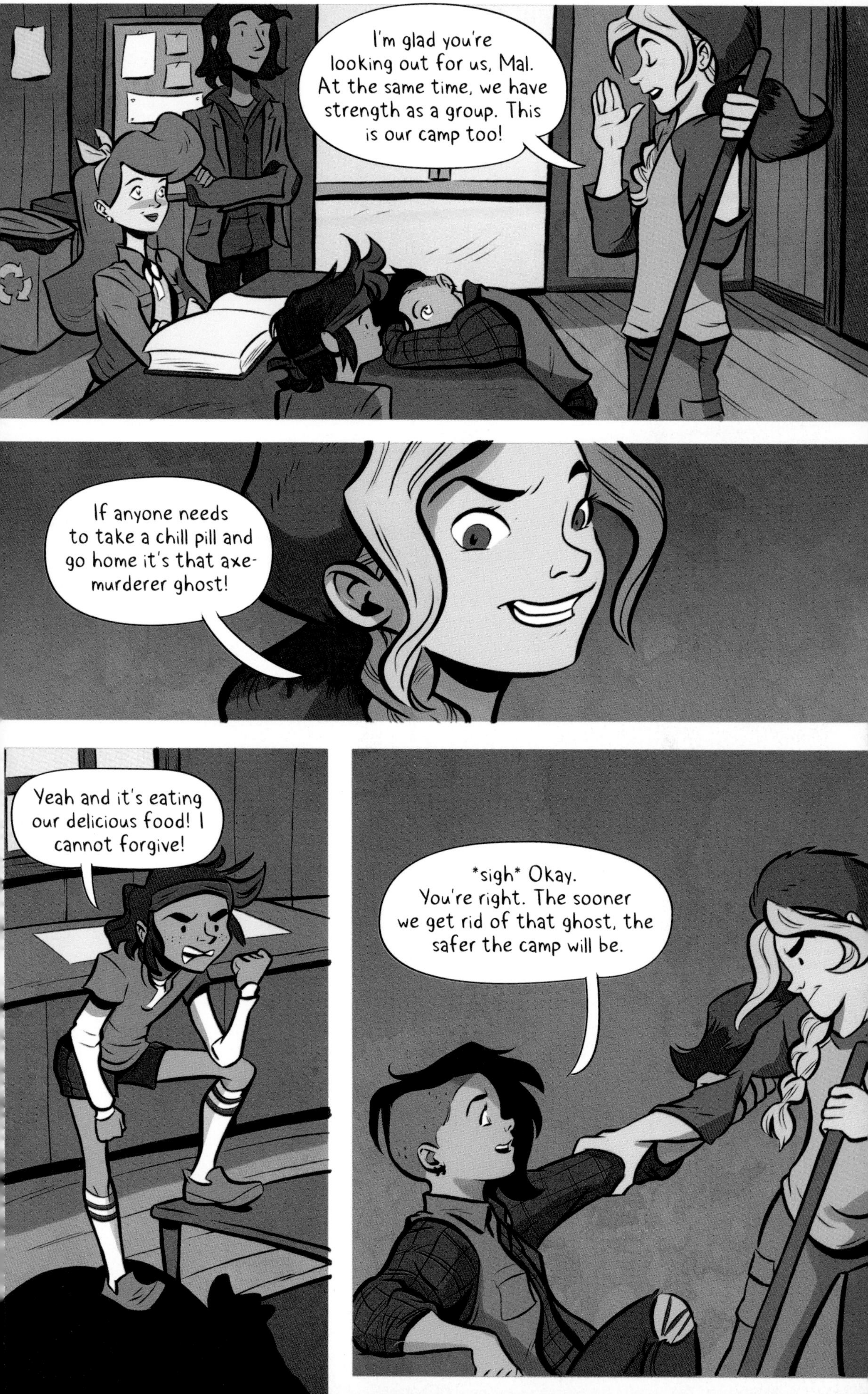
I'm glad you're looking out for us, Mal. At the same time, we have strength as a group. This is our camp too!
If anyone needs to take a chill pill and go home it's that axe-murderer ghost!
Yeah and it's eating our delicious food! I cannot forgive!
sigh Okay. You're right. The sooner we get rid of that ghost, the safer the camp will be.

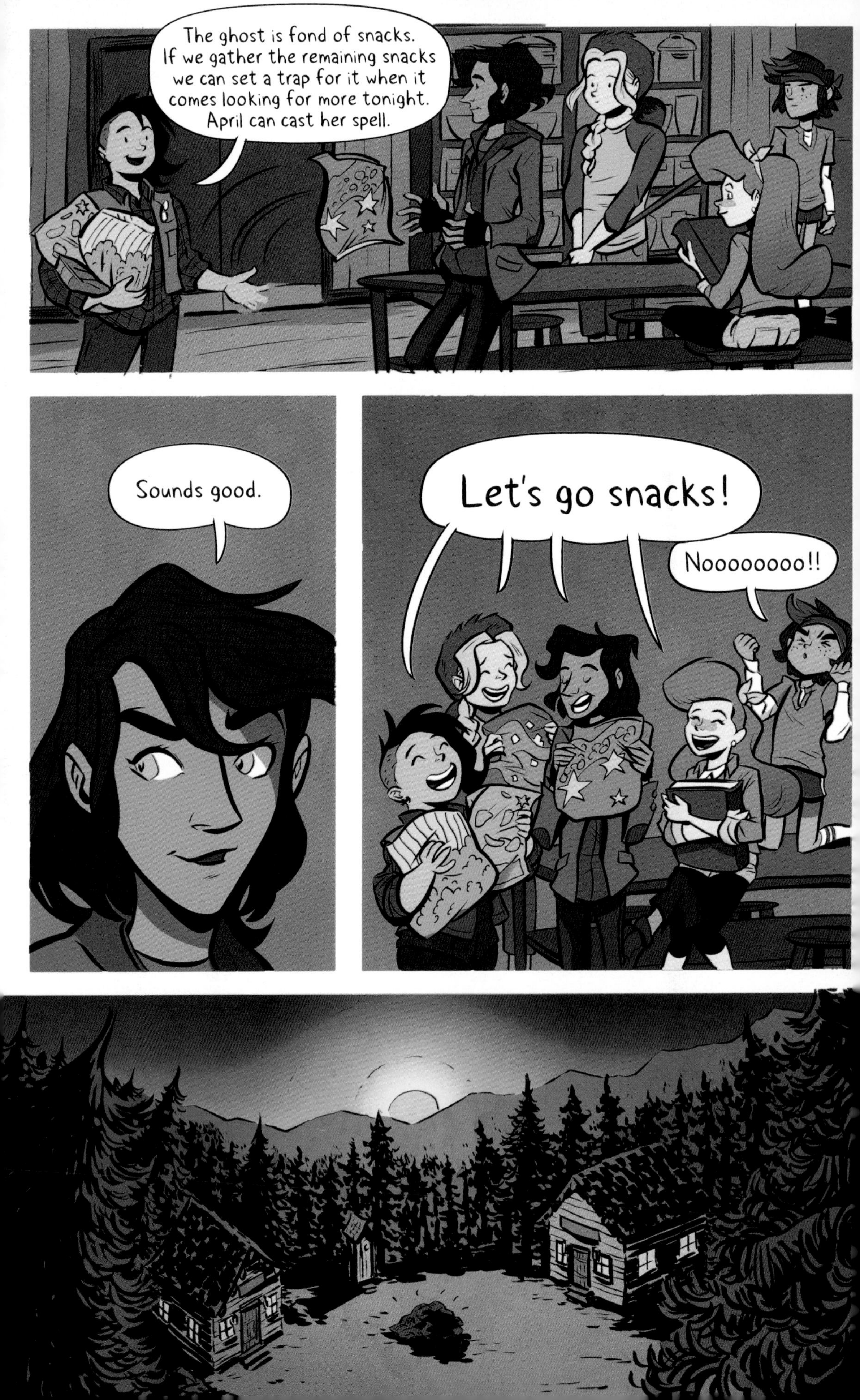
The ghost is fond of snacks. If we gather the remaining snacks we can set a trap for it when it comes looking for more tonight. April can cast her spell.
Sounds good.
Let's go snacks!
Noooooooo!!

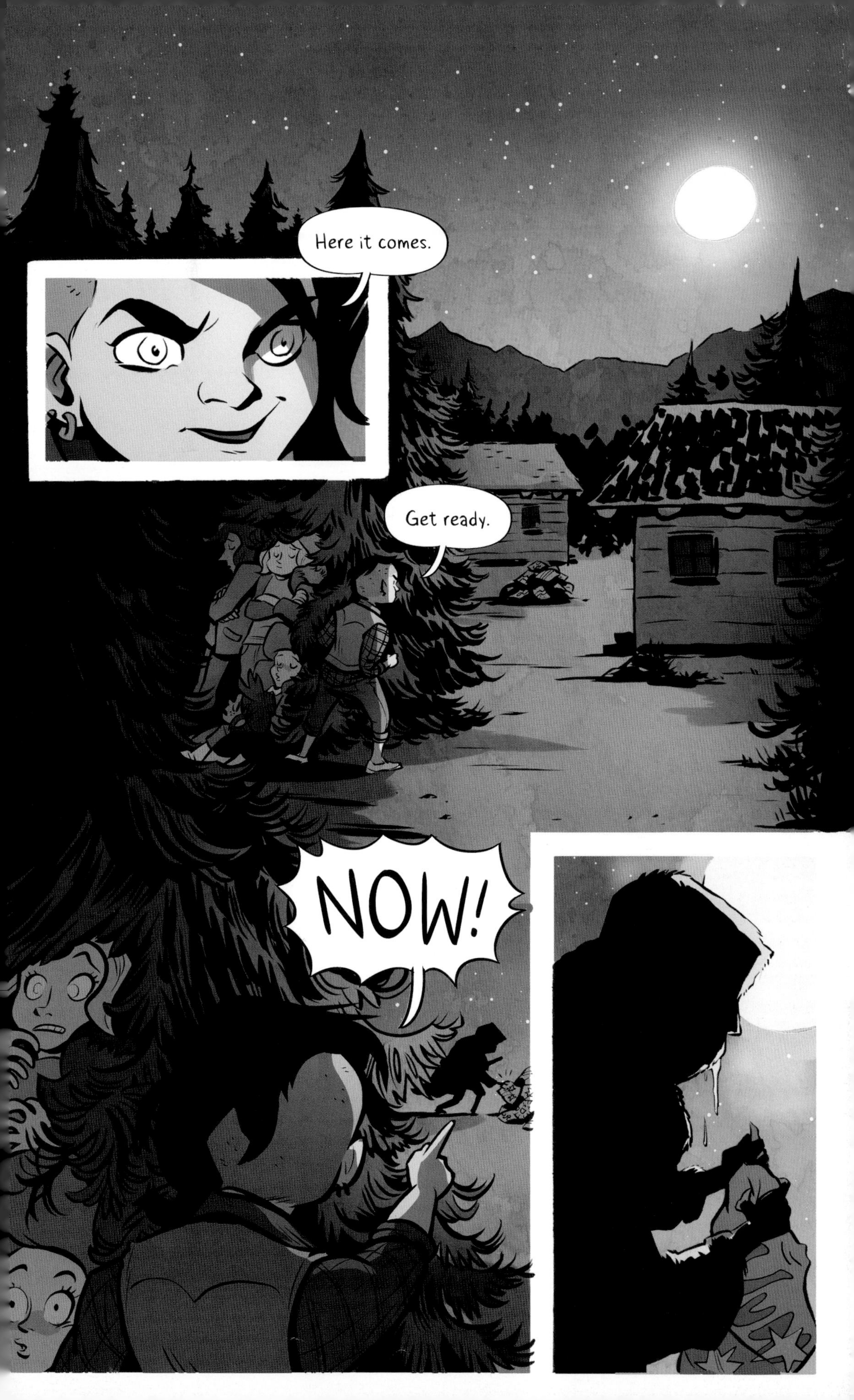
Here it comes.
Get ready.
NOW!

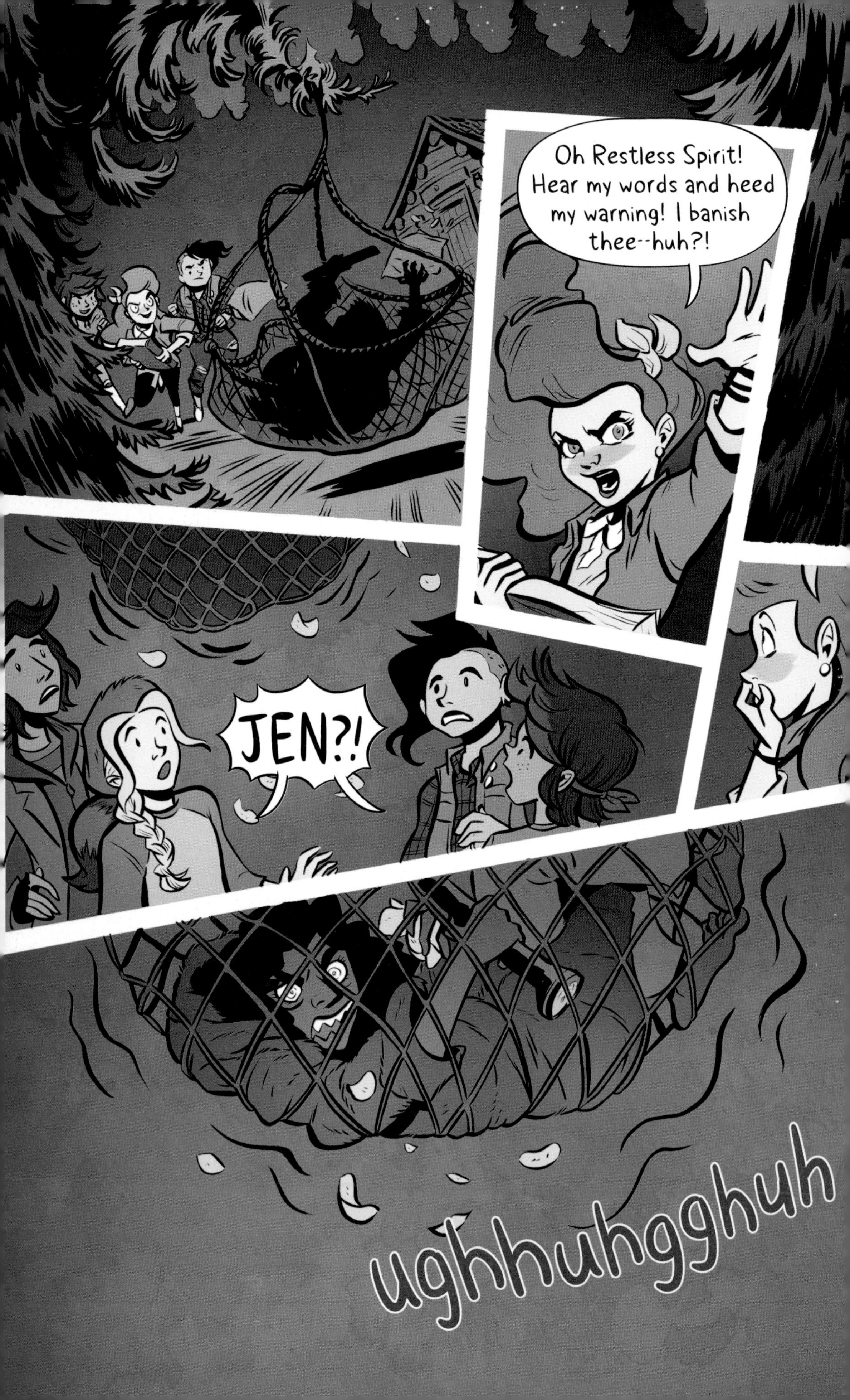
Oh Restless Spirit! Hear my words and heed my warning! I banish thee--huh?!
JEN?!
ughhuhgghuh

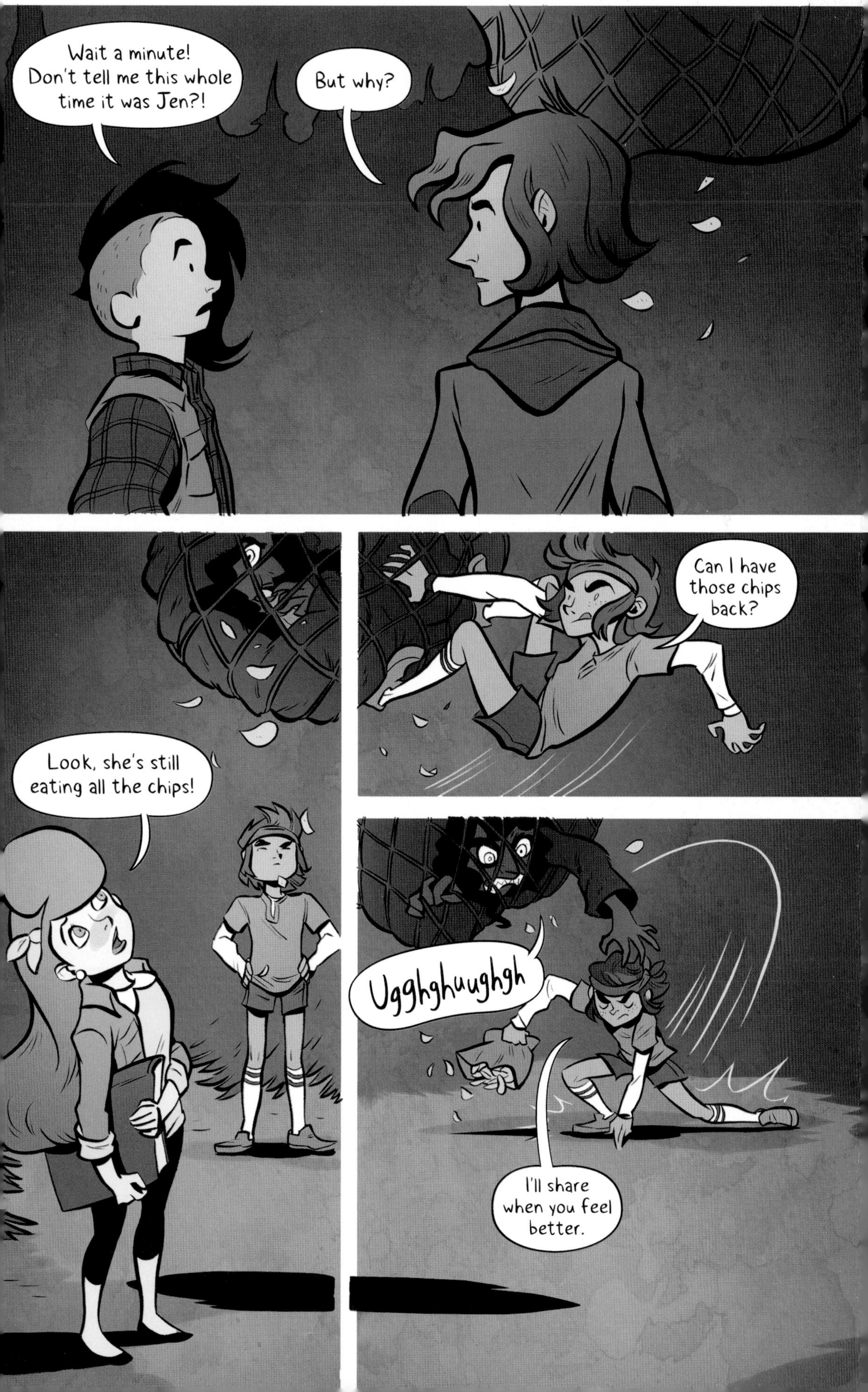
Wait a minute! Don't tell me this whole time it was Jen?!
But why?
Can I have those chips back?
Look, she's still eating all the chips!
Ugghghuughgh
I'll share when you feel better.

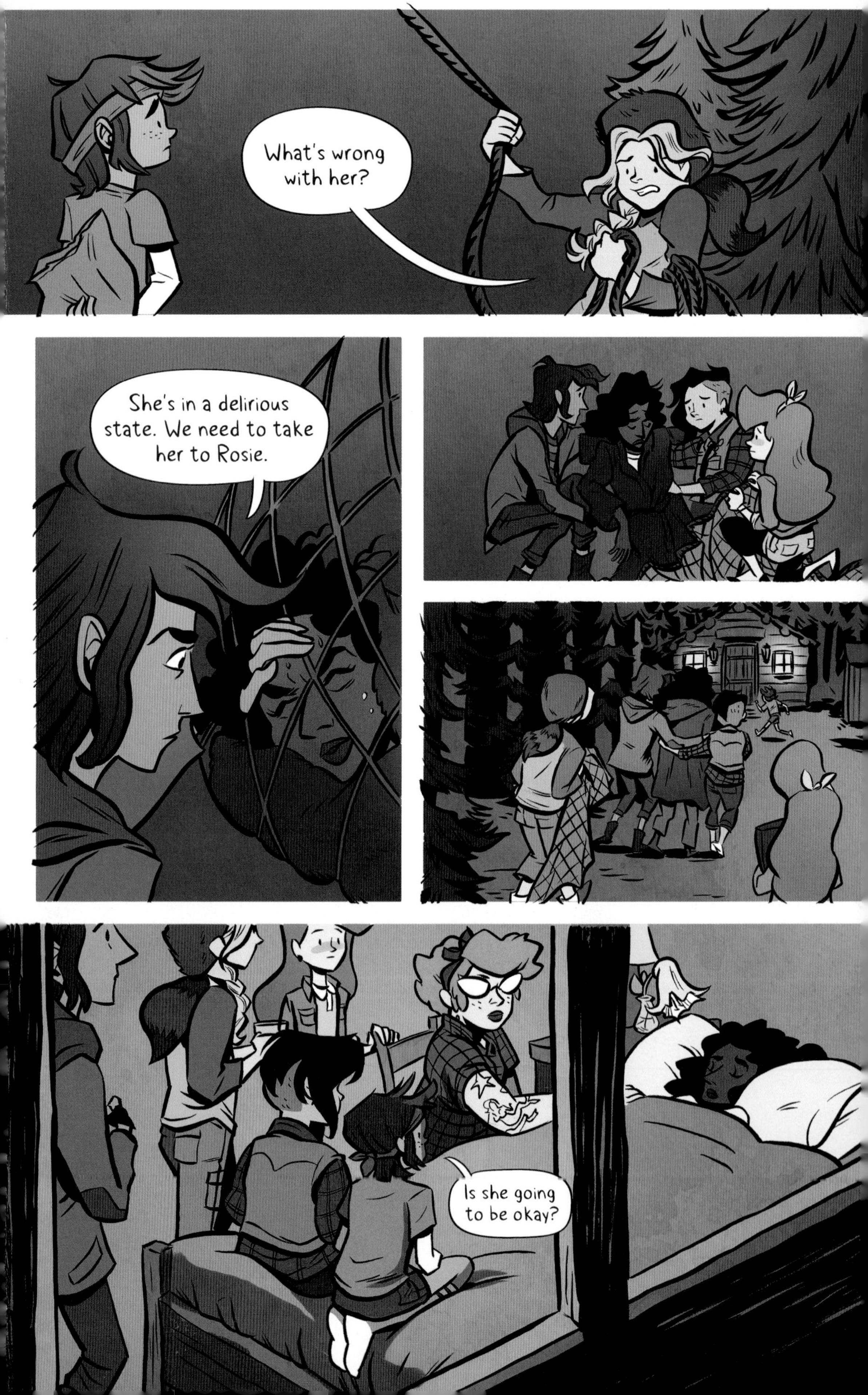
What's wrong with her?
She's in a delirious state. We need to take her to Rosie.
Is she going to be okay?

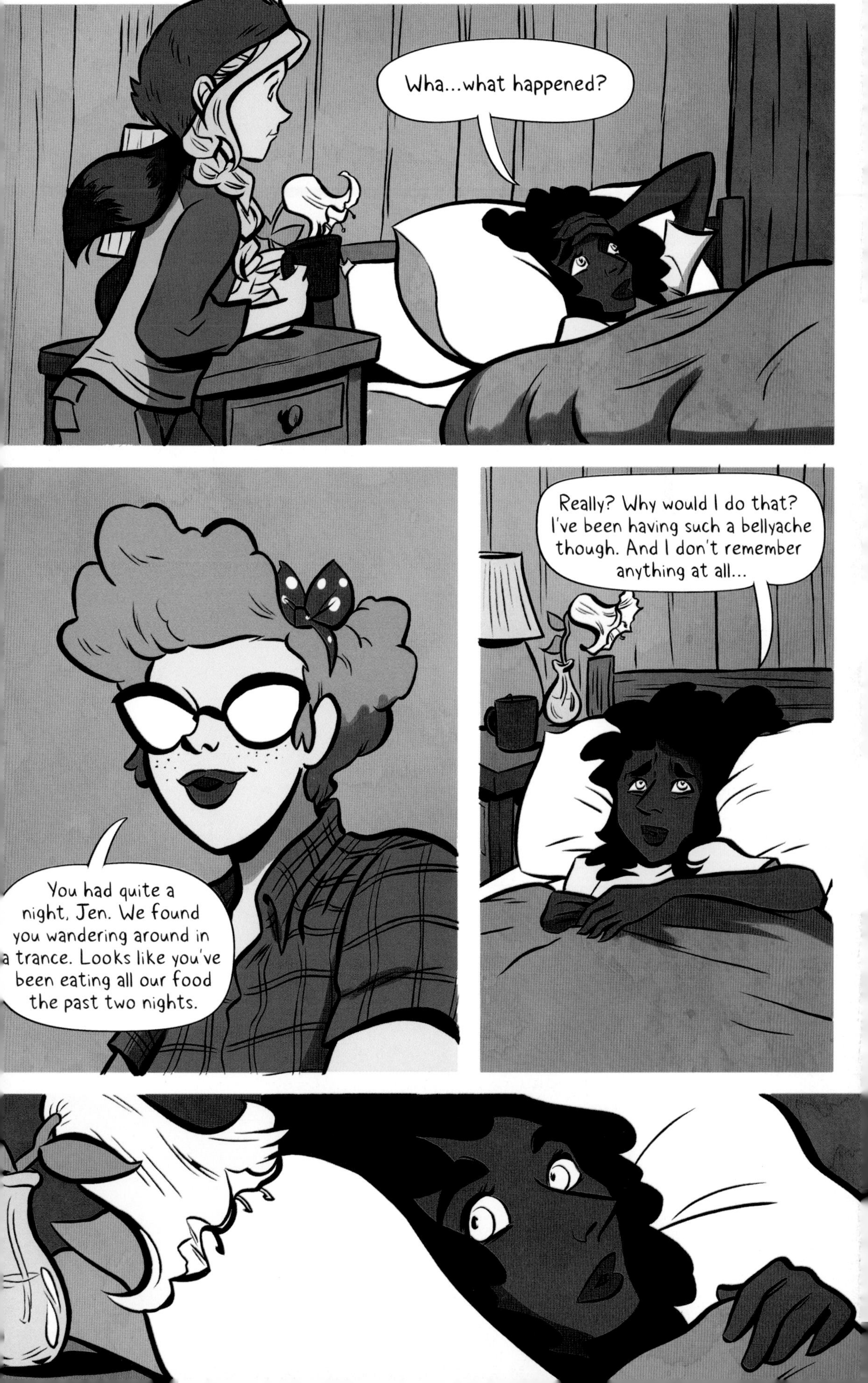
Wha...what happened?
You had quite a night, Jen. We found you wandering around in a trance. Looks like you've been eating all our food the past two nights.
Really? Why would I do that? I've been having such a bellyache though. And I don't remember anything at all...

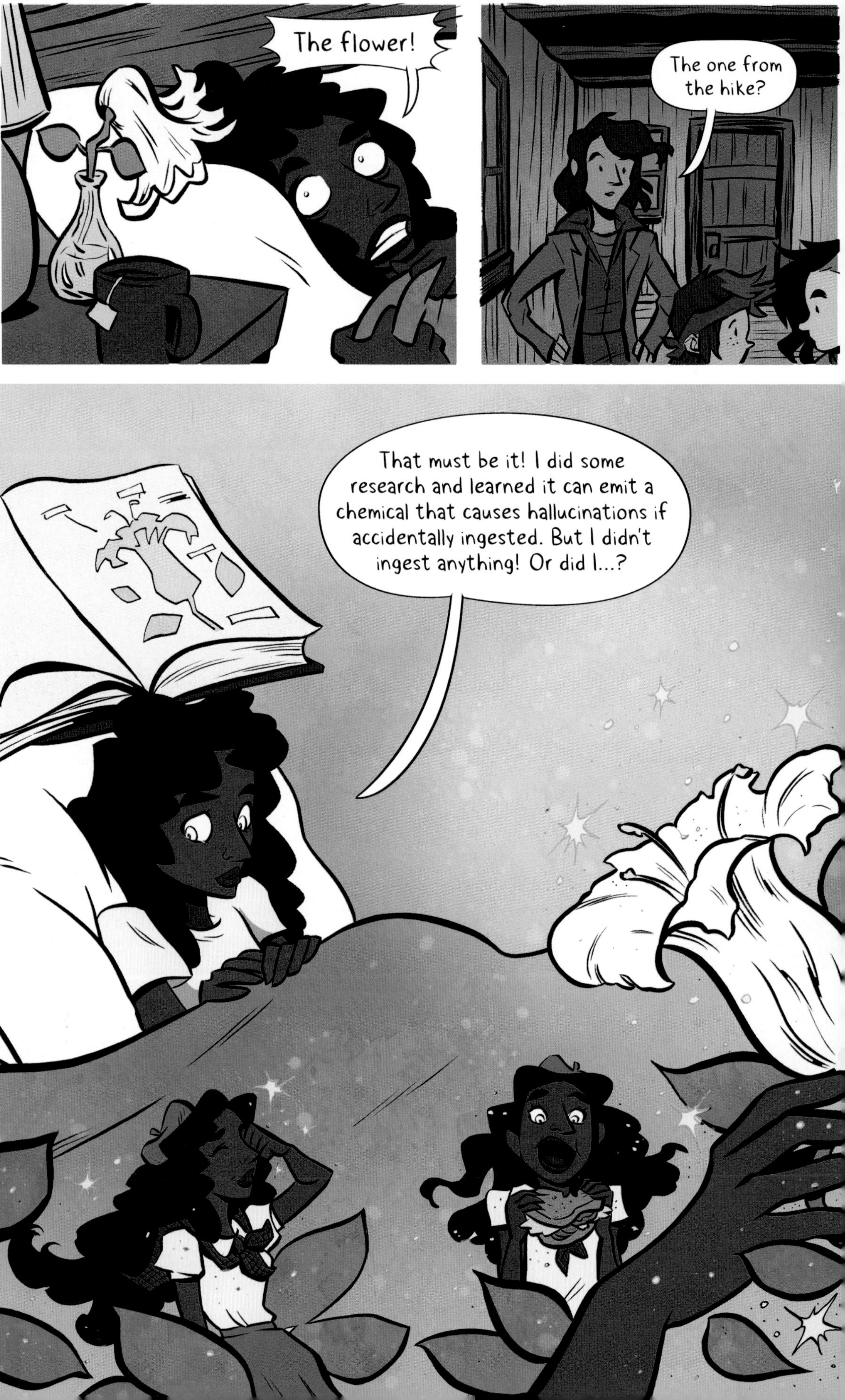
The flower!
The one from the hike?
That must be it! I did some research and learned it can emit a chemical that causes hallucinations if accidentally ingested. But I didn't ingest anything! Or did I...?

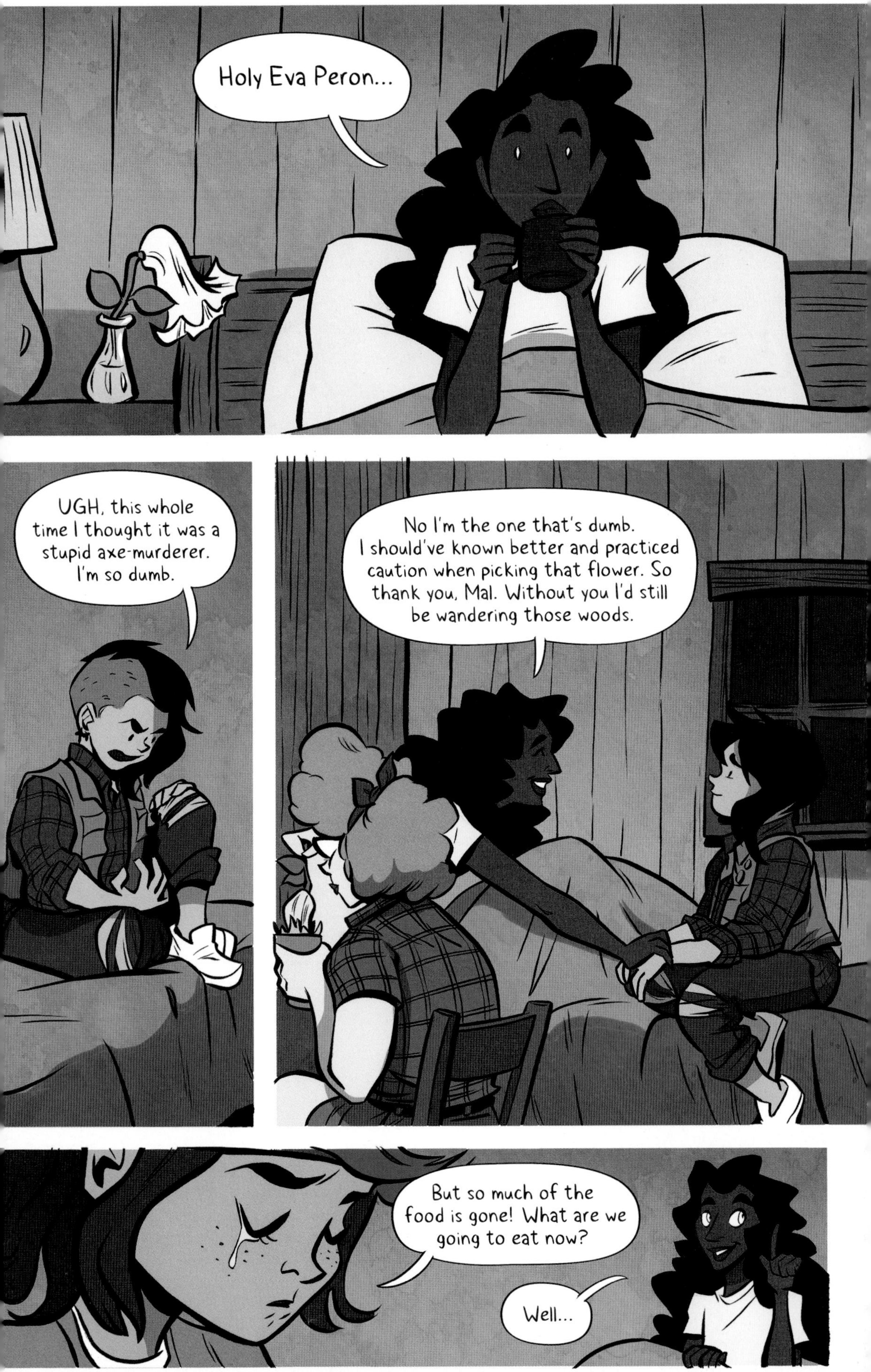
Holy Eva Peron...
UGH, this whole time I thought it was a stupid axe-murderer. I'm so dumb.
No I'm the one that's dumb. I should've known better and practiced caution when picking that flower. So thank you, Mal. Without you I'd still be wandering those woods.
But so much of the food is gone! What are we going to eat now?
Well...

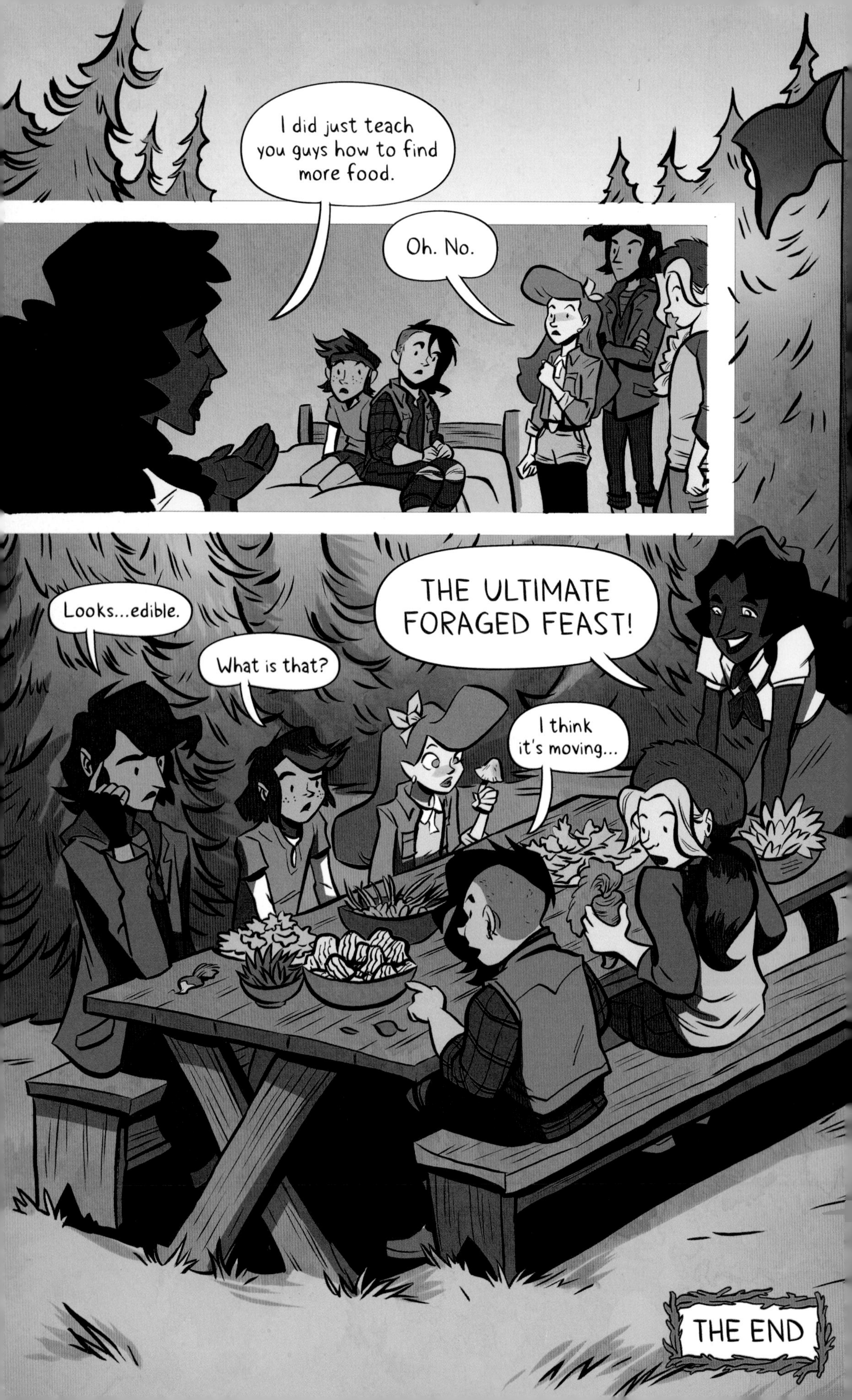
I did just teach you guys how to find more food.
Oh. No.
Looks...edible.
What is that?
THE ULTIMATE FORAGED FEAST!
I think it's moving...
THE END

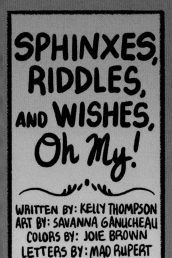

SPHINXES, RIDDLES, AND WISHES, Oh My!

WRITTEN BY: KELLY THOMPSON
ART BY: SAVANNA GANUCHEAU
COLORS BY: JOIE BROWN
LETTERS BY: MAD RUPERT

HEY, GUYS!

RIPLEY? JEN?

JEN! YOU OKAY?

I'M ALRIGHT, MOLLY, JUST A TWISTED ANKLE.

AND LOTS OF LEAVES... AND DIRT...

SO MUCH DIRT IN SO MANY PLACES.

YOU GUYS! SO MUCH HAS HAPPENED!

I SINGLE-HANDEDLY SAVED JEN FROM CERTAIN DOOM!!!

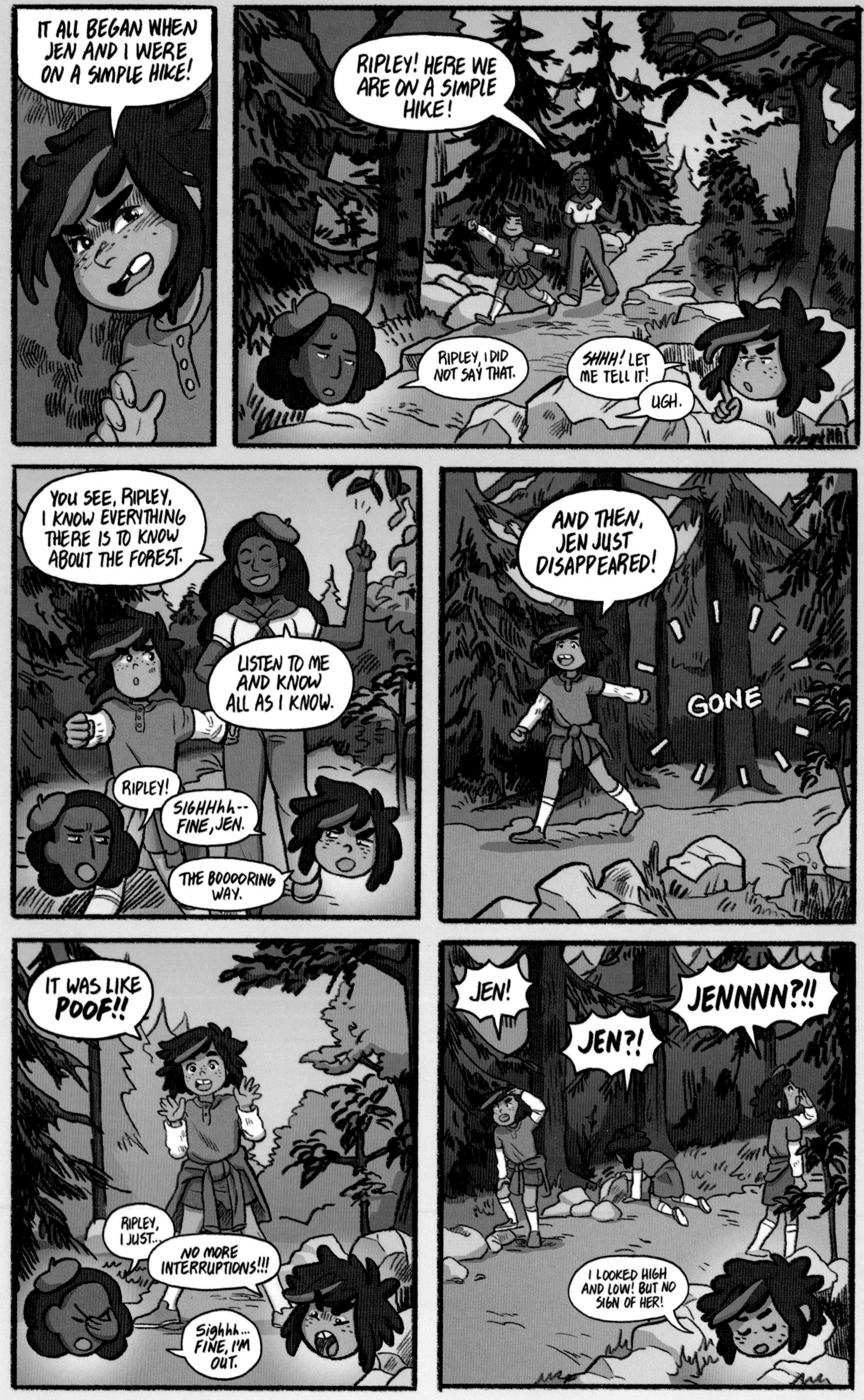
IT ALL BEGAN WHEN JEN AND I WERE ON A SIMPLE HIKE!
RIPLEY! HERE WE ARE ON A SIMPLE HIKE!
RIPLEY, I DID NOT SAY THAT.
SHHH! LET ME TELL IT!
UGH.
YOU SEE, RIPLEY, I KNOW EVERYTHING THERE IS TO KNOW ABOUT THE FOREST.
LISTEN TO ME AND KNOW ALL AS I KNOW.
RIPLEY!
SIGHHhh-- FINE, JEN.
THE BOOOORING WAY.
AND THEN, JEN JUST DISAPPEARED!
GONE
IT WAS LIKE POOF!!
RIPLEY, I JUST...
NO MORE INTERRUPTIONS!!!
Sighhh... FINE, I'M OUT.
JEN!
JEN?!
JENNNN?!!
I LOOKED HIGH AND LOW! BUT NO SIGN OF HER!

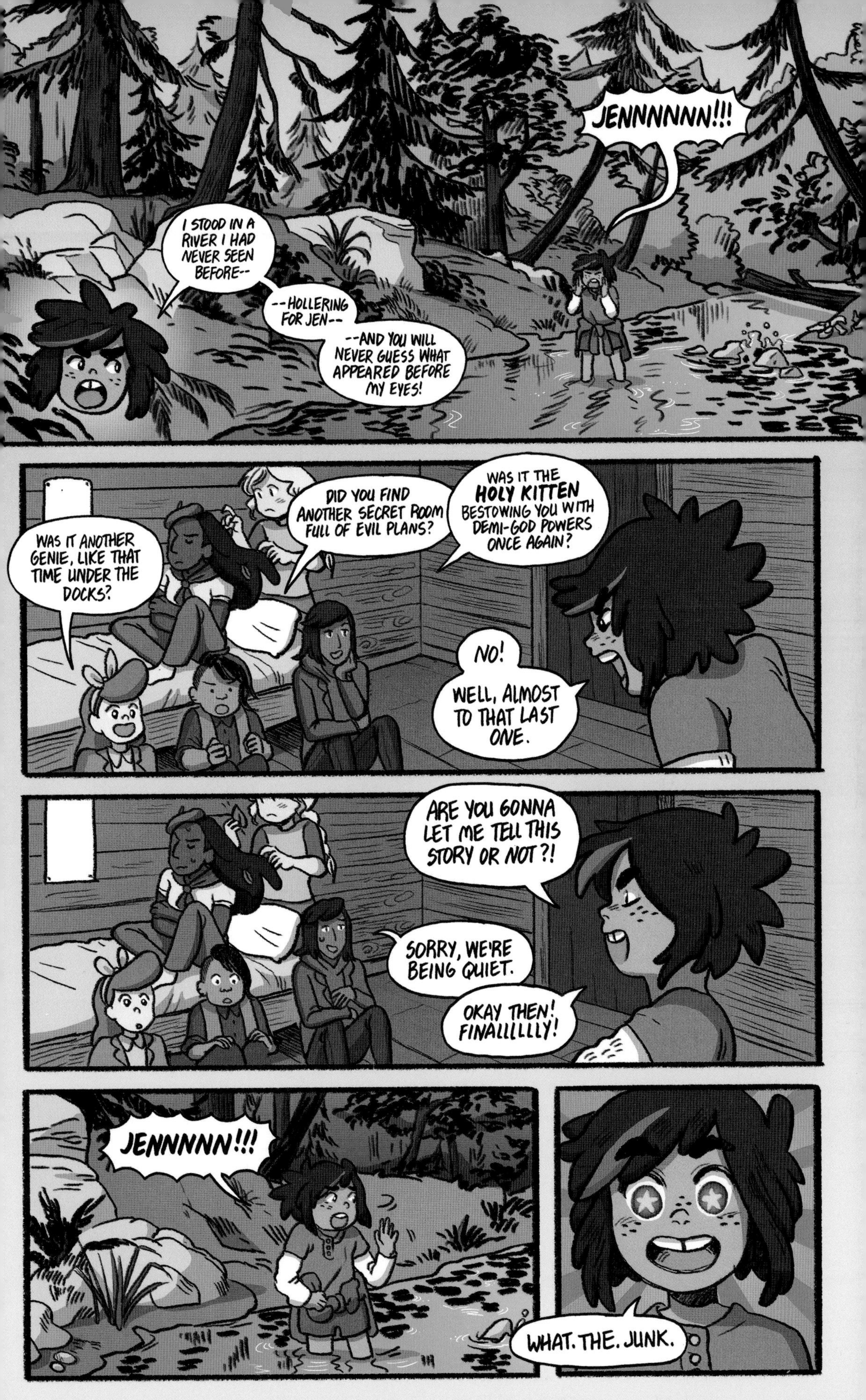

I STOOD IN A RIVER I HAD NEVER SEEN BEFORE--
--HOLLERING FOR JEN--
--AND YOU WILL NEVER GUESS WHAT APPEARED BEFORE MY EYES!
JENNNNNN!!!
WAS IT ANOTHER GENIE, LIKE THAT TIME UNDER THE DOCKS?
DID YOU FIND ANOTHER SECRET ROOM FULL OF EVIL PLANS?
WAS IT THE HOLY KITTEN BESTOWING YOU WITH DEMI-GOD POWERS ONCE AGAIN?
NO!
WELL, ALMOST TO THAT LAST ONE.
ARE YOU GONNA LET ME TELL THIS STORY OR NOT?!
SORRY, WE'RE BEING QUIET.
OKAY THEN! FINALLLLLY!
JENNNNN!!!
WHAT. THE. JUNK.

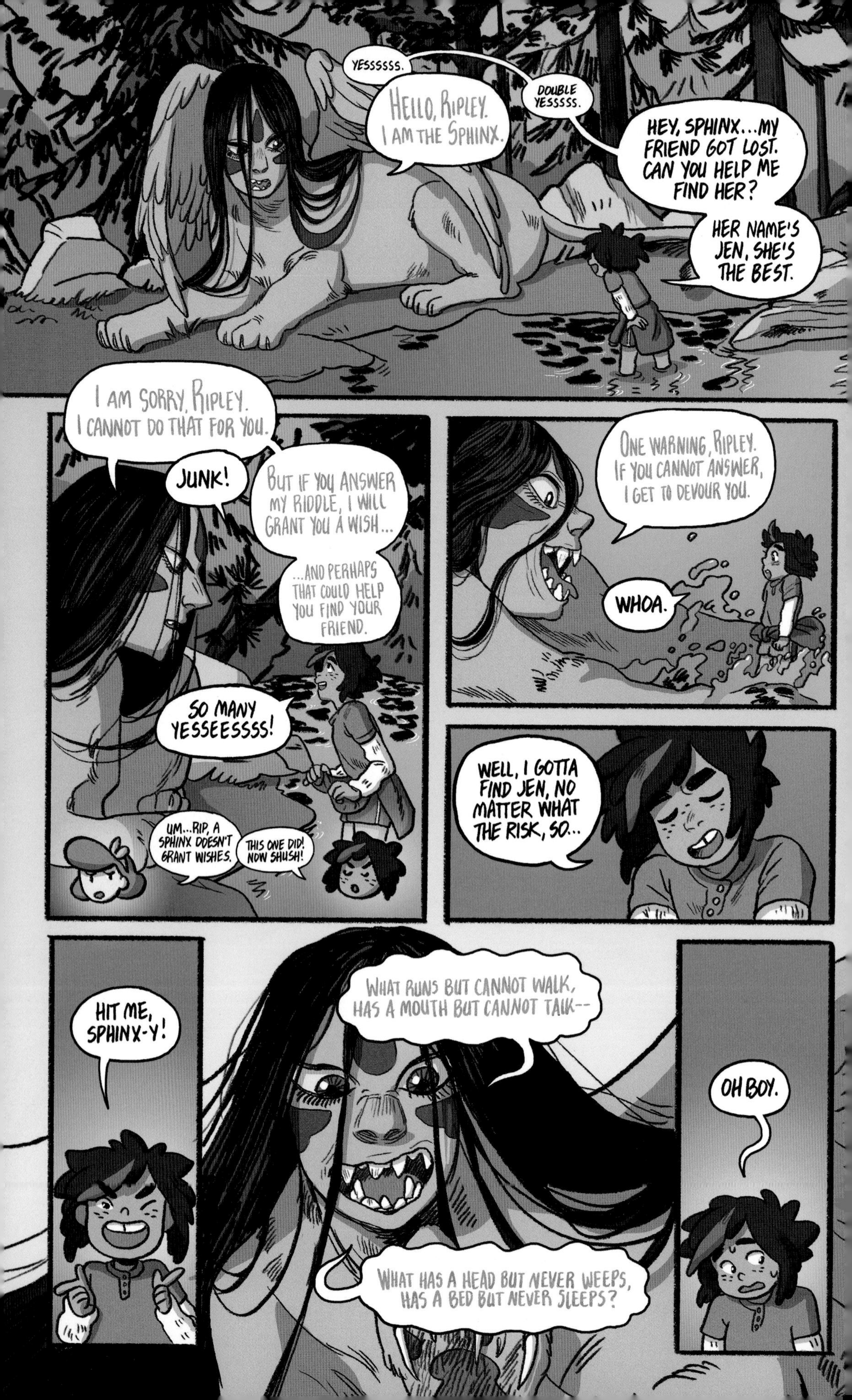
YESSSSSS.
HELLO, RIPLEY. I AM THE SPHINX.
DOUBLE YESSSSS.
HEY, SPHINX...MY FRIEND GOT LOST. CAN YOU HELP ME FIND HER?
HER NAME'S JEN, SHE'S THE BEST.
I AM SORRY, RIPLEY. I CANNOT DO THAT FOR YOU.
JUNK!
BUT IF YOU ANSWER MY RIDDLE, I WILL GRANT YOU A WISH...
...AND PERHAPS THAT COULD HELP YOU FIND YOUR FRIEND.
SO MANY YESSEESSSS!
UM...RIP, A SPHINX DOESN'T GRANT WISHES.
THIS ONE DID! NOW SHUSH!
ONE WARNING, RIPLEY. IF YOU CANNOT ANSWER, I GET TO DEVOUR YOU.
WHOA.
WELL, I GOTTA FIND JEN, NO MATTER WHAT THE RISK, SO...
HIT ME, SPHINX-Y!
WHAT RUNS BUT CANNOT WALK, HAS A MOUTH BUT CANNOT TALK--
WHAT HAS A HEAD BUT NEVER WEEPS, HAS A BED BUT NEVER SLEEPS?
OH BOY.

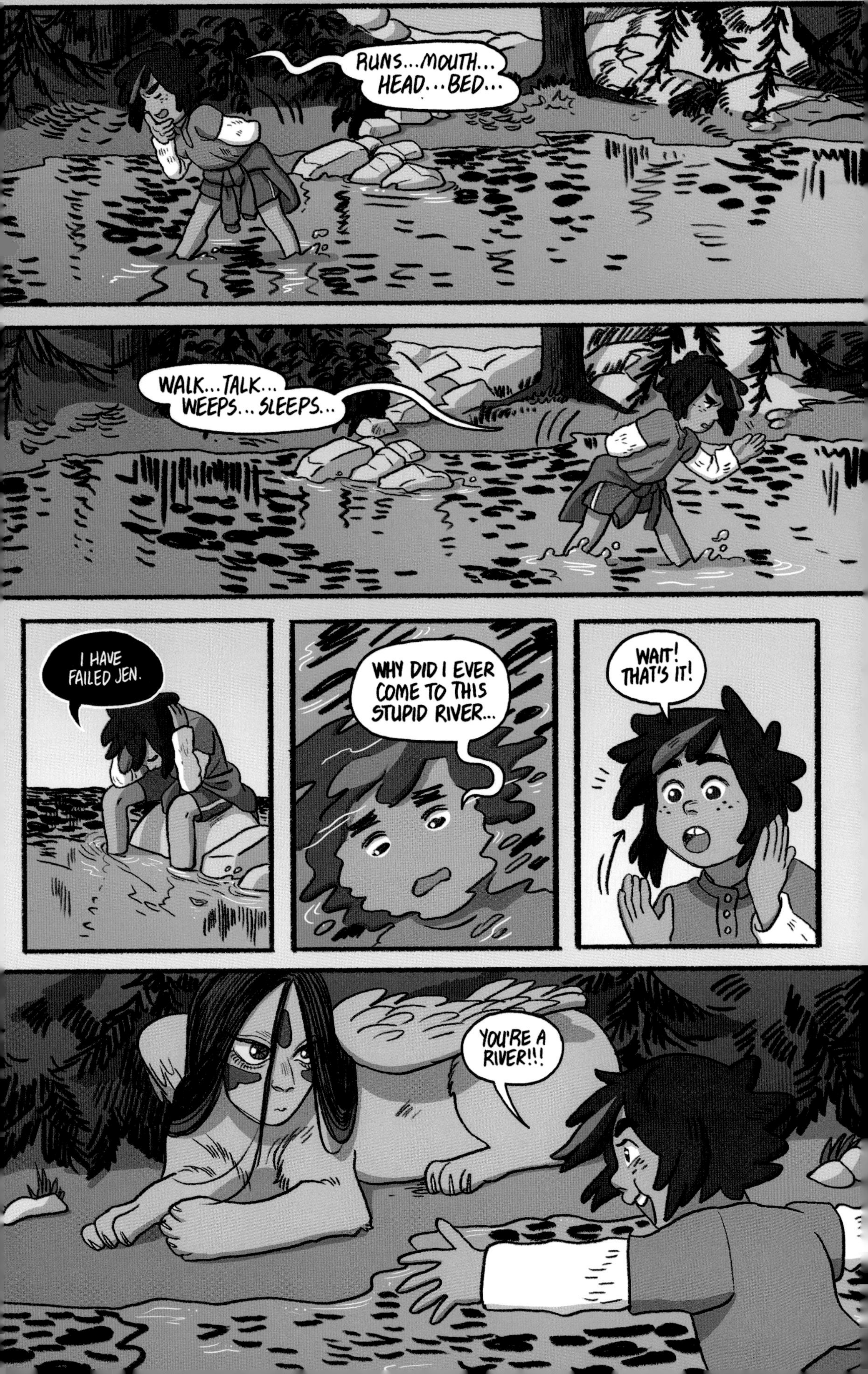
RUNS...MOUTH...
HEAD...BED...
WALK...TALK...
WEEPS...SLEEPS...
I HAVE FAILED JEN.
WHY DID I EVER COME TO THIS STUPID RIVER...
WAIT! THAT'S IT!
YOU'RE A RIVER!!!

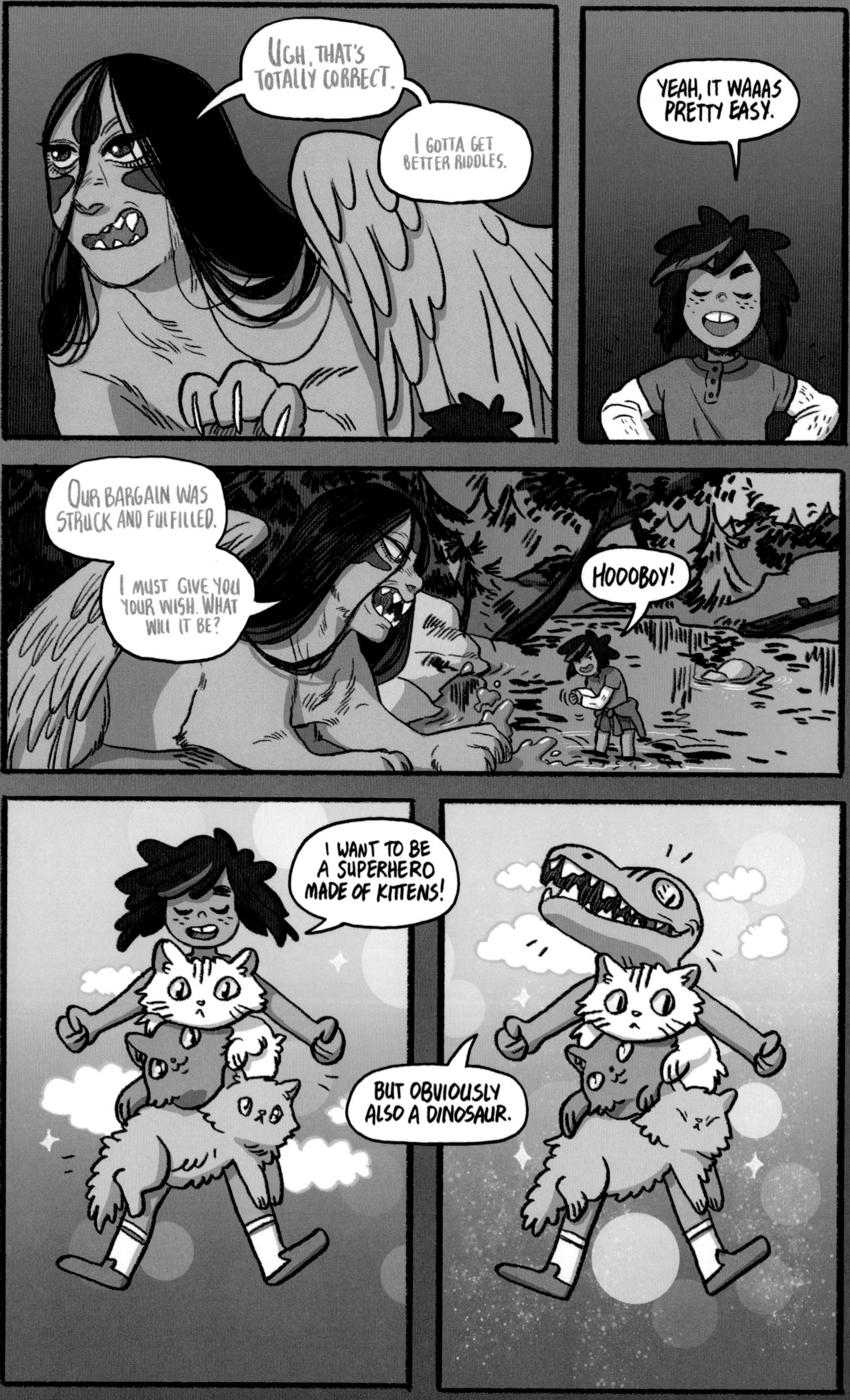
UGH, THAT'S TOTALLY CORRECT.
I GOTTA GET BETTER RIDDLES.
YEAH, IT WAAAS PRETTY EASY.
OUR BARGAIN WAS STRUCK AND FULFILLED.
I MUST GIVE YOU YOUR WISH. WHAT WILL IT BE?
HOOOBOY!
I WANT TO BE A SUPERHERO MADE OF KITTENS!
BUT OBVIOUSLY ALSO A DINOSAUR.

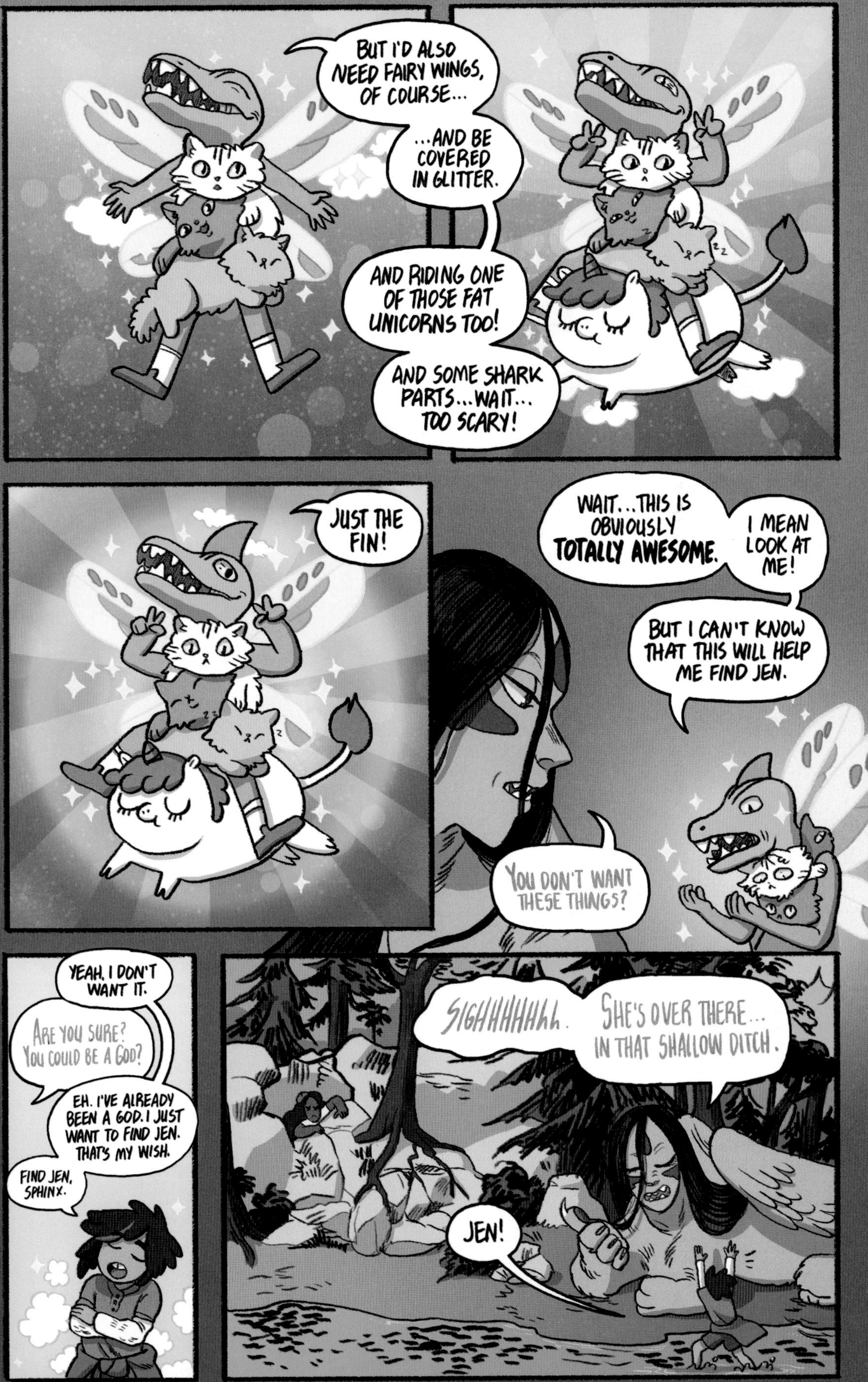
BUT I'D ALSO NEED FAIRY WINGS, OF COURSE...
...AND BE COVERED IN GLITTER.
AND RIDING ONE OF THOSE FAT UNICORNS TOO!
AND SOME SHARK PARTS...WAIT... TOO SCARY!
JUST THE FIN!
WAIT...THIS IS OBVIOUSLY TOTALLY AWESOME.
I MEAN LOOK AT ME!
BUT I CAN'T KNOW THAT THIS WILL HELP ME FIND JEN.
YOU DON'T WANT THESE THINGS?
YEAH, I DON'T WANT IT.
ARE YOU SURE? YOU COULD BE A GOD?
EH. I'VE ALREADY BEEN A GOD. I JUST WANT TO FIND JEN. THAT'S MY WISH.
FIND JEN, SPHINX.
SIGHHHHHHH.
SHE'S OVER THERE... IN THAT SHALLOW DITCH.
JEN!

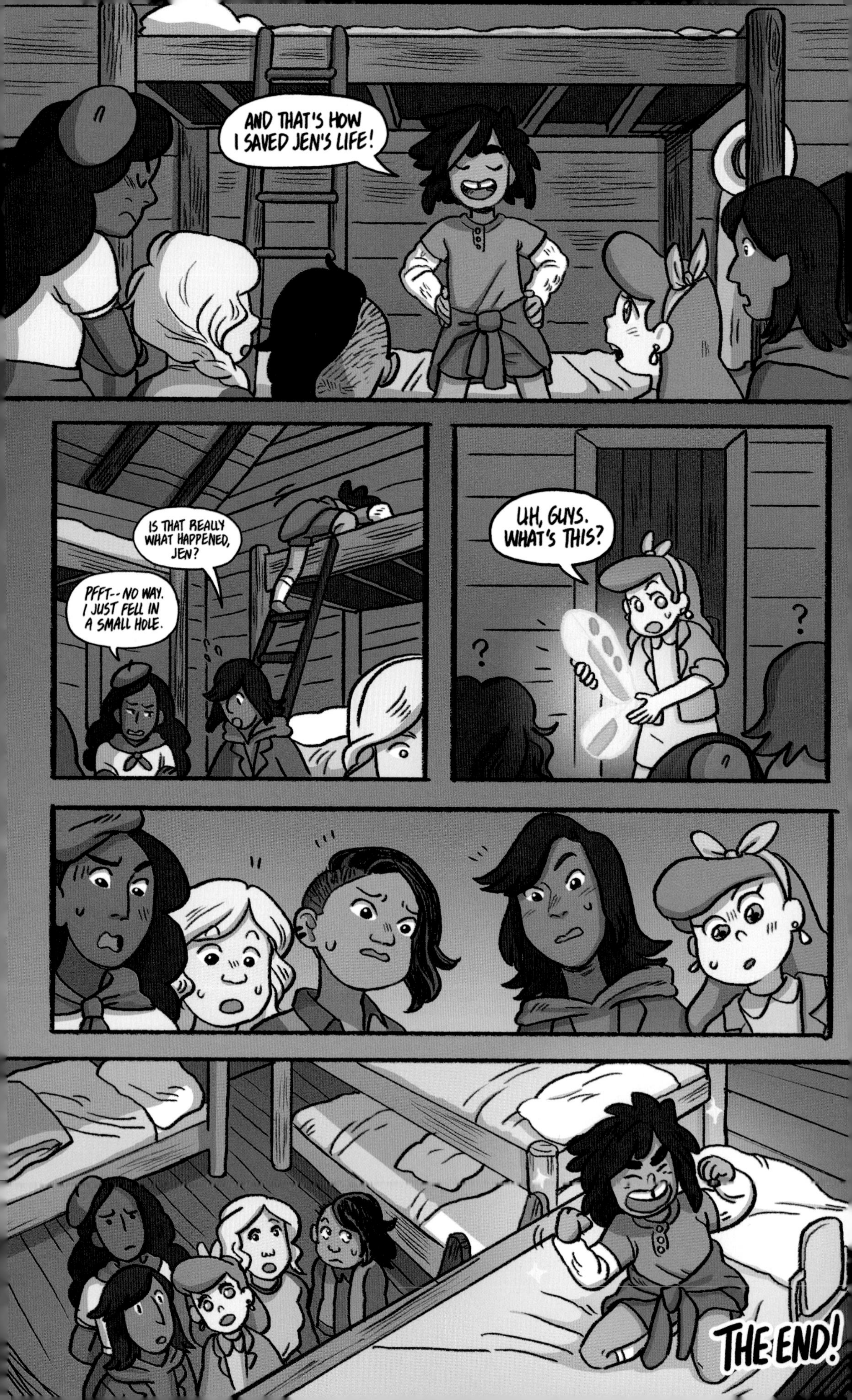
AND THAT'S HOW I SAVED JEN'S LIFE!
IS THAT REALLY WHAT HAPPENED, JEN?
PFFT-- NO WAY. I JUST FELL IN A SMALL HOLE.
UH, GUYS. WHAT'S THIS?
THE END!

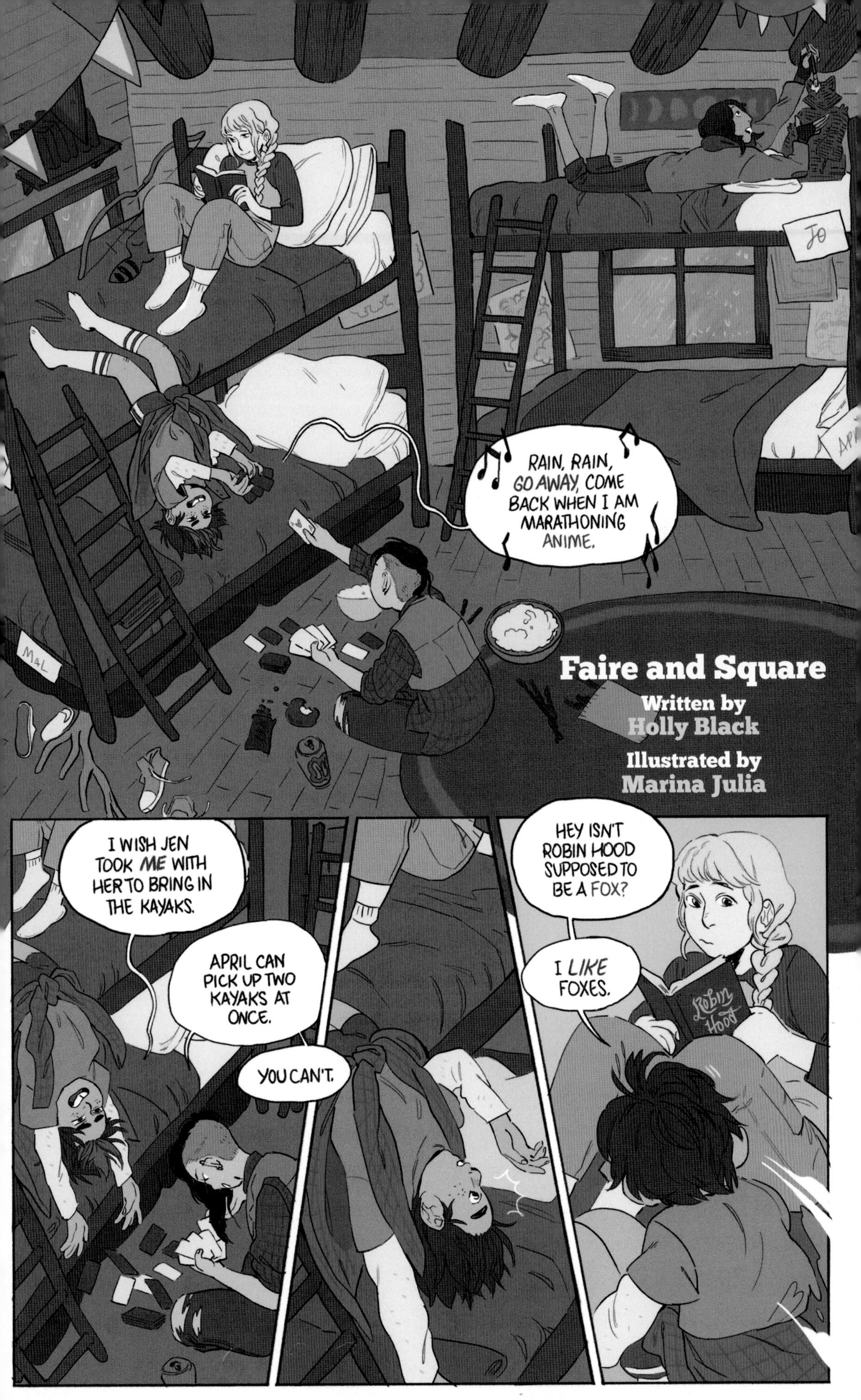
RAIN, RAIN, GO AWAY, COME BACK WHEN I AM MARATHONING ANIME.
Faire and Square
Written by
Holly Black
Illustrated by
Marina Julia
I WISH JEN TOOK ME WITH HER TO BRING IN THE KAYAKS.
APRIL CAN PICK UP TWO KAYAKS AT ONCE.
YOU CAN'T.
HEY ISN'T ROBIN HOOD SUPPOSED TO BE A FOX?
I LIKE FOXES.
Robin Hood

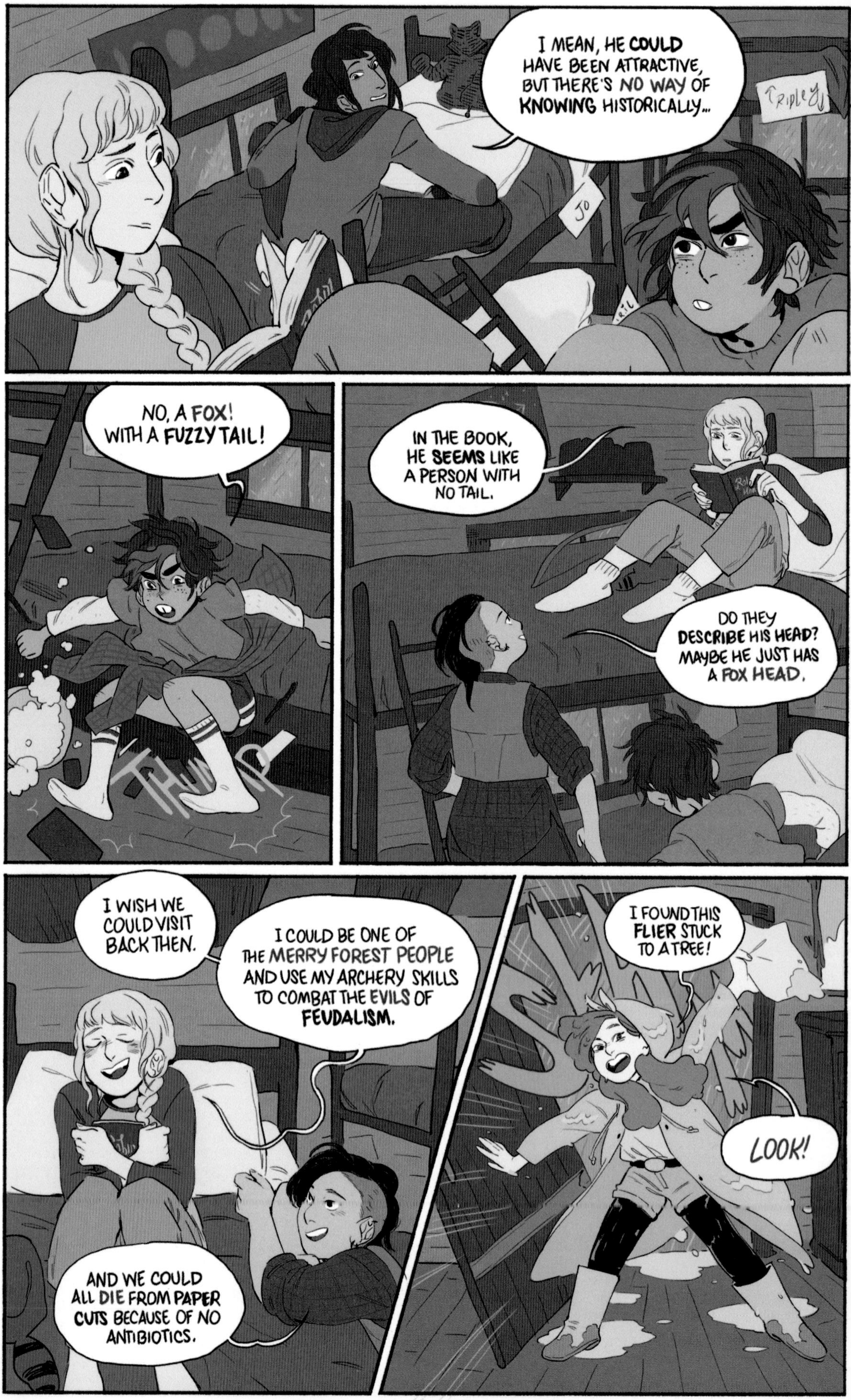
I MEAN, HE COULD HAVE BEEN ATTRACTIVE, BUT THERE'S NO WAY OF KNOWING HISTORICALLY...
Ripley
JO
NO, A FOX! WITH A FUZZY TAIL!
THUMP
IN THE BOOK, HE SEEMS LIKE A PERSON WITH NO TAIL.
DO THEY DESCRIBE HIS HEAD? MAYBE HE JUST HAS A FOX HEAD.
I WISH WE COULD VISIT BACK THEN.
I COULD BE ONE OF THE MERRY FOREST PEOPLE AND USE MY ARCHERY SKILLS TO COMBAT THE EVILS OF FEUDALISM.
AND WE COULD ALL DIE FROM PAPER CUTS BECAUSE OF NO ANTIBIOTICS.
I FOUND THIS FLIER STUCK TO A TREE!
LOOK!

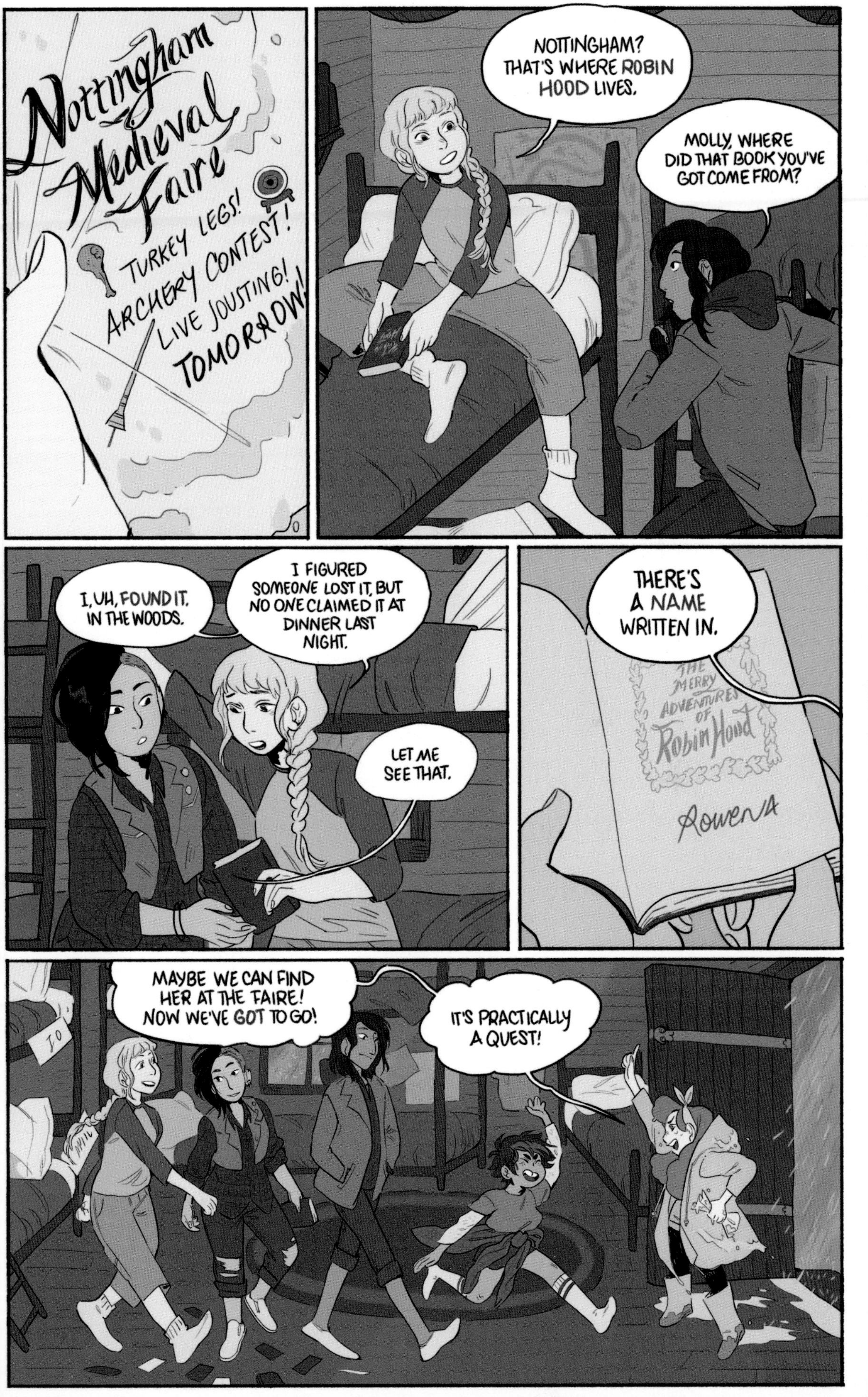
Nottingham Medieval Faire
TURKEY LEGS!
ARCHERY CONTEST!
LIVE JOUSTING!
TOMORROW!
NOTTINGHAM? THAT'S WHERE ROBIN HOOD LIVES.
MOLLY, WHERE DID THAT BOOK YOU'VE GOT COME FROM?
I, UH, FOUND IT. IN THE WOODS.
I FIGURED SOMEONE LOST IT, BUT NO ONE CLAIMED IT AT DINNER LAST NIGHT.
LET ME SEE THAT.
THERE'S A NAME WRITTEN IN.
THE MERRY ADVENTURES OF Robin Hood
ROWENA
MAYBE WE CAN FIND HER AT THE FAIRE! NOW WE'VE GOT TO GO!
IT'S PRACTICALLY A QUEST!

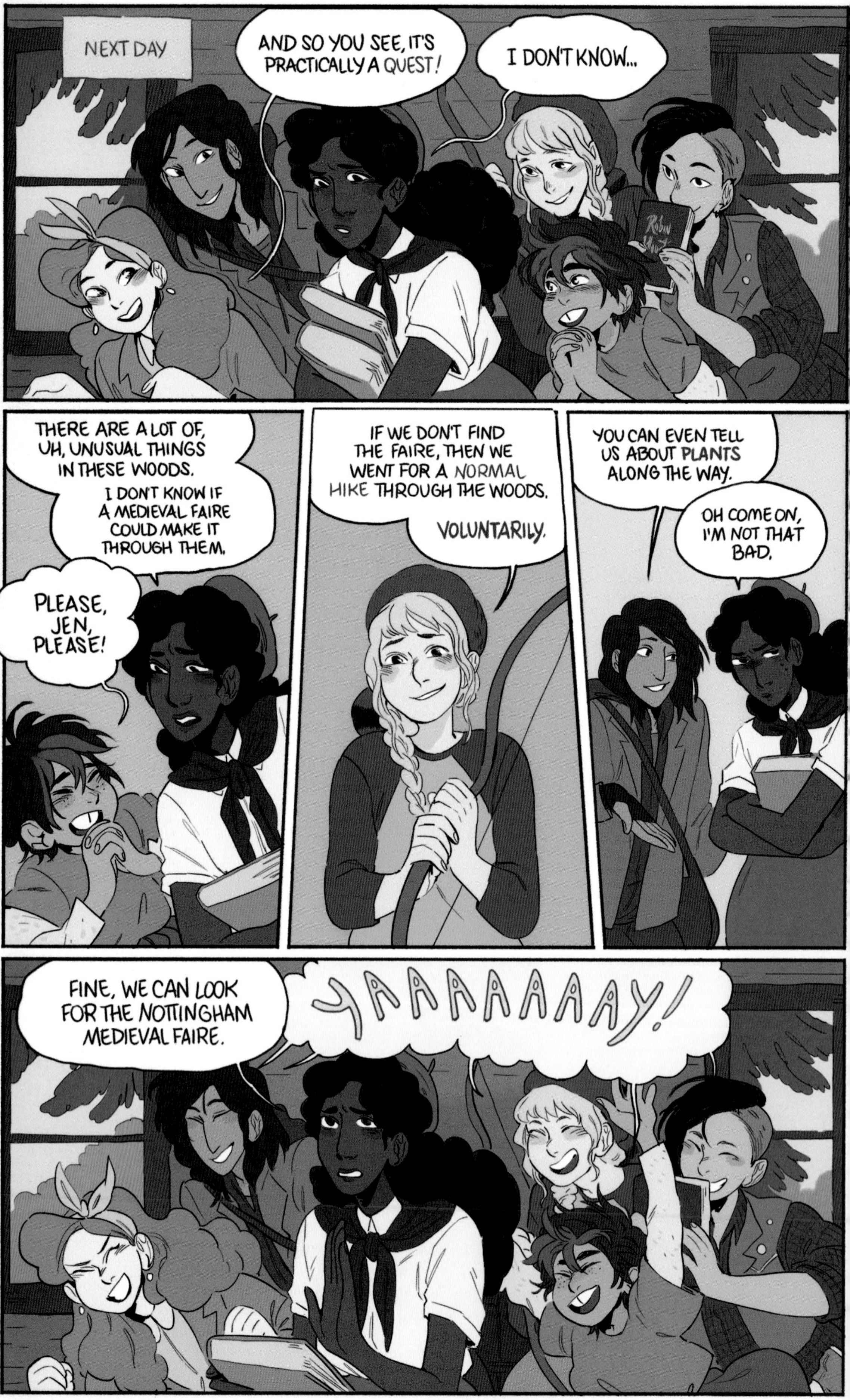
NEXT DAY
AND SO YOU SEE, IT'S PRACTICALLY A QUEST!
I DON'T KNOW...
THERE ARE A LOT OF, UH, UNUSUAL THINGS IN THESE WOODS.
I DON'T KNOW IF A MEDIEVAL FAIRE COULD MAKE IT THROUGH THEM.
PLEASE, JEN, PLEASE!
IF WE DON'T FIND THE FAIRE, THEN WE WENT FOR A NORMAL HIKE THROUGH THE WOODS.
VOLUNTARILY.
YOU CAN EVEN TELL US ABOUT PLANTS ALONG THE WAY.
OH COME ON, I'M NOT THAT BAD.
FINE, WE CAN LOOK FOR THE NOTTINGHAM MEDIEVAL FAIRE.
YAAAAAAAY!

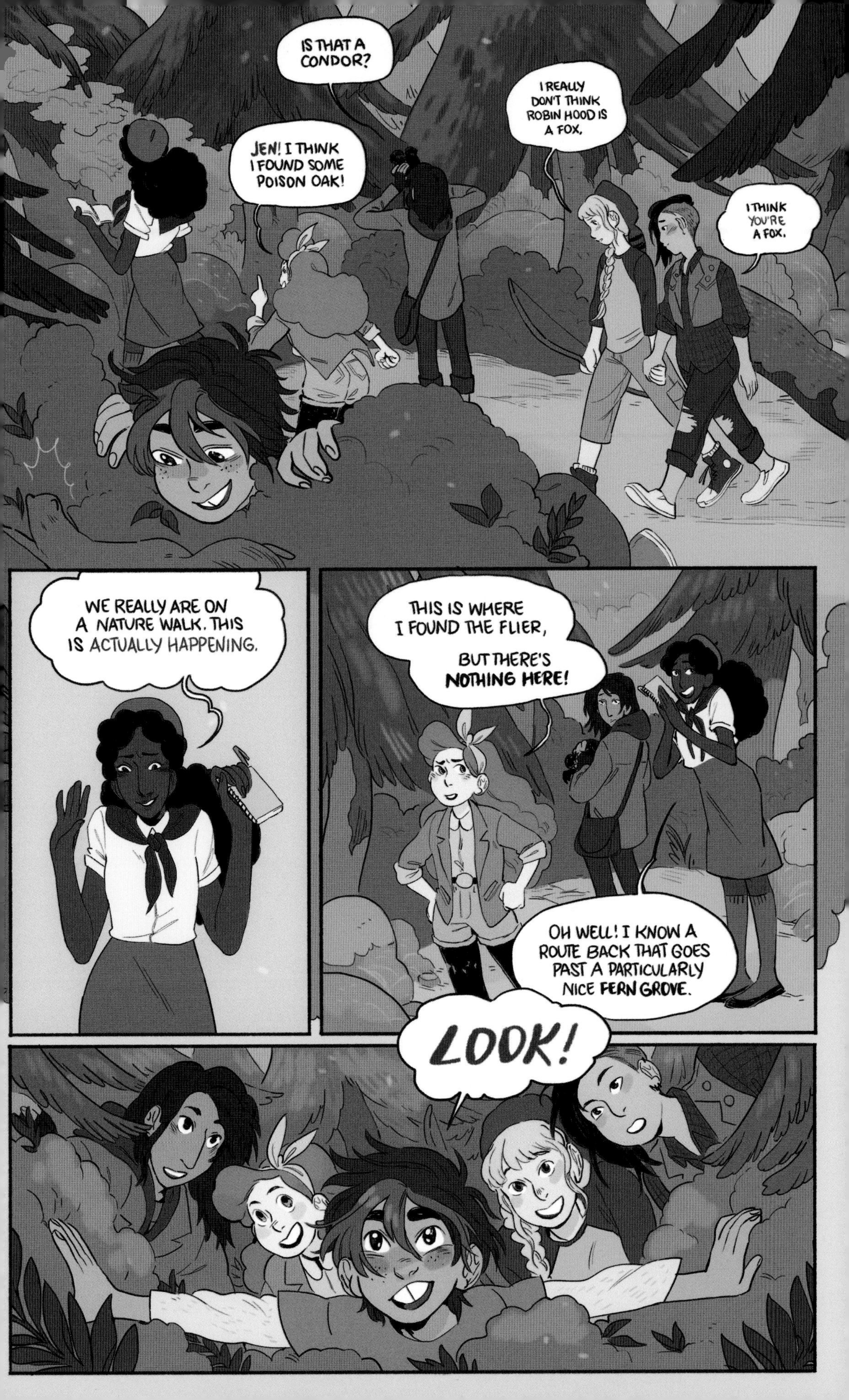
IS THAT A CONDOR?
JEN! I THINK I FOUND SOME POISON OAK!
I REALLY DON'T THINK ROBIN HOOD IS A FOX.
I THINK YOU'RE A FOX.
WE REALLY ARE ON A NATURE WALK. THIS IS ACTUALLY HAPPENING.
THIS IS WHERE I FOUND THE FLIER,
BUT THERE'S NOTHING HERE!
OH WELL! I KNOW A ROUTE BACK THAT GOES PAST A PARTICULARLY NICE FERN GROVE.
LOOK!

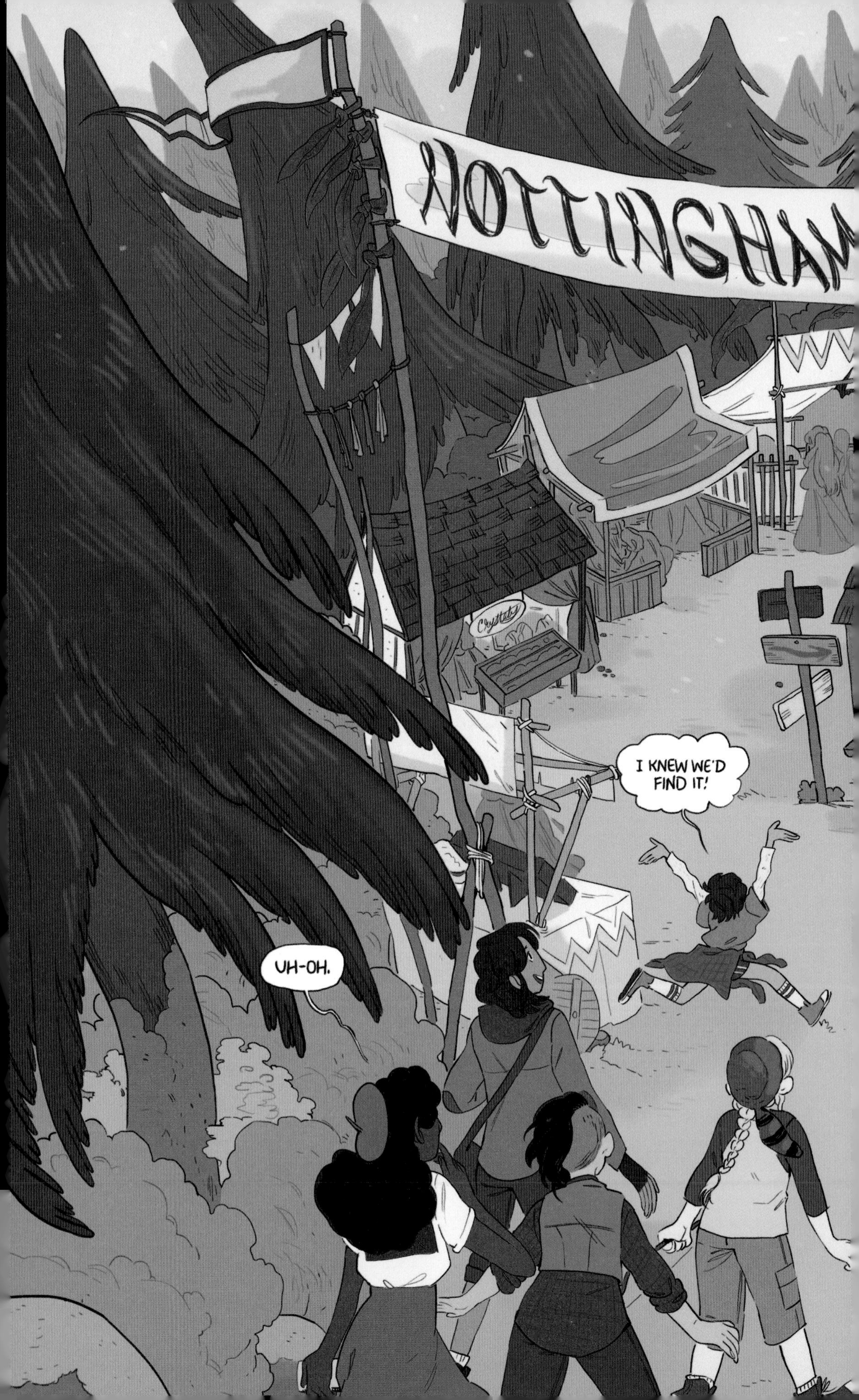
NOTTINGHAM
I KNEW WE'D FIND IT!
UH-OH.

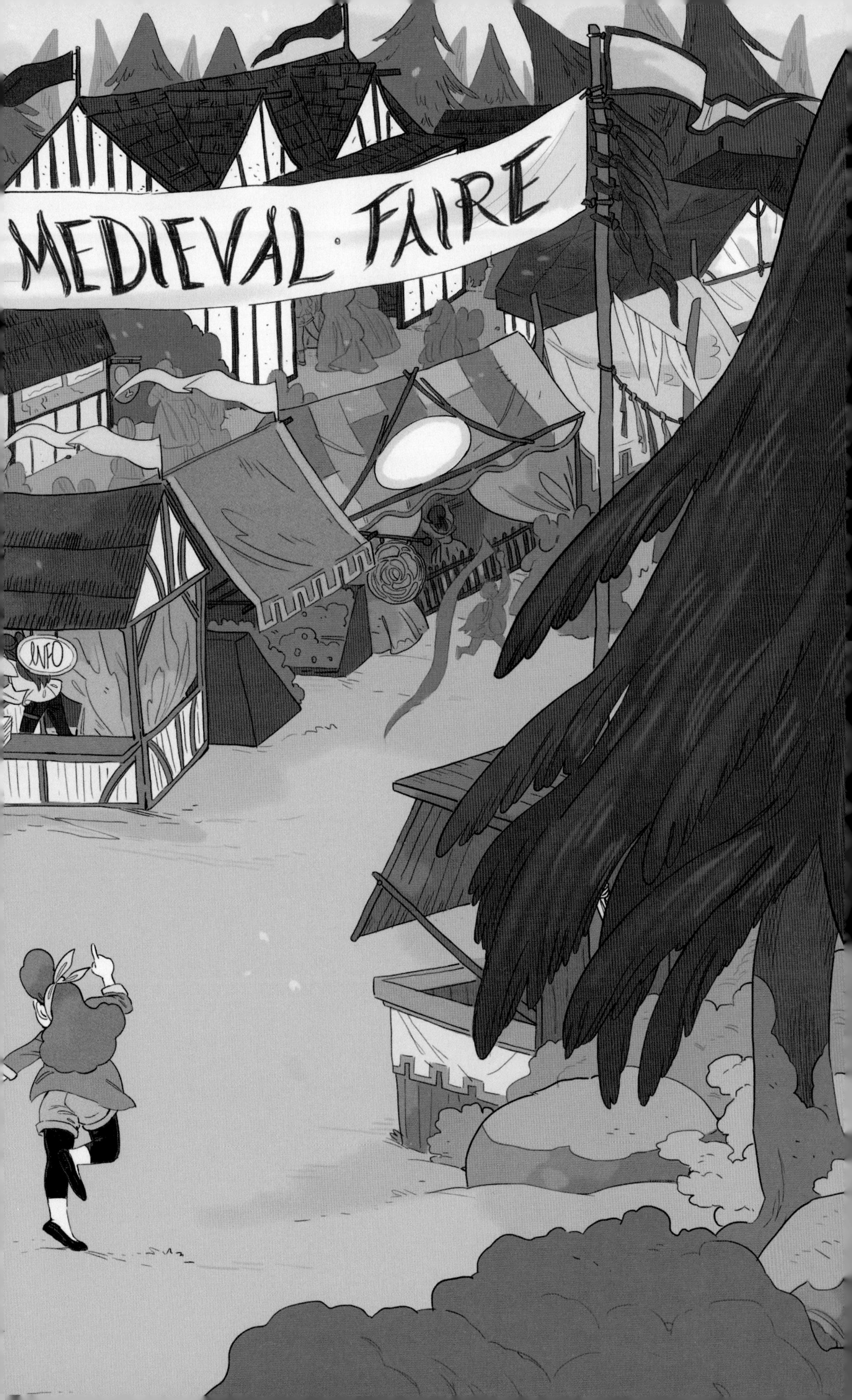
MEDIEVAL FAIRE
INFO

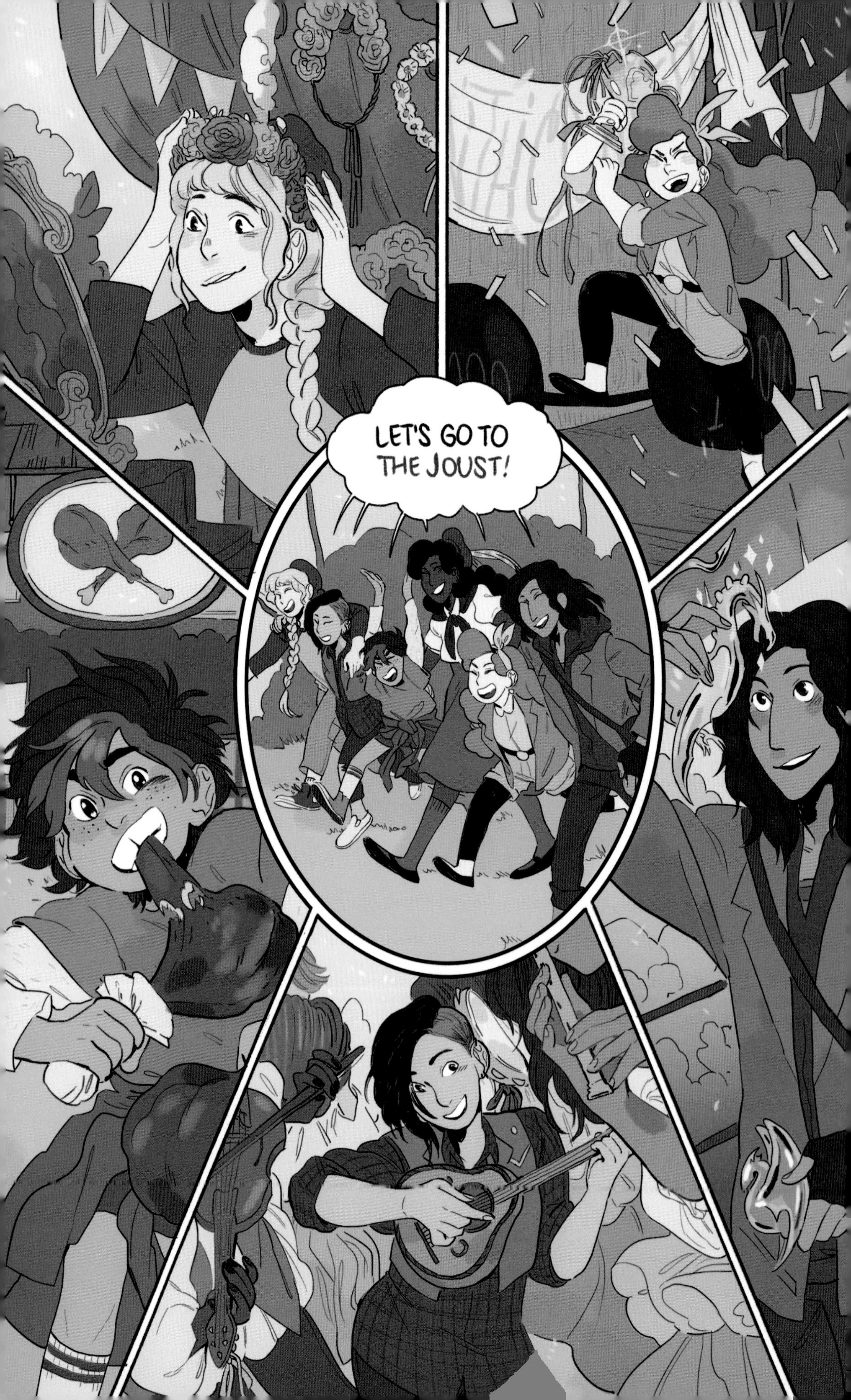
LET'S GO TO THE JOUST!

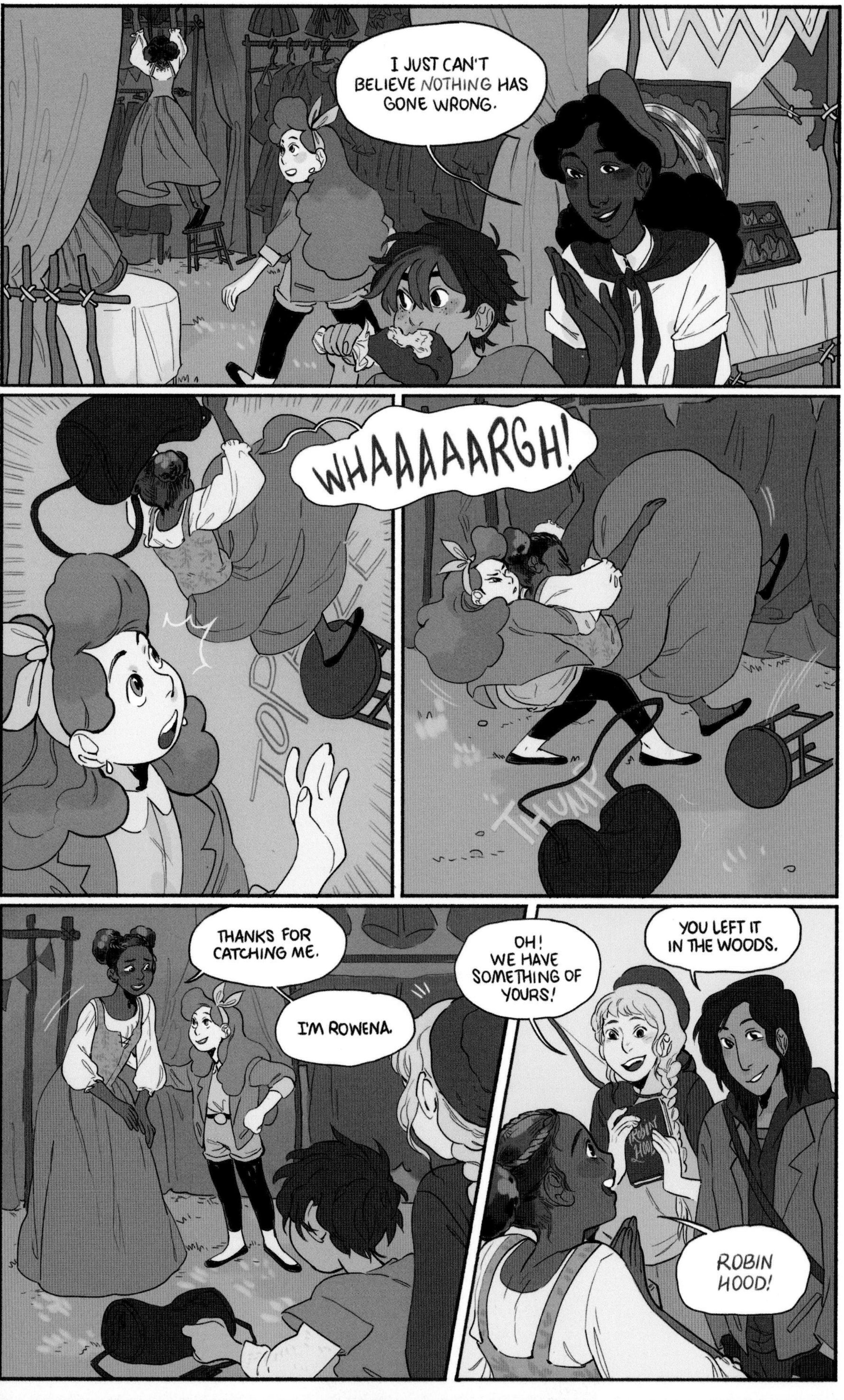
I JUST CAN'T BELIEVE NOTHING HAS GONE WRONG.
WHAAAAARGH!
TOPPLE
THUMP
THANKS FOR CATCHING ME.
I'M ROWENA.
OH! WE HAVE SOMETHING OF YOURS!
YOU LEFT IT IN THE WOODS.
ROBIN HOOD
ROBIN HOOD!

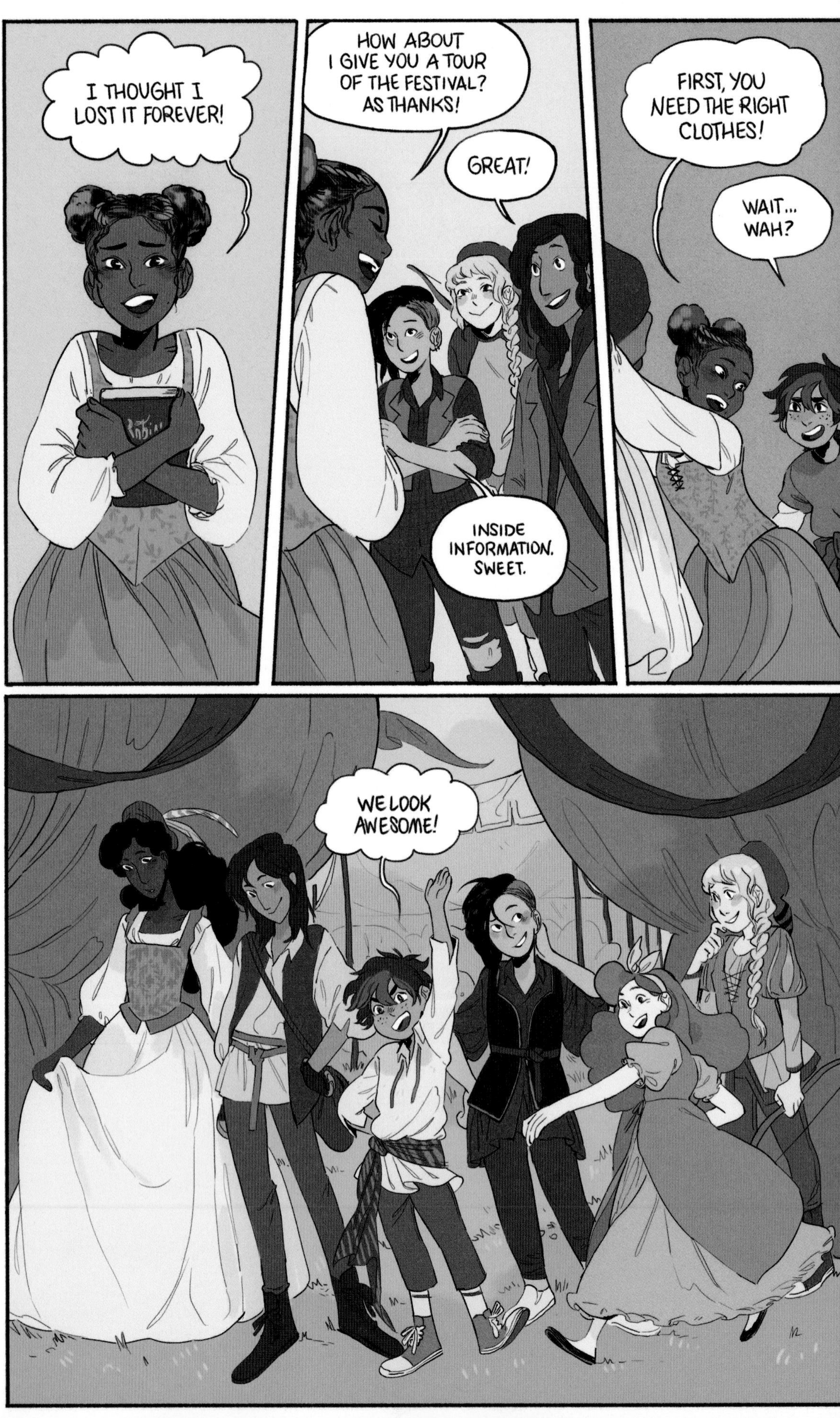
I THOUGHT I LOST IT FOREVER!
HOW ABOUT I GIVE YOU A TOUR OF THE FESTIVAL? AS THANKS!
GREAT!
INSIDE INFORMATION. SWEET.
FIRST, YOU NEED THE RIGHT CLOTHES!
WAIT... WAH?
WE LOOK AWESOME!

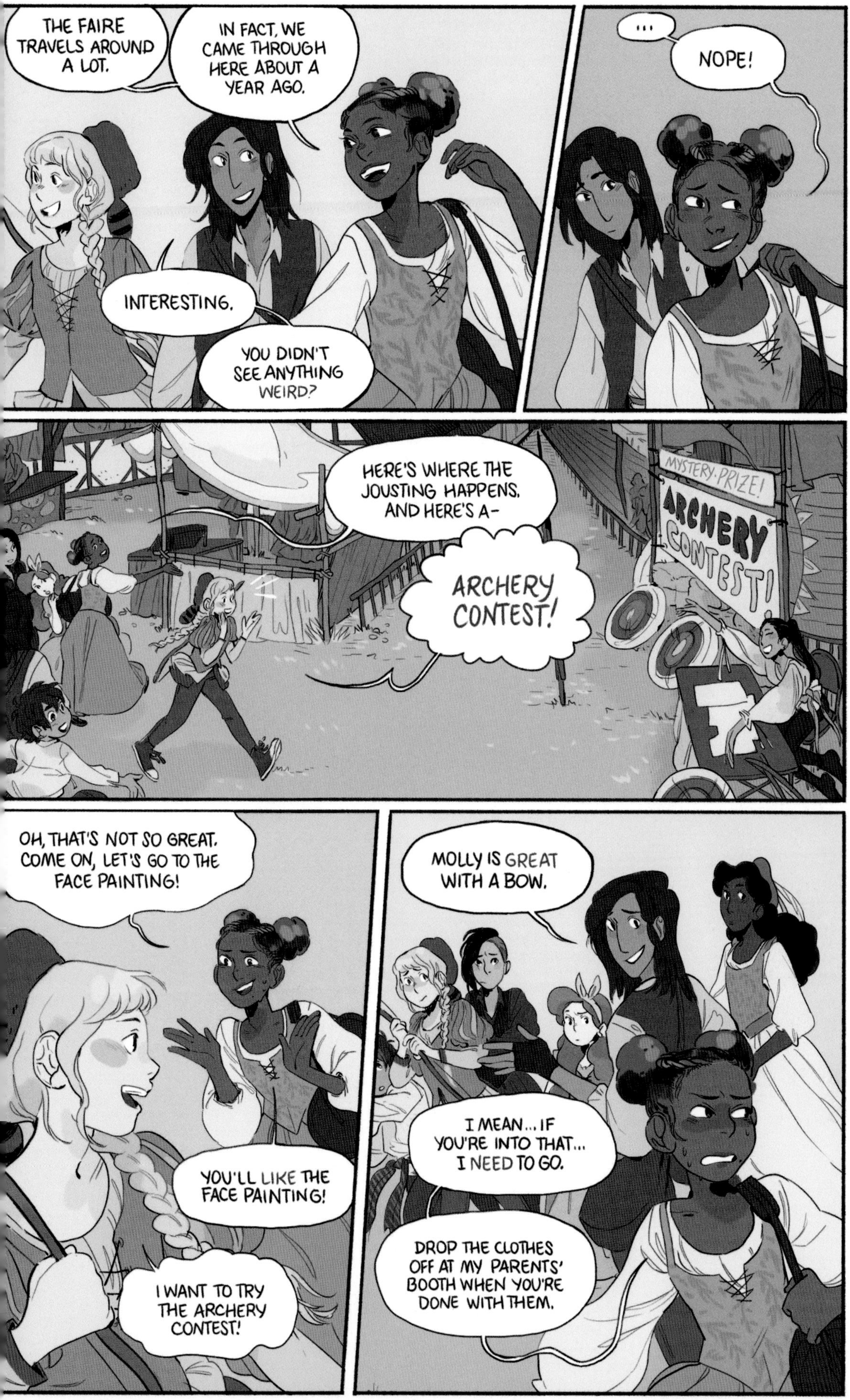
THE FAIRE TRAVELS AROUND A LOT.
IN FACT, WE CAME THROUGH HERE ABOUT A YEAR AGO.
INTERESTING.
YOU DIDN'T SEE ANYTHING WEIRD?
...
NOPE!
HERE'S WHERE THE JOUSTING HAPPENS. AND HERE'S A-
ARCHERY CONTEST!
MYSTERY PRIZE!
ARCHERY CONTEST!
OH, THAT'S NOT SO GREAT. COME ON, LET'S GO TO THE FACE PAINTING!
YOU'LL LIKE THE FACE PAINTING!
I WANT TO TRY THE ARCHERY CONTEST!
MOLLY IS GREAT WITH A BOW.
I MEAN... IF YOU'RE INTO THAT... I NEED TO GO.
DROP THE CLOTHES OFF AT MY PARENTS' BOOTH WHEN YOU'RE DONE WITH THEM.

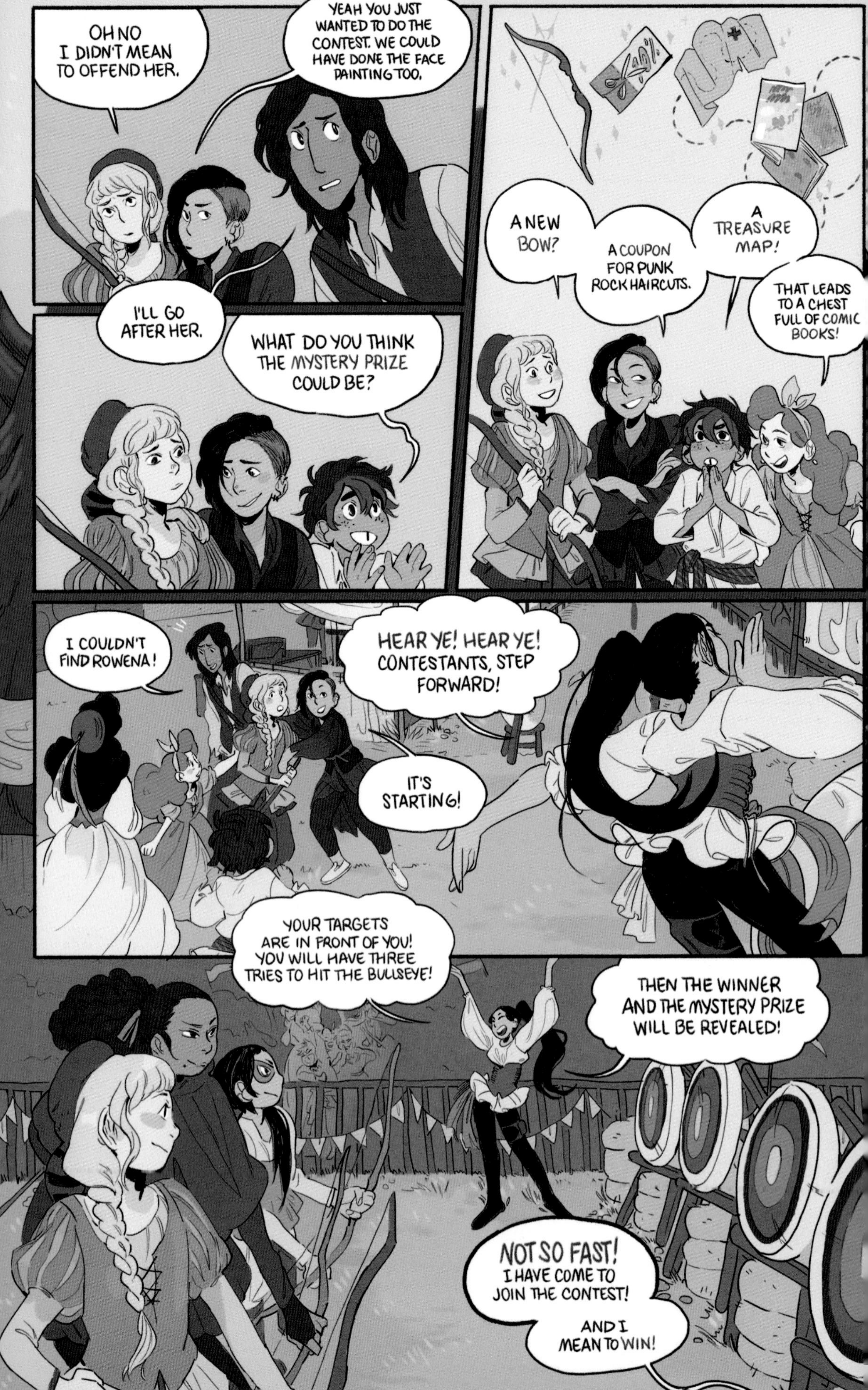
OH NO I DIDN'T MEAN TO OFFEND HER.
YEAH YOU JUST WANTED TO DO THE CONTEST. WE COULD HAVE DONE THE FACE PAINTING TOO.
A NEW BOW?
A COUPON FOR PUNK ROCK HAIRCUTS.
A TREASURE MAP!
THAT LEADS TO A CHEST FULL OF COMIC BOOKS!
I'LL GO AFTER HER.
WHAT DO YOU THINK THE MYSTERY PRIZE COULD BE?
I COULDN'T FIND ROWENA!
HEAR YE! HEAR YE! CONTESTANTS, STEP FORWARD!
IT'S STARTING!
YOUR TARGETS ARE IN FRONT OF YOU! YOU WILL HAVE THREE TRIES TO HIT THE BULLSEYE!
THEN THE WINNER AND THE MYSTERY PRIZE WILL BE REVEALED!
NOT SO FAST! I HAVE COME TO JOIN THE CONTEST!
AND I MEAN TO WIN!

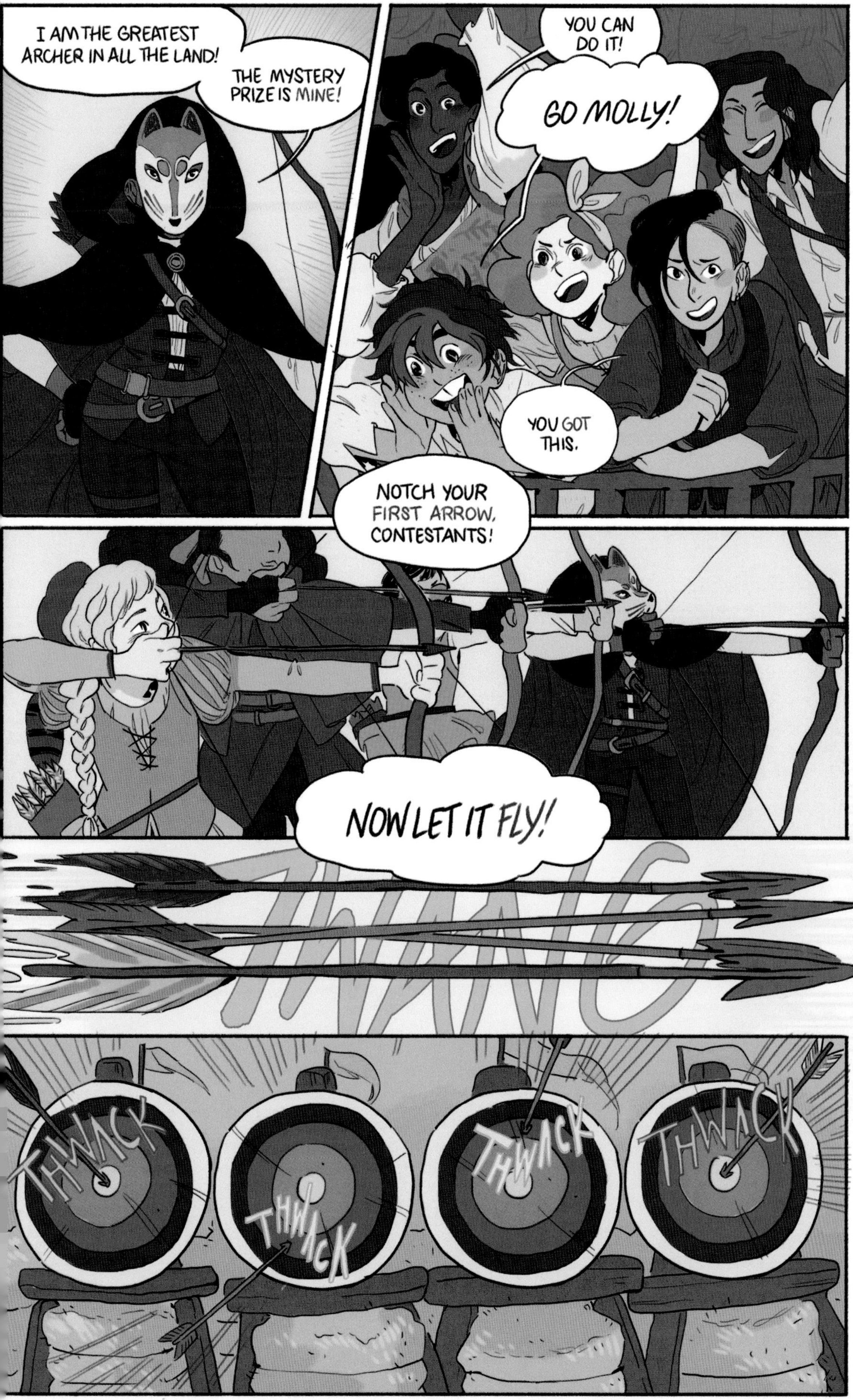

I AM THE GREATEST ARCHER IN ALL THE LAND!
THE MYSTERY PRIZE IS MINE!
YOU CAN DO IT!
GO MOLLY!
YOU GOT THIS.
NOTCH YOUR FIRST ARROW, CONTESTANTS!
NOW LET IT FLY!
THWANG
THWACK
THWACK
THWACK
THWACK

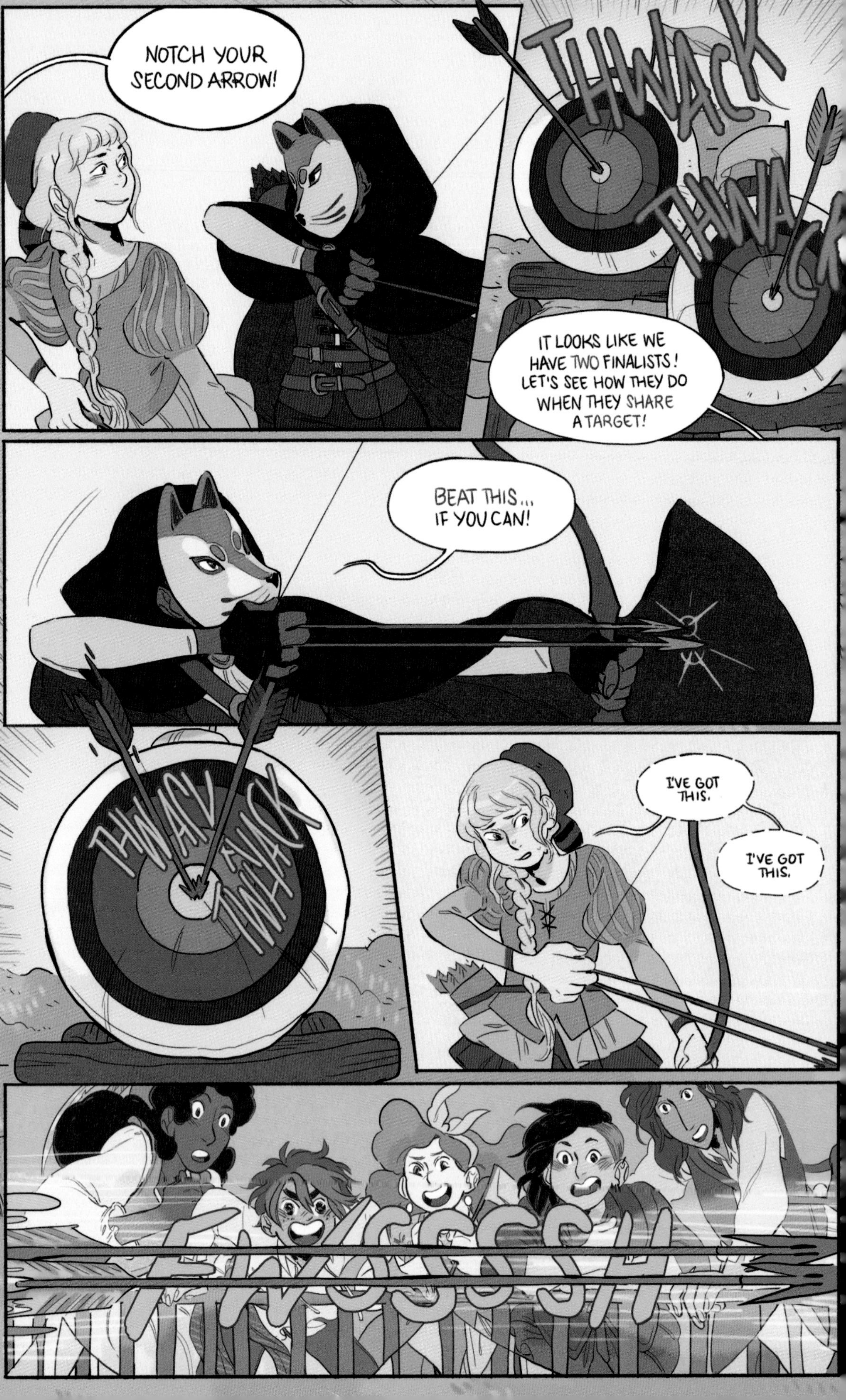
NOTCH YOUR SECOND ARROW!
THWACK
THWACK
IT LOOKS LIKE WE HAVE TWO FINALISTS! LET'S SEE HOW THEY DO WHEN THEY SHARE A TARGET!
BEAT THIS... IF YOU CAN!
THWACK
THWACK
I'VE GOT THIS.
I'VE GOT THIS.

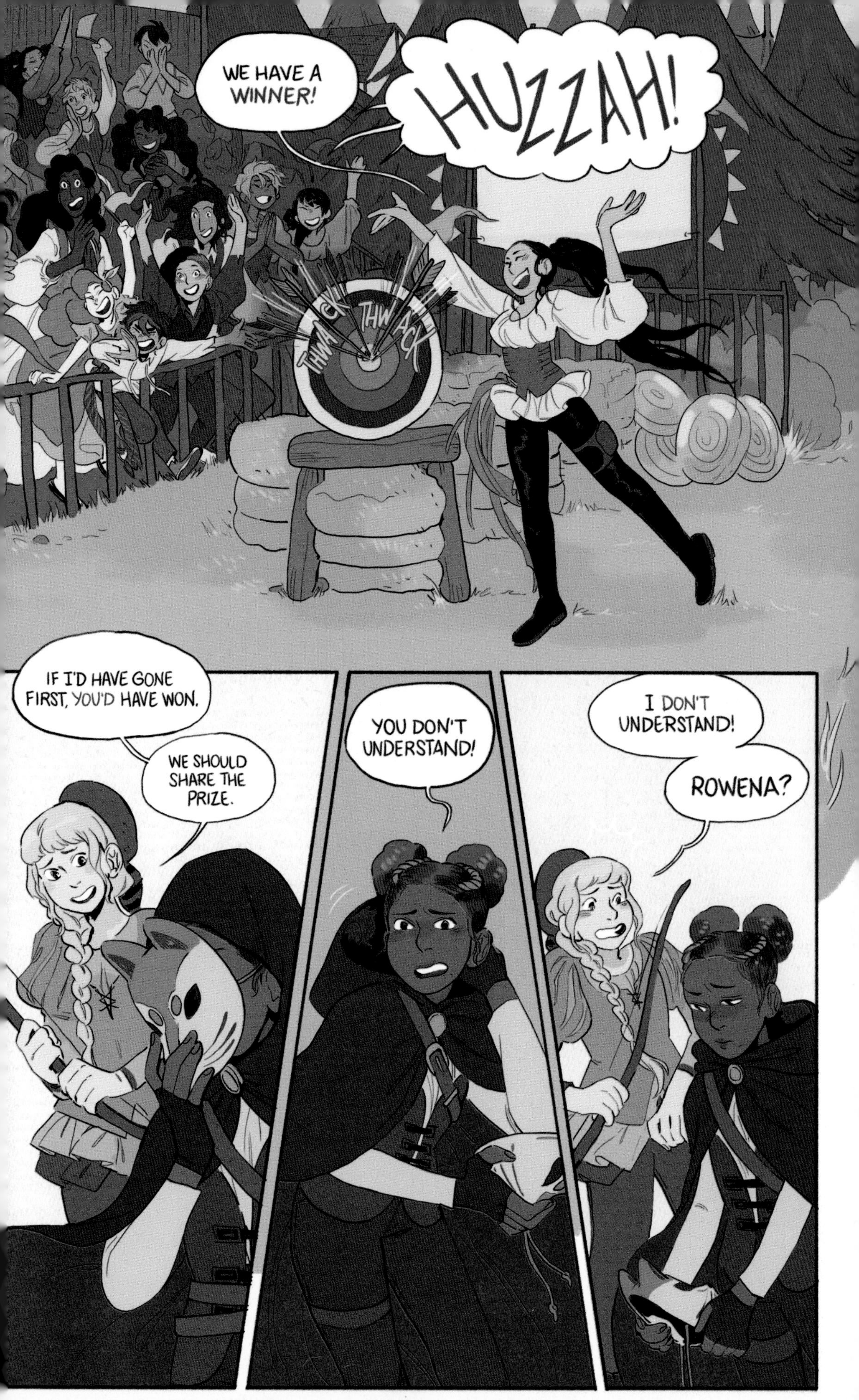
WE HAVE A WINNER!
HUZZAH!
THWACK
THWACK
IF I'D HAVE GONE FIRST, YOU'D HAVE WON.
WE SHOULD SHARE THE PRIZE.
YOU DON'T UNDERSTAND!
I DON'T UNDERSTAND!
ROWENA?

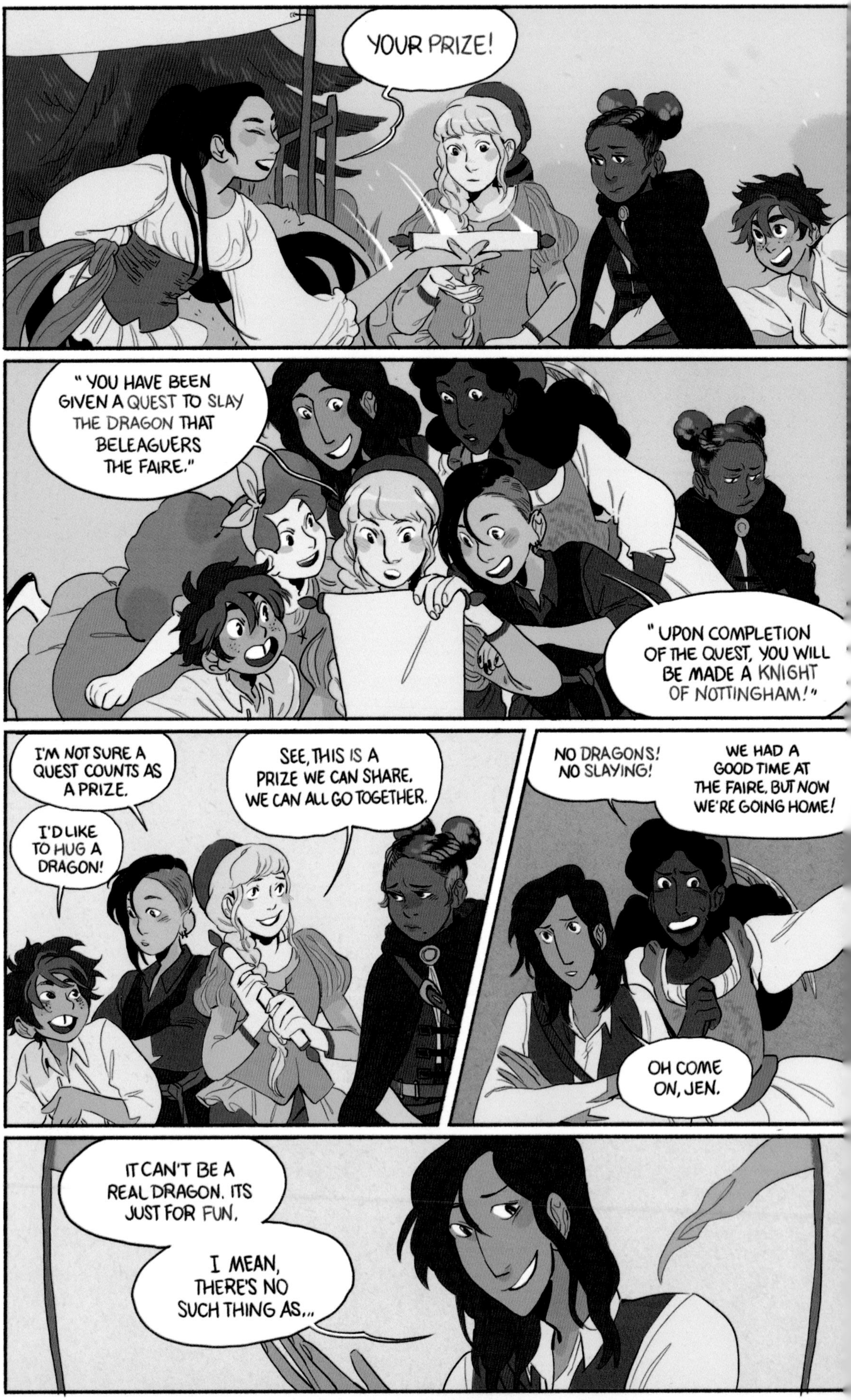
YOUR PRIZE!
" YOU HAVE BEEN GIVEN A QUEST TO SLAY THE DRAGON THAT BELEAGUERS THE FAIRE."
" UPON COMPLETION OF THE QUEST, YOU WILL BE MADE A KNIGHT OF NOTTINGHAM!"
I'M NOT SURE A QUEST COUNTS AS A PRIZE.
I'D LIKE TO HUG A DRAGON!
SEE, THIS IS A PRIZE WE CAN SHARE. WE CAN ALL GO TOGETHER.
NO DRAGONS! NO SLAYING!
WE HAD A GOOD TIME AT THE FAIRE, BUT NOW WE'RE GOING HOME!
OH COME ON, JEN.
IT CAN'T BE A REAL DRAGON. ITS JUST FOR FUN.
I MEAN, THERE'S NO SUCH THING AS...

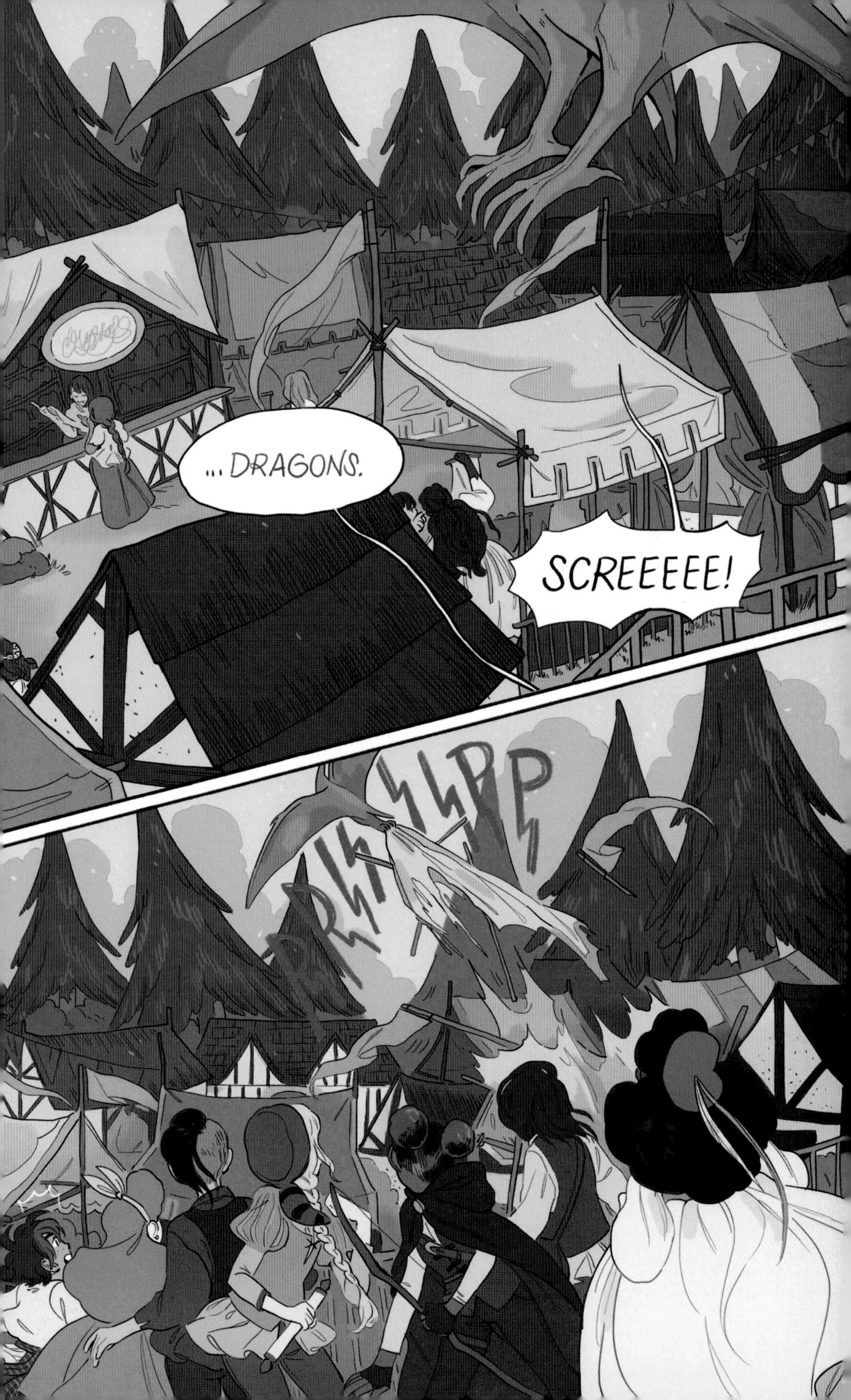
...DRAGONS.
SCREEEEE!

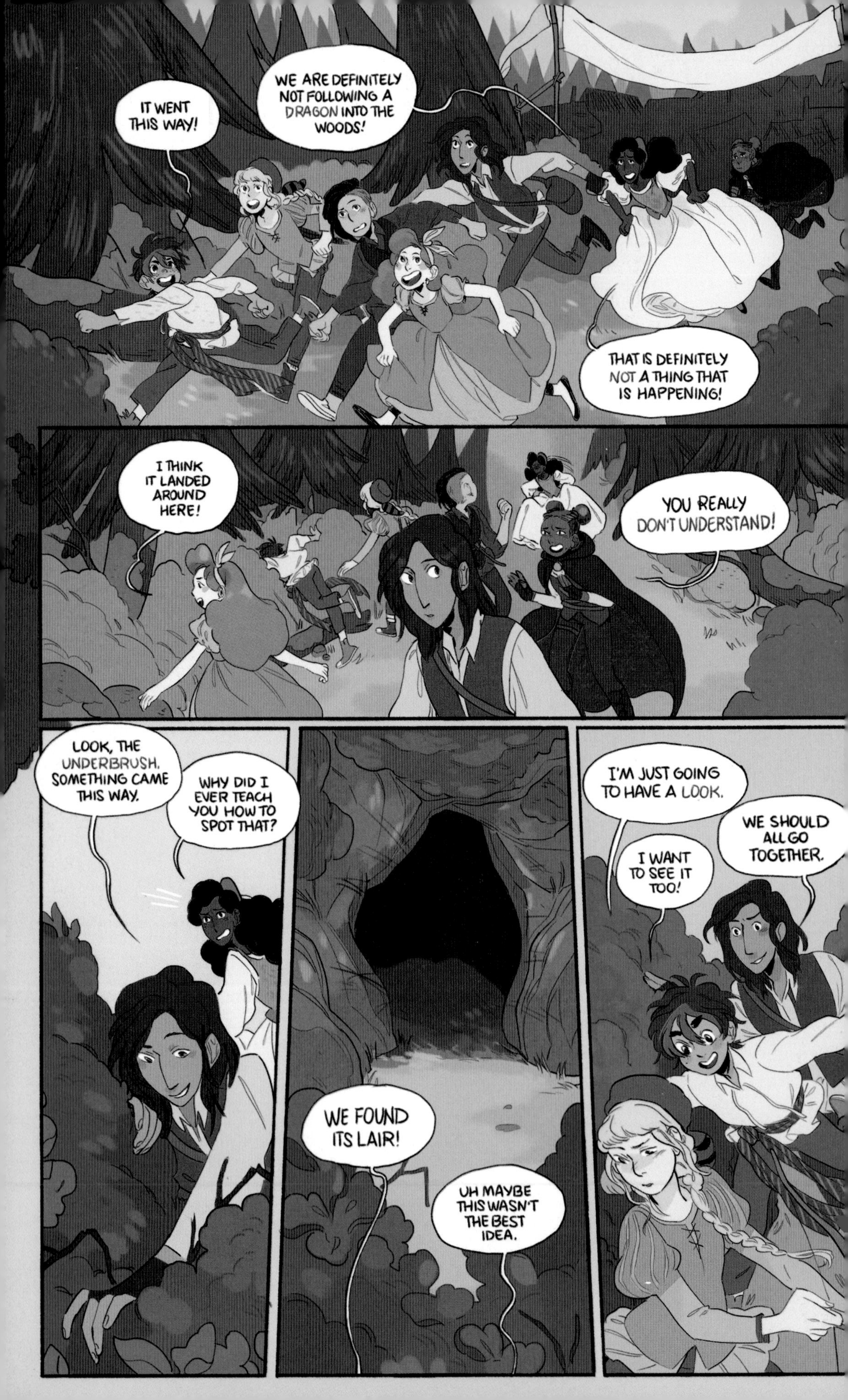
IT WENT THIS WAY!
WE ARE DEFINITELY NOT FOLLOWING A DRAGON INTO THE WOODS!
THAT IS DEFINITELY NOT A THING THAT IS HAPPENING!
I THINK IT LANDED AROUND HERE!
YOU REALLY DON'T UNDERSTAND!
LOOK, THE UNDERBRUSH. SOMETHING CAME THIS WAY.
WHY DID I EVER TEACH YOU HOW TO SPOT THAT?
WE FOUND ITS LAIR!
UH MAYBE THIS WASN'T THE BEST IDEA.
I'M JUST GOING TO HAVE A LOOK.
I WANT TO SEE IT TOO!
WE SHOULD ALL GO TOGETHER.

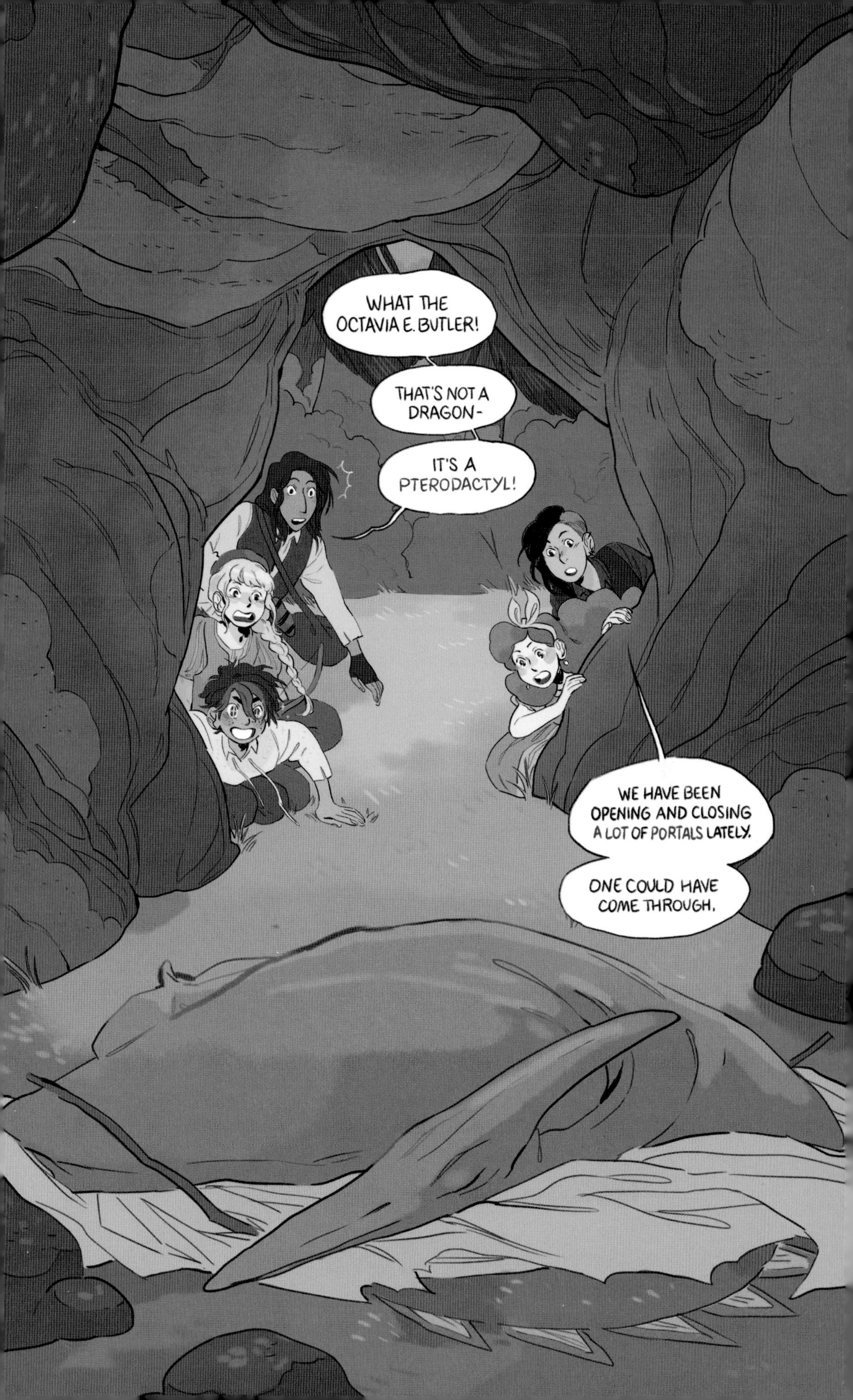
WHAT THE OCTAVIA E. BUTLER!
THAT'S NOT A DRAGON-
IT'S A PTERODACTYL!
WE HAVE BEEN OPENING AND CLOSING A LOT OF PORTALS LATELY.
ONE COULD HAVE COME THROUGH.

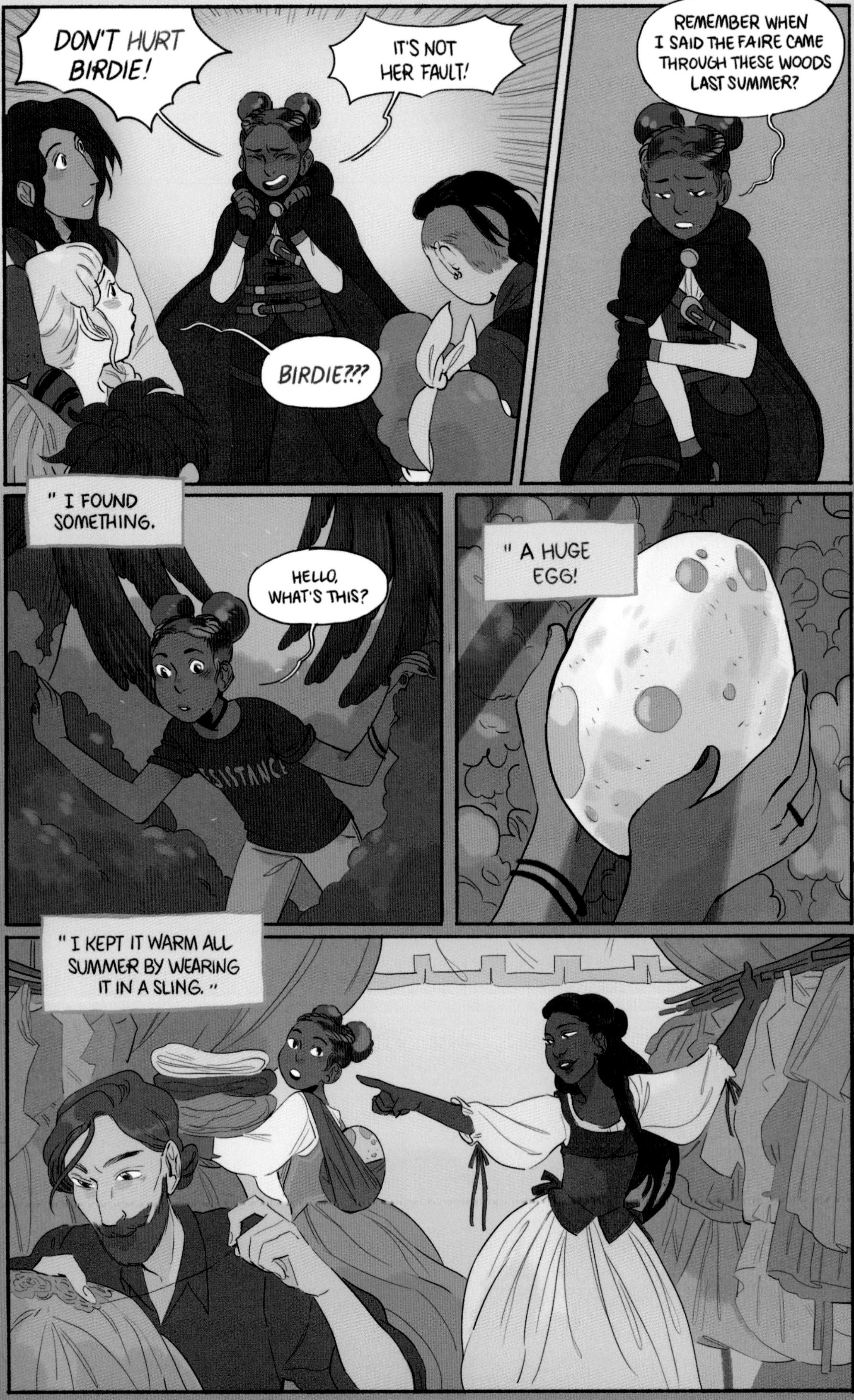
DON'T HURT BIRDIE!
IT'S NOT HER FAULT!
BIRDIE???
REMEMBER WHEN I SAID THE FAIRE CAME THROUGH THESE WOODS LAST SUMMER?
" I FOUND SOMETHING.
HELLO, WHAT'S THIS?
" A HUGE EGG!
" I KEPT IT WARM ALL SUMMER BY WEARING IT IN A SLING. "

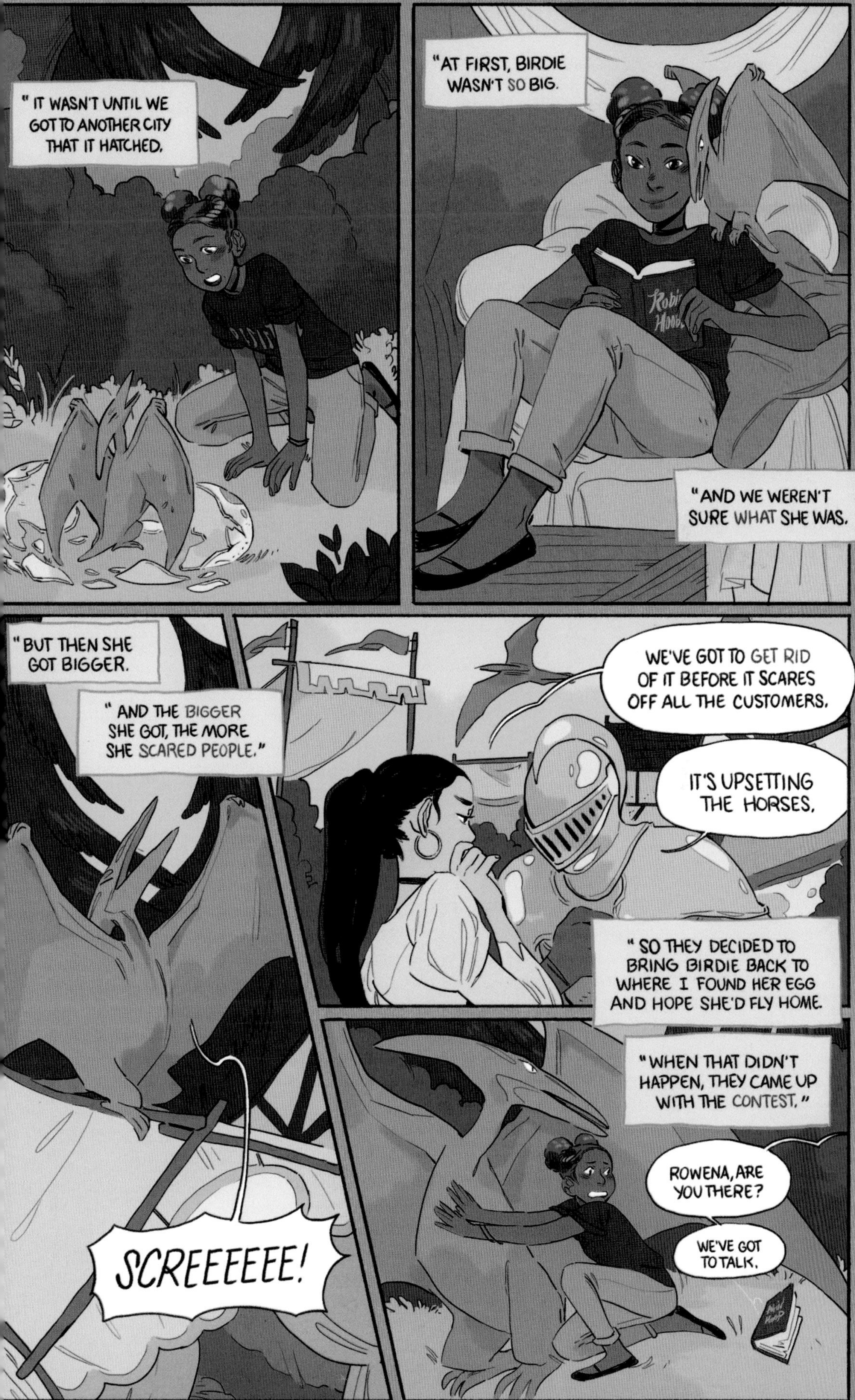
" IT WASN'T UNTIL WE GOT TO ANOTHER CITY THAT IT HATCHED.
"AT FIRST, BIRDIE WASN'T SO BIG.
"AND WE WEREN'T SURE WHAT SHE WAS.
"BUT THEN SHE GOT BIGGER.
" AND THE BIGGER SHE GOT, THE MORE SHE SCARED PEOPLE."
SCREEEEEE!
WE'VE GOT TO GET RID OF IT BEFORE IT SCARES OFF ALL THE CUSTOMERS.
IT'S UPSETTING THE HORSES.
" SO THEY DECIDED TO BRING BIRDIE BACK TO WHERE I FOUND HER EGG AND HOPE SHE'D FLY HOME.
"WHEN THAT DIDN'T HAPPEN, THEY CAME UP WITH THE CONTEST."
ROWENA, ARE YOU THERE?
WE'VE GOT TO TALK.

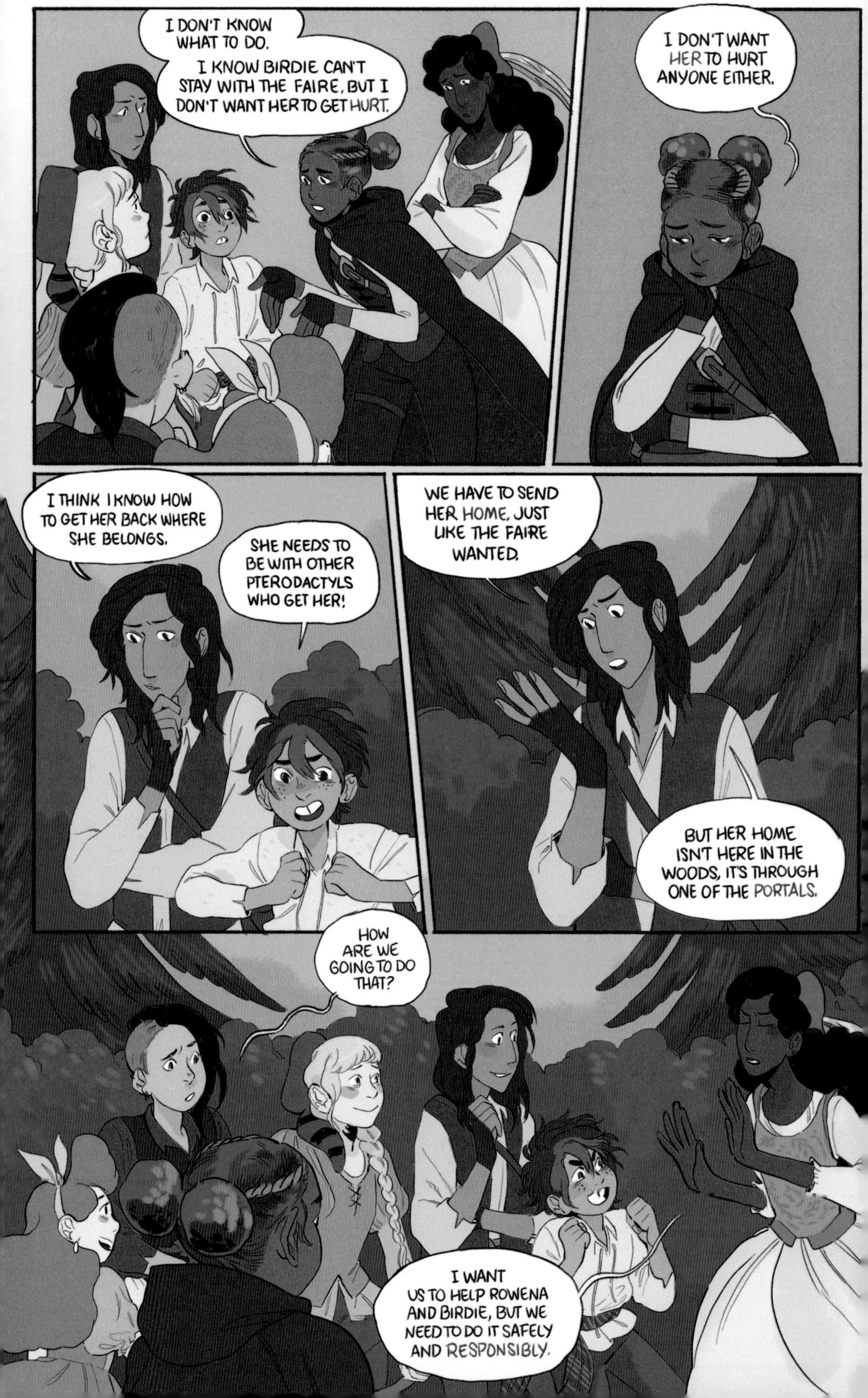
I DON'T KNOW WHAT TO DO.
I KNOW BIRDIE CAN'T STAY WITH THE FAIRE, BUT I DON'T WANT HER TO GET HURT.
I DON'T WANT HER TO HURT ANYONE EITHER.
I THINK I KNOW HOW TO GET HER BACK WHERE SHE BELONGS.
SHE NEEDS TO BE WITH OTHER PTERODACTYLS WHO GET HER!
WE HAVE TO SEND HER HOME, JUST LIKE THE FAIRE WANTED.
BUT HER HOME ISN'T HERE IN THE WOODS, IT'S THROUGH ONE OF THE PORTALS.
HOW ARE WE GOING TO DO THAT?
I WANT US TO HELP ROWENA AND BIRDIE, BUT WE NEED TO DO IT SAFELY AND RESPONSIBLY.

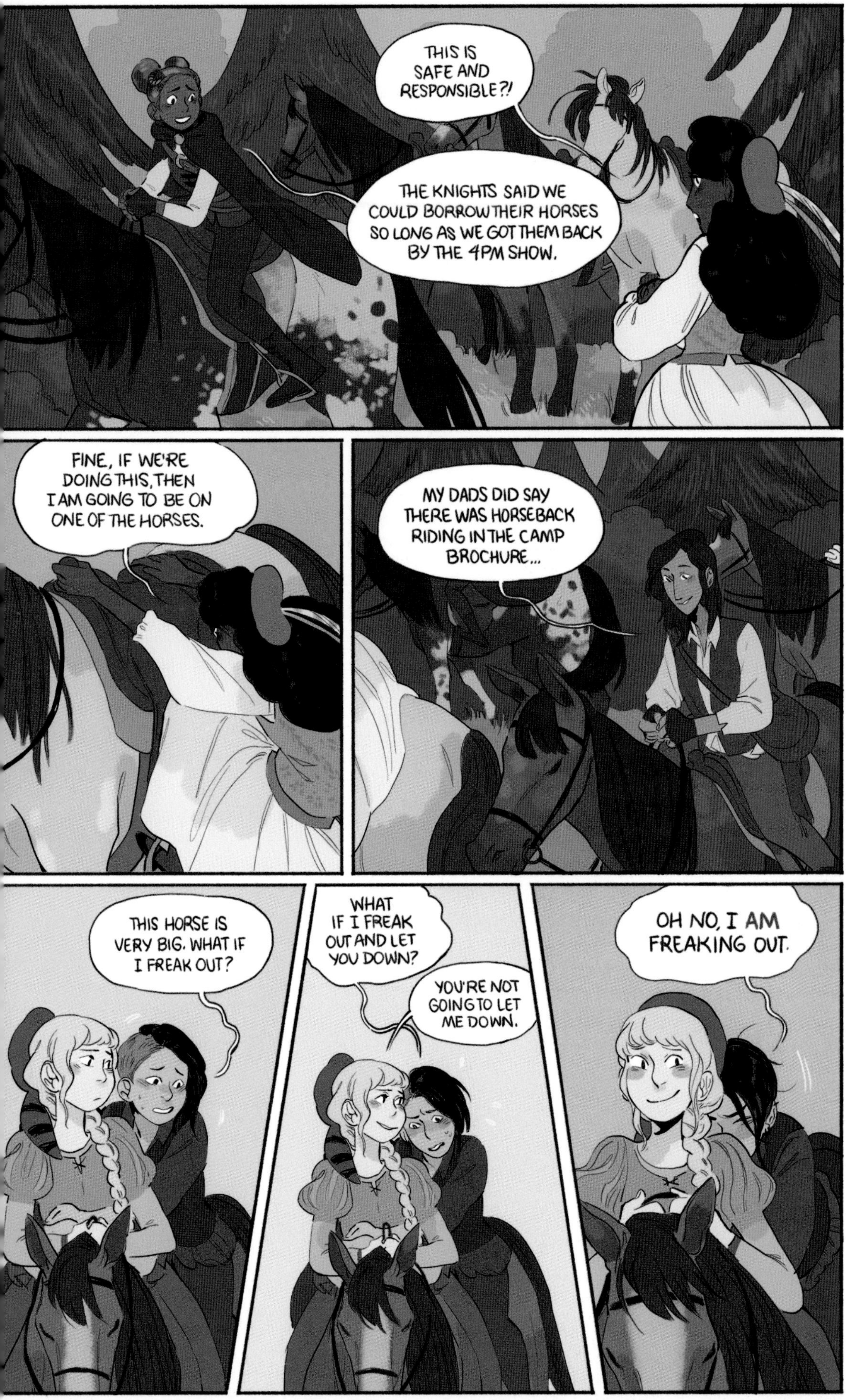
THIS IS SAFE AND RESPONSIBLE?!
THE KNIGHTS SAID WE COULD BORROW THEIR HORSES SO LONG AS WE GOT THEM BACK BY THE 4PM SHOW.
FINE, IF WE'RE DOING THIS, THEN I AM GOING TO BE ON ONE OF THE HORSES.
MY DADS DID SAY THERE WAS HORSEBACK RIDING IN THE CAMP BROCHURE...
THIS HORSE IS VERY BIG. WHAT IF I FREAK OUT?
WHAT IF I FREAK OUT AND LET YOU DOWN?
YOU'RE NOT GOING TO LET ME DOWN.
OH NO, I AM FREAKING OUT.

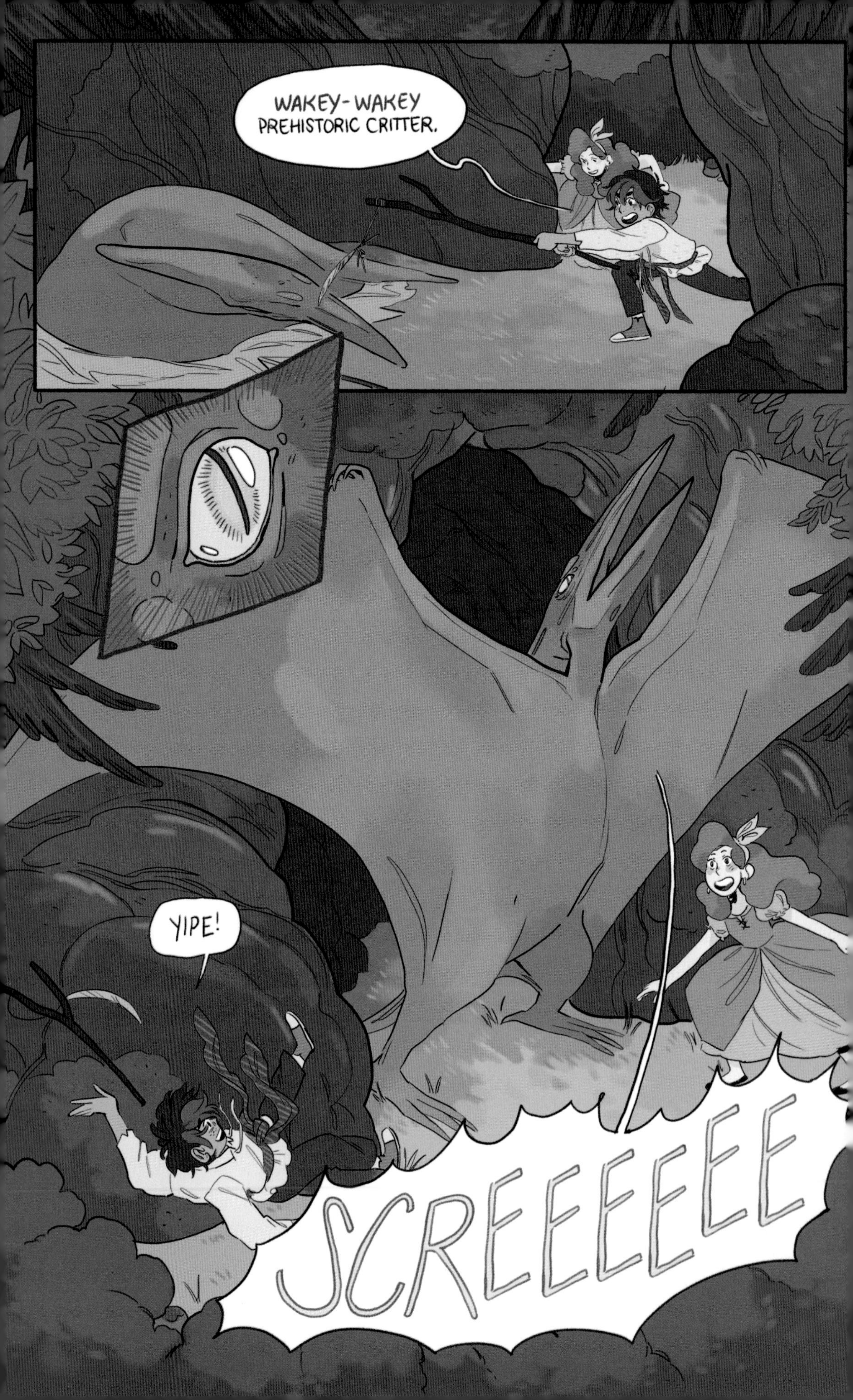
WAKEY-WAKEY PREHISTORIC CRITTER.
YIPE!
SCREEEEEEE

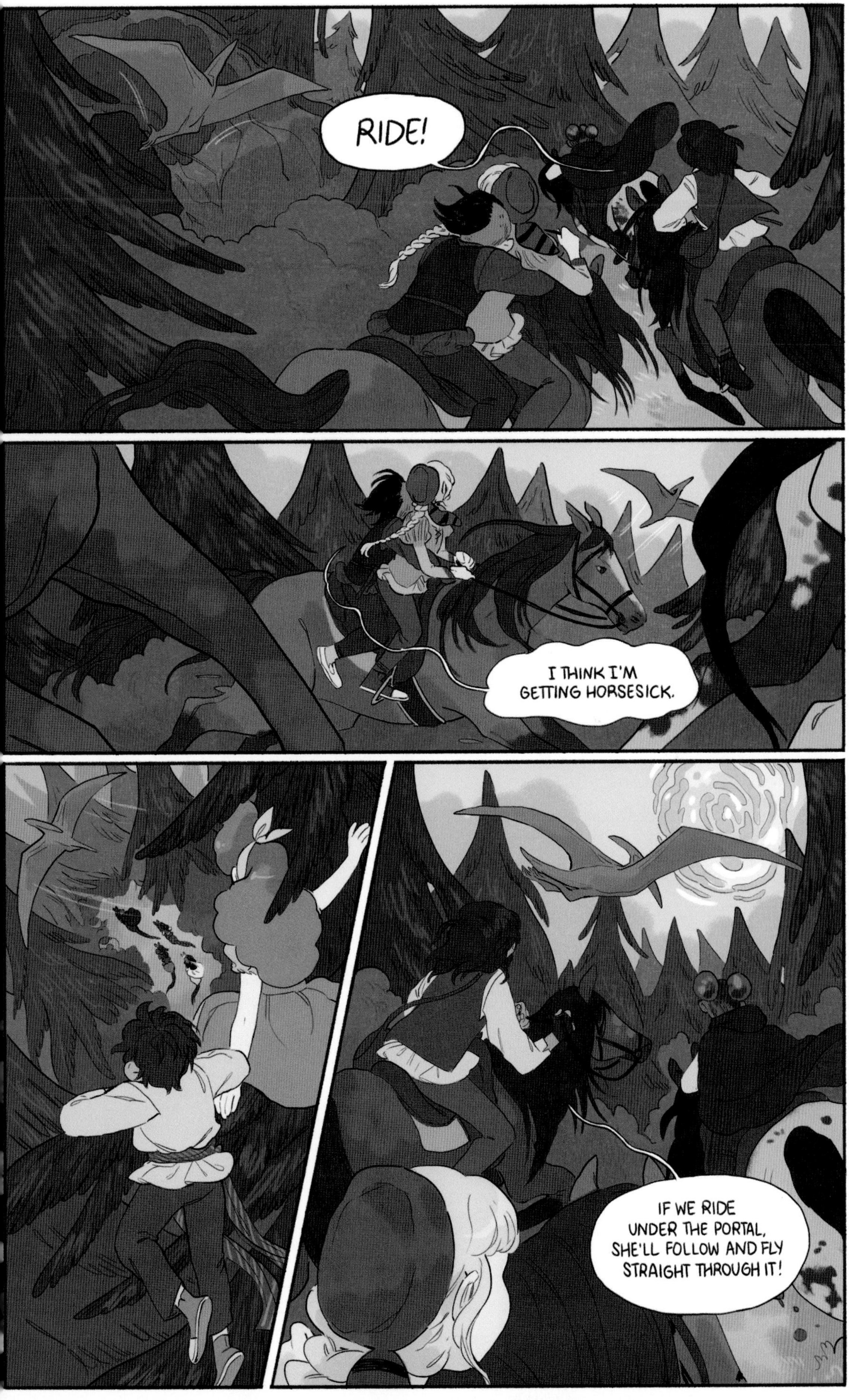
RIDE!
I THINK I'M GETTING HORSESICK.
IF WE RIDE UNDER THE PORTAL, SHE'LL FOLLOW AND FLY STRAIGHT THROUGH IT!

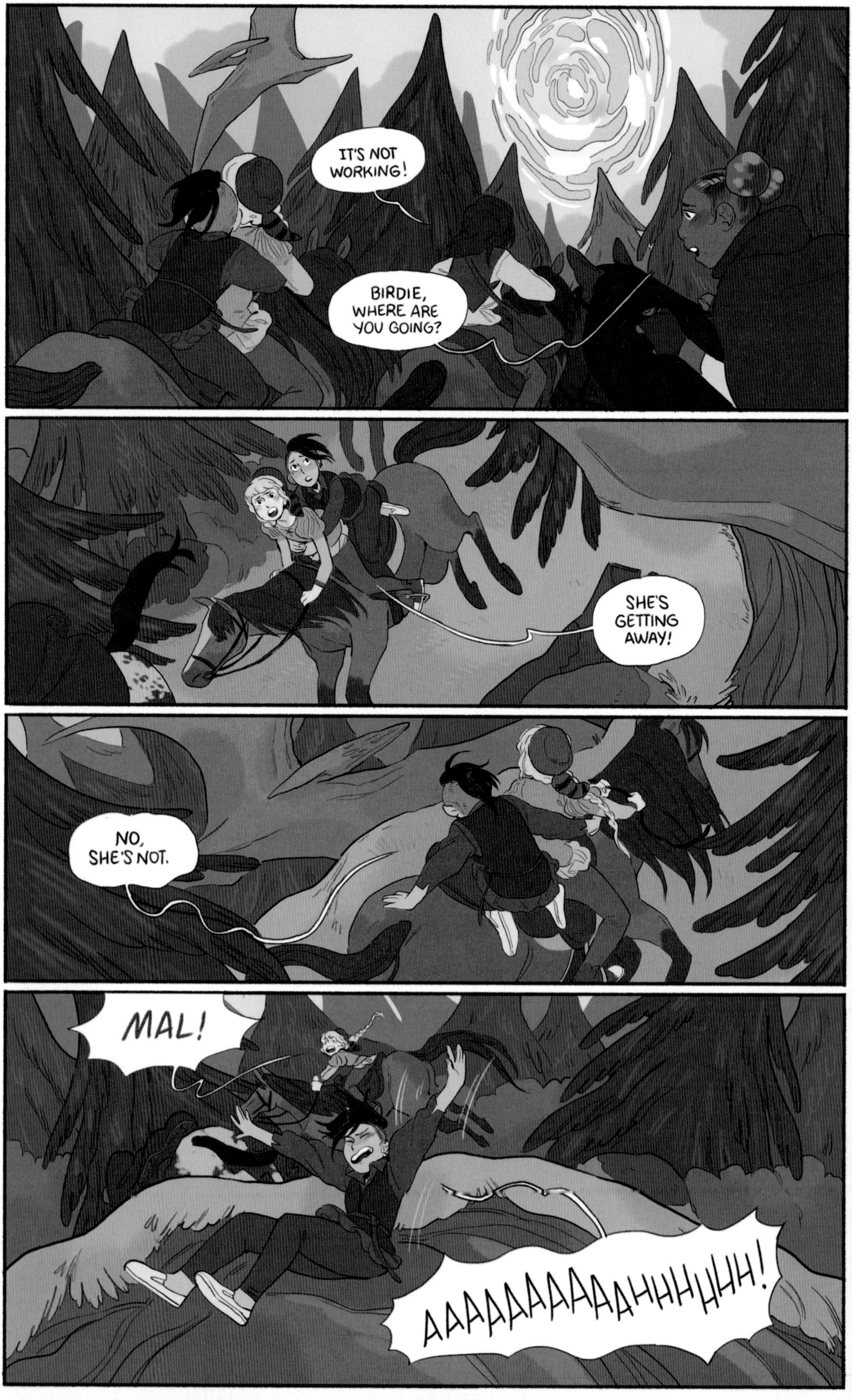
IT'S NOT WORKING!
BIRDIE, WHERE ARE YOU GOING?
SHE'S GETTING AWAY!
NO, SHE'S NOT.
MAL!
AAAAAAAAAAHHHHHHH!

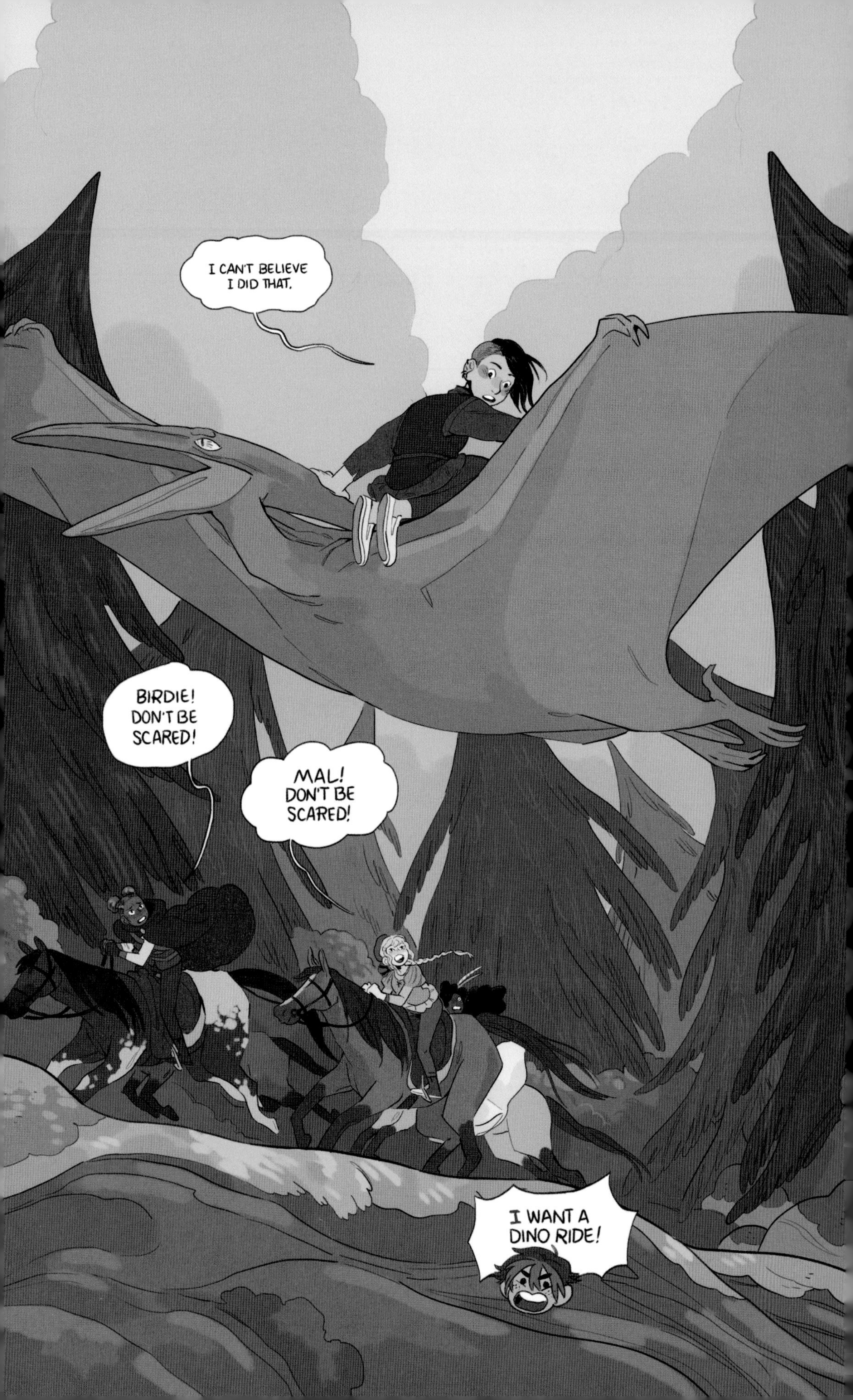
I CAN'T BELIEVE I DID THAT.
BIRDIE! DON'T BE SCARED!
MAL! DON'T BE SCARED!
I WANT A DINO RIDE!

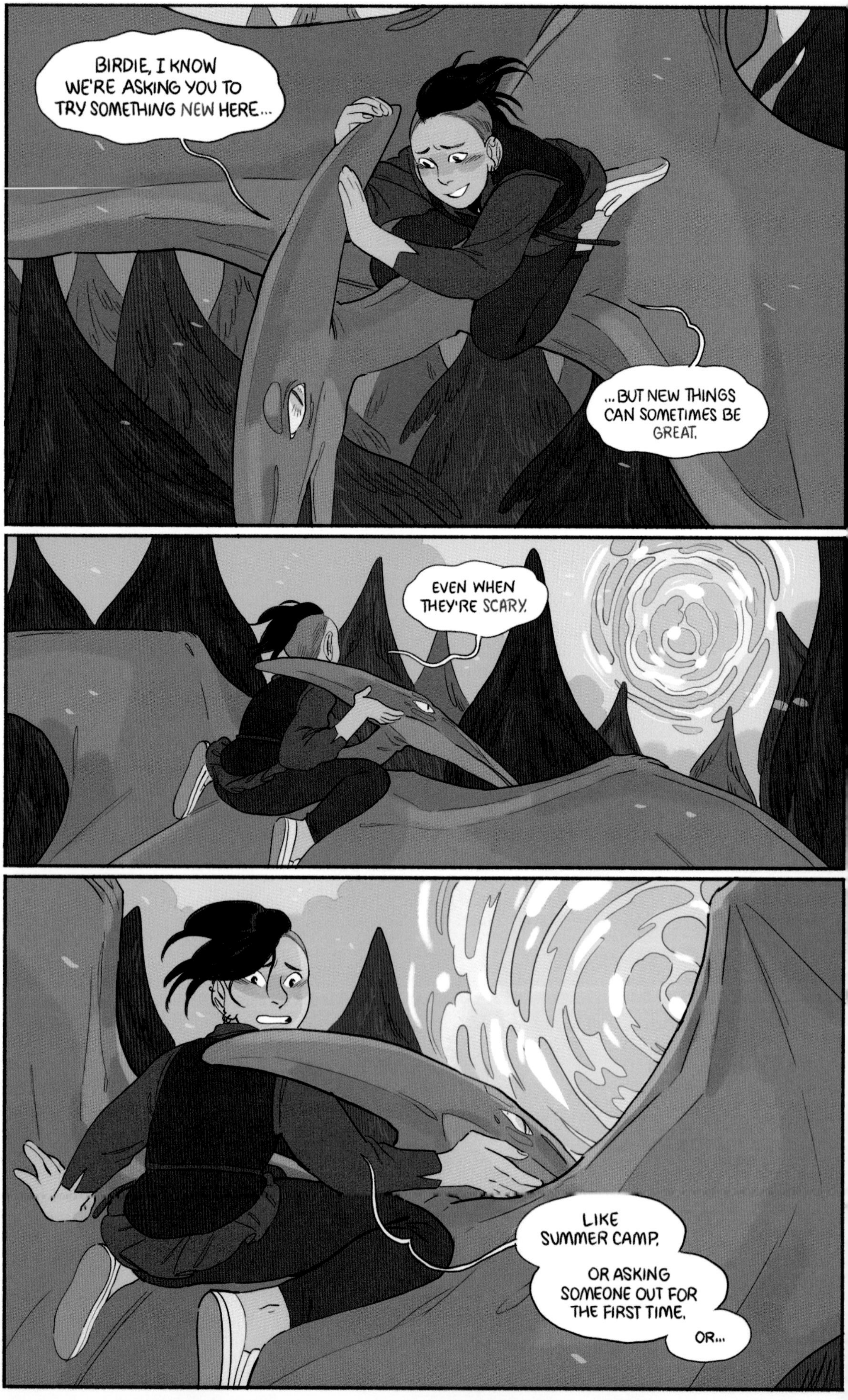
BIRDIE, I KNOW WE'RE ASKING YOU TO TRY SOMETHING NEW HERE...
...BUT NEW THINGS CAN SOMETIMES BE GREAT.
EVEN WHEN THEY'RE SCARY.
LIKE SUMMER CAMP.
OR ASKING SOMEONE OUT FOR THE FIRST TIME.
OR...

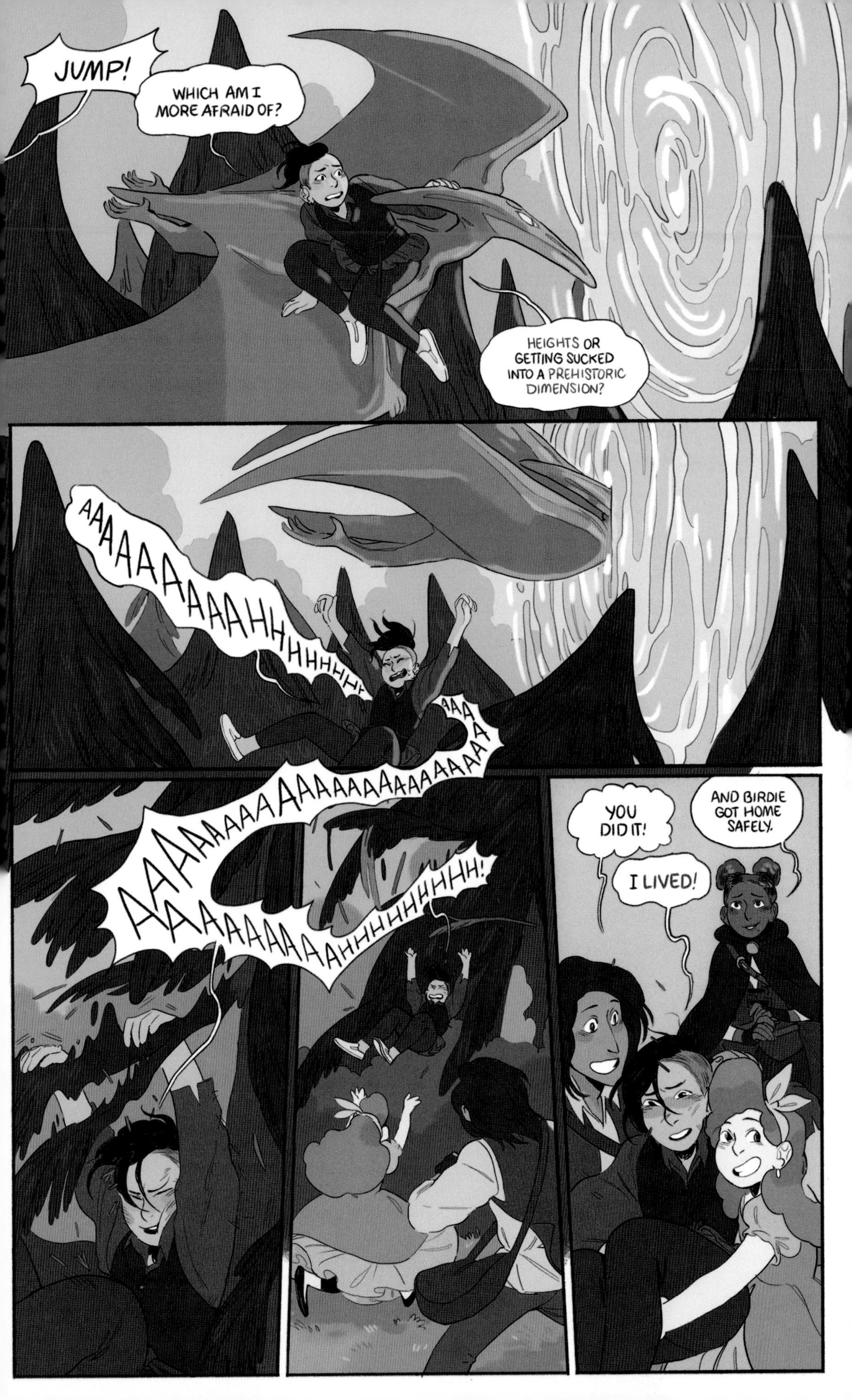
JUMP!
WHICH AM I MORE AFRAID OF?
HEIGHTS OR GETTING SUCKED INTO A PREHISTORIC DIMENSION?
AAAAAAAAAAHHHHHHH
AAAAAAAAAAAAAAAAAAAAAAAAAAAAAAAAAAAAAAAHHHHHHHHHHH!
YOU DID IT!
AND BIRDIE GOT HOME SAFELY.
I LIVED!

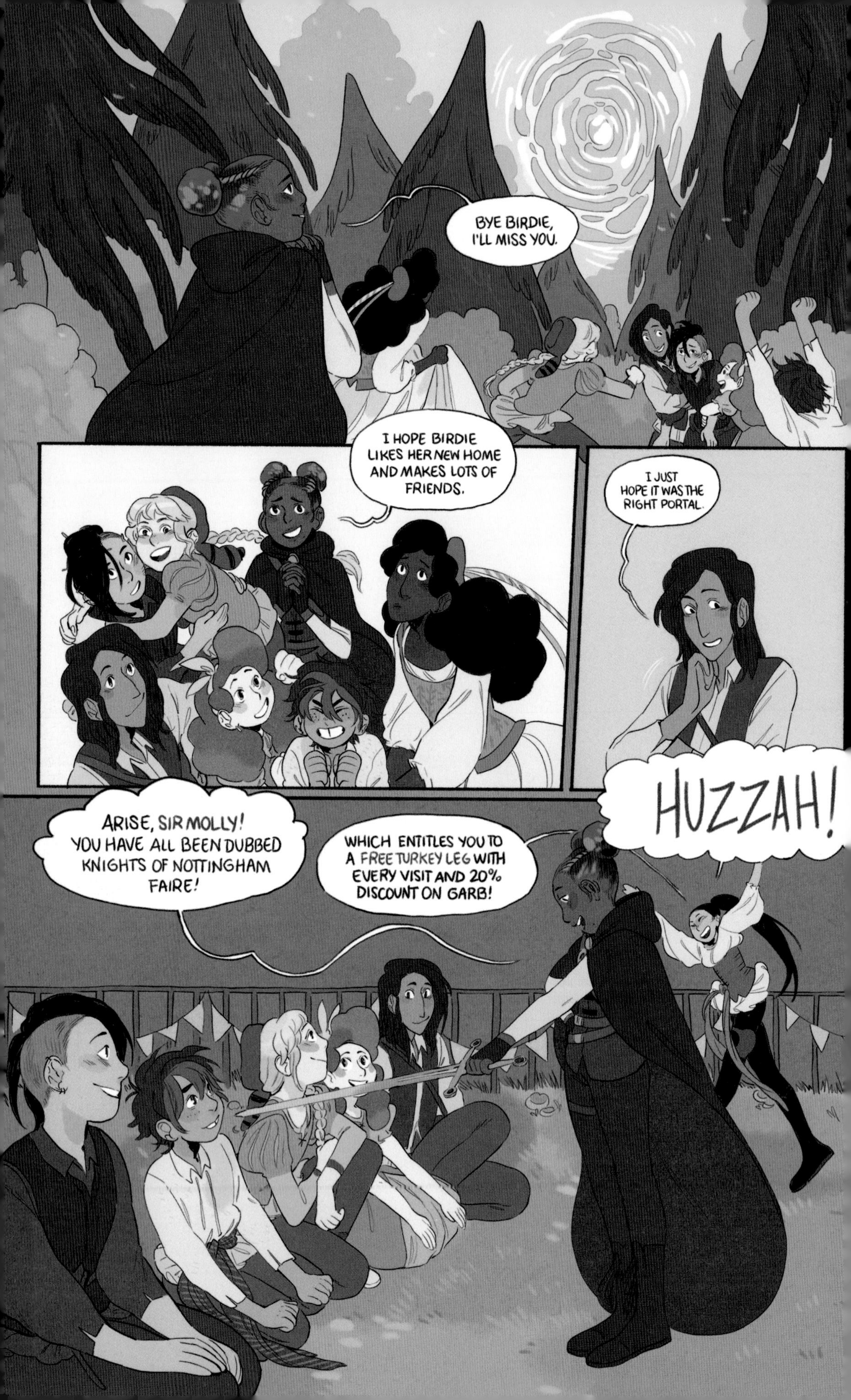

BYE BIRDIE, I'LL MISS YOU.
I HOPE BIRDIE LIKES HER NEW HOME AND MAKES LOTS OF FRIENDS.
I JUST HOPE IT WAS THE RIGHT PORTAL.
ARISE, SIR MOLLY! YOU HAVE ALL BEEN DUBBED KNIGHTS OF NOTTINGHAM FAIRE!
WHICH ENTITLES YOU TO A FREE TURKEY LEG WITH EVERY VISIT AND 20% DISCOUNT ON GARB!
HUZZAH!

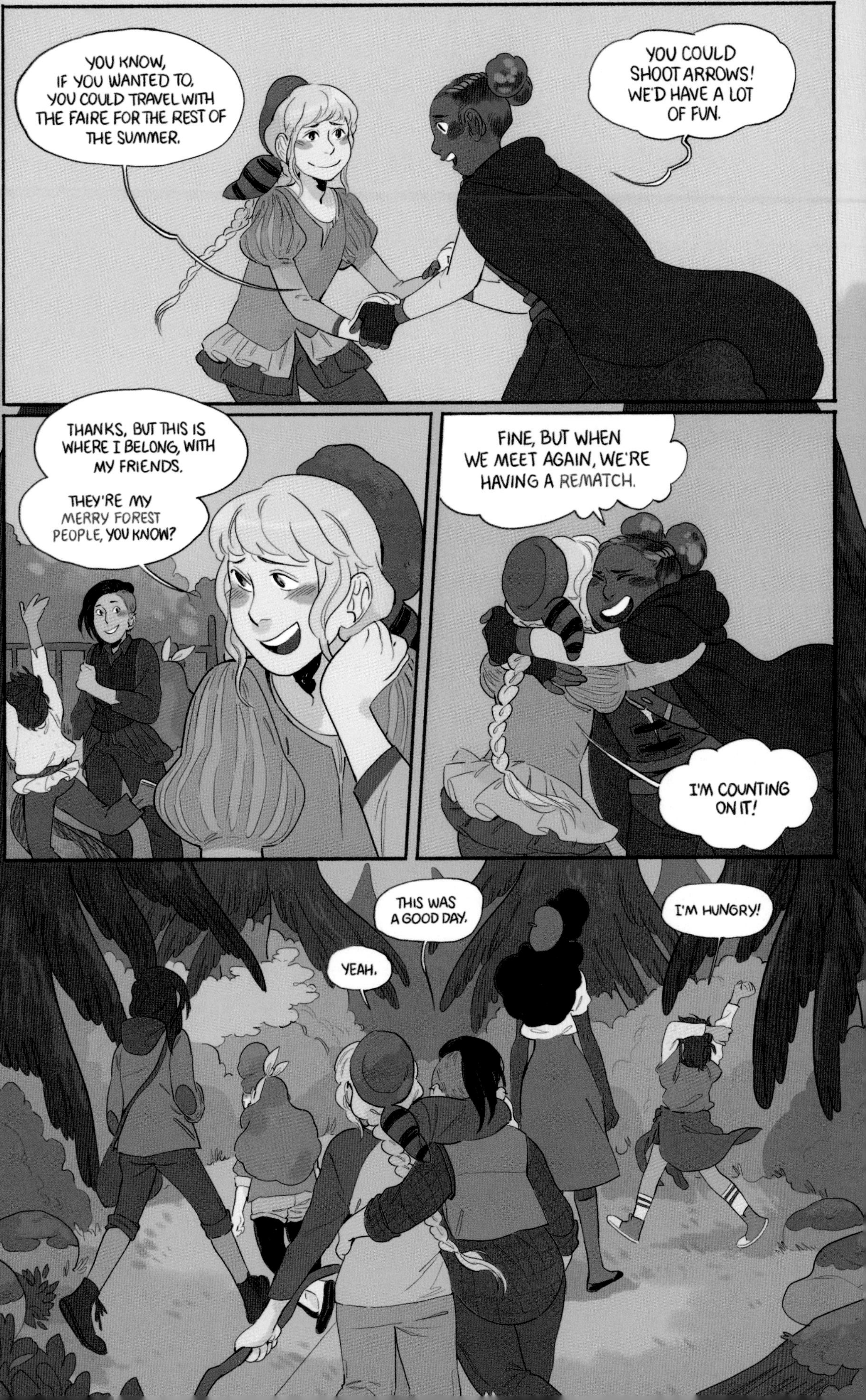
YOU KNOW, IF YOU WANTED TO, YOU COULD TRAVEL WITH THE FAIRE FOR THE REST OF THE SUMMER.
YOU COULD SHOOT ARROWS! WE'D HAVE A LOT OF FUN.
THANKS, BUT THIS IS WHERE I BELONG, WITH MY FRIENDS.
THEY'RE MY MERRY FOREST PEOPLE, YOU KNOW?
FINE, BUT WHEN WE MEET AGAIN, WE'RE HAVING A REMATCH.
I'M COUNTING ON IT!
THIS WAS A GOOD DAY.
YEAH.
I'M HUNGRY!

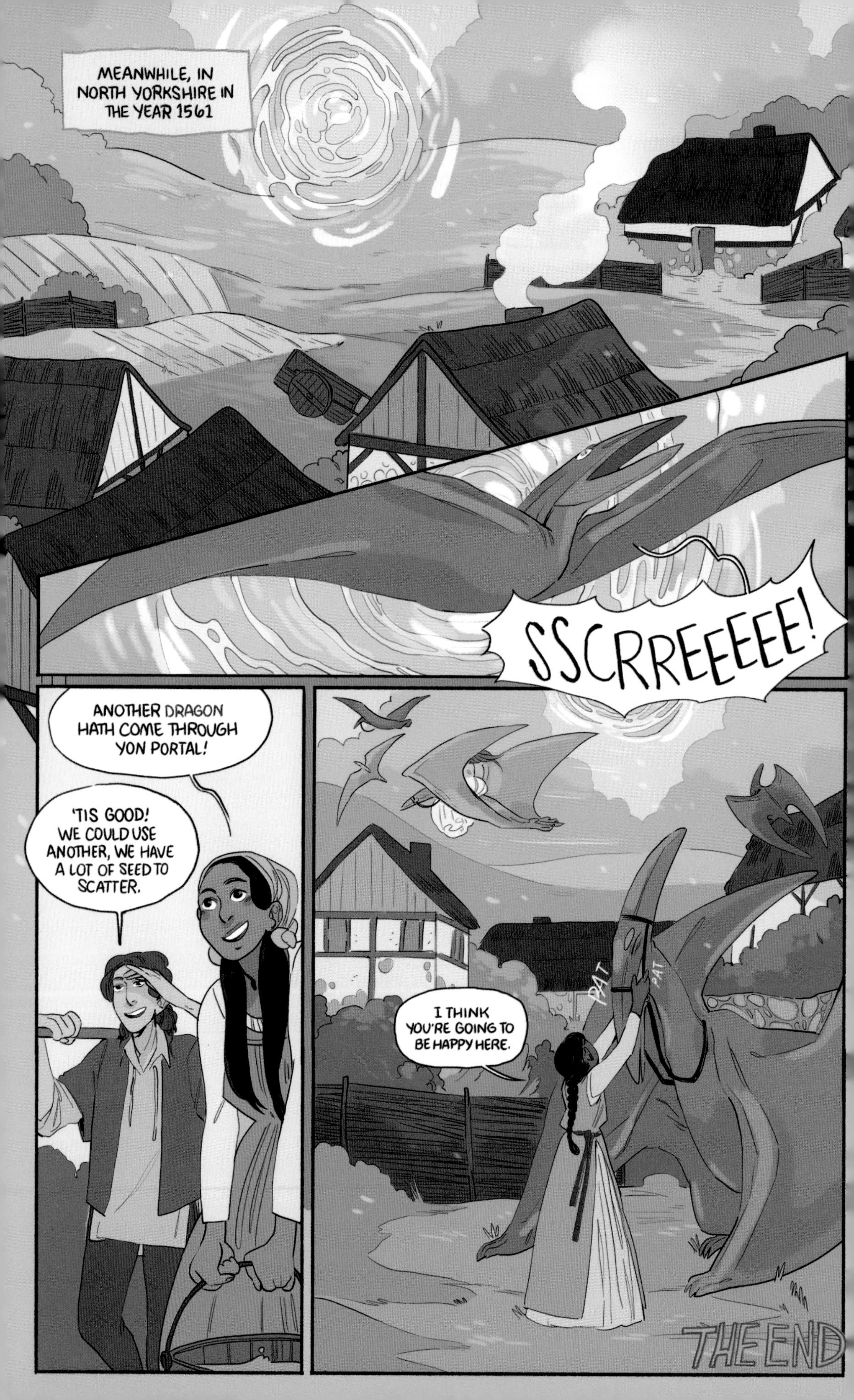
MEANWHILE, IN NORTH YORKSHIRE IN THE YEAR 1561
SSCRREEEEE!
ANOTHER DRAGON HATH COME THROUGH YON PORTAL!
'TIS GOOD! WE COULD USE ANOTHER, WE HAVE A LOT OF SEED TO SCATTER.
PAT PAT
I THINK YOU'RE GOING TO BE HAPPY HERE.
THE END

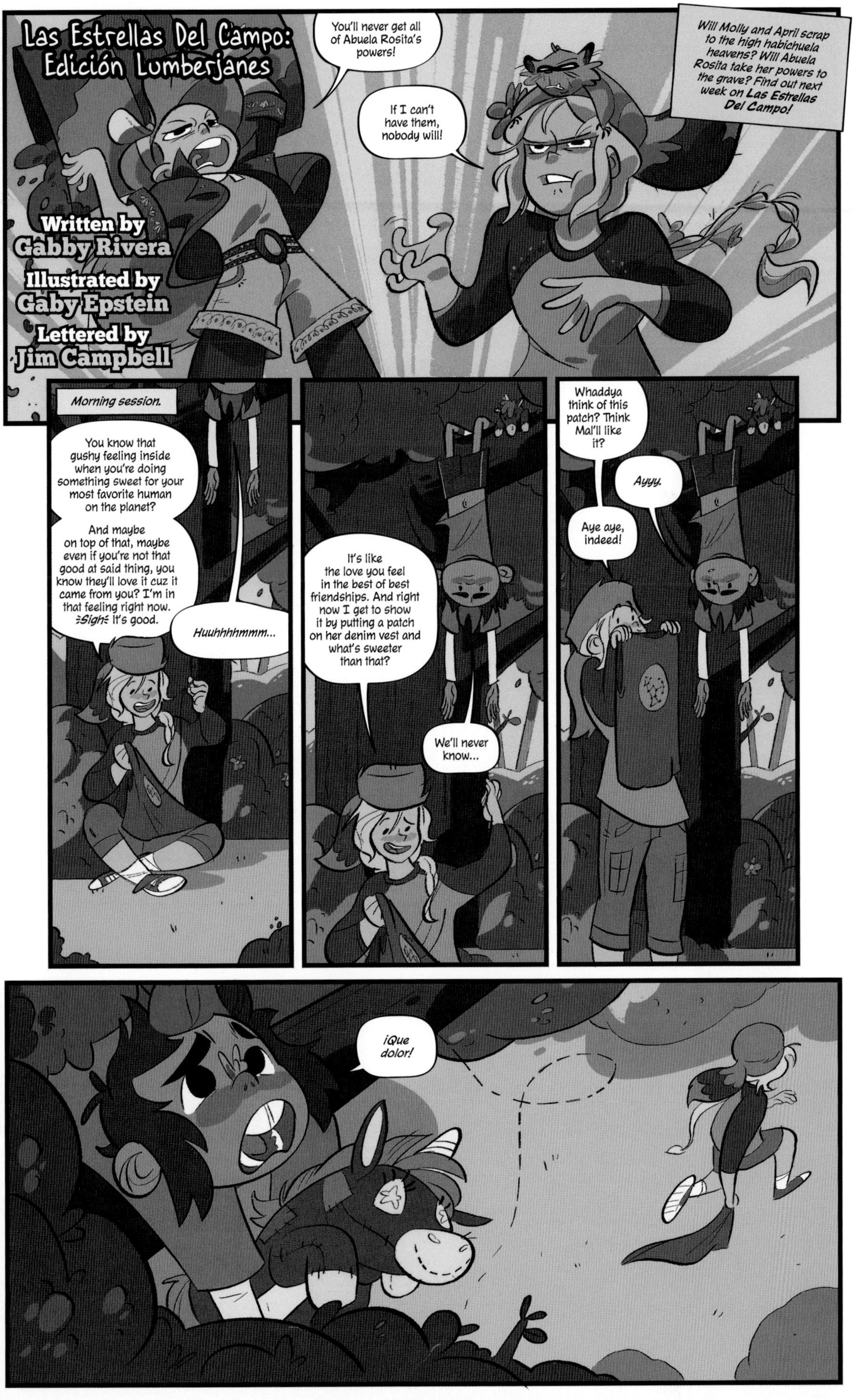

Las Estrellas Del Campo: Edición Lumberjanes
You'll never get all of Abuela Rosita's powers!
If I can't have them, nobody will!
Will Molly and April scrap to the high habichuela heavens? Will Abuela Rosita take her powers to the grave? Find out next week on Las Estrellas Del Campo!
Written by Gabby Rivera
Illustrated by Gaby Epstein
Lettered by Jim Campbell
Morning session.
You know that gushy feeling inside when you're doing something sweet for your most favorite human on the planet?
And maybe on top of that, maybe even if you're not that good at said thing, you know they'll love it cuz it came from you? I'm in that feeling right now. *Sigh* It's good.
Huuhhhhhmmm...
It's like the love you feel in the best of best friendships. And right now I get to show it by putting a patch on her denim vest and what's sweeter than that?
We'll never know...
Whaddya think of this patch? Think Mal'll like it?
Ayyy.
Aye aye, indeed!
¡Que dolor!

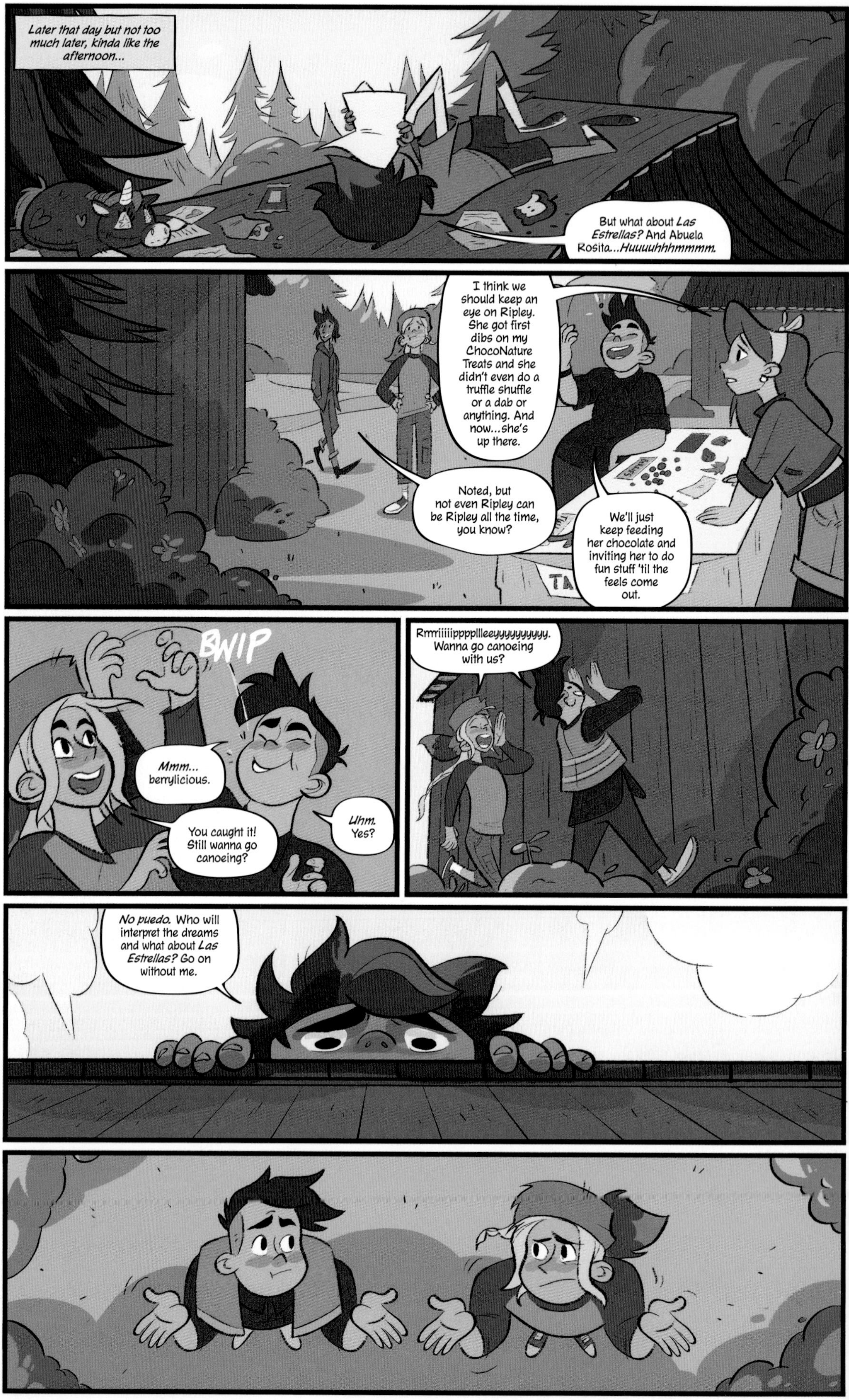
Later that day but not too much later, kinda like the afternoon...
But what about Las Estrellas? And Abuela Rosita...Huuuuhhhmmmm.
I think we should keep an eye on Ripley. She got first dibs on my ChocoNature Treats and she didn't even do a truffle shuffle or a dab or anything. And now...she's up there.
Noted, but not even Ripley can be Ripley all the time, you know?
We'll just keep feeding her chocolate and inviting her to do fun stuff 'til the feels come out.
BWIP
Mmm... berrylicious.
You caught it! Still wanna go canoeing?
Uhm. Yes?
Rmriiiiippppllleeyyyyyyyyyy. Wanna go canoeing with us?
No puedo. Who will interpret the dreams and what about Las Estrellas? Go on without me.

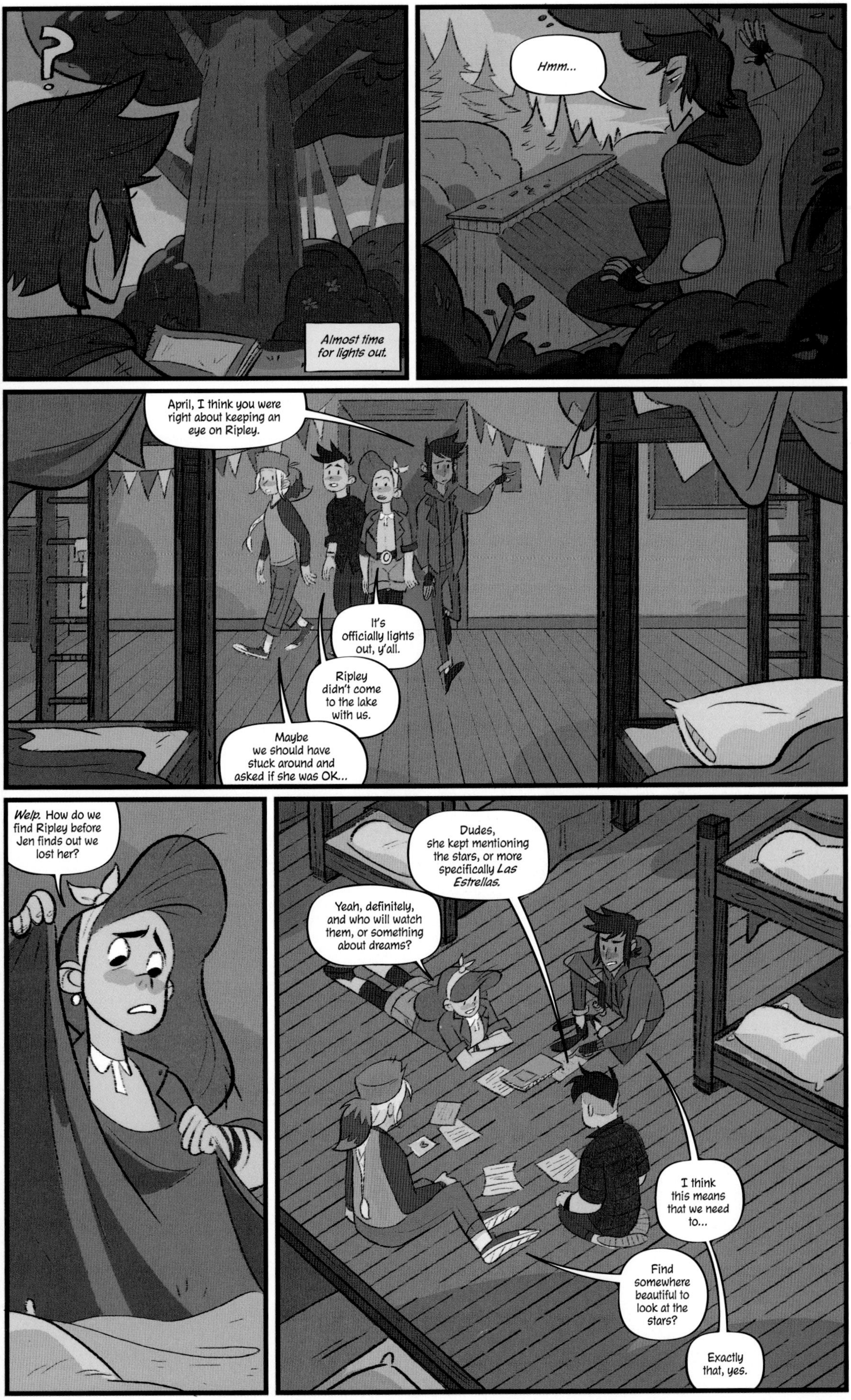
?
Almost time for lights out.
Hmm...
April, I think you were right about keeping an eye on Ripley.
It's officially lights out, y'all.
Ripley didn't come to the lake with us.
Maybe we should have stuck around and asked if she was OK...
Welp. How do we find Ripley before Jen finds out we lost her?
Dudes, she kept mentioning the stars, or more specifically *Las Estrellas.*
Yeah, definitely, and who will watch them, or something about dreams?
I think this means that we need to...
Find somewhere beautiful to look at the stars?
Exactly that, yes.

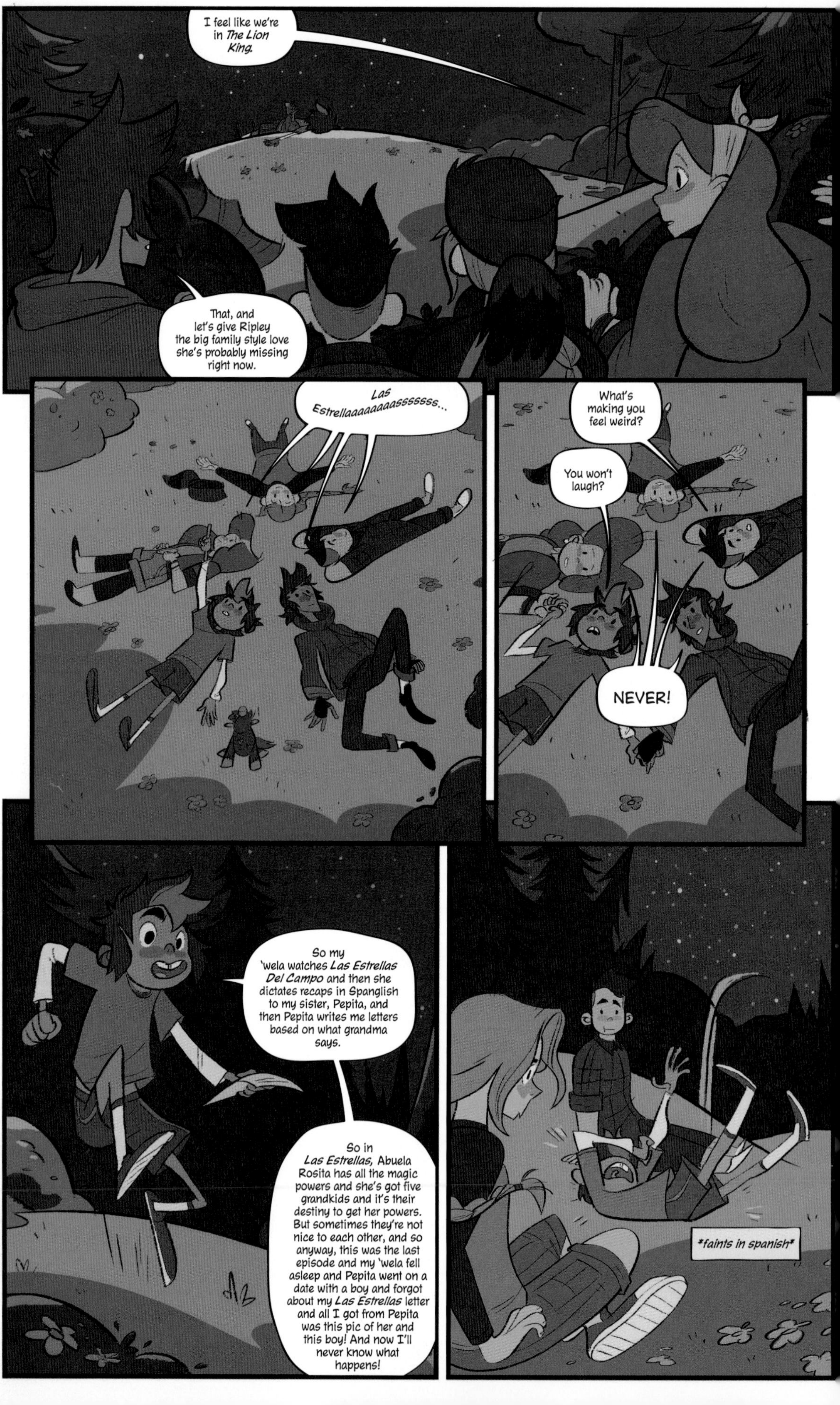
I feel like we're in *The Lion King*.
That, and let's give Ripley the big family style love she's probably missing right now.
Las Estrellaaaaaaaasssssss...
What's making you feel weird?
You won't laugh?
NEVER!
So my 'wela watches *Las Estrellas Del Campo* and then she dictates recaps in Spanglish to my sister, Pepita, and then Pepita writes me letters based on what grandma says.
So in *Las Estrellas*, Abuela Rosita has all the magic powers and she's got five grandkids and it's their destiny to get her powers. But sometimes they're not nice to each other, and so anyway, this was the last episode and my 'wela fell asleep and Pepita went on a date with a boy and forgot about my *Las Estrellas* letter and all I got from Pepita was this pic of her and this boy! And now I'll never know what happens!
faints in spanish

≥sigh≤ I love telenovelas.

You know, Ripley, the stars are always here for us. Like since the beginning of time, they've watched over us, teaching us about the universe, and giving us a whole world of stories to tell.

And that includes you and *Las Estrellas Del Campo.*

But how can I tell the stories if I missed the ending?

You get to make it up. Anything you want. And we, your humble but totally bodacious players, will act out every scene you can imagine.

I didn't think I'd ever get the chance to test out my Soraya Montenegro faces.

I totally want to see all of those.

Of course! I get to make it up! My own novela on my own network like Ripleyvision or Ripleymundo.

Oooh, Ripleymundo has a nice ring to it.

I'll be Abuela Rosita Ripley. Now, in the novela, I have five grandkids but I think the four of you will be ok. Or maybe I can play the grandma *and* the fifth grandkid, but that might get confusing...

Ripley remember, it can be whatever you want!

You could even be all five grandkids.

Is there like a cool uncle? I could be the cool uncle.

Should we start sketching out a script? Or wait, maybe I can take out some A/V equipment...

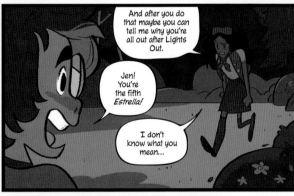

And after you do that maybe you can tell me why you're all out after Lights Out.

Jen! You're the fifth *Estrella!*

I don't know what you mean...

...but I've always loved the constellations, especially Orion's belt. Solid. Strong. Shiny.

Heck yes! Just like you.

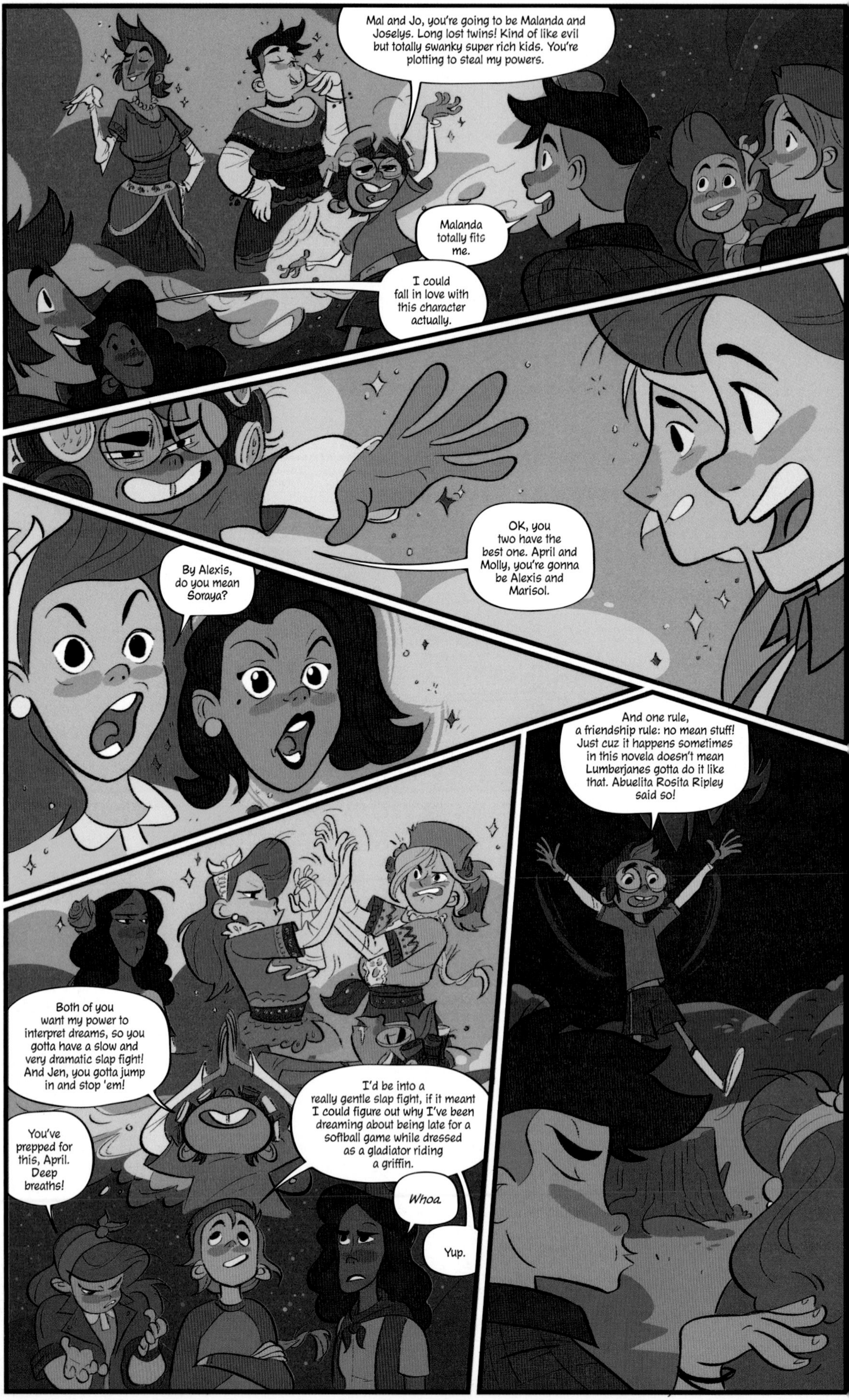

Mal and Jo, you're going to be Malanda and Joselys. Long lost twins! Kind of like evil but totally swanky super rich kids. You're plotting to steal my powers.
Malanda totally fits me.
I could fall in love with this character actually.
OK, you two have the best one. April and Molly, you're gonna be Alexis and Marisol.
By Alexis, do you mean Soraya?
And one rule, a friendship rule: no mean stuff! Just cuz it happens sometimes in this novela doesn't mean Lumberjanes gotta do it like that. Abuelita Rosita Ripley said so!
Both of you want my power to interpret dreams, so you gotta have a slow and very dramatic slap fight! And Jen, you gotta jump in and stop 'em!
You've prepped for this, April. Deep breaths!
I'd be into a really gentle slap fight, if it meant I could figure out why I've been dreaming about being late for a softball game while dressed as a gladiator riding a griffin.
Whoa.
Yup.

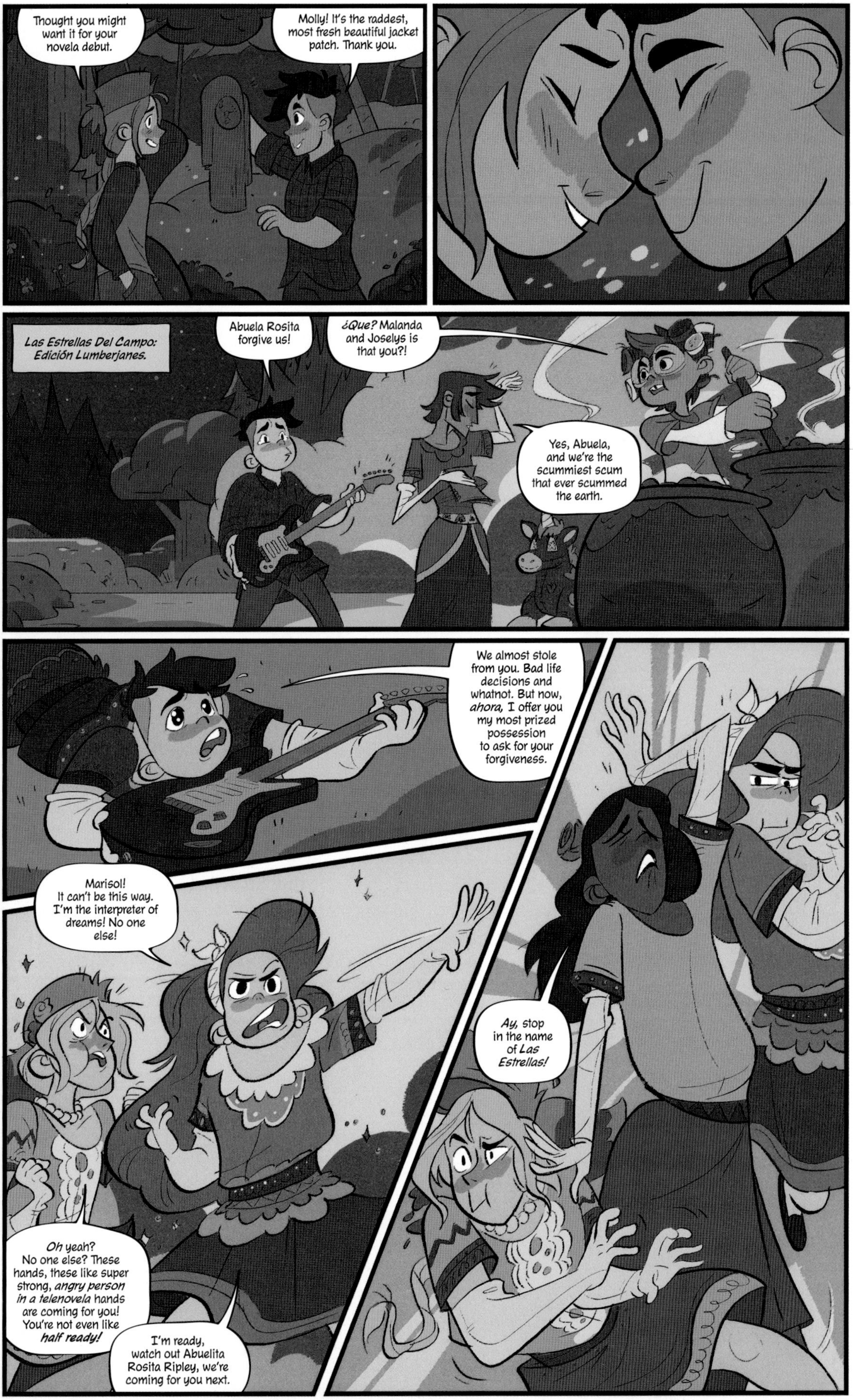
Thought you might want it for your novela debut.
Molly! It's the raddest, most fresh beautiful jacket patch. Thank you.
Las Estrellas Del Campo: Edición Lumberjanes.
Abuela Rosita forgive us!
¿Que? Malanda and Joselys is that you?!
Yes, Abuela, and we're the scummiest scum that ever scummed the earth.
We almost stole from you. Bad life decisions and whatnot. But now, *ahora,* I offer you my most prized possession to ask for your forgiveness.
Marisol! It can't be this way. I'm the interpreter of dreams! No one else!
Oh yeah? No one else? These hands, these like super strong, *angry person in a telenovela* hands are coming for you! You're not even like ***half ready!***
I'm ready, watch out Abuelita Rosita Ripley, we're coming for you next.
Ay, stop in the name of *Las Estrellas!*

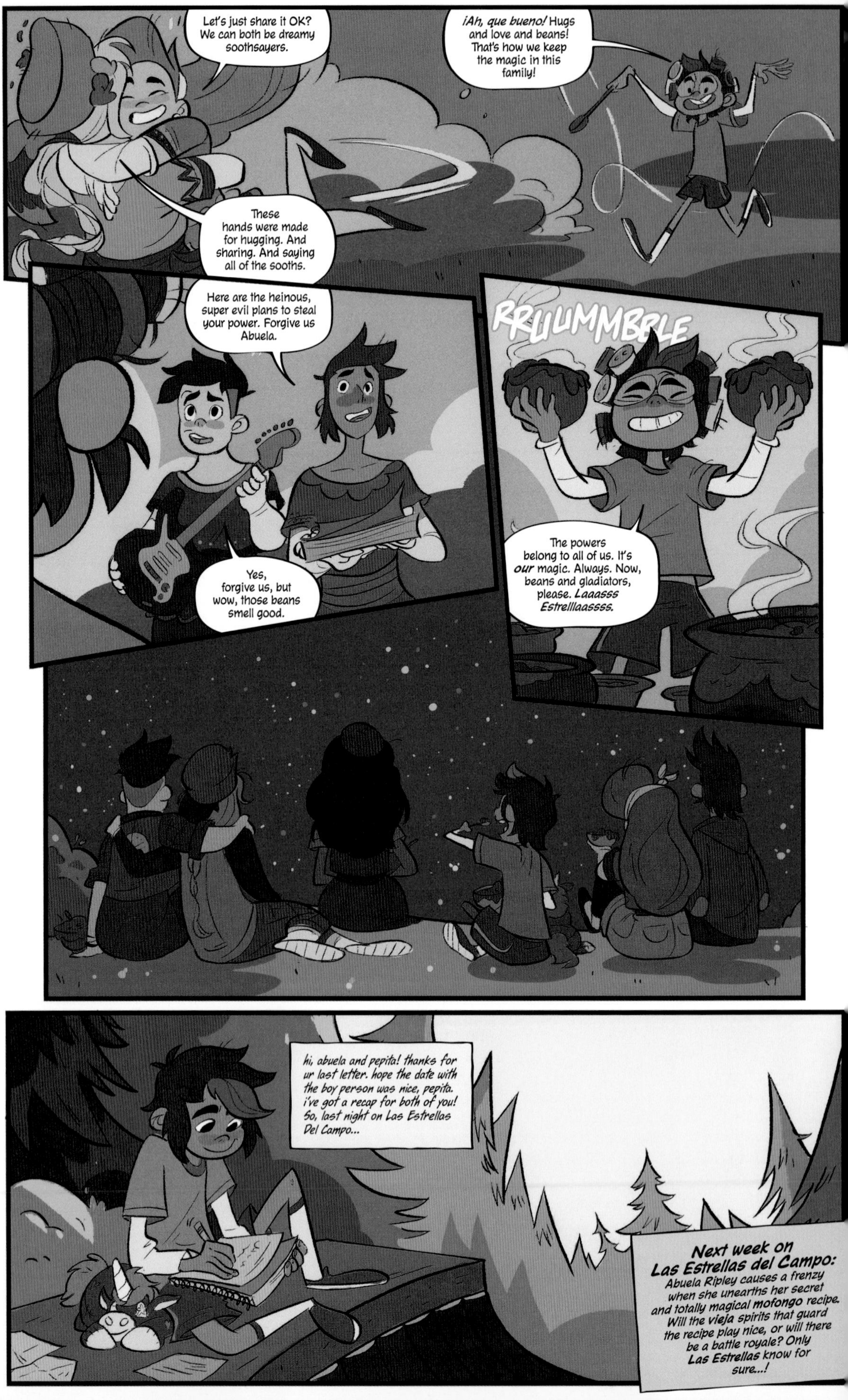
Let's just share it OK? We can both be dreamy soothsayers.
These hands were made for hugging. And sharing. And saying all of the sooths.
¡Ah, que bueno! Hugs and love and beans! That's how we keep the magic in this family!
Here are the heinous, super evil plans to steal your power. Forgive us Abuela.
Yes, forgive us, but wow, those beans smell good.
RRUUMMBRLE
The powers belong to all of us. It's our magic. Always. Now, beans and gladiators, please. Laaasss Estrelllaassss.
hi, abuela and pepita! thanks for ur last letter. hope the date with the boy person was nice, pepita. i've got a recap for both of you! So, last night on Las Estrellas Del Campo...
Next week on Las Estrellas del Campo: Abuela Ripley causes a frenzy when she unearths her secret and totally magical mofongo recipe. Will the vieja spirits that guard the recipe play nice, or will there be a battle royale? Only Las Estrellas know for sure...!

COVER GALLERY

Lumberjanes "Heart to Heart" Program Field

BEYOND BAY LEAF PIN

"The Truth is Out of This World"

To tell a story that delights and amazes both the teller and the audience is a worthy and admirable skill. Whether your story-telling craft comes in the shape of tall tales told on the anglers' dock; or spooks shared around a campfire, lit from below with eerie light; or carefully crafted word after beautiful, painstaking word typed on a typewriter or etched with quill and ink, the stories you tell are the legacy you leave behind.

What types of stories do you most like to hear? Are they fables and myths, that connect only metaphorically to your everyday life? Are they the gossip of the day, starring your friends and family members (only good things, we hope)? Are they epic poems of old, or diaries of important historical figures? What about high-concept fantasy? Or do you prefer realistic fiction about girls and children much like you?

These stories matter to us because we can relate to them--they take people who are far away from us, in time and in greatness and in circumstances, and they bring them near to us again. They show us who we are, through the guise of introducing us to someone else, and they teach us who we want to be by allowing us to live vicariously through our heroes and learn from their mistakes. They give us the freedom to explore different aspects of ourselves, and to escape the stresses of our lives. They exercise our imaginations and our empathy, and they fill in the gaps of long and boring rainy days.

Think about the stories that interest you, and what it is in them that piques your interest and whets your appetite. What types of stories would you like to tell, and leave for generations to come?

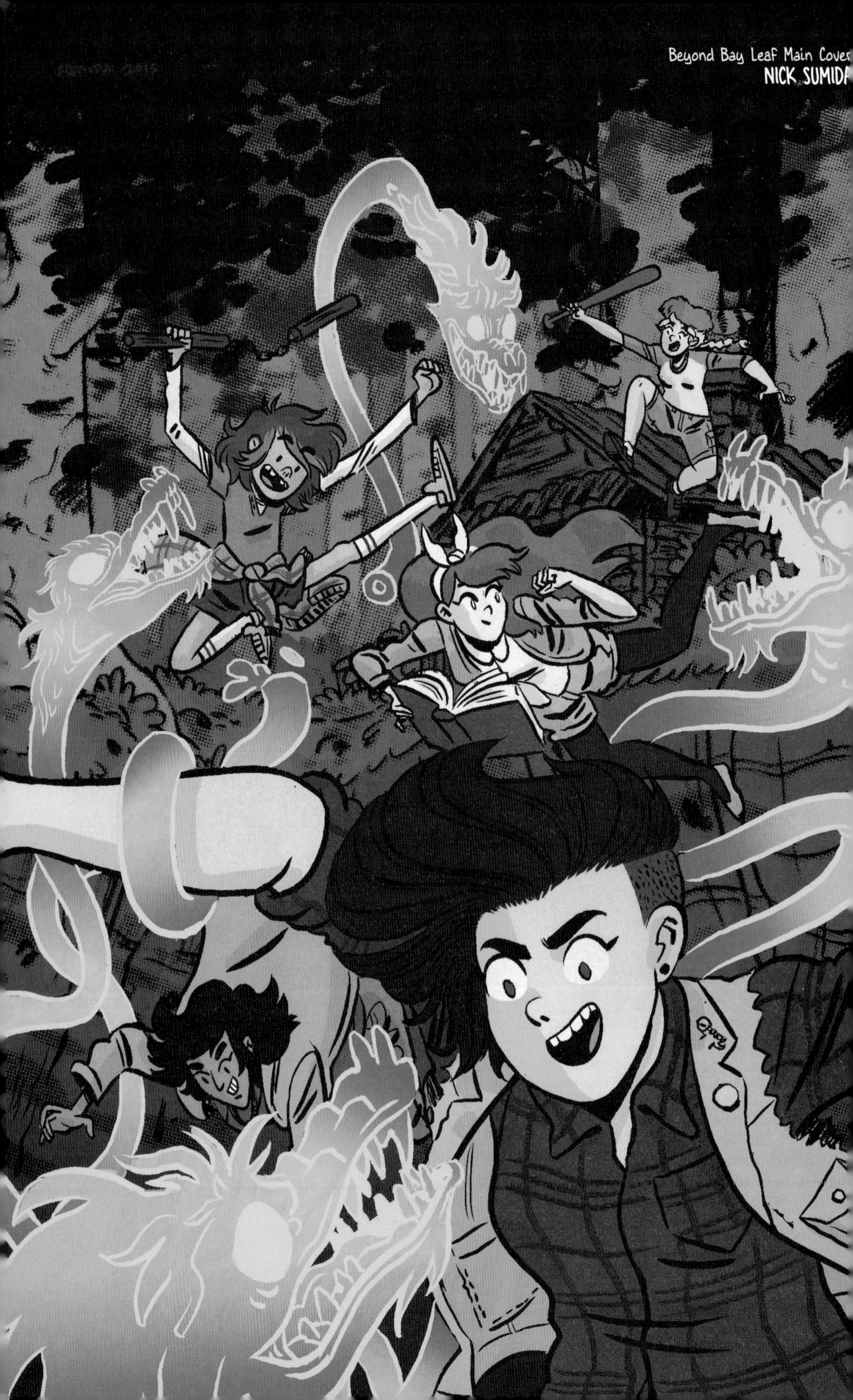

Beyond Bay Leaf Main Cover
NICK SUMIDA

eyond Bay Leaf Variant Cover
VA ESKELINEN

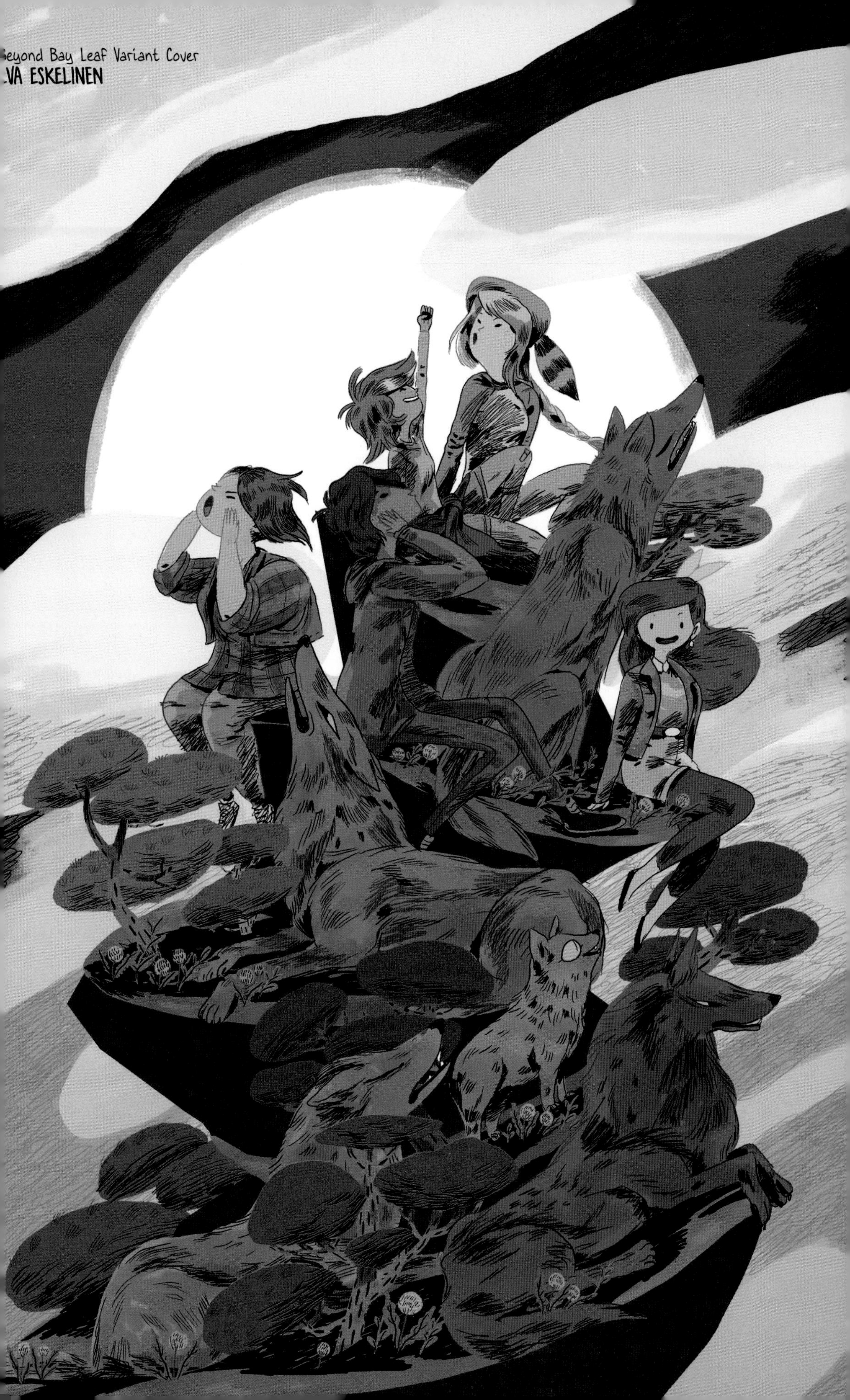

Beyond Bay Leaf Fried Pie Variant Cover
CARA MCGEE

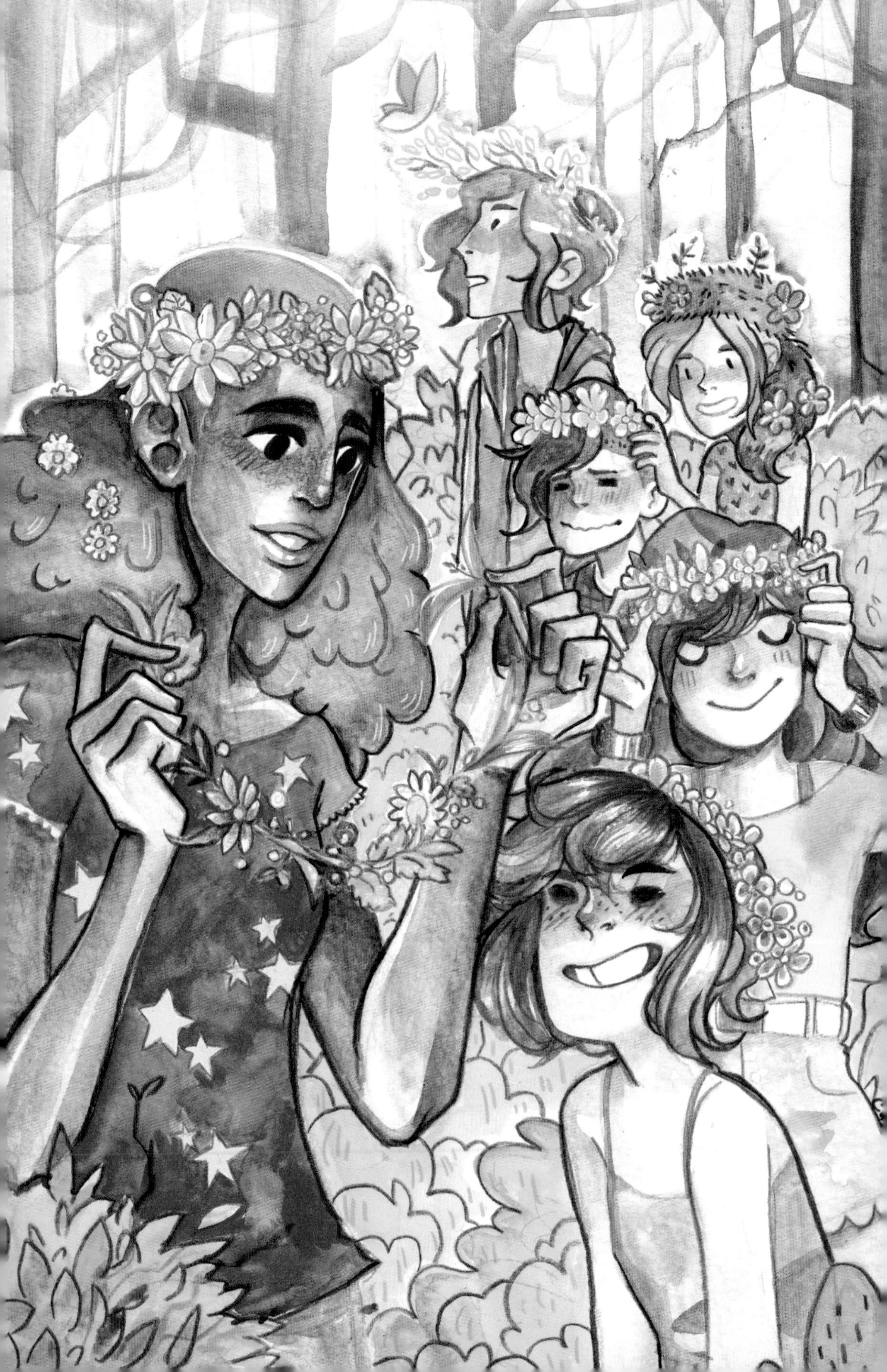

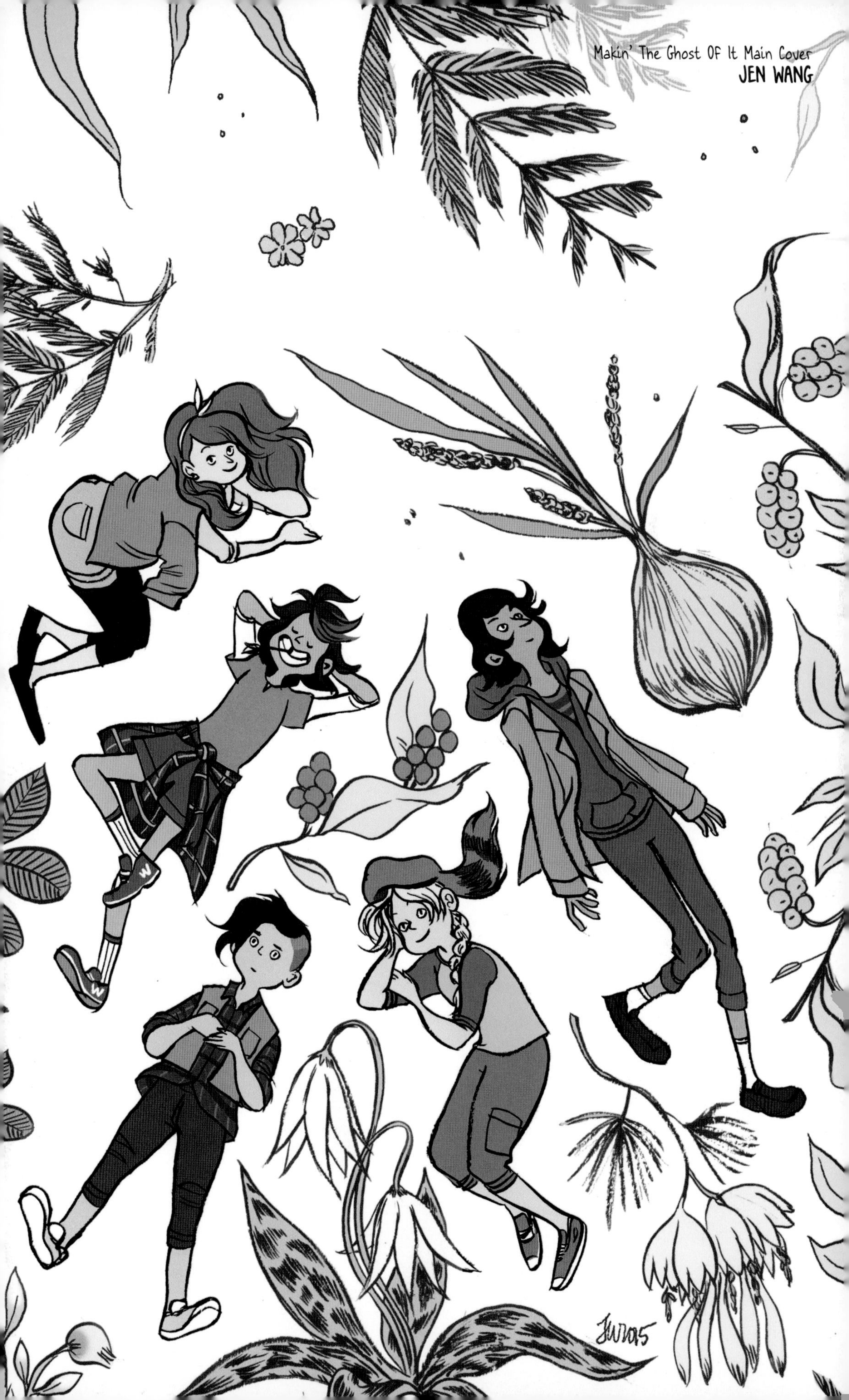

Makin' The Ghost Of It Main Cover
JEN WANG

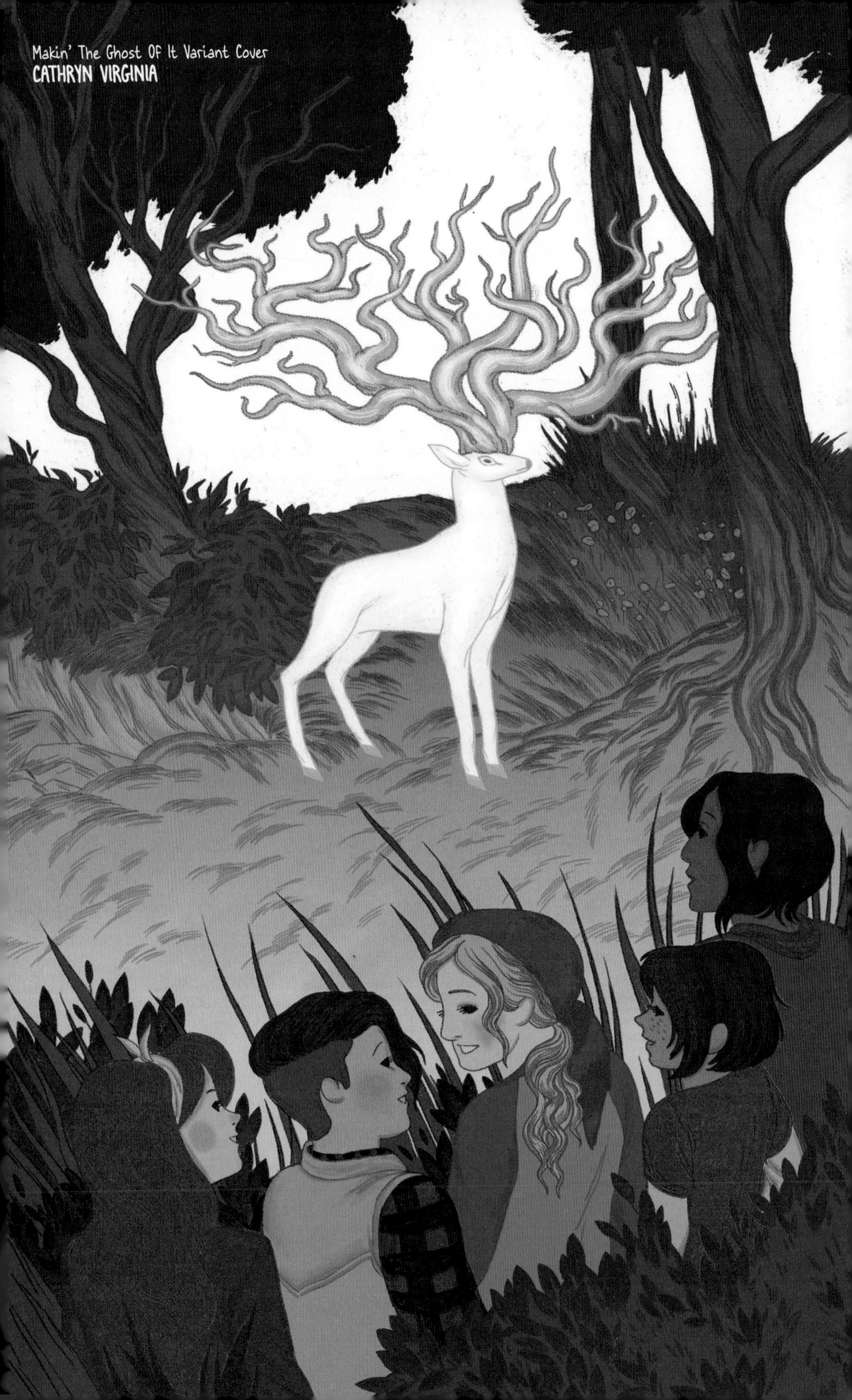

Makin' The Ghost Of It Variant Cover
CATHRYN VIRGINIA

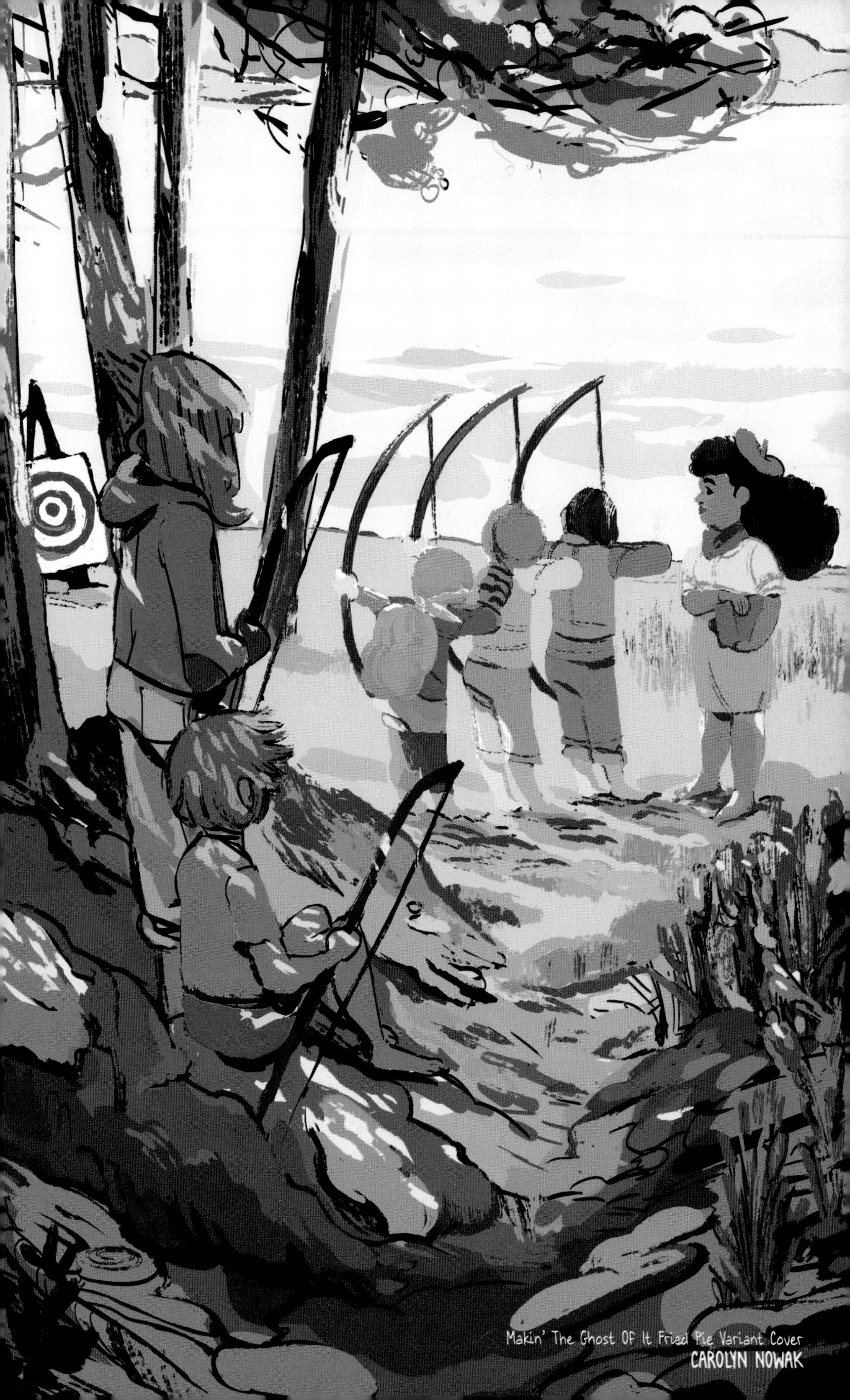
Makin' The Ghost Of It Fried Pie Variant Cover
CAROLYN NOWAK

Faire And Square Main Cover
RU XU

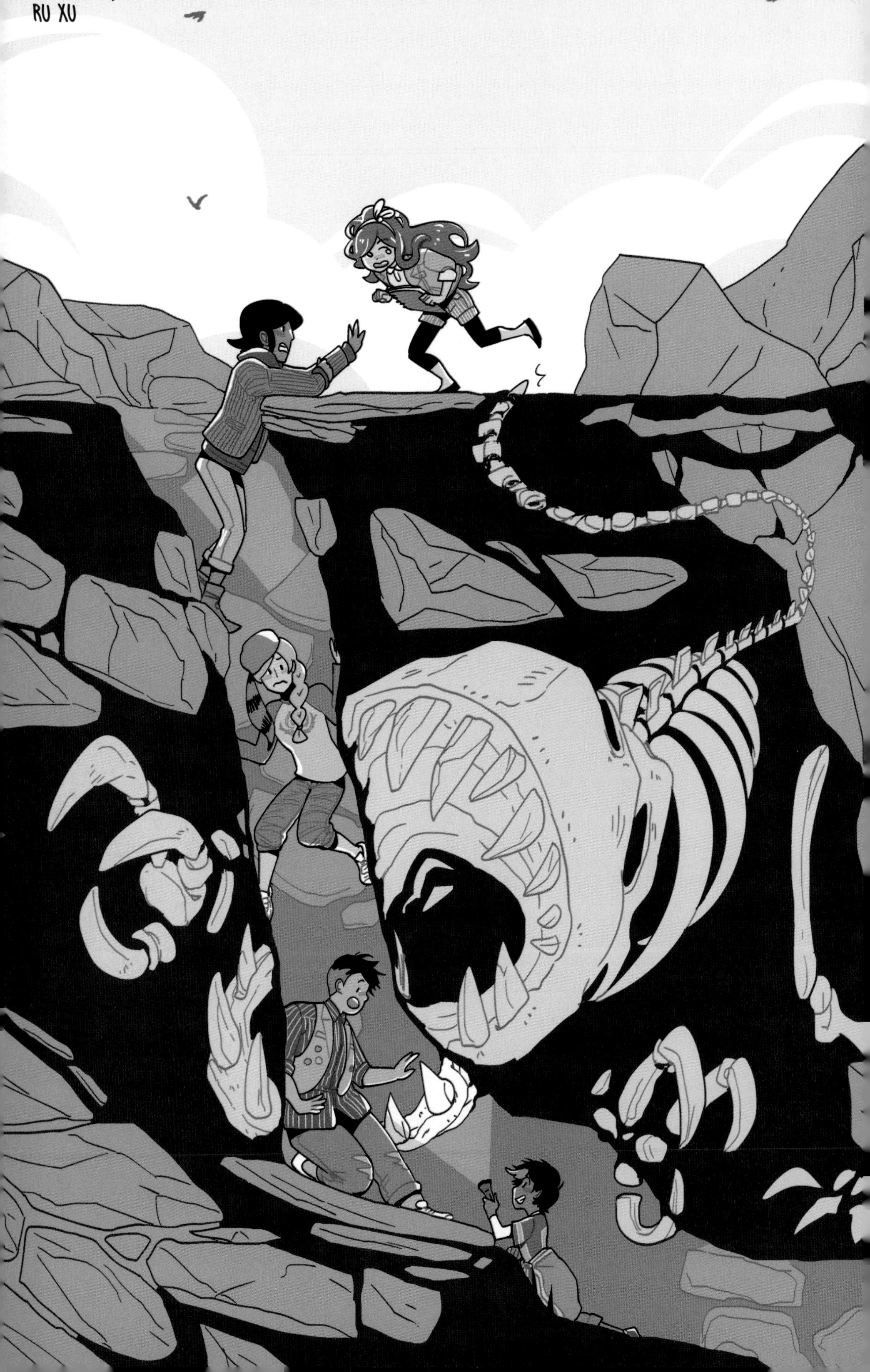

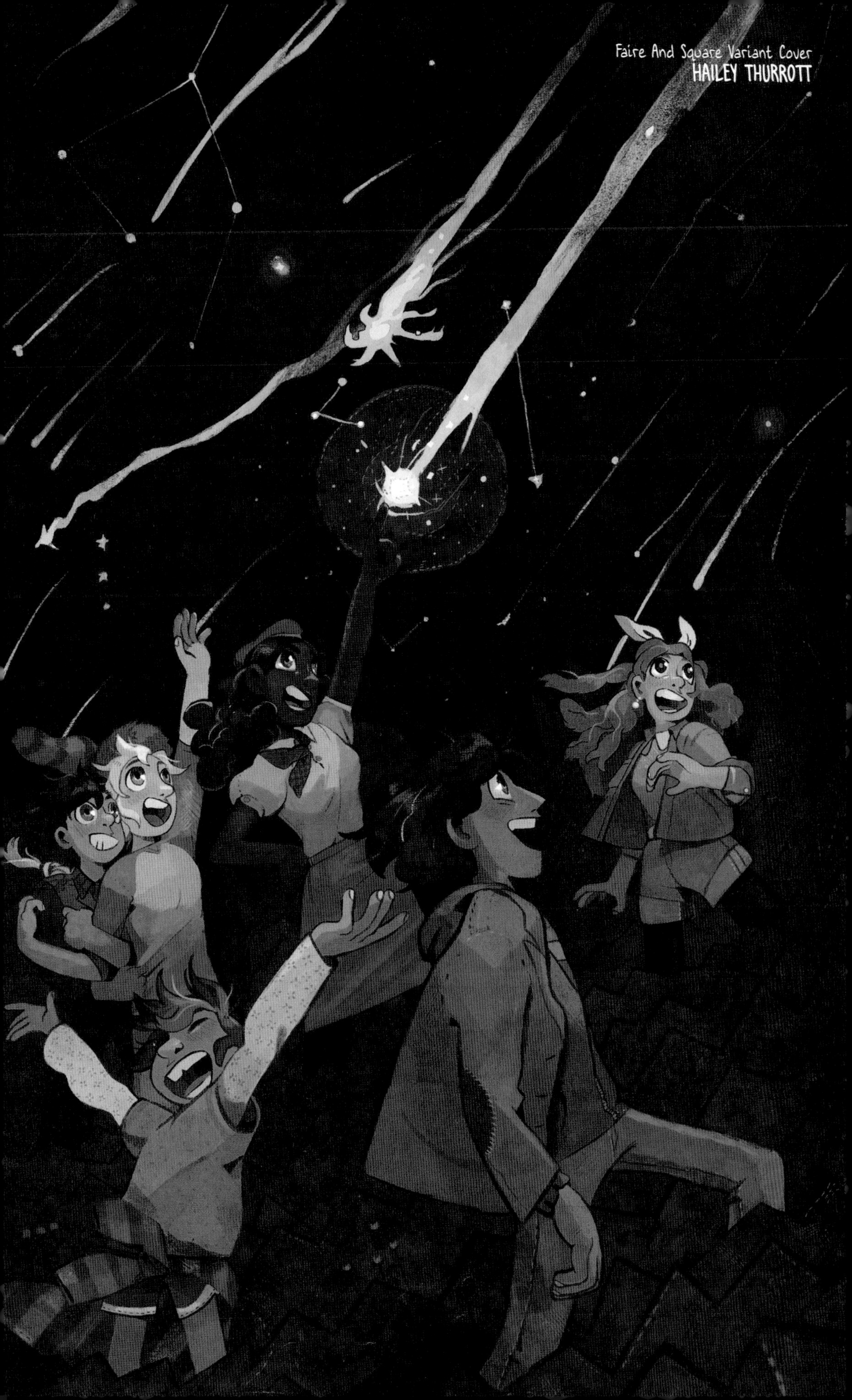

Faire And Square Variant Cover
HAILEY THURROTT

DISCOVER
ALL THE HITS

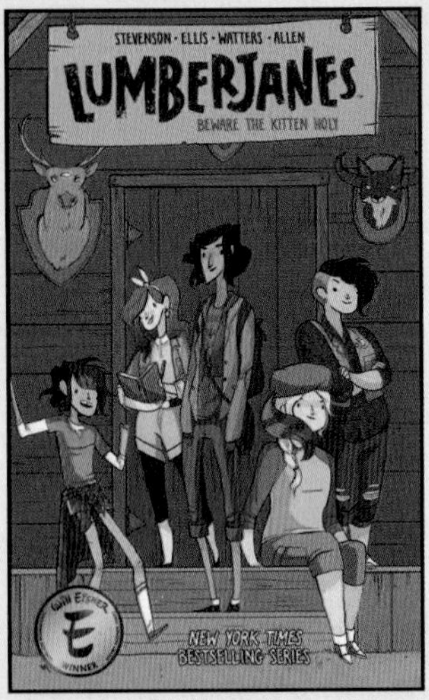
STEVENSON · ELLIS · WATTERS · ALLEN
LUMBERJANES
BEWARE THE KITTEN HOLY
NEW YORK TIMES BESTSELLING SERIES

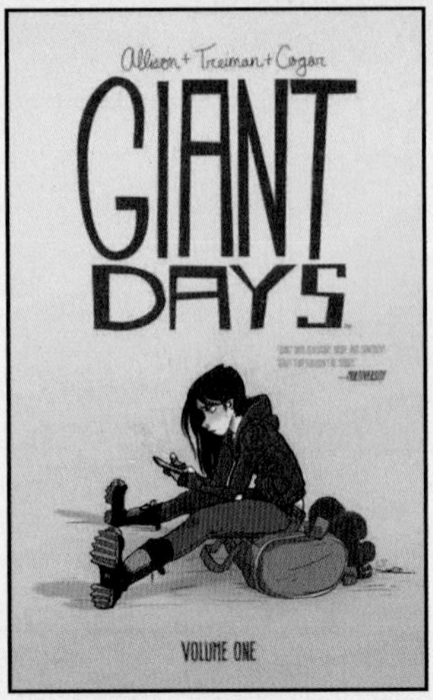
Allison + Treiman + Cogar
GIANT DAYS
VOLUME ONE

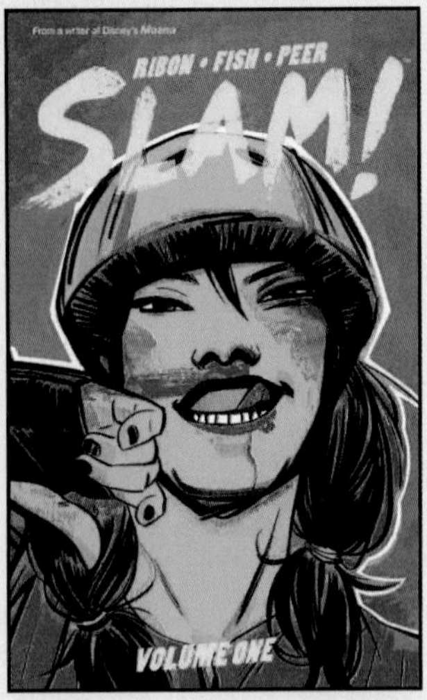
RIBON · FISH · PEER
SLAM!
VOLUME ONE

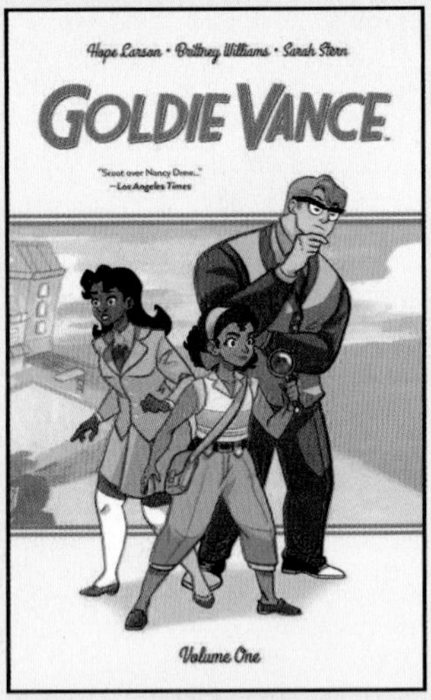
Hope Larson · Brittney Williams · Sarah Stern
GOLDIE VANCE
Volume One

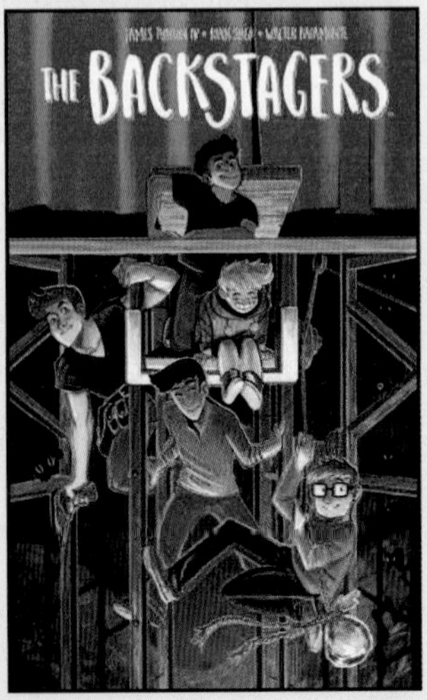
THE BACKSTAGERS

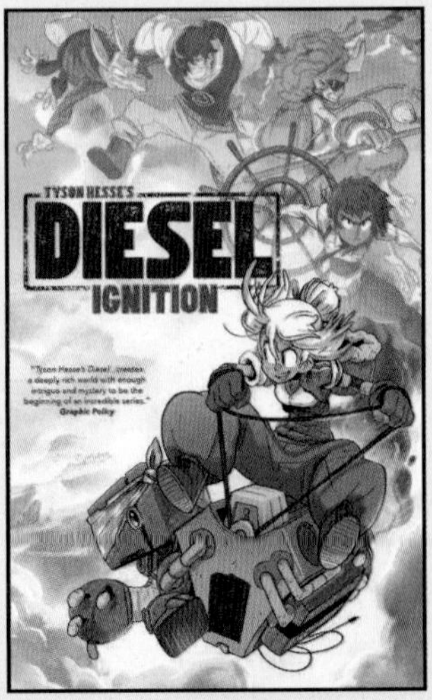
TYSON HESSE'S
DIESEL
IGNITION

Lumberjanes
Noelle Stevenson, Shannon Watters, Grace Ellis, Brooklyn Allen, and Others
Volume 1: Beware the Kitten Holy
ISBN: 978-1-60886-687-8 | $14.99 US
Volume 2: Friendship to the Max
ISBN: 978-1-60886-737-0 | $14.99 US
Volume 3: A Terrible Plan
ISBN: 978-1-60886-803-2 | $14.99 US
Volume 4: Out of Time
ISBN: 978-1-60886-860-5 | $14.99 US
Volume 5: Band Together
ISBN: 978-1-60886-919-0 | $14.99 US

Giant Days
John Allison, Lissa Treiman, Max Sarin
Volume 1
ISBN: 978-1-60886-789-9 | $9.99 US
Volume 2
ISBN: 978-1-60886-804-9 | $14.99 US
Volume 3
ISBN: 978-1-60886-851-3 | $14.99 US

Jonesy
Sam Humphries, Caitlin Rose Boyle
Volume 1
ISBN: 978-1-60886-883-4 | $9.99 US
Volume 2
ISBN: 978-1-60886-999-2 | $14.99 US

Slam!
Pamela Ribon, Veronica Fish, Brittany Peer
Volume 1
ISBN: 978-1-68415-004-5 | $14.99 US

Goldie Vance
Hope Larson, Brittney Williams
Volume 1
ISBN: 978-1-60886-898-8 | $9.99 US
Volume 2
ISBN: 978-1-60886-974-9 | $14.99 US

The Backstagers
James Tynion IV, Rian Sygh
Volume 1
ISBN: 978-1-60886-993-0 | $14.99 US

Tyson Hesse's Diesel: Ignition
Tyson Hesse
ISBN: 978-1-60886-907-7 | $14.99 US

Coady & The Creepies
Liz Prince, Amanda Kirk, Hannah Fisher
ISBN: 978-1-68415-029-8 | $14.99 US

BOOM! BOX™

AVAILABLE AT YOUR LOCAL COMICS SHOP AND BOOKSTORE
To find a comics shop in your area, call 1-888-266-4226
WWW.**BOOM-STUDIOS**.COM